# KILLING PILGRIM

## A MARKO DELLA TORRE NOVEL

# ALEN MATTICH

SPIDERLINE

This edition published in 2014 by
House of Anansi Press Inc.
110 Spadina Avenue, Suite 801
Toronto, ON, M5V 2K4
Tel. 416-363-4343
Fax 416-363-1017
www.houseofanansi.com

Distributed in Canada by
HarperCollins Canada Ltd.
1995 Markham Road
Scarborough, ON, M1B 5M8
Toll free tel. 1-800-387-0117

House of Anansi Press is committed to protecting our natural environment.
As part of our efforts, the interior of this book is printed on paper that contains
100% post-consumer recycled fibres, is acid-free, and is processed chlorine-free.

18  17  16  15  14    1  2  3  4  5

Library and Archives Canada Cataloguing in Publication

Mattich, Alen, 1965–, author
Killing pilgrim : a Marko della Torre novel / Alen Mattich.
Issued in print and electronic formats.
ISBN 978-1-77089-109-8 (pbk.). —ISBN 978-1-77089-418-1
(html)

I. Title.

PS8626.A874K55 2014          C813'.6          C2013-903901-5
C2013-903902-3

Jacket design: Alysia Shewchuk
Text design and typesetting: Alysia Shewchuk

Canada Council    Conseil des Arts
for the Arts      du Canada

ONTARIO ARTS COUNCIL
CONSEIL DES ARTS DE L'ONTARIO

*We acknowledge for their financial support of our publishing program
the Canada Council for the Arts, the Ontario Arts Council, and the Government of
Canada through the Canada Book Fund.*

Printed and bound in Canada

MIX
Paper from
responsible sources
FSC® C004071

For Pippa, Tilly, Kit, and Bee

## STOCKHOLM, FEBRUARY 1986

THE MONTENEGRIN HAD been smoking, fiddling with the car's tuner, searching out something other than inane pop music or indecipherable talk radio, when Pilgrim and his wife walked past, unaccompanied.

He hadn't seen them leave the building because, he shamefully realized, he hadn't been looking. Every time before, Pilgrim's chauffeured car had drawn up outside. But that night there was no car.

The Montenegrin reached under the seat and brushed the smooth metal of the Smith & Wesson revolver with his finger. It had become a talisman. At first, he hadn't been sure of the gun. He would have preferred a smaller-calibre pistol with an efficient silencer, one of the official standard issues. But he hadn't dared risk smuggling a weapon across Europe, not now that he was working alone, even though he'd worried about the quality of equipment he'd be able to get his hands on in Sweden.

But the boy had done well. Not only had he found a pristine weapon, but he'd taken the Montenegrin to an isolated spot in a forest two hours west of Stockholm where he could test it to his heart's content, assured of privacy.

The Montenegrin slipped the gun into his coat pocket and got out of the stolen Opel, shutting the door behind him quietly. He followed the couple on foot, at a discreet distance, as he'd learned to do over long years of practice.

Pilgrim and his wife walked to the nearest metro station, where they waited for a train in the direction of the city's shopping district. People recognized the man but left him alone, though one youth made a mocking two-fingered sign behind his back. Pilgrim's face was unmistakable, round, with a beak nose and hooded eyes, like a vulture's. The wife was unexceptional. Small, dowdy, utterly forgettable, though by now the Montenegrin was familiar with her too, having even watched her do her shopping at the local supermarket like any other middle-aged Swedish housewife, filling a basket with milk, vegetables, a roll of aluminium foil, and toilet paper.

The Montenegrin bought a ticket and waited at the other end of the platform. The train was full but not crowded. He stood well away from the couple but within sight. Pilgrim seemed agitated, glancing frequently at his watch. His wife patted his arm, a gesture that spoke of long familiarity with her husband's impatience. They went three stops on the green line from the old town, with its island of narrow cobbled streets and its mustard-coloured stone buildings with gas lamps, and got off in a nondescript part of Stockholm marked by nineteenth-century apartment blocks lined with restaurants and shops on a long, straight avenue. Except for the cold, the city reminded the Montenegrin of Belgrade.

He joined the flow of passengers leaving the station, keeping Pilgrim and his wife in sight as they and a handful of others hurried to a cinema a block away.

Pilgrim walked to the front of the queue, as was only natural, but his wife gently upbraided him for his rudeness, making him take his place at the back. Pilgrim looked both irritated and chastened, but when he got to the ticket window he paid like everybody else and disappeared into the theatre.

The Montenegrin checked the running time to see when the show would end. It was something frivolous about Mozart, a summer comedy for the dead of winter, according to the poster. Popular. Maybe because there wasn't much else to do in Stockholm. It was an expensive town in which to drink, eat, smoke.

He took the metro back to the car. It was a short drive, but it took him a while to find somewhere to park that was out of sight but within easy access. His sense of direction had failed him in this unfamiliar town; he ended up on the wrong side of the cinema from the metro stop, on a parallel side street farther away than he'd intended.

He walked back towards the theatre and stood silent sentry at a shop window diagonally opposite, in clear sight of its entrance. He was early, but he wanted to be ready if Pilgrim walked out before the end of the film. So he waited, half-staring at the darkened display, illuminated solely by street-light, struggling not to shiver despite the new blue overcoat and cheap knitted cap he'd bought a couple of weeks before in Copenhagen, where he'd briefly stopped to find a car with Swedish plates.

Several times he glanced around the intersection, but the streets were mostly empty. There wasn't much snow on the ground, but it was cold enough for him to feel the fine hairs in his nose start to freeze.

He stamped his feet, the dance cold people do when they're waiting, but resisted the temptation to walk some warmth back into his legs. The film would be ending soon.

He pressed his fingers to his neck, feeling for his pulse, using the psychological tools he'd been taught to force himself to relax. Nerves were inevitable, expected, even for a professional. They kept him sharp, alert. But unfettered, they caused mistakes.

It worried him that he hadn't had time to plan properly, to get a clear idea of each subsequent move. Normally he'd have been directing a team from a safe distance. He'd have had people doing fieldwork for weeks in advance, with a whole intelligence portfolio at his disposal. Then there would have been a separate squad, given exact instructions, down to the colours of their ties. They wouldn't know why, but they'd know when and where, to the minute and metre. And if they got it wrong... they were deniable. All with criminal backgrounds and a good reason to keep their mouths shut.

Not now. This time he was standing at the front with no one behind him. The intelligence, the fieldwork, and the execution were all down to him. No safety net. No support. Just an unwritten promise in return for success.

No, he wasn't quite alone. But he didn't count the boy, whom providence had seemingly sent. Despite his youth, the boy was capable and smart, even if he smoked dope most evenings or went out to sell it. The boy was a piece of luck.

It was also lucky that Pilgrim and his wife had decided to take the metro to the cinema that evening. And that they'd gone unaccompanied by a bodyguard.

Even professionals get lucky, the Montenegrin reminded himself.

Every day since he'd arrived in Stockholm, he'd driven to Pilgrim's apartment building well before dawn, waiting and watching. Then he would shadow the man and his two uniformed bodyguards, tracing the short route to his nearby offices. Once, Pilgrim had caught the Montenegrin off guard by returning home unaccompanied mid-afternoon. A missed opportunity.

Most evenings, the Montenegrin would sit in his car, engine running, smoking cigarettes, watching. Pilgrim would return home flanked by a pair of uniformed men, different ones from the morning team. Usually he'd go out again, collected by a chauffeured car, mostly alone, though his wife had gone with him once or twice. He'd come back the same way, the driver getting out and opening Pilgrim's door and then escorting him to his building.

At first the Montenegrin worried he'd draw attention to himself, sitting in a parked car in this affluent Old Stockholm neighbourhood for hours on end. But then he noticed other men doing the same, in similar cars, cheap Opels, rusty Volvos, Fords. It puzzled him at first, but then he realized that husbands were dropping off their wives for their night cleaning jobs. Some worked for only a couple of hours, and the husbands would wait. Others came back early in the morning. He was just another waiting husband, another poor immigrant.

It was the third week of this slow, methodical surveillance. He had another month to work out how to get the job done in a way that got him out of the country, safe and anonymous.

Maybe if he spoke Swedish as well as the boy did. He got by on his English and German but...No, it didn't matter what language he spoke. Even if he succeeded, he'd never escape Pilgrim's security.

Except that evening there was no security.

It was after eleven o'clock when the film ended. His feet were numb. He should have bought felt-lined boots, like the Korean-made pairs he'd seen the Kurdish immigrants wearing in the suburb where he was staying. The cinema doors opened and people spread into the deserted street like oil from a ruptured pipe. The crowd broke up into couples and small groups, some of whom passed the Montenegrin, talking animatedly before dispersing into the night.

He felt a sudden panic when he saw people emerging from around the corner. He'd been stupid not to check for a second exit. He swore under his breath but restrained himself from racing round to see whether Pilgrim had used it. If Pilgrim was going to the same metro station he'd arrived at, he would have to pass the front of the cinema anyway.

Pilgrim. The Montenegrin didn't understand why the man had been given that code name. Or who chose it. Pilgrim seemed neither religious nor holy.

But where was he? The Montenegrin grew anxious. Maybe he'd been absorbed into the departing crowd. He'd worn a nondescript overcoat and hat, was of average height and build. Bundled up against the cold, he could have been any middle-aged man.

The Montenegrin's thoughts adjusted to failure, returning to what he needed to do over the coming days, weeks, willing patience on himself. But he couldn't suppress the ripple of regret. He grimaced at the acres of time he would have to spend on dull surveillance, the mountain of work ahead. He'd wait until the crowd disappeared and then drive back to the suburbs. Sleep and then start again early tomorrow.

The Montenegrin was cold. Even the short walk back to the car would be a chore.

But his discomfort, his gloom, evaporated in an instant, his focus narrowing sharply when he saw, from across the light flow of traffic, Pilgrim exit the cinema. The man and his wife were among the last to leave.

They and another couple stopped under the cinema's rigid awning, talking in a huddle, as people did in these cold places. There was a lack of formality in the encounter, though it wasn't overly animated, suggesting they saw each other frequently. The couples exchanged kisses and broke off.

The younger couple walked towards the Montenegrin, but Pilgrim and his wife turned in the opposite direction. Whatever they were doing, they weren't taking the route they'd come by.

It could be that they were going to walk home. Or perhaps they were heading to the other metro station, just beyond the stairs he'd parked by. One stop less for them to travel.

The Montenegrin crossed two roads—he resisted taking

the shorter diagonal route for fear of drawing attention to himself—putting himself directly behind Pilgrim and his wife as they ambled down the long main avenue, which was lined with young trees, their bare dark trunks made stark by the street lights. His gloveless hand was in his pocket, securing the revolver's heft against his thigh.

The couple was fifty metres ahead of him. A plan coalesced as he drew closer.

His shirt was clammy with sweat. White fluorescent street lamps cast a hard steel light on the night. The couple came to a tall white church with a domed tower, where Pilgrim again showed his impulsiveness by crossing the road without using a crosswalk, his wife scurrying behind. For a moment the Montenegrin wondered whether the man had sensed he was being followed, but then saw that the couple had been drawn to a shop's illuminated window display. The Montenegrin continued on his side of the road, walking past the church and not crossing until he'd reached the traffic lights, waiting patiently for a green signal, as he'd seen Swedes do.

He took a few strides off the main road onto a smaller, perpendicular street, but stopping close enough to the intersection that he'd be able to see when Pilgrim and his wife walked past. It was risky. It meant they'd be out of sight. But it also meant they wouldn't notice him when they resumed their walk.

He stood in front of a lit stationer's window, wishing his daughter had the physical ability to hold the expensive Faber-Castell coloured pencils on display. He tried to push her out of his thoughts. To focus. Solo surveillance was hard. Teams of three or four, or better yet two teams of three, were ideal. How he wished he had the people to do this job properly. Professionally.

He mocked himself for wishing the impossible. Why not just wish his wife back to life?

A young man brushed past him, absorbed in the headphones of his Sony Walkman, a miracle of Japanese engineering.

Maybe he'd buy one for his daughter. That was something she might enjoy more than pencils. He breathed steadily, consciously, the crisp air making him cough.

He looked up and saw Pilgrim and his wife crossing the intersection, continuing along the main avenue, walking a little more briskly now.

The Montenegrin looked around to make sure no one else was following. The street was nearly empty. He turned the corner, lengthening his stride so that he caught up with them before they'd made it halfway along the block.

He was now directly behind the couple, though they hadn't noticed him. With an assured smoothness, he put his arm over the man's shoulder, and said *"Hej"* in a hearty tone. Pilgrim and his wife looked up at the Montenegrin, startled.

They smiled as if to show they knew him, yet doubt creased their foreheads. It often happened to famous people. People recognizing them, but not knowing quite why, thinking perhaps they were old acquaintances. The woman said something to him in Swedish. The Montenegrin smiled apologetically, shrugging his shoulders. He exhaled a little sigh of relief. He'd confirmed the target. There was no mistake.

The couple kept glancing nervously at the silent stranger in the cheap coat. He stepped away from them and they walked, perhaps slightly faster, though it was hard to tell.

Pilgrim and his wife hadn't gone more than a couple of metres before the Montenegrin started following again, hand deep in the overcoat pocket, gripping the butt of the gun, index finger straight beside the trigger. With a practised thumb he cocked the gun as he drew it out of his pocket, and in a smooth move he slid his finger between the trigger and its guard.

The red and white muzzle flame was brief and bright against the city's hollow, artificial light.

The first bullet took Pilgrim down. The second, fired immediately after, was wasted.

Pilgrim fell hard, in the way the Montenegrin had seen other men fall, not even twitching once he'd hit the ground.

They were at the bottom of an alley that led up to a set of stairs, near the top of which the Montenegrin had parked his car. He jogged away from the dead man, along the alley and then up the stairs, which he took two at a time, keeping his right hand in his pocket to prevent the still-warm gun from falling out, and gripping the rail with the other.

Halfway up, he stopped, thinking he could hear footsteps behind him.

But from below, there rose only the echo of a woman's screams.

He counted as he climbed. Eighty-nine steps.

Soon people would be coming. Very soon.

The car wasn't far now. He knew this was only the start of a very long night. But it had been a good beginning. A lucky one.

Behind him Pilgrim lay prone, his wife kneeling, keening by his side.

Olof Palme, prime minister of Sweden, was dead.

## ZAGREB, AUGUST 1991

**A**T FIRST ONLY a single air-raid siren wailed in the distance, some-where to the east. But like the baying of dogs, its call was rapidly taken up, so that within moments the whole of Zagreb was caught up in the fearful ululation.

Marko della Torre watched from the window of his office as nervous pedestrians stopped, looked skyward as if sniffing the air, and then rushed away, heads bowed, ducking the invisible enemy. He felt a bead of sweat run under his arm to his scarred elbow.

Zagreb's sticky summer heat was made even more oppressive by the fear of looming war, which piled up like impossibly high and ever blacker thunderclouds. So far, all the city's air-raid warnings had been false alarms. It had been less than two months since Croatia and Slovenia declared their independence from Yugoslavia. The country had been cobbled together after the First World War from a collection of the Balkans' Slav nations, anchored by the relatively large and powerful Serbia. But any sense of brotherhood was riven by two alphabets, three religions, innumerable dialects, and a history of mutual loathing. From the first days, the country's smaller republics had chafed under Serb hegemony. The Nazi invasion during the Second

World War triggered a civil war. Tito's Communist Partizans won and for nearly half a century bound the country through fear and ideology. And an effective secret police apparatus, for which della Torre worked.

After Tito died, an unwieldy rotating presidency from the country's various republics kept things going for a decade. But a crumbling economy, endemic corruption, and a deep vein of cynicism collided with the end of Communism, and the richer, western republics of Slovenia and Croatia had decided to go their own way.

Slovenia took over control of its borders from the federal police and military units. The Yugoslav government had responded by sending its air force to attack the rebels and commanding its military units to recover the federal government's authority.

But the federal authorities acted without any great conviction. Yugoslavia had one of the biggest armies in the world, out of all proportion to the country's modest size. Slovenia's force was limited to little more than traffic policemen and farmers called up from the reserves. And yet, after ten days of desultory bombings and small, localized engagements, the Yugoslav army was ordered to withdraw. Slovenia was allowed to secede because nearly the whole of the population was ethnically Slovene.

Croatia wasn't so lucky. There was no way its proclamation of national sovereignty would go unchallenged. One in eight of its inhabitants considered themselves ethnic Serbs. And Serbia effectively ran both the federal government and the Yugoslav army. There was an impasse. Croatia might have declared independence along with Slovenia, but its rulers made no effort to physically enforce their new country's sovereignty. The Croat government rightly feared the Yugoslav tanks and fighters.

So far the federal presidency in Belgrade was too split to make any authoritative decisions. And anyway, the Europeans had brokered a temporary truce. Though that was going to end in a few weeks.

Meanwhile Serbian leaders were consolidating their power over the federal system. They made up most of the army's officer class, and held most of the senior posts in the government bureaucracy, and Serbia was the heartland of heavy industry. Even the rulers of compliant republics were fearful of what would come once the Serbs decided to make their own greater nation. Especially the Bosnians. Bosnia was a microcosm of Yugoslavia, wedged between Serbia and Croatia and made up of Serbs, Croats, and Bosnian Muslims. They knew that whatever storm broke elsewhere, it would hit them like a holocaust.

Once the Serbs were sure of their strength, air raids were sure to follow the sirens. And with them, the tanks and the big guns.

Della Torre watched and waited for the all-clear. But the sirens kept on with their urgent nagging. He spread the slats of the thin metal Venetian blinds with his fingers and looked skyward. Were those vapour trails? The thought made him pull back from the window. The Croat government had taken over all the Yugoslav federal buildings in Zagreb, including his. Especially his.

Della Torre figured the federal forces might have a special interest in destroying the UDBA's regional headquarters in Zagreb. The UDBA was Yugoslavia's notorious department of internal security. The secret police. It held plenty of documents the Yugoslavs would want incinerated. Besides, Serb staffers had long since vacated the building. Della Torre doubted the Yugoslav pilots would be particularly concerned for the welfare of any Croats working there. And not just because people in every walk of Yugoslav life hated the UDBA. It was time to leave. Before he got bombed. Or before the all-clear sounded and he got caught.

The corridor was empty. Everyone had gone down to the basement shelter. Officially he was still on sick leave, nursing a not very old bullet wound in his elbow. The bandage was off, but his scar was puckered and pink.

He should have stayed away, but the combination of a deep thirst, being broke, and knowing there was a three-quarters-full bottle of Bell's nestled in the locked bottom drawer of his filing cabinet had made him tempt fate. If Anzulović spotted him, he'd come to the erroneous conclusion that della Torre was ready to return to work. Ready to drink and ready to work were entirely different states of being.

Captain Anzulović was in charge of UDBA's Department VI and was della Torre's boss. Department VI had been created five years earlier as a sop to Yugoslavia's increasingly activist parliament. In Tito's time the parliament had been a nursery for the dim but well-behaved sons and brothers of the dictator's old cronies. After his death they'd started to find a spine and a conscience. One of their bravest acts was to insist on the creation of an agency that could monitor the UDBA. Someone to watch the watchers everyone feared. The UDBA tried to neuter the department by making it part of the apparatus and then sticking it in Zagreb, well away from the heart of the organization. But they'd underestimated Anzulović, drafted in from the Zagreb police force.

Anzulović hired the most competent people he could find, including Marko della Torre, a smart young specialist in international law whom he had poached from the Zagreb prosecutor's office. In Department VI, della Torre was given responsibility for reviewing the UDBA's program of assassinating Yugoslav dissidents in foreign countries. No other secret police force in the world was as successful at killing people beyond its borders—not the KGB, not the Stasi, not the Securitate, not Savak, not even Mossad. The CIA didn't even register as competition. Della Torre's job was to find and prosecute any UDBA operations done outside the scope of Yugoslav laws. Killings done for the personal motives of people in power.

Della Torre slipped out of his office into the high, long corridor, trying to keep his heels from clicking on the terrazzo floor. He was halfway down the hall, almost at the emergency staircase, when a familiar voice stopped him dead.

"Where are you going?" It came from behind the frosted glass window of a half-open door.

"I thought maybe I'd see whether they'd done up the bomb shelter. You know, new wallpaper and carpet to cover up the bloodstains, that sort of thing," della Torre said.

"Nope, still looks like Frankenstein's cellar. Come on in."

"Don't you think maybe it's worth going down—"

"Why? Do you suppose the bombers are flying from Belgrade via Reykjavik? They could have sent Zeppelins, bombed us, and been back by now if anything was happening," Anzulović said, irritated.

As they spoke, the warning gave way to an all-clear. Della Torre cursed under his breath as he hovered near the door, feebly trying to hide the bottle of Bell's behind his back.

"See? Anyway, don't stand there looking like a lemon. Come in," Anzulović said. "Sit. And shut the door behind you."

Della Torre slipped the bottle onto the floor behind the chair leg as discreetly as he could.

Anzulović allowed himself a half grin. "You shouldn't have. Though it'd be rude not to."

He reached a long arm into a low cupboard on one side of his desk, from which he pulled out two dusty cut-glass tumblers. One had a hairline crack.

"I was only stopping in to say hello. As part of my convalescence. You know, until the doctors say I'm fit for work," della Torre said.

"And to pick up your medicine? Sort of prescription I like," said Anzulović.

It was only a little past ten in the morning, but della Torre poured two fingers into each glass. The whisky was warm and

burned just the right way. Anzulović offered della Torre a cigarette from his pack of Lords and lit a match for them both.

From the corridor came sounds of people returning to their
offices.

"How's the funny bone, by the way?"

Della Torre rubbed his elbow. "Keeping me in stitches." He
knocked back what remained in his glass. "Well, thanks for
taking an interest. I'll let you know when my sick leave's over.
Assuming there still is an office..."

"Or that you've still got a job," Anzulović said, finishing the
sentence. "Well, the office is moving."

He blew smoke through the tufts of hair growing out of his
nostrils so that he looked like he was stoking a miniature brush
fire. He was in his mid-fifties, nearly twenty years older than
della Torre, but already looked ripe for retirement. The saddle-
bags under his eyes made his hangdog face look even more
basset-like.

"So have I still got a job?" della Torre asked.

"Good question. All those nasty bits of the UDBA that everyone hates so much, they're being absorbed into the Croat
Interior Ministry."

"A new, better UDBA, eh? *Plus ça change*...What about us?"

"You can imagine how hard the new, improved UDBA fought
to keep us with them," Anzulović said dryly. "And oddly
enough, now that the Croat government has power over the
security apparatus, they're no longer very keen on having an
anti-corruption unit either."

"Funny, that. So where's this leave us?" della Torre asked.

"We, my dear Gringo..." Della Torre still disliked that nickname, though after twenty years he'd become inured to it. The
kids at school had started calling him that when he and his
father had moved back to Zagreb from America. They were
obsessed with cowboys and Indians—everyone in the country
was—and anybody who'd lived in America had to be one or

the other. The name stuck, and now the only people who used his given name were his wife and his father. And Harry, the English woman he'd met in London. "We are being absorbed into military intelligence."

The Croat military had been patched together from the various local and regional police services. Their personnel weren't known for their brains or insight.

"And because I know how happy this will make you, I'll let you in on a little secret. The military intelligence unit is being run by your number one fan: Colonel Kakav."

Della Torre choked, whisky fumes scorching his lungs.

"Of the Zagreb police?"

"The one and only."

Della Torre slumped in his chair. Kakav was a bureaucrat attached to the Zagreb police. He was an oleaginous, self-serving political coward with considerable resentment against the state security apparatus. And, lately, della Torre.

Earlier that spring, a senior Zagreb police detective called Julius Strumbić had been shot by an UDBA agent. Namely, one Marko della Torre. It was Kakav's life ambition to nail an UDBA agent and here he had one. "Shit."

"Ah, you put your finger right on it. Or, rather, in it. Kakav was very eager that you be part of his team. Mentioned it more than once."

"Because then it's that much easier to hang me high?"

"Probably." Anzulović wasn't showing much sympathy.

"I thought that little misunderstanding had been sorted out. Didn't Strumbić write an affidavit to the effect that it was an accident and we're friends again?"

"He wrote a statement but he still hasn't signed it. Like you, he's officially on leave. Post-traumatic stress for getting shot twice in less than six months."

"There's no one more deserving," della Torre said.

Strumbić set new standards for police corruption, even in a

force as dirty as Zagreb's. He'd amassed huge wealth and had never been caught.

Anzulović cocked a bushy eyebrow at della Torre. "I thought you said it was an accident."

It really had been an accident. A complicated accident.

He had been selling third-rate files to Strumbić, making just enough to keep smoking his Lucky Strikes. Everything was fine, except somewhere in among the dross was a document somebody cared about. It got back to people in Belgrade that it had come from della Torre, and they called the Dispatcher, Tito's old fixer in Zagreb. The Dispatcher specialized in making problems go away. He'd arm-twisted Strumbić into setting up della Torre for a bunch of Bosnian killers.

It was only through a happy accident that della Torre didn't end up in a shallow grave. He hadn't intended to use violence to find out from Strumbić what was going on. But the crappy Bulgarian knock-off pistol went off on its own and shot Strumbić in the leg. And then della Torre stole Strumbić's money, his coat, his cigarettes, and his BMW and ran. To Italy. And then to London. Where he found himself having to deal with the UDBA, Strumbić, his ex-wife, and the Bosnians.

For the next several months, della Torre hid out in London — from the Bosnians, from Strumbić, from the entire Zagreb police force, who didn't take kindly to one of their own being shot.

He thought about the file at the heart of all the trouble. An operation called Pilgrim. Finding and assembling that file had been an accident. Like shooting Strumbić.

"It was," della Torre said. "Do you think they'll try to prosecute me?"

"Kakav? He's enough of an idiot. But he'll probably just use the charges against you as leverage. Make you jump when he says jump. Don't worry. Strumbić will sign. Eventually. Knowing him, he's just waiting to see where his best advantage lies. Unfortunately, I'm not in a great position to twist his arm," Anzulović said.

"So it's either Kakav making me dance or Goli Otok. Or whatever they've replaced it with." Goli Otok had been Yugoslavia's gulag, a hellish island prison off the Dalmatian coast, run by the UDBA. Its reputation had grown so vast and ugly that a couple of years before, the Yugoslav government, embarrassed by international attention and shocked by the findings of a Department VI investigation, had finally shut it down.

"Look on the bright side. If you're rotting in prison, it means you won't have to be standing on the front lines when the shooting starts."

"Thanks. I've had enough of standing around with a bull's eye painted on my back."

"Well, then, you're in luck. A nice little war means that whoever it is in Belgrade that wants you dead is probably a bit distracted right now."

"You really believe that?" Della Torre sat forward in his chair, hopeful.

"No. But has anyone taken a potshot at you over the past couple of months?"

"No. But I thought that was because you'd put some security on me."

"You mean those guys we had drive by your place a couple of times a day? Only lasted for a couple of weeks. Though I suspect the Zagreb cops might have taken an interest in your welfare," Anzulović said. He was doodling circles with his cigarette butt in a crystal ashtray the size of a dinner plate and heavy enough to break a foot. It had, for once, been emptied. "What I suggest, Gringo, is that all those files, all that stuff that got you into trouble, that business about Pilgrim or whatever it was called, that you forget about it. Ever hear the phrase 'let sleeping dogs lie'?"

"Maybe."

Pilgrim. He'd put some of the pieces of the puzzle together. He knew it had something to do with nuclear centrifuges exported from Sweden to Belgrade and then onwards. Somewhere.

And that it had involved the Montenegrin. He took his nickname from his home, the tiny republic to the south. *Montenegro* meant "black mountain." It was a land of blood feuds and vendetta. It was almost as if even his UDBA colleagues were too afraid to evoke his real name, needing the comforting distance of a pseudonym. He'd led some of the organization's most effective assassination squads and was, for a time, head of the secret police's wetworks.

Had the Montenegrin wanted him dead, della Torre knew that by now he'd be a yellowing black-bordered photograph in the back pages of an old evening newspaper.

That was the extent of his knowledge. And yet it was enough for somebody to want to have him killed.

"Then don't go poking them with sticks. Because, knowing my luck, you won't be the only one who ends up getting bitten. Right?"

"Right." Della Torre screwed the cap back on the bottle of Bell's, now less than half full, and got up. "I guess I'll be back in touch once the doctors figure I'm all right."

"Did I say you could go?"

"Oh, sorry, how remiss," della Torre said, unscrewing the cap.

"No, not that. You're back on duty."

"But—"

"No buts. Even if I hadn't caught you prowling around right now, I'd have had somebody dig you out of your flat."

"Don't I—"

"No, you don't. Remember when I said that Kakav was going to take great pleasure in making you jump? Well, he said jump. There's an order from him to find you and send you to Istria."

"For what?"

"Ours is not to question and all the rest...You're to talk to the captain of the Poreč police."

"About what?"

"Gringo, I was not made privy to that. Maybe you should ask Kakav."

"Can't I just phone?"

"Kakav said go. So you will go. If you know what's good for me," Anzulović said. "Remember, I like an easy life. A quiet life."

Della Torre shrugged. He'd lived most of his life in the system. At university, in the army, in the prosecutor's office, in the UDBA, he'd always had to deal with incomprehensible, stupid orders handed down from one oblivious bureaucrat to another until they landed in his lap. Sometimes he could pass them down to someone lower on the food chain. Sometimes he couldn't.

"Okay, I'll go."

"Nice of you to be so obliging. And while you're there, you're expected to stay at your father's."

"Oh, I see. It's a cost-saving exercise. Send the guy who has family there to do the work so that we don't have to put him up in a hotel or pay for his meals," della Torre said.

"I'm sure it's something like that."

"Did he say what sort of toothpaste he wants me to use?"

"No point getting smart with me, Gringo. Your arm good enough to drive?"

"Should be," della Torre said.

"Good. Otherwise I'd have to put you on a bus."

"So does this mean we'll be getting paid again?"

"We've been on payroll since the start of the month."

"So I can afford to buy myself some cigarettes?"

"Don't get too ambitious."

"Do I get to keep my UDBA rank? Or is it back to where I was when I left the army?"

"No, it's the same. Otherwise I'd be a private second class," Anzulović said. "Where did you finish up in the commandos? Hard to believe they took you, of all people."

"Somebody had a sense of humour," della Torre said. "I managed lieutenant. Funny to think I'd be your boss if we were knocked back."

"Wouldn't it just. Be straight out of *Sergeant Bilko*," Anzulović said.

Della Torre nodded, though the reference didn't mean anything to him. The man's obsession with Hollywood was surely his only real weakness.

"Right. If you set off now, you can get to your father's for a late lunch. Tomorrow you can do whatever it is you need to do in Poreč. Think of it as a working holiday. I expect you back at the start of next week."

"Any nice cars left in the pool?"

"I sold them all. Use yours. The old UDBA petrol card ought to work. We'll be getting new IDs and uniforms when we move offices, which will be as soon as Kakav figures out where he put his thumb."

"Thanks. If you don't hear from me again, it's because my brakes failed going around a clifftop bend." His Yugo was aptly named. Like the country, it was a car designed to fall apart at the worst possible time and in the bloodiest, most destructive way possible.

"Avoid clifftop bends. You're back here at the start of next week. Understand?"

Anzulović made it clear the interview was over. Della Torre didn't say goodbye. He just shut the door behind him. He was most of the way down the corridor before he remembered the half-bottle of whisky he'd left on Anzulović's desk.

# 3

DELLA TORRE TOOK the long way to his father's house, navigating the slow road down Istria's precipitous east coast. He'd always preferred this route, even in the summer, when traffic crawled behind German caravans and overladen Czech Škodas. It wasn't a problem that August afternoon. Traffic was as light as on a drizzly Sunday in January. Looming war was keeping tourists away.

As the road climbed he took in the deep blue waters of Kvarner Bay, the green haze of Cres Island, and farther still the stony white starkness of the Velebit range on the mainland. He could see rising black smudges, high in the distance: smoke from fires lit by Serbs who'd declared independence from Croatia in their pocket of territory just inland from the coast.

The Serbs called the territory Krajina. It was a borderland within Croatia that the Austro-Hungarians had created as a frontier buffer against the Turks. The Austrians had populated the area with displaced Serbs, and now their descendants were trying to secede from Croatia, just as Croatia was struggling to break free from Yugoslavia. In doing so, the Krajina Serbs all but cut Croatia in half, blocking the main road that connected the long, thin slice of the republic's Dalmatian coastline to the main body of the country up north. The dark columns of smoke marked his course south from Zagreb until he'd crossed the coastal mountains.

Della Torre turned into Istria's verdant interior. Stands of poplar stood among oak forests, orchards, wheat fields, and everywhere vineyards rose out of the rich red earth. The countryside was guarded by hilltop villages, each a little fortress of white walls with a church tower rising from the centre like a sentry against the pirates who used to pillage these lands in centuries past. The farmers wouldn't be harvesting their grapes for another month; they'd wait for the berries to absorb the sun's full sweetness so that they would not need to add sugar to the juice to aid fermentation. It was always a delicate balance; a late storm could yet ruin the crop. But for the coming weeks they could do nothing but wait and hope. And wonder whether, even if it was a good vintage, there would be a market for their wine.

Come the time, maybe he'd take a few days off and help his father with the picking. Della Torre hadn't done it in years. He'd hated the work as a boy and young man; it was hard, backbreaking effort. But he was starting to feel nostalgic. Honest work, his father called it.

Somewhere in there was an unspoken criticism of della Torre's UDBA job, a subject neither father nor son ever broached. Maybe it was because in his years as an academic in Zagreb, the state's long shadow had loomed over everything della Torre senior wrote, everything he said, much of what he'd allowed himself to think. And then to have his son become a servant of the pitiless, arbitrary machine that maintained the state . . .

Della Torre drove past the village where his grandparents, aunt and uncle, and cousins lived. He seldom saw them. Even within families, Istrians were reserved.

The Yugo's rattle lessened as he turned onto the newly asphalted road taking him the final two kilometres to his father's house. The car had somehow survived another four-hour trip without falling apart. It wasn't old, but it was as reliable as a wooden horseshoe.

He stopped at the high iron gates that opened onto a walled courtyard. Della Torre found the key, hidden behind a loose stone in the wall. It was as big as a revolver and just as heavy. He fed it into the massive lock. The gates were well balanced and on oiled steel rollers, so they opened easily and noiselessly. He drove into the courtyard, which had been paved with smooth white Istrian stone by some distant ancestor three centuries before.

He parked the car in an old ox shed, stopping only to wonder at the new blue Volkswagen Golf that stood alongside his father's decrepit Renault 4 and an equally old canvas-sided truck. Those vehicles couldn't have been much younger than della Torre, and he was coming on for thirty-seven years old. The Golf was a rental and had Zagreb plates. He wondered if his father had a guest, or perhaps he'd borrowed the vehicle from a cousin in Poreč who managed the local branch of a car rental company. Sometimes he did that when he was planning a longer trip, say to Trieste or Zagreb or Ljubljana.

Della Torre went back to shut the gates and replace the key. As he did, he took in a lungful of the smells that told him, better than his eyes could, where he was. Hay and ancient dung from the barns behind the house. A faint whiff of wine spilled on the cellar floors and gone sour over the years. His own sweat from the searing heat of the afternoon sun. Engine oil and petrol from the ox shed. The distant, overripe sweetness of fallen fruit in the orchard. Wheat from a field just beyond the house. The hot earth, as deeply coloured as rust. And fresh-baked bread.

He walked over to the house. It was built from the same marble-white blocks of stone that paved the courtyard. The house's bottom storey was a tall wine cellar; he climbed an

outdoor staircase to a large vine-covered terrace onto which
the main door to the house opened. In the middle of the terrace, which was as big as a town garden, was the wellhead to
a giant cistern. Water was a precious commodity in Istria, and
though the house was connected to the mains, the cistern still
fed a walled vegetable garden abutting the building.

The green-shaded terrace immediately softened the heat
of the sun, heavy clumps of grapes, plump but still a greenish
blue, almost touching his head.

"What a nice surprise," his father said, rising to give him a
hug. He'd been sitting on a stone bench built into three sides of
the terrace wall. A heavy wooden table was laid out in front of
him. On it was a carafe of wine and the remains of lunch: a few
slices of the local cured ham and cheese next to a few spears of
raw red pepper, a handful of cherry tomatoes, and a half-eaten
slice of homemade bread. Two places had been laid.

"Looks like you were expecting me," della Torre said, and
then noticed the dregs of wine in the tumbler and the crumbs
of cheese on the unoccupied plate.

"How could I have been expecting you when you don't pick
up the phone and you don't answer your messages?" Dr. Piero
della Torre's eyebrows came together for a brief moment, a
sign of irritation that his son remembered well from his youth.
"No, I wasn't expecting you, but you're welcome to join us."

The older man smiled contentedly, in a way that caught his
son by surprise. Not that his father was a grim man. But since
his mother's death—when della Torre wasn't yet a teenager—
his father's every expression had been smudged by grief, sometimes only just apparent in the distant corners of his eyes, but
always there. Even after a quarter of a century, laughing over
the old Laurel and Hardy films they both loved, della Torre
could sense a distant sorrow in the older man. Or maybe it was
a reflection of his own feelings when they were together.

"Sorry. I've been . . . I've been distracted. I'd have called to say

I was coming, but I didn't know until this morning. I've barely packed anything. I'll be here for a few days, if you don't mind."

"Of course I don't mind."

Della Torre sat in the chair opposite the older man and washed the used tumbler in front of him with water from a second carafe, draining the contents into a ring of holes drilled into the stone floor. Into the same glass he then poured wine the yellow-orange colour of petrol, and helped himself to the remains of his father's lunch.

"So, who else is here? Old man Brnobić?" della Torre asked. Brnobić was a cousin, a retired priest, and his father's chess and drinking companion. They were divided on any number of subjects, from politics to religion to culture, but were brought together by loneliness and intelligence.

"No. Haven't managed to see him for a little while. I've been busy."

"I guess with Libero getting older you're needing to do more of the work yourself. Time you found yourself someone else to help around here. I hope you've still got somebody coming to tidy the house."

Over the years various middle-aged women from the local villages had come to gossip and do basic housework for him. They'd come once a week for a few months, and then his father would chafe under their intrusion and tell them they weren't needed, until the mess got the better of him. Then the women would come again.

"Libero's fine. And I've managed to do a bit of sorting in the house," his father said.

"Oh really," della Torre said, trying not to show his skepticism.

Having knocked the edge off his hunger and thirst, della Torre took a closer look at the older man. Now in his late six-ties, he was showing signs of age. He'd been retired from the university for nearly a decade, and the hard work on the farm was beginning to be beyond him. His eyes were watery. Not quite the bloodshot eyes of an alcoholic, but maybe heading in that direction. The jowls were heavier than della Torre remembered. The back was rounded from a lifetime of bending over manuscripts. Like many long-time bachelors, his father softened his own company with too much drink, hoarded too much junk, lived in his own dust. Della Torre knew something of that existence too. But the older della Torre's writing kept him busy. Kept him alive.

There were still hints of the man he'd been. His shoulders were still broad and strong. He was, after all, the son of farmers and knew how to work the soil himself. Even stooped, he was nearly as tall as his son. There was something of a Roman emperor to his aquiline nose, the high forehead, and the short hair, now gone silver-grey.

His forearms spoke of residual strength. Della Torre remembered when as a teenager he'd once asked his father to open a recalcitrant pickle jar. The old man hadn't been much older than della Torre was now. He'd watched as his father gripped the jar, muscles straining until the glass buckled, exploding in his hands like a crushed egg. He'd cut himself slightly, the vinegar making him wince. He'd grinned and said, *"Pour encourager les autres."*

Now the silver hairs on those forearms against the tanned, wrinkled skin betrayed his age. Yet there was a surprising liveliness to the old man's smile that della Torre hadn't seen in a long time.

"How's the elbow?" his father asked.

"Better. Mostly healed. It's a bit stiff. They think they'll keep the metalwork in, though I could probably ask for it to be taken out eventually. It's as normal as you can expect for somebody who never uses his left arm," della Torre said.

"So they've given you another holiday, then?"

"Something like that. I've got to go back early next week."

"Fine," his father said. Usually he welcomed della Torre's

company, wanting him to stay as long as possible. He liked it even better when della Torre's wife...ex-wife, Irena, was with him. Though it had been a while since he'd stopped asking when she was coming.

"How's the work?" della Torre asked.

As an academic, his father had specialized in middle European Slavic languages. But during recent years he'd re-made himself as an impartial commentator on Yugoslav polit-ical developments. Business was good. Interest was constantly growing.

"Not bad. I'm writing commentary for U.S. policy journals. The Americans have suddenly discovered us. But..."

Della Torre followed the path of his father's gaze, twisting in his chair to look back towards the house. The younger man's mouth fell open, as if a hinge in his jaw had come loose.

There, on the step leading from the farmhouse's front door onto the terrace, stood a woman wearing a green print bikini top that matched the vines crawling up the overhead trellis. She'd wrapped a similarly patterned sarong low around her hips, so he couldn't tell if she was wearing anything under-neath. Her heart-shaped face was freckled, and her copper hair fell loose around her bare, pale shoulders. If there was a blem-ish, it was her nose, its ridge a little too prominent and margin-ally bent to one side. But della Torre forgave the flaw when she smiled at him. It was the sort of smile that made men weak at the knees.

"Hi," she said in American-accented English, as she walked barefoot towards father and son.

**4**

"**MY SON, MARKO**, who you've been asking so much about," Piero said in his accented but clear English, nodding towards della Torre. "This is Rebecca Vees. She's the American researcher I told you about, the one who's interested in my work. She's been staying with me."

Della Torre stood up quickly, almost knocking his chair backwards as he did.

"How do you do," she said.

"Yes. How do you do," he echoed.

Della Torre was mesmerized by the softness of her naked flesh between breasts and hips. It took him an awkward moment before he noticed she was holding a hand out towards him. Her hand was cool and small, but her grip had substance and there was a roughness to the skin. He recovered a semblance of composure, enough to step back from the table and offer up his seat.

"I'm afraid it seems I took your chair," he said. "And your plate and glass too."

"Never mind, I'll sit next to Piero. The stone's nice and cool anyway," she said.

Her eyes opened wide as she spoke to him. She turned to

della Torre's father and lay some bound papers she'd been holding in her hand on a clear corner of the table.

Piero? Hearing her use his father's Christian name came as an aftershock to della Torre. Istria was old-fashioned. People still used formal language between the generations. Okay, so on closer inspection he could tell she wasn't quite as young as she'd first seemed, when she'd been framed by the front door's white stone architrave and lit by sunlight filtered green through the vine leaves. There were fine wrinkles in the corners of her eyes, and the backs of her hands looked like they were familiar with physical work. Even so, she couldn't have been past her early thirties; she was at least four or five years younger than he was.

She sat on a flat, long cushion bleached with age, next to his father. So close they touched.

"I'll get you another glass," della Torre said, making a move for the house.

"Don't bother. I've had lunch and I don't drink much in the afternoon," she said, smiling brightly at him.

She picked up the folder and turned to della Torre's father. "This is as much as I came up with back in the States, but they're only rough notes. I hadn't really intended to work on them. Only if something came up."

"I'm sure we can do a bit of work on it over the next few days," his father said, tilting his head back so that he could read the notes through the bottom edge of his glasses.

"I'm researching the development of the Glagolitic alphabet," she said, turning to the son.

"So you study Slavonic languages, like my father," della Torre said, struggling to regain his composure.

"I'm no specialist. I'm beginning to research the subject."

"Oh, are you an academic?" he asked.

"Sort of," she said, not elaborating.

"Where?"

"At George Mason," she said, that smile never leaving her lips.

He shook his head. "Where is it?"

"In Virginia," she said. "Ever been there?"

"Never," he said, trying to refresh his memory of American geography from primary school. Once upon a time he could name every state and its capital. Now he had only a rough idea of where Virginia was. Somewhere to the east and south.

"It's very nice," she said. "Rolling hills, beaches, and the Blue Ridge Mountains. You should come sometime. I'll show you around."

"That's a kind offer," he said. "So are you doing a doctorate or post-doctoral work?"

"Your notes here give you away," the older man said to Rebecca, interrupting the conversation. "They show that you come at your analysis from the Russian. You've been deceived by some false friends, words from different languages that sound the same but have different meanings. Very naughty to start with the presumption of Russian when approaching middle European Slavic languages. It's like the mistake people often make in thinking the word *histrionic* is related to the word *hysteria*. *Hysteria* comes from the Latin for *womb*. But *histrionic* is from *Histria*, which the Romans called Istria. The most famous actors were from Histria, and so *histrionic* refers to an ability to act, and not to womb or women."

Della Torre couldn't resist a little indulgent smile at his father. Piero loved explaining the etymology of *histrionic* because it often came as a surprise, even to linguists.

Rebecca smiled. "I said they were very rough," she said by way of apology.

"Oh, never mind. You're not a specialist. But I think a little more reading is in order before you start to build a thesis of any sort. And work on your Slovak. Very important for this. Not to mention Serbo-Croat."

"You speak Serbo-Croat?" della Torre asked. His father had long argued that it was spurious to claim that Serbian and Croatian were separate languages; they were no more separate than American and British English, albeit with different alphabets. The differences were trivial, a matter of accent and a handful of words and a deep-seated enmity of two peoples. His father's views may have been correct for a philologist, but they didn't win him many friends among nationalists on either side.

"Not really. My background is in Russian, but I've taken an interest in western Slavic languages. That's why I'm here. I invited myself a while ago, and your father's just too kind to turn down a stranger."

The memory precipitated from a fog in a distant corner of his mind. His father had mentioned an American research student some time ago, but della Torre had been too preoccupied to give it much thought. He had been on the run. From hired killers, from the Zagreb cops, from the UDBA. He'd driven through Istria on his way to London, via Venice, moving as quickly and secretly as he could. But he'd felt a pang on his way past his father's house, not knowing when he'd ever see his father or the house again. So he'd taken an enormous risk in calling the old man. He wasn't sure what he'd expected. Maybe some deep, longed-for . . . what? Whatever he'd been hoping for, he hadn't gotten it. Instead, he'd spent worried moments listening to gossip, conversational filler — and, he now remembered, something about an American researcher.

"I'll find some references for you," Piero said. "You'll be able to look them up when you get back to Washington. But that's for later; it's a side issue to the work you're doing."

"Time for a little break," Rebecca said. "We got right down to it from the minute I showed up, and haven't stopped since. Isn't that right, Piero?" She lowered her head and looked up at the older man through her eyelashes.

For a moment della Torre could have sworn he'd seen his

father's cheeks colour. The old man kept his eyes on the notes in front of him. His prominent widow's peak was more apparent than ever; the hair was almost completely white, in marked contrast to his deeply tanned skin. No, della Torre decided, he'd been mistaken; it was probably just the afternoon heat.

"You've been staying here?"

"For a little more than a week now. It's terrific. I love how you can really feel history in the place. You can almost taste it," she said, running her bottom lip under her teeth in a way that sent an electric current up della Torre's spine.

History. She was right. Maybe there was too much of it. A history of armies and of destruction. The ruins of a Roman hamlet lay under his father's wheat field. Bits of stone wall and the detritus of an ancient civilization pushed up through the soil now and again. And his family history was tied to it.

His father had bought the house as a ruin, a project for the two of them, when they'd come back from the U.S. after della Torre's mother died. They'd rebuilt it, at a time when these old stone houses were being abandoned in favour of new, concrete structures, the local architecture replaced with anodyne modern Mediterranean villas that wouldn't have been out of place in Spanish or Greek resorts.

But when they'd finished, people came from all over Istria to marvel at their work. No doubt some laughed up their sleeves that these Yugo-Americans had spent so much time and money on an old house when a new one would have been so much cheaper and easier to build. But even they had admired the quality of the restoration and the household conveniences they'd only ever seen on television: a machine to wash dishes, a big shower that never ran out of hot water, air conditioning in almost every room.

The house had been state of the art a quarter of a century before. But, like his father, it had grown tired in the intervening years.

Rebecca pulled her head closer to the old man's so that they were reading the papers together. It gave della Torre another chance to look at her closely. The pale skin, marked by small freckles; the curve of her breasts. He felt a pang. Could it be he was jealous?

She looked up suddenly, catching the younger della Torre scrutinizing her. Again that smile.

"So how long are you here?" she asked.

"Just the weekend. I'm due back in Zagreb on Monday."

"What a coincidence. I need to get to Zagreb next week too. I'd like to do a bit of research in the library there. Maybe we can make the trip together," she said.

Della Torre senior looked up sharply, his head drawing back as if in reproach. "I didn't realize you'd be leaving so soon."

"You've been so kind, Piero, but I really can't encroach any further on your hospitality. I've been here too long already. I'd only intended to spend a few days. Besides, there are a couple of people I promised to look up in Zagreb," she said.

Della Torre thought he could read hurt in his father's expression.

"I need to be in Poreč tomorrow, might make a day of it. So I'll stay out of your hair while I'm here," della Torre said. "Right now, if you don't mind, I'm going to have a shower. It was a hot drive."

"If you don't mind, I'll join you," she said. Della Torre's look of panic made her laugh. "I mean on the drive down to Poreč. I need to pick up one or two things and it'll make a nice change from the brain work."

"I can drive you," della Torre's father said, hurriedly. "We can all go to Poreč tomorrow."

Della Torre shrugged. "Like I said, I'll probably be making a day of it, so I'll take my own car. Anyway, it's nice to meet you," he said to Rebecca.

"The pleasure is all mine."

.    .    .

The house was considerably tidier than when della Torre had seen it last. Papers still covered the dining-room table, but now they were in ordered stacks. Surfaces looked like they'd been dusted. The kitchen had been scrubbed and the perennially dripping faucet had been mended. Books were back on their shelves and shutters had been opened for the first time since he and his father had hung them, despite the heat of the day.

He went to put his overnight bag in his room but stopped short. Rebecca's clothes were folded on a chair, and her suitcase was at the end of the double bed, the one he and Irena had bought.

He carried on through to a small interconnected room. It had been his study and model-making room when he'd been a teenager, and it had a single bed that he'd used as a sofa. The room wasn't air-conditioned, but enough cool air flowed through the louvred door from his bedroom. He'd be comfortable for the three nights he was there.

Della Torre dropped his bag on the bed and went through another door to the hall that led to the bathroom. Rebecca's toiletries were on the shelf. Nothing elaborate, but feminine enough for della Torre to feel Irena's absence. He'd call her when he got back to Zagreb.

He took a long, cool shower and then headed back to his room with a towel wrapped around his waist. Rebecca was in the hall.

"Sorry. Have you been waiting for me to get out?" he asked.

"Nope. Besides, I'm the one who should be apologizing for taking your room. You can have it back if you like," she said, running her gaze up and down his damp torso.

"That's fine. It'll seem like old times sleeping in my little bed," he said. "If you don't mind me parking myself next door. Sound travels between the rooms and I'm told I sometimes snore."

"Just as long as you don't smoke. Then again, maybe I won't mind if you do." She paused. "Well, if you have all your things, I was going to take a little siesta. I've grown used to them. A cool shower and a lie-down these hot afternoons."

The sarong she'd tied around her waist slipped lower still. His eyes traced an invisible line that arrowed down her belly from her navel.

"Don't let me stop you," he said, shutting the door behind him.

His hand rested on the doorknob for a long time before he pulled on some shorts. He lay on his bed, thinking, while she showered. But the heat of the day, the journey, and the wine at lunch lulled him to sleep before she finished.

It was late in the afternoon when he woke. He pulled on an old T-shirt that fit better than it had in years. He must have lost weight since getting shot.

He made his way downstairs barefoot and found a pair of his father's plastic sandals by the front door—they wore the same size shoes. There was no sign of life in the house. Della Torre guessed his father would be in his study, reading and drinking watered-down wine or cold beer, as he did most afternoons. In the evenings he moved on to grappa or slivovitz, the fierce local plum brandy, while watching Italian television or listening to the World Service or sometimes American or German short-wave broadcasts.

As it was, the old man drank too much. Della Torre wondered how much worse it would be if his father didn't have his writing to keep him focused and sober at least part of the time. Maybe with Rebecca around he'd been drinking less.

Della Torre stepped out onto the terrace and wandered down into the courtyard and through an arched wooden door in the garden wall, into the well-tended vineyards. This was another thing that kept his father going—the vines. He still sprayed them by hand, finishing the day coated in the harsh blue-green mixture of copper sulphate and lime used to kill the fungus that rotted grapes.

The grapes were already ripening; they'd need harvesting early this year. Della Torre wondered if there'd be a market for the wine. It wouldn't matter much for his father, who sold only a little to the cooperative. But the farmers would suffer.

He'd hung a Lucky off his lower lip, stopping to strike a match, when he heard footsteps. Light ones, barely brushing the ground. He turned.

"I saw you going for a walk. Thought I might join you. Hope you don't mind," she said, though something in her voice suggested she was indifferent to what he wanted. She stood in the next row of vines, mostly hidden by the broad leaves.

"By all means," he said, shrugging. He reached for the cigarettes and offered one to her through the wire that held up the plant's tendrils. She smiled and shook her head.

"I don't think you said whether you were doing a doctorate or post-doc work," he said.

"No," she said.

"No?"

"No, I didn't say." That smile again. "Your father tells me you're a lawyer. Any special sort of law or just the usual accidents and contracts?" she said with what he thought might be irony. He couldn't be sure; she was almost invisible behind the foliage. What exactly had his father told her?

"I work for the prosecutor's office. I investigate suspected cases of fraud in our legal system, where corruption may have caused innocent people to be, um, jailed." It was the standard shorthand he used to get around the fact that he worked for the UDBA. But the essence of what he'd told her was close to the truth. "Or I used to. Now it looks like I've been drafted into the Croatian army."

They'd reached the end of the row and could see each other clearly. Della Torre turned right so that they walked side by side between blocks of vines.

"Accidents of justice. Contracts taken out wrongly," she said. "Something like that."

"So how does an American end up working for the—" She paused for a long beat. "—for the prosecutor's office and then joining the Croatian army? I didn't know Croatia had an army."

"Dad told you I was American?" he said.

His father had always been circumspect about his son's other nationality. It was no secret that they'd lived in America for much of della Torre's childhood, but no one in Yugoslavia, apart from his father and his wife, knew he was an American citizen. Nobody in the UDBA. He was certain of it. He kept his passport updated by travelling to Rome and applying to the American embassy there. Only della Torre and his mother had taken citizenship. His father had decided he'd be best off sticking to a green card. As a young academic he'd had to join the Communist Party, and he'd never officially renounced it. Americans didn't look favourably on citizens who were Communists.

Rebecca didn't answer but merely smiled at him. "I take it you're a member of the Communist Party. You'd have to be to hold a senior position. Wouldn't you?" There was something in the way she said "Communist," the crisp, sharp, legal tone that made his muscles tighten and his head pull back.

"What else did my father tell you about me?"

"Not much. That you're married but live apart from your wife. That you don't have any children and this might have something to do with why your wife no longer wants to live with you. That you've never wanted to go back with him to visit the States since you moved here as a kid. Not even to visit your mother's grave. Speaking of which, he didn't talk much about your mother. What happened to her?"

"I'm the wrong person to ask," della Torre said abruptly.

"Sorry. I understand," she said.

He was starting to realize what disturbed him about her smile. It wasn't reflected in her eyes.

"I think he doesn't quite understand why you don't leave, now that the war's coming," she said.

"No. Neither do I," said della Torre. He'd tried. Earlier that year, he'd run away to London, escaping the hired Bosnian killers. For a short while he thought he'd be able to make a new life for himself there with Harry Martingale. But he'd failed. And got shot along the way.

"He didn't tell me what you did to your arm," she said.

He looked down at the pink wound. His arm wouldn't quite straighten, but it was throbbing less than it had since he'd got shot.

"An accident," he said.

"Like the ones you investigate?" she asked.

"Not quite as..." He let his thought trail off.

"As final?" she asked.

He shrugged. They'd walked into his father's orchard, at the end of which was a small wheat field. Della Torre helped himself to a peach. It hung heavy, ripe, so that he took it gently, not wanting to bruise the flesh. The hot, still air was luscious with its sweet scent. He offered the peach to Rebecca, but she shook her head. He bit into it and the juice ran down his chin; he leaned forward to keep it from dripping on his shirt.

In the distance, his father's farmhouse hung above a sea of green vines, an island of white stone turned pink in the evening light. Now in shadow, the earth under their feet was a deep blood red. Above, a high mare's tail streaked the sky. A storm was coming.

**5**

DELLA TORRE SAT in the back seat of the Renault 4. The complete lack of sound insulation meant having to shout over the rattling engine, so they stayed quiet after the first feeble attempts at conversation.

His father had insisted on driving them to Poreč. They'd have a great time in town, he said at dinner the night before. He'd already shown Rebecca the sights on an earlier trip: the Byzantine basilica, some Roman ruins, and the graceful Venetian palazzos. They could go to the beach while della Torre did his business at the police station. And then they could meet up for lunch at a favourite fish restaurant on the quayside, overlooking the harbour and the island of St Nikola beyond.

Della Torre would rather have gone alone, left the two to their own devices. But he saw that his father had become set on his plan, and so he dutifully gave in.

His father drove the car with intense concentration, hunched over the wheel, which he gripped hard with both hands when he wasn't shifting gears. And he aimed to shift as little as possible. The senior della Torre had discovered long ago that the car functioned well at exactly 35 kilometres an hour, a speed that required little braking or slowing for corners. Fortunately for other drivers, he used only small country lanes unless he absolutely couldn't avoid the bigger roads. And fortunately for his passengers, it was only 15 kilometres to Poreč.

The road through the fields from the house was newly paved—a blessing, given the Renault's almost complete lack of suspension. Only a few years back it had still been a rutted dirt track. Coming into a long corner, they disturbed a flock of starlings warming themselves on the asphalt. As the car approached, the birds lifted off and flew at waist height in the direction of Poreč, hovering directly in front of the car like a black cloud, following the road through every curve.

His father didn't waver, even as the distance between the birds and the car narrowed. And then, as if in slow motion, the birds were scooped along the bonnet. Still beating their wings, they slid the length of the car until they reached the windscreen. Then, tail feathers up, their orifices pressed flat against the glass, they slid up and over the roof. Della Torre looked behind him. The birds did little cartwheels as they fell off the top of the car and into its slipstream. As soon as they were in still air again, they fell back into formation. And so the Renault passed through the whole flock, bird by astonished bird.

The absurdity hit della Torre, and he laughed out loud. His father didn't seem to have noticed the strange occurrence, and Rebecca stared straight ahead as if she wasn't sure what she'd just experienced.

Della Torre looked into the rear-view mirror, catching his father's eyes. There was a humour in them. More like the person della Torre remembered from before his mother had died. The spirit of joy had crept back into the old man. Years spooled back and happy memories resurfaced. And then, with a jolt, he realized his mistake. He hadn't been looking into his father's eyes. He'd been looking into his own.

They dropped della Torre off at the police station on the edge of the old town. He showed his ID to the sergeant at the front desk, who immediately sat up. An UDBA document commanded fear and revulsion, like a tattooed face.

The sergeant hadn't been expecting him but sent della Torre up to the station captain's office anyway. The captain hadn't arrived yet, so della Torre made himself comfortable on the sofa after getting a uniformed secretary to make him a cup of coffee. It wasn't a particularly nice coffee—too much sugar and too gritty—but at least the office's upright fan worked. Della Torre had dozed off by the time the captain arrived.

"Ah, Comrade della Torre," he said twice before della Torre responded.

Caught by surprise, della Torre couldn't remember the captain's name, so he just stood up and shook the man's hand.

"Captain, how good to see you. Hope you don't mind that I made myself at home. One of your typists very kindly brewed up a cup of coffee. I'd been told to get here sharp or somebody'd be wearing my ears on a necklace," della Torre said.

"Very sorry. I'd have been in earlier, but I had to drive my wife down to Rovijn to see her sister, and by the time I'd picked up her order from the butcher's and got it home, well, you know how it is." He was flustered.

Usually nothing very interesting happened in this part of the world. Mostly tourists getting into car accidents and the occasional theft. Specialist squads down in Pula or Rijeka dealt with the serious stuff, such as drug trafficking or crime rings, while political matters were left for the UDBA. Or had been.

Della Torre shrugged. Both men stood there looking at each other for a while.

"So, how is it in Zagreb?" the captain finally asked.

"Gloomy. The war's coming and nobody knows how to avoid it."

"Yes." The captain nodded. "We've started losing tourists and gaining refugees. Something tells me they won't be nearly as good for the economy. And it'll make us busier."

Della Torre raised his hands in what he hoped was a sympathetic gesture. Though it could also have been taken to mean "So what?"

They fell silent again. Della Torre really knew no way around the question, so he attacked it straight on.

"You wouldn't know why I'm here by any chance, would you?" he asked.

"You don't know?" the captain said.

"No. Frankly, I was hoping you might tell me."

"I only got word last night that somebody from Zagreb would be coming sometime today," he said, shrugging his shoulders. "I wasn't expecting anyone till the afternoon. They usually don't come until the afternoon. Had I known it was you, I'd have arranged something. We could have met up over a coffee somewhere civilized, maybe brought the old girl along, you know how she likes to talk family. But she's in Rovijn till Sunday."

Della Torre belatedly remembered that the captain's wife was a distant cousin. Everybody in Istria seemed to be a cousin. Or married to one.

"I'm sorry to have missed her." Della Torre tried to remember whether he was sorry or not, but the woman wouldn't come into focus. It probably meant she wasn't too bad.

"Actually, since you're here, I might as well fill you in. You're family and all, and I can trust you," the captain said, though as he said it, he wiped his hand on his trouser leg and wouldn't raise his eyes from della Torre's Italian blue silk tie.

He shut the office door and pulled out a couple of shot glasses and a bottle of homemade slivovitz from his filing cabinet.

"I know it's early, but a little sip can't hurt, can it?"

Della Torre acquiesced. It was traditional to have a swallow of something strong, coffee or alcohol or both, before sitting down to talk business. Whatever the time.

"I'm not quite sure how to say this, but I think we're being put into a difficult position here. A really hard one," the captain said, the words inadvertently bumping up against each other.

"Yes, I'm afraid it's the same everywhere," della Torre said. "Having to choose between Croatia and Yugoslavia — this new Shangri-La or the country you've been taught all your life is your homeland and which you're sworn to defend."

The captain nodded in a slightly embarrassed way. "Yes. Yes, of course there's that. But there's something else too."

"Oh?" said della Torre.

"Well, you see, they've been taking my officers, my policemen. Zagreb, that is..."

"I guess they're building up units for the war. Maybe, with God's grace, we won't need them. But we have to have an army when we're being faced with the JNA," della Torre said, trying to justify what was happening everywhere, the mobilization of Croat men. The JNA, Yugoslavia's national army, would be a formidable enemy.

"Oh, of course. That's only right. We all have to muck in. No, it's just that..."

He paused.

"That Poreč needs experienced senior officers to stay at their posts?" della Torre prompted.

He was sympathetic. He'd have felt the same way as the middle-aged man in front of him. In fact, della Torre felt exactly as he suspected this other man did. Nobody wanted to go to war, to be in the sights of a Serbian machine-gunner. Here was a veteran cop, used to handing out parking tickets and signing insurance forms for Germans who'd had their cameras stolen. Not for B-movie heroics.

But the captain bridled at della Torre's implication.

"No. It's not what you think. If those people in Zagreb want me to do my patriotic duty, they can have me. My kids are all grown up, and hell, I might even be useful. I may not be a great leader of men but I can navigate bureaucratic bullshit, and unless things have changed from my national service days, there's plenty of bullshit in the army," he said. "No, the problem is they're sending my men, Istrian boys, to the front lines and they're filling the posts here with kids from Zagreb and out east. Connected kids, if you know what I mean. You look at their surnames and ask them a few questions, and the lot of them have a father or an uncle in Parliament or high up in government."

"I'm sorry. I didn't mean to cast aspersions," della Torre said.

That the politicians in Zagreb were protecting their kin by giving them soft jobs well away from the action while making Istrians stand in their place was an ugly revelation, but maybe not surprising. If there was anywhere likely to stay safe from the impending war, it was Istria. The province had precious little strategic value except as a holiday resort, and no Serb population to speak of. And if things got too hot there, it was only a short ferry ride to Venice.

"No, I can see why you thought I might be looking to . . . you know, to get out of army service. I mean, who wouldn't," the captain apologized in turn. "I know there's nothing you can do about it. But it worries me. And it's not just because they're looking for a safe place to hide their sons. Zagreb doesn't trust us. Maybe they sent you to listen for rumblings of discontent. I've spent the last thirty years in the force keeping my mouth shut. Hell, I kept it shut even before that, when I was a kid. But if we're going to be a new country, if all those checkerboard flags are meant to mean something other than a new bunch of the same old, it'd be nice to feel that they weren't operating the same way as the Communists. Beg pardon." He excused himself, with a look of surprise and shock at what he'd just said.

Once upon a time, talk like that would have been a ticket to Goli Otok. Would it still? And if not, what taboo would replace it? In a country where even jocular priests might say, offhandedly, "May God fuck your mother," and mothers shout at their wayward children, "Your mother's cunt," what would be forbidden once people were allowed to slander the Party? Would turning your back on Croat nationalism get you shot?

The policeman poured himself and della Torre another finger's width and then shrugged. "Maybe the next time you come here, there'll be somebody else in this office. Maybe things really aren't changing."

Della Torre nodded sadly. He knew the captain spoke the truth. There were high hopes that by gaining independence Croatia might prove to be more noble than the thoroughly rotten country it was seceding from. But the people who'd taken control of the Croat government were Communists from the old administration. The old crooks were being replaced by not-so-new ones. He'd noticed how one or two UDBA men, from the dirty parts of the service, had shown up in senior posts in the new Croat government. Istria would be used as a fief by whatever faction, whatever political interests came out on top. A rich, quiet province to be milked and used as the politicians wanted.

"No one will hear anything from me. At least nothing that's going to make your life any more difficult," said della Torre. "I think I'm in the same position as you now. Dangling a little. They sent me here without even telling me why. Who knows what they'll want from me when I get back."

The captain got the same woman to make them coffees and dig up some biscuits. The two men talked a little more about the upcoming grape harvest and whether the rains would hold off. But it was a distracted conversation, and before long the press of ordinary police business impinged.

When they parted, della Torre held the man's hand in his a long time and asked that the captain remember him to his wife. He meant it. They were family here.

.    .    .

When della Torre got to the restaurant, his father was sitting alone at a table with a bottle of beer in front of him. He was toying with roasted nuts in a small dish, slouched in his chair, looking old again, worn, staring into the distance across the harbour. Shipwrecked on that big covered terrace. The waterfront had been abandoned, like della Torre had never seen before, not in high summer. The only other people there were a couple of older Germans sitting in silence over their coffees a few tables away.

"Oh, hello, Marko," Piero said, looking up and noticing his son only at the last minute. "You get everything done?"

"I don't know. I'm really not sure what I was meant to be doing," della Torre said honestly. "You're alone?"

"Well, Rebecca wanted a swim and I thought it'd be a good chance to get one or two things done in town."

"Where'd she go?"

"St Nikola," his father said, waving over to the pine-covered island on the other side of the harbour. Years before, it had been taken over by German, Austrian, and Italian nudists. "She said she was swimming there and taking the midday boat back. She has a little waterproof rucksack that she swims with. Ingenious."

"She must have some stamina," della Torre said.

His father hemmed in answer.

The waiter came over and della Torre ordered a lemonade. There was no point in getting tanked up this early in the day; he could still feel the afterburn of the slivovitz.

"So what do you think it's going to be, Dad?"

"What?"

"The thing you seem to spend your life on these days." His father seemed unsure how to answer, so della Torre continued: "The state of the nation."

"Oh." His father looked relieved at the question. He sat up a little, giving himself space to wave his hands around, which he did when he became animated by a subject of close personal interest. "They've let the Slovenes go, but Croatia's another matter. The Serbs want all the Serbs in Croatia to be part of Greater Serbia, which means chopping the republic into bits, especially if they want access to the Adriatic. Which they do. The army is led mostly by Serbs, so it'll go that way. Croatia hasn't got a chance unless it can pull the Germans and the Americans into the fight. The Germans are supportive, but they won't fight. The Americans would fight, but now that the Soviets are falling apart, they're not so interested. The Russians will support the Serbs, though they've got plenty on their own plate."

"Will it be war?"

"It is war. The only question is whether our dear and noble Croatian leaders roll over and allow the Serbs to take big chunks of Croat territory or whether they put up resistance. If they roll over, the crisis will keep flaring up for decades. If they put up a fight it'll be quicker and bloodier. But the result will be the same, unless Croatia can get the Germans actively involved or make the Americans think it's worth their while to help. The Americans might respond to being bribed. Except we have nothing to bribe them with. There's no oil and not a hell of a lot else besides pretty scenery, and they have enough scenery of their own. We might be able to use moral suasion, but a lot of innocent people would have to die first before a sense of outrage forced the Americans to notice. Or we could try blackmail."

"Blackmail? You mean like catching the ambassador in a clinch with a male prostitute?"

"Probably something bigger than that. But don't ask me what. I can't even imagine," his father said with an elaborate shrug.

"Maybe if we told them Elvis is still alive and living in a Belgrade brothel," della Torre said.

His father waved a hand at his son. "Don't be absurd."

"Or that the Yugoslavs helped to fake the moon landings," della Torre said.

"Could you imagine if Yugoslavia had had a space program?" His father shook his head.

"We'd be world experts in fireballs and crash landings."

"The space capsules would have all come with cigarette dispensers and ashtrays, and we'd have invented a way of propelling them with slivovitz," his father added, throwing himself into the joke.

"And when they got there, our astronauts would have spent their time trying to claim asylum so they didn't have to come back. Though the lack of cafés might have put them off." Della Torre called the waiter over and was met with a surly shrug. "Maybe we could threaten to destroy the American service industry by sending them all our waiters."

"Ah, well, they know how to smile in theory, that's all that counts."

Della Torre grew more serious. "So we're screwed one way or another," he said. They'd had variations on this conversation for years.

"These are the Balkans. The Balkans are always screwed," Piero said.

"I guess at least Istria will be fine."

"You think so? The Serbs might not take much of an interest, but when the Croats over there—" He waved his arm in the direction of the east. "—get pushed out of their lands, they're going to want to go somewhere. And they're going to want to find a new bunch of people to tell what to do."

"Yes. I got that message already this morning."

"Back when it was a struggle between Zagreb and Belgrade, they left us alone. Once Belgrade wins that particular fight, Zagreb will have plenty of time to devote itself to other problems. Besides, they'll need to tax somebody. Look, you can see them over there. The Serbs." The senior della Torre motioned towards the sea, where a warship sat silhouetted against the horizon.

"Looks like a cruiser," Rebecca said from behind them. Both men half stood from their chairs.

"Dad said you were coming in on the midday boat."

"I decided to swim back. It was easy, no current and warm water. St Nikola was quite dull. Sea urchins and Mediterranean pines all get a bit samey after a while," she said.

"You mean one prick's much like another," della Torre said.

Rebecca cocked her eyebrow. "Something like that," she said.

She took a towel out of a bag next to the senior della Torre, squeezed the water out of her hair, and then pulled on a long shirt.

"Shall we order some food?" Piero said.

6

WHEN THEY GOT back to the house, della Torre decided on a shower and a siesta.

His skin was dripping when he shut the door from the hall to the little room behind him. With the shutters closed and a breath of cool air coming through the slats from the room next door, he was at last comfortable.

He threw himself on the single bed. The springs complained under his weight.

"So, did you get what you needed to do done this morning?"

She was speaking from her room, though he could hear her clearly through the louvred door.

"To tell you the truth, I'm not really sure what I was meant to be doing this morning," he replied, hardly having to raise his voice above a normal tone.

"They sent you all the way from Zagreb but didn't tell you what they wanted you to do?"

"No. I belong to the army now. So there's going to be a lot more of this in my life."

"Didn't you ask?"

"Oh, I asked. They'll probably send me back when they've remembered what they forgot to tell me. I don't mind."

There was a silence.

"You know, your picture doesn't do you justice," she said. "You're even better looking in person."

"Ummm. Thanks," he said.

He was at a loss for which picture she could possibly be referring to. The only one on display in the house was the one his father had taken of him on his twelfth birthday. He was standing next to his mother at the university campus in Ohio where his father had taught. They'd been on their way to a restaurant for lunch, a rare treat. Or maybe coming back from it. It was his mother's last photograph.

The only other possibility was that Rebecca had found a passport-sized snap somewhere in the room, the kind that was used for official documents.

"It's pretty nice and cool in this room. Have you got air conditioning there?"

"It's fine," he said. His heart started to beat a little faster.

"Well, if you wanted to get a little...cooler, you're welcome to join me."

"Thanks," he said and after a huge effort of will, he added: "But I think I'd better not."

"If you change your mind..."

She stopped talking after that. But he heard her moving on the bed regularly and breathing in time. She made a sound like a suppressed cough. He lay there, willing Rebecca to say something to him. Eventually he spoke to her, but it was too late. She was asleep.

·    ·    ·

Della Torre woke early the next morning. On the way to the bathroom, he saw his father standing by an open window looking over the terrace, watching Rebecca. At first della Torre didn't register what she was doing. It looked like a dance, like she was falling through the air in regular undulating movements punctuated by staccato jerks. Something modern. Sometimes she picked up a long stake for vines, using it as part of her choreographed movements.

"Does that every morning," his father said with a gently mocking tone. "Like she's Bruce Lee."

Della Torre nodded. Tai chi and other martial arts were popular in the West as exercise. In London earlier that summer, he'd frequently seen people, especially young women, practising similar moves in the park on weekend mornings.

He knew a little about it. He'd had some training in martial arts during his time in the commandos. The men who'd taught him had themselves spent years learning their skills in North Korea. There was a whole cohort of Yugoslav commandos who'd been through combat courses run by the North Koreans. They were unimaginably tough, brutal men who seldom talked about their experiences in that strange, distant country. Nothing their charges went through, they said, would even approach the pain they themselves had endured. This the younger men took as bravado. But, the trainers continued, what they themselves had suffered was small discomfort compared to what their North Korean peers were subjected to. Only a handful of the Yugoslav commandos in North Korea had died because of the training. Not more than one in twenty or thirty. Whereas the mortality rate for the North Korean commandos was one in four or even three.

As he watched Rebecca, della Torre realized she wasn't an amateur using the martial arts movements as another way of staying lean and healthy. The exactness and speed of her repetition, the steady, inexorable increase in pace, told him she'd been doing this for years and had learned from professionals.

He knew the dance she did could be put to deadly effect.

"She's the real thing, Dad," della Torre said. And when his father gave him a puzzled look, he added, "Let's just say that if you've got it in mind to have somebody's legs broken, she's your man. To move that fast and with that much control is very, very hard, I promise you. If you came at her with a knife, you'd be dead. If you had a gun, you'd better be shooting straight."

.    .    .

He passed the rest of the weekend swimming, eating, and reading novels, trying to stay out of the way, though Rebecca sought him out. They had gone, without Piero, to a little-frequented stony cove a twenty-minute drive south of the port. His father had decided to stay back at the house. "To write," he said.

When they got there, they waded in the water and then sat under the shade of a broad pine tree. Rebecca sat facing him, knees drawn up, feet apart so that he had to look away from the cleft barely covered by her bikini bottom. She talked about movies della Torre hadn't heard of. He knew nothing about the music she mentioned, but they had similar tastes in trash novels. They talked a little about travelling. He was curious about her experiences in the Soviet Union. She asked him what it had been like to serve in the Yugoslav army, her questions making it clear she knew what she was talking about, though she wouldn't be drawn out on why. She deflected all conversation about her family, her friends, her history. At most, she gave anodyne answers.

He felt frustrated at having been sent to Istria on a pointless errand, and that while there he'd managed to wedge himself between his father and whatever brief contentment had befallen him.

On Sunday he told them he'd be leaving for Zagreb early the following morning.

"I'll come too," Rebecca said. "It's time I got going."

Della Torre's father made a frail effort to dissuade her. But she was adamant. Della Torre was intrigued at how firm she could be without being the least bit abrasive.

"But where are you staying in Zagreb?" the old man demanded, as if such a problem was insurmountable and might persuade her to stay in Istria.

"I'm sure there are hotels," she said. "I stayed in one when I came. It's probably still there."

"They're so expensive. No, you have to stay at my apartment. I insist."

Della Torre was surprised. His wife . . . ex-wife, Irena, lived in his father's apartment. There was a spare room, but he wasn't sure what she'd think about having a stranger drop in on her. She'd go along with it, of course. But he didn't think it'd be fair.

"That's a very kind offer. Maybe I'll take you up on it," Rebecca said.

His father looked pleased at the small victory.

"She can stay with me. Your place wouldn't do," della Torre said reluctantly.

"My flat's much nicer," his father argued.

"Yes, but Irena's living there. I'm sure Rebecca would be happy enough to stay with me."

"It's my apartment. I'm sure Irena wouldn't mind for a few days. Besides, I can choose who stays there," his father said, a hint of petulance in his voice. He'd always liked Irena and it surprised della Torre that he would put her in an awkward position.

"I think maybe Marko is right," Rebecca said, putting a hand on the older man's forearm. It looked to della Torre as if she was stroking it, very faintly. "You've done more than enough for me already, Piero. When you come to the States, you'll let me return the favour. Promise?"

Della Torre's father was beaten and didn't offer up any more resistance. That night, he was the first to turn in.

7

## STOCKHOLM, FEBRUARY 1986

THE MONTENEGRIN GOT to the top of the stairs and looked back down the alley, past a skeleton of builders' scaffolding, and saw nothing. He hurried along the street at the top of the little hill until he found the car.

The blue Opel started with some gentle prompting. He'd worried about the cold. The boy had said the Swedish winter could freeze and crack engine blocks.

The Montenegrin swore as the inside of the car's glass started to cloud up. He turned the heater on full, pulling away before the window had defrosted.

He listened hard for the sound of sirens, but heard none.

He drove carefully, avoiding black ice. Once the glass had cleared, he took a turn around a block to see if anyone was on his tail. No one. He crossed the bridge and drove out to the suburb with the low-rise tower blocks. It was mostly immigrants who lived there: Kurds, Turks, some Ethiopians, and various east Europeans and Balkans.

He pulled up in front of the building. The lock on the entrance was broken and the overhead light flickered. Graffiti wasn't unusual in this part of Stockholm, but the area didn't look obviously poor, just a little less well kempt. He climbed the three flights to the apartment's landing. There were only four apartments to a floor. It wasn't a big building, but it was anonymous; the neighbours all kept to themselves. The boy had said the residents were mostly itinerant. They came and went. Some families doubled up for a while, and then there'd be a whole new group of people a few weeks later.

He'd been given keys to the place by a contact in Belgrade. It was an UDBA safe house, most recently used by one of the agency's tame criminals, the head of a Serbian gang that ran drugs and guns to Sweden, except he was cooling his heels in a Malmo prison for illegal possession of a firearm, downgraded from armed robbery. He was six months into a fifteen-month term. Long for possession, but short for armed robbery.

When the Montenegrin had first arrived in the city, late in the evening, he'd expected an empty apartment, but instead he found it occupied by a skinny boy sprawled on a sofa, wearing only a pair of underwear and a red and green tartan blanket draped over his shoulders. Smoking hash out of a water pipe, the boy had greeted him in Swedish, barely taking his eyes off the television.

For a moment the Montenegrin had frozen, uncertain about how to react. In his good English he'd demanded who the boy was and what he was doing there. The boy had replied in a slurred, incomprehensible mix of Swedish and English. The Montenegrin realized his plans would have to change. Whether the boy belonged there or not, he'd have to find somewhere else to stay. He'd cursed at the stupidity of it all, of having no fallback plan, of being alone, of having been deceived by the people in Belgrade, who'd said the apartment was empty and reliable. He'd sworn in Serbo-Croat, quietly. But not so quietly the boy didn't hear. The boy had replied in the same language, accented but clear.

They talked. The boy was Kosovar, with mixed roots, a Serb first name but an Albanian surname. He'd grown up in Sweden and ran odd jobs for the Serbian gangster now in prison. He was the Serbian's boy, he said, leaving it to the Montenegrin to interpret what that meant.

He was pretty, dark skinned with dark brown eyes and long black hair like a girl's. His lanky frame made him look about fifteen, though he said he was eighteen.

The Montenegrin was tired. It had been a long drive from Copenhagen. He didn't know Stockholm or where he might find a room. The boy had said he'd do whatever it was the Montenegrin wanted if he could stay the night on the sofa, assuming immediately that the Montenegrin had rights to the place. The Montenegrin stayed. And so did the boy.

It wasn't a big place and had little in the way of furniture. A bed and chest of drawers in the bedroom, where the Montenegrin slept. A sofa, an easy chair, and a small table with a couple of chairs, as well as the big TV, in the sitting room. There was a bathroom and a kitchenette.

The following morning the boy was up and dressed and eager to please. He knew Stockholm well, could he act as a guide? If this stranger borrowing the apartment didn't speak Swedish, perhaps he could help with any arrangements he needed to make.

The Montenegrin had sent him out with some money to buy breakfast, giving himself time to think about what to do with this unexpected nuisance. The boy came back promptly with a cup of good coffee and a proper breakfast. And all the money. He'd gotten it free, he said, because he knew how.

That day the Montenegrin had driven around Stockholm, using the boy as a guide. The boy knew quick ways around town. He had taken the Montenegrin to a cheap but good Turkish restaurant and told him about the Stockholm police, about how to avoid them and what they looked for, what attracted their attention. The Montenegrin had let him stay another night in the flat. The boy slept on the sofa, drifting off in front of the television after smoking some dope.

The third day, the boy had guided him once again, asked him whether he needed any equipment. A gun, maybe?

The Montenegrin demurred, not wishing to bring the boy into his confidence. The boy had gone out that afternoon anyway and come back with the Smith & Wesson and a couple of boxes of bullets, quoting a cheap price. The Montenegrin had worried that he was being set up. But there was something about the boy that made him seem trustworthy. The boy assured him the gun was in factory mint condition, only ever test-fired. The Montenegrin stripped it down, had a look at the barrel and the revolving chambers, and had to agree. He needed a gun and he'd hoped to pick one up from a Yugoslav underworld contact he'd been given on arrival. The boy suggested driving to his secret place outside of Stockholm, where the Montenegrin could test the gun before buying it, though he'd have to pay for the bullets.

The Montenegrin had told the boy nothing about himself or what he was doing there. Not even a lie. The boy had seemed content to know nothing. It was enough to be allowed to come and go, to smoke dope while watching television. The Montenegrin had figured him for a dealer; the boy kept a gram scale for postage. He didn't seem to have any source of income, but he had enough money to live off, to go out to eat whenever he wanted. But there was no evidence of any drugs other than the small quantity he kept for his own use. At first the Montenegrin had feared the boy's dope smoking would attract the police's attention. But he relaxed as he realized the boy was astonishingly discreet. If he had any family or friends in Stockholm, he showed no signs of it.

Indeed, the boy had told him he was alone in Stockholm. He knew people through the Serb, had contacts but no friends. They were all back in Malmo, where he'd grown up. But he couldn't be bothered to go back. The boy didn't explain why.

Just that he was happy to wait where he was for the Serb to get out of jail. His parents had moved back to their small Kosovor village when they'd saved up enough money to build themselves a house. The boy didn't like it there. Too boring.

Apart from the dope smoking, the Montenegrin had found the boy to be surprisingly bright. Clever and useful, as capable and smart as he was pretty. So the Montenegrin had kept him around. He'd paid him for his help, a couple of weeks ahead. He'd also paid a generous commission for the gun. It was good money.

When the Montenegrin let himself back into the apartment, the boy was sitting on the floor, leaning back on the threadbare brown sofa, watching TV. He was wearing a red-and-grey-striped jersey and jeans. The Montenegrin had made it clear he didn't want the boy walking naked around the apartment.

He was watching an American movie with Swedish subtitles. He pressed the mute button on the remote control, knowing the Montenegrin didn't like the sound of the television. The boy's eyes rolled upwards towards the man, an ember falling from his hashish joint onto the front of his jersey.

"Shit," he said, without much feeling. The jersey had a number of small black dots on the chest where it had been burnt. "Want a smoke?" he asked, knowing the answer.

"We need to go," said the Montenegrin.

"What? Now, man? This time of night? I was just getting comfortable."

"Now. Is your bag still packed?"

"I think so. Yes, it is," the boy slurred.

"Good. I'll get the rest of my things together. We need to make it so that this apartment will be fine for a couple of months without anyone coming in. Understand?"

"It's cool. Nobody's going to come. Everything's sorted. I told you that."

He'd warned the boy they'd have to leave town quickly, on

short notice. The boy had understood. The Montenegrin had said he'd drive the boy to Malmo, though if he preferred, he'd get him a flight from Copenhagen to Belgrade or Zagreb, with enough money to live for a while on the Adriatic coast.

"Time to go. In a couple of months the beaches will be full of pretty girls and you'll have the money to enjoy them. Until then you can smoke dope and watch TV."

"Spliffs in Split." The boy laughed. "You done with Stockholm?"

"I'm done."

"Yeah? That was quick. I thought you said you might be around for a couple of months."

"I got lucky."

"What about the money? I mean, I can't really pay you back. The money's been invested, if you know what I mean," the boy said, more alert now that he was talking finance.

"The money's yours. Hope you invested it wisely."

"The best. Paid for another couple of bricks."

"You're not taking them with us."

"They'll keep where I've stored them."

"You're not afraid somebody will steal them?"

"Nobody knows about it."

"What about me? Anybody know about me?"

"You mean other than the people across the hall? I think they're illegal. I think they're going to move pretty soon," the boy said. His glassy eyes reflected the silent explosions on the television.

"No, I didn't mean them. Did you tell any of your friends?"

"Why should I?"

The Montenegrin believed him. Dealing with the Yugoslav mafia taught people to keep their mouths shut.

The Montenegrin cleared the bedroom. He used a small dusting cloth to wipe any flat surfaces he was likely to have touched. He wiped down the bathroom and sitting room and the kitchen as well. He wiped up any hair he found in the apartment, mostly the boy's. His own he'd had cut short before coming to Sweden.

It was a routine he'd done every morning before leaving for the stakeout, giving the whole apartment a clean in case he'd have to leave quickly during the day.

"Nice of you to give the place a tidy, but I don't think anyone's going to thank you," the boy said, watching him idly through heavy-lidded eyes.

The Montenegrin put all the perishable food he could find into a plastic garbage bag. He pocketed a couple of cans of cat food.

"Why'd you buy cat food?" the boy asked, having roused himself enough to follow the Montenegrin to the kitchen, where he helped himself to a couple of slices of white processed bread before slumping back onto the sofa.

"Didn't know what it was."

"Picture of a cat on the package didn't give you a clue?"

"I wasn't paying attention."

"So what do you need it for now?" the boy asked.

The Montenegrin left the question unanswered. The boy didn't press the issue.

The Montenegrin threw his toiletries into the bag. He then unplugged all of the electrical appliances, including the stove, but left the fridge running. He'd thought about that for a bit. The wall of ice that almost completely blocked up the freezer convinced him not to risk flooding the place by defrosting it. When it came to switching the television off, the boy complained.

"Hey, man. That's not cool. That's a good movie."

"Time to go."

"Oh, man, come on. Let's go tomorrow."

"No. Now."

The Montenegrin tied the top of the garbage bag. He'd stripped his bedding and placed it in another bag, along with the towels in the bathroom. His clothes and other personal items were in his fake leather suitcase. The boy had packed the few possessions he had into a duffel bag, clean and dirty clothes mixed together, the scales and a little hash wrapped in foil. Where the boy kept his money, the Montenegrin didn't know or care, but he didn't carry it on himself.

The boy looked up at him, too stoned to be properly petulant. His eyes were bloodshot. The Montenegrin bent down and lifted the boy up onto his feet. He wasn't heavy. The Montenegrin wasn't rough, but he was firm enough to let the boy understand there was no point in sitting back down.

The boy struggled into his heavy black coat and pulled on his hat. The Montenegrin handed the boy his duffel bag. He put his suitcase and the garbage bags onto the landing, and then went back in to give the door handles and the light switch a last wipe.

The stairwell was cold after the warmth of the apartment.

The boy carried his own duffel bag, the red and green-checked blanket hanging over his shoulder, while the Montenegrin took his suitcase and the two garbage bags.

They went down without seeing anyone and loaded their things in the car. The boy sat in the passenger seat, bundled up in his coat, blanket over his knees, shivering with cold. The Montenegrin turned on the engine and pulled away. It was less than an hour since Olof Palme had died.

## ZAGREB, AUGUST 1991

**D**ELLA TORRE WISHED he'd kept his apartment a little tidier, but Rebecca didn't seem to mind. Or not too much, anyway. Though she asked whether he'd ever washed the floor. He was sure he had, but he couldn't remember when.

Rebecca had given him a lift back to Zagreb. The Yugo wouldn't start, wouldn't even turn over. It was a crap car, but he'd never known it to die so completely.

The trip in Rebecca's rented Golf was considerably more pleasant than the one to Istria had been. He was thankful Rebecca ran the air conditioner the whole way, indifferent to how much fuel it consumed, though della Torre could have done without her music or her refusal to allow him to smoke in the car.

But when they got to his apartment, della Torre felt a ripple of shame. It had the same bachelor mustiness, clutter, and slow decay as his father's house. He didn't often have visitors.

"You can put your things in this room. In theory it's my study."

"It's where paper comes to die, isn't it," she said. The room was taller than it was wide. Faint, diffuse light filtered past the sides of the blinds, making it feel cave-like. Stacked files on a long desk and a tall bookcase overflowing with volumes and yet more files only added to the oppressive gloom.

"Well, I suppose some of these things could do with a bit of clearing out."

"Don't tell me, you inherited the talent for stacking from your father."

"Anyway, the sofa folds down like this." Della Torre pulled a lever by the side of the sofa and pushed down on the back. Nothing happened. "Like this," he said, with effort. Once again he failed.

"Want me to try?" she asked.

Together they got the back of the sofa down, making a mostly flat surface. In Yugoslavia, sitting rooms almost always doubled as bedrooms, and everyone had at least one of these sofas.

"I'm sure it's more comfortable than it looks," Rebecca said.

"Oh, you can lie on it for minutes at a time," della Torre said. "I've got to go into the office. I'll give you a spare key. I'd say help yourself to anything in the fridge, but I wouldn't vouch for it."

"I can fend for myself."

"I'm sure you can."

"I've got some people to see as well," she said.

"Do you know where the university is?"

"I've got a good map. Though I might just take it easy this afternoon," she said.

Della Torre felt guilty about leaving her so abruptly.

"I don't think I'll have that much to do in the office. Really, it's just to check in. I'll be back in a couple of hours and maybe then I can show you around town a little."

"Sounds nice," she said. She broke into that smile of hers and gave him a peck on the cheek. He detected a faint scent of jasmine on her skin. Not perfume. Perfumes, even the expensive ones, made his eyes water and itch. Maybe it was her shampoo or a lotion. "And thanks for letting me stay."

"Oh, don't thank me. You can thank my father," della Torre said on the way out.

.    .    .

The fan in Anzulović's office was running full tilt. He'd sold the office's portable air conditioners cheaply during the late winter months, when he needed the cash to keep Department VI's employees paid.

"I'm thinking that maybe it was a mistake selling all of the cooling units," he said to della Torre by way of a hello.

"You think?"

"Maybe it wouldn't have been so bad to let a couple of people starve instead. You know, the useless time-servers."

"I could have given you some names."

"You'd have been top of the list." Anzulović was slumped in his chair. Boxes were stacked on one side of the office and out into the hall.

"Looks like the move's on," della Torre said.

"Today or tomorrow, I'm told. I'll believe it when I'm in the new building with all my stuff. Until then, we're in limbo as far as I'm concerned."

"You know where we're moving to? Police headquarters?"

"No. They want us to be incognito, like a proper spy agency. It's in a modern building on Ilica, south side at the corner of the square, with the women's underwear shop on the ground floor."

"Great. If we all wear trench coats, sunglasses, and hats, we'll fit right in with the local perverts," della Torre said.

There wasn't much della Torre needed to pack. His filing cabinet was locked. He filled a couple of plastic crates with his law books, random items of stationery, a stapler, a calculator, and his electric typewriter. He'd long been promised a computer but ended up using the one in the secretary's office when he needed to record data on a floppy disk. He wondered whether to take the indestructible rubber plant. He was sure somebody snuck into his office to water it; he could never remember doing so himself. He didn't count the dregs of coffee or soft drinks he routinely drained into the soil.

"It's got air conditioning," Anzulović said, turning his face into the fan. "Anyway, I don't feel like wasting precious energy talking to you. I'm glad you're back. I won't ask if you got anything." He paused. "Did you get anything?"

"From the local cops? What exactly was I supposed to get?"

"Food poisoning, maybe. How the hell should I know?" said Anzulović.

"All I got was an earful about how the Istrian police are being pulled out and stuck on the front lines in Krajina, while their positions are being filled by the sons and brothers of Zagreb's great and good."

"You mean the ones who can't get their kids out of the country to study in some third-rate Italian or English school."

"Just so," said della Torre, wishing he could somehow catch more of the fan's breeze. The angle was wrong and he couldn't see how it'd be right unless he sat between it and Anzulović. "Oh, I picked up an American."

"A what?"

"An American. An American researcher who'd been staying at my father's."

"Americans. Had some here the other day. Kakav was showing them around. Not that I got an introduction. At least I think they were Americans. Looked it. Though they could have been Australian. Or Canadian. Pretty sure they weren't Japanese."

"Oh," della Torre said, his surprise showing. It wasn't so long since inviting Americans to the UDBA's offices would have been as sacrilegious as herding pigs through a mosque. "So what does Kakav want with the non-Japanese?"

"We're looking for friends everywhere, didn't you know?"

Anzulović said, shrugging. "Speaking of Kakav, he's got something for you. I think I might have mentioned it last week."

"All you mentioned last week was that he'd have something else for me to do once I got back from Istria. Am I supposed to write up that trip, by the way? If I am, I'll have to be creative, because I'm not going to report the conversations I had."

"If you want to write it up, go ahead. I don't remember Kakav asking for a report. Just that when you got back he wanted you to go away again," Anzulović said.

"Likes me around, does he?" della Torre said. "Let me guess. Back to Istria. He wants me to ask the cops there whether they like milk in their coffee."

"No, you're heading in the other direction. Vukovar," Anzulović said. Vukovar was at Croatia's eastern limits, on the great Danube River. Serbia was on the opposite shore. Conditions had become as tense there as they were in Krajina.

"Any idea what he wants me to do there? Or can I just go home and watch TV for a couple of days and pretend I've been?" Della Torre was unenthusiastic about making the trip. At the best of times it was a long drive, but the looming war meant having to negotiate traffic tied up by police roadblocks, dull scenery along the way, and crazy people when he got there.

"This time he wants you there for a reason. I think. Anyway, he's got somebody he wants you to talk to. Or who wants to talk to you."

"You're keeping me in suspense."

"Zlatko Horvat."

"The pizza man?"

Horvat was an extreme specimen of an increasingly common variety of expat Croat. The kind who'd left the country decades before as poor nobodies, but through hard work and good luck had done well for themselves abroad. And all the time they were in America or Australia or Canada or wherever, nostalgia for the old country had festered and grown into a utopian nationalism. Networks of deracinated countrymen dreamt of what Croatia would be like without the Yugoslav yoke. And they, with their vast experience of how things are done in proper developed countries, could show their countrymen the way forward. So they came back rich, superior, and determined to meddle in politics.

"Yup."

"What am I supposed to talk to him about?"

"The weather. How the hell do I know? You both lived in the middle of America. Maybe he wants to reminisce."

"He was in Canada."

"There's a difference?"

"Snowshoes," della Torre said. "Any more details?"

"Comrade Colonel Kakav said, and I quote, 'When that della Torre gets back from Istria I want him in Vukovar. He's to talk to Mr. Zlatko Horvat. Make sure he's there by Tuesday.' And that was the length and breadth of all the useful information I got out of our dear leader. May I remind you to be polite to Mr. Horvat. He may be a Nazi, but he's a friend of our president's and a generous contributor to the Croatian cause. And if he wants you to stand him a beer, well, you're standing him a beer."

"Shit."

"Better you than me, that's all I can say. You might as well go today. The sooner you're there, the sooner you can come back."

"Shit."

"You should have someone look at that echo of yours. It sounds like shit," Anzulović said, lighting a cigarette, sweat glistening on his forehead.

"I guess I'm going to Vukovar. Do we have a car I can use? Mine broke down in Istria."

"How'd you get here?"

"The American drove me."

"Well, get someone to drive you to Vukovar. We're all out of cars. I can fix you a ride on a military transport, or you can take a bus. But until we're properly part of military intelligence, we're not part of the car pool."

"That's swell."

"You're resourceful," Anzulović said airily.

"Thanks."

"Oh, and while you're out there, you can do me a favour."

"What, like jump in the Danube?"

"The chief of police in Osijek is a guy called Josip Rejkart. I'd like you to go to his office and talk to him and other people there. See what's happening. Don't mention my name. I'll get the Zagreb police to call to say they're sending you to..." Anzulović paused. "...to do a survey on the use of paper clips on the front line."

"Close friends, are you?"

"We are, in fact. I trained him as a detective when he was in Zagreb. He's a nice guy. Smart. But if he knows I sent you, he'll make sure you only see the rosy side of things, because he knows I'm worried about him. I've been trying to get him transferred out of there for the past couple of months."

"So you think he'll be more forthcoming to a stranger?" Della Torre sounded doubtful.

"Maybe not, but at least if you don't tell him anything at first, you might be able to see stuff he wouldn't otherwise show you if he knew you were one of my people. And some of his cops might be willing to grumble."

Della Torre shrugged. It sounded like another aimless mission, like the one he'd just made to Poreč. On the other hand, he knew it was the only real way to get a sense of how things actually were. To go and smell the air. Talk to people. See how their hands shook when they picked up their coffee cups. How they lit one cigarette off another. See how many houses were empty and boarded up. Whether the shops had customers and if they had anything on their shelves. Small clues that created a picture.

His trip to Istria had been almost worthless. Almost. And yet talking to the police captain in Poreč had told him something he wouldn't have gotten from a newspaper or a telephone call.

Della Torre had to find a car. He excused himself and went back to his mostly packed-up office.

He called Irena at her apartment—his father's apartment—not expecting to get through to her. He didn't. He tried her at her office at the university, knowing that too was a long shot. She wasn't there either. The best prospect was getting her at the hospital, though that always entailed having to phone at least three times, listening to it ring until he lost count, at which point somebody would finally pick up. Then there were even odds that they wouldn't bother to take a message, much less look for her. But now and again he managed to get through to Irena. And this was one of those times.

"Lucky I was just passing," Irena said.

"And that that Albanian nurse of yours decided it was just as easy to call you over as it was to hang up." The Albanian nurse was meant to be an administrator, but she was like a blood clot to the normal functioning of the hospital.

"She's busy."

"Painting her nails? I've never seen her do anything other than read fashion magazines or primp," della Torre said.

"So this is a call to tell me I've got staffing problems, is it?"

"No, I was wondering if I could ask a favour."

The phone went quiet.

"Hello?" he said, thinking the connection had broken.

"Oh, I'm still here," she said. "I'm just waiting to hear what favour it is that you want of me. I was under the impression you'd used them all up."

"Just a little teeny-weeny one. Could I borrow your car?"

"No."

"Please."

"No."

"Just for a couple of days. I'm being sent to Vukovar and my Yugo died in Istria. Dad said he'd give it last rites."

"Vukovar?"

"Yes. Arse end of everywhere, and I'd like to get there in a bit of comfort."

Irena owned a new Volkswagen Golf, like the one Rebecca had driven. It was one of the few advantages of being a senior consultant at the hospital. The occasional private patient and a donation from a grateful family had earned her enough to buy the car. It was smooth to drive and, most importantly, had air conditioning. He decided cool air was worth the cost of petrol. Especially since he was planning on using the UDBA fuel card. He hoped it still worked.

"Two days," she said after a long pause.

"Two days. Promise. I'll bring it back on Wednesday."

"If there's the smallest scratch, you pay in flesh and blood."

"You're sounding—"

"Like Shylock?" It was something she only ever joked about with him. A residual, bitter joke. Jews were widely despised by Croats, even though there were so few of them left. They had been all but wiped out during the Second World War, murdered in their thousands together with Serbs and gypsies by Croatia's fascists. But the Serbs didn't like Jews or gypsies much either. Both of Irena's parents were Jewish. Her mother's parents had survived, thanks largely to her grandfather's ability to apply his skills as a professor of medicine to the needs of peasants and their livestock in a cluster of small forest villages. Her father's parents, lower-middle-class semi-skilled workers, and his four siblings had perished, together with all his cousins and aunts and uncles. He never spoke about how he'd survived.

"Well, now that you mention it, can I choose which pound and how I give it to you?"

She ignored him. "When do you want it?"

"I always want it."

"The car, stupid."

"Now. Ish," he said. "The sooner I go, the sooner I get back."

"I've got to go down to my office at the university in half an hour. I'll meet you at Alegoria with the keys." Alegoria was the café around the corner from his flat. "But you have to go to mine to pick up the car."

"Deal."

.    .    .

When della Torre arrived at the café, Irena was already sitting in the shade on the patio. She wore a thin-strapped summer dress that showed off her shape beneath. Her hair was shiny and black and hung down below her shoulders, though there was grey in it too. Wrinkles fanned from the corners of her eyes, giving them a look of gentle amusement. She was what they called petite, girl-like, and people who knew her only by reputation were surprised when they met her. Though she was four years younger than della Torre, by dint of hard work and intelligence she had achieved considerable stature in the university's medical faculty.

They kissed on both cheeks, close but without romance.

"You order?" he asked.

"No. Their fridge broke down and I didn't feel like a coffee."

"I think I might have a cold beer at home if you're happy to share it. There must be some ice in the freezer too. If there isn't, we can just chip off the frost. There's plenty of that."

"Okay. I suppose I'll feel like moving in a minute," she said, looking firmly planted in her seat, fanning herself with a menu.

"Fine by me. Have you got the keys?"

She handed them over.

"I'll be going away for a month or two," she said. "Just so you know."

"Back to London," he said.

"No, I won't be leaving the country. Anyway, I need the car back before the end of the week."

"Two days, no more. I promise."

"And don't smoke in it."

It wasn't a rule he much liked. Smoking made the journey go quicker.

"So you're not going back to David?" David was the English doctor she'd grown close to in London. The one who'd pulled the bullet out of della Torre's elbow.

"He might come to visit."

"Oh. So that night didn't mean anything," he said.

It wasn't long after they'd got back from London. She'd run away there too, separately from him, but they'd returned together. His elbow had been hurting and he'd run out of pain-killers, so he'd gone up to her apartment to raid her extensive medical cabinet. She'd only just got home after a thirty-six-hour shift. She fed him pills and an omelette, and they got through a pitcher of wine. They woke up the next morning in the same bed, both naked — it had been a hot, sultry night. Not that they were particularly embarrassed. They'd been together long enough for there to be no surprises. But neither remembered much of what might have happened in the time between the booze and the hangover. Della Torre preferred to think it had been a meaningful night.

She hadn't wanted to talk about it then, and she ignored him now.

"Anyway," she said, rising out of the chair, "Let's get that beer before I melt."

They left the café terrace and walked the half block to della Torre's building. Della Torre unlocked the door to his flat. Irena was immediately behind him when they saw her. Neither said anything.

Rebecca was standing in the hall, dressed in one of della Torre's new shirts. One of the ones he'd bought in London, with French cuffs and mother-of-pearl buttons. Only one of those buttons was done up, somewhere midway between Rebecca's navel and the hollow at the base of her neck. The rest of the shirt was pulled back, exposing the fallen autumn leaf of hair between her thighs.

She made no effort to cover herself up.

"Ummm. Irena, this is Rebecca. She's a friend of my father's, an American student friend," he said in English.

"Is she this friendly with your father?" Irena asked in Croat before switching to English. "How do you do?"

"And Rebecca, this is Irena, my ex-..."

"Wife," Irena filled in.

"My wife," della Torre corrected himself.

"I've heard all about you. You're the doctor, aren't you?" Rebecca said without showing the least bit of embarrassment.

"Yes. Though not a gynecologist."

"Oh? What do you do, then?"

"Chests," she said, deadpan. "Anyway, it was nice to meet you, but I must be going. I'm sure you and Marko have plenty to...discuss."

Irena kissed della Torre.

"The car's up the street a little way, in the shade. And don't worry about the beer," Irena said. "I think your need will be greater than mine."

**DELLA TORRE HAD** never liked going east. The Zagreb–Belgrade highway was mostly straight and went through flat land. For the first hour or so there were some distant hills to the north, but eventually they disappeared too.

The late afternoon heat shimmered in front of him, while in the far distance a layer of brooding cloud stretched from one end of the horizon to the other. If there was a small mercy, it was that at least he was driving with the sun to his back.

The conflict with the Serbs in Croat territory was metastasizing. The cancer had started with the Serb rebellion in Krajina, near the Dalmatian coast, but it had spread fast and wide. A swathe of borderland south of Zagreb, to his right as he drove east, was contested. And the region of Vukovar, where he was headed, had become a series of flashpoints. Within these Serb pockets there were Croatian villages. Undoubtedly Serb families lived in those Croat villages. How far down, he wondered, could Yugoslavia be atomized? Or was it every man for himself?

Della Torre's UDBA ID got him through the police road-blocks, though he knew it wouldn't work forever. Eventually he'd run into a cop who both hated the UDBA and knew it no longer existed.

The closer he got to the border with Serbia, the more signs he saw of chronic nervousness. Traffic thinned. There were more police cars around. When he turned off the main highway, heading north, he could see that many houses were closed up, shutters drawn and locked, gates closed. Barns had been emptied. A few courtyards still had chickens scrabbling, and here and there he saw a chained dog. He didn't envy the people who called these fertile flatlands home, though they were some of the wealthiest in Yugoslavia.

He was about to turn off the Osijek road to Vukovar, where the Zagreb police's admin girl had booked him into a hotel, then changed his mind. It was early enough in the evening to catch Anzulović's friend Rejkart in the office, or at least one of his lieutenants, but also late enough that they'd want to get rid of him quickly. That suited della Torre. He'd repeat his performance at the Poreč police station. Show up. Quick, meaningless chat. And duty done. It was all a matter of form. For Anzulović's sake, he knew he ought to be as thorough as possible. But he also knew it was largely a pointless exercise. Sort this out, see Horvat the following day, and he'd be back in Zagreb for dinner later that night. Maybe he'd take Rebecca out. If he could think of a decent restaurant.

He remembered from a previous trip the way to the large concrete and glass office block that served as the regional police headquarters in Osijek, and parked on the street. He didn't want an aggrieved relative of one of the police's temporary guests to run a house key down the side of Irena's car.

He passed a man smoking and lounging against a tree in front of the police station, dressed in combat fatigue trousers and a tight black T-shirt showing off a bodybuilder's chest and arms. His hair was too long for the army, but plenty of young men were dressed as paramilitaries these days. He gave della Torre a dead-eyed look as he passed.

In the building, della Torre pulled out his UDBA ID and slid it towards a booking sergeant who was manning the main desk. The sergeant had a big face, thick neck, and oddly shaped head—tight around the forehead, so that it looked like it'd been compressed by an iron band. He picked up della Torre's ID and held it at arm's length.

"Uh-huh?" he said, handing it back to della Torre.

"I'd like to see your boss, Captain Rejkart."

"Have you got an appointment?"

"I'm not sure," he said.

"On what business?"

"That I'll discuss with the captain."

"Uh-unh," the sergeant said, giving della Torre the faintest nod. "You can wait over there."

He waved at a public seating area full of old men in black suits, white shirts, and porkpie hats. Farmers with creased, tanned faces, or their wives, in patterned headscarves and dark calico dresses, waiting to find out what was to be done with their sons or brothers or nephews.

"If I remember correctly, you've got a slightly more comfortable waiting room over there," della Torre said, lifting his chin towards a door behind the sergeant's desk.

The sergeant stared at him for a moment and then gave another little nod, unlocking the wooden barrier to let della Torre through. Della Torre took two steps and then stopped, half turning.

"Oh, and you were going to make that phone call. You know. The one to your boss. To tell him he's got a visitor," della Torre said.

The room was stuffy; there were a couple of municipal armchairs and an overflowing ashtray on a table. But della Torre was alone, which suited him. Either they'd see him quickly to get rid of him or keep him waiting to show him how little they thought of him. He sat down and dove into the trashy English paperback he hadn't had a chance to read in Istria, the one with a man's hand on a woman's ass on the cover. He didn't notice the door open.

"A criminology textbook?" the man said. He was round-headed, solidly built, in suit trousers and a short-sleeved shirt. He wore no tie. His light-coloured and thinning hair was cut like a military man's. He came at della Torre the same way he might have approached a suspect. There was nothing friendly about him.

Della Torre stood up.

"No. It's about horses and sex. Maybe sex with horses. I don't know, I haven't gotten that far yet." He held out his hand. "Chief Rejkart?"

"'Fraid not, sir. The boss is tied up this afternoon. You'll have to do with me, Captain...?"

"Della Torre."

"Of course. Slipped my mind. I'm Lieutenant Boban, one of the chief's deputies. And I'm afraid I can't spare you much time either. We're a bit busy these days, with everybody wanting to shoot everybody else. Maybe a quick coffee. I've got to go down to Vukovar to sign off on some of our guys for the end of the day. Locals keep cutting the phone lines, and you can't say anything on the radio without having half the world listen in, so one of us has to drive down to check things out once a day. But first I've got to find a car, and I'm already running late."

Boban gave della Torre a curt smile. As friendly as a fish on a marble slab, della Torre thought.

"Coffee it is, then," he said to the lieutenant.

They went to a corner café. The sun bore down on them from the west, the air creased with heat and suffused with dust and the smell of warm asphalt and hay from the not-too-distant countryside. Towards the east, clouds had piled higher. They passed the bodybuilder in the black T-shirt and fatigues, still leaning against a tree, smoking, watching them.

Boban walked with broad strides, silent the whole way. It was clear to della Torre they didn't want him underfoot in the police station. Normally, a coffee would have been brewed by a secretary while they chatted in a private office.

"So, what might Zagreb be interested in?" Boban asked once they'd sat at the bar and ordered. He glanced at his watch.

"Oh, just to get a measure of how things are going. Captain Rejkart's thoughts on the state of the world. That sort of thing."

Della Torre hated going to these far-flung stations and asking banal questions. At least this time he sort of knew what he was expected to find out. He'd have to sidle into it backwards.

"Well, the local Serbs aren't very happy and neither are the local Croats," Boban said, his blue-green eyes sharp and cold. "And on top of that, we've got people coming here from god knows where with big sticks that they poke into wasps' nests."

"So I hear."

"Zagreb sends someone who over an afternoon makes the Serbs crazy, and then we spend the next three weeks trying to calm them down. Be nice if they left us alone to keep the peace for a change." Boban looked at his watch for the third time in as many minutes.

Della Torre figured he wasn't going to get anywhere as a dignitary, so he tried another tack: honesty.

"Lieutenant, I haven't been sent from Zagreb to give you a hard time. To tell you the truth, this is just a side trip, a favour for a friend of Rejkart's to see how he's getting along. This friend's worried about him. I'm really here to see a guy called Horvat in Vukovar. You've probably heard about him."

Boban drew back a little and his eyes narrowed. Not much, but enough to tell della Torre it was probably a mistake to have mentioned Horvat's name.

"I'm sorry, I can't really help you, Captain. I'm sure there are formal channels..." Boban edged off the bar stool, having emptied the thimble-sized cup of its contents.

"You said you're looking for a car. Haven't you got a driver?" della Torre said quickly.

"If there's a car free, I take the car. If there's a driver, I let him drive and I get to do a bit of work."

"What do you guys use here, Zastavas?"

"What else? As far as I know, only the UDBA have Mercedes-Benzes or BMWS. Provincial police, we're lucky we have something better than a donkey and cart."

"Air-conditioned?"

Boban laughed. "Sure. Yugoslav air conditioning. You get a nice breeze every time the donkey farts."

"Lieutenant, I've got a Golf. With air conditioning. And I haven't got any plans this evening. You have a driver and an air-conditioned car at your disposal. No obligation. I'll take you out to your men in Vukovar and back."

The suggestion caught Boban off guard. The penetrating blue-green eyes shifted from della Torre to the mirror behind the café bar. It would be a real temptation. Driving around in a Zastava on a hot August afternoon wasn't pleasant. On the other hand, he didn't know or trust this captain who'd been foisted on them by Zagreb. Della Torre could sense the struggle.

Comfort won out.

"I can't promise you any conversation," Boban said carefully. "I've got some paperwork to catch up on."

"No problem."

"I'll bring a portable radio. Can we plug it into your lighter socket?"

"Yes. One little rule," della Torre said, stubbing his cigarette out in a glass ashtray. "No smoking in the car."

"That's a clincher for me. I don't smoke and it's impossible to get our police drivers not to. Impossible. They'd strike."

"Deal, then," della Torre said, holding out his hand.

Boban considered it for a moment, as if della Torre was

offering him a piece of evidence from a crime scene. A severed limb, perhaps. But he shook it anyway.

.    .    .

Boban directed the way down from Osijek. They took the highway and then minor roads to avoid impromptu roadblocks by local vigilantes. But other than that he said nothing as he went through papers in the briefcase, occasionally marking them with a cheap red Biro. Della Torre realized he had no right to feel irritated, but Boban treated him exactly as he might have done a police chauffeur. No pleasantries when he said "Next left" or "Ignore the sign." The radio squawked away in the background.

They skirted Vukovar and carried on parallel to the Danube towards the Croat-Serb border, until Boban told della Torre to turn off onto a gravel track between long, flat fields of stubble. In the distance were a fringe of trees and a pair of half-built houses.

"Slowly," Boban said.

Della Torre slowed down while Boban stared intently out the window. They were about two hundred metres from the buildings when Boban said, "Stop."

Della Torre stopped.

Boban sat and stared hard into the field on his side of the car. The short stalks stuck up from the ground. Birds filled the fields, picking up loose wheat seeds, suggesting a recent harvest.

"I'm going to walk from here," Boban said, getting out of the car and shutting the door behind him. "You just drive on up to the houses. I'll be there in five minutes,"

Della Torre pulled away faster than he'd intended, spraying gravel behind him. A police car was parked in front of the larger of the two buildings. They were the unfinished skeletons of a pair of two-storey houses, one a bit larger the other, separated by a cemented yard that could comfortably hold two cars side by side. Like most new buildings in Croatia, they were made of red cinder blocks, though they remained unrendered. They were both roofed but had no doors or windows.

With the police car sitting in front of the larger building and a big pile of builders' sand spread in front of the other one, della Torre parked between the houses. He had a pretty and uninterrupted view of the Danube, no more than fifty metres down a little slope. The iron-coloured river was calm, broad but not overwhelming. A forest lined the opposite bank, with a row of poplars standing sentry.

Della Torre got out of the car, leaving the door open, breathing in the smell of cut straw in the evening air. Three uniformed policemen looked from him to Boban in the distance. A tall young man with short sandy hair approached della Torre.

"Mr—" he started to say.

"Captain," della Torre answered sharply.

"Mr. Captain—"

"Captain della Torre," della Torre interrupted.

"Mr. Captain della Torre, can I maybe give you a bit of advice?" The man was a typical Croat policeman. Someone who otherwise would be tending a small holding in a quiet village.

"What sort of advice might that be?"

There was the flat sound of a hammer striking brick and, nearly simultaneously, the hollow thump of something punching through a thin sheet of metal, followed soon after by the sound of two cracks in the distance and their echoes. Della Torre watched as his car door slammed shut without the whisper of a breeze in the air.

Della Torre stared at the car door, bewildered, wondering if a ghost had passed, and then bent down to take a closer look. Something about it was wrong.

The policeman grabbed della Torre by his mostly healed arm and tugged him behind the building.

"What the—?"

"There's a shooter, sir. On the opposite side. I was going to suggest you might want to move your car before it got hit. But I guess I was too late," the cop said apologetically.

Boban, meanwhile, had arrived at the half-built houses.

"Why the hell did you idiots let the captain park in a clear line of fire?" Boban said, running to the car. Without pulling the door shut, he started the engine and reversed so that the Golf stood next to the police car in the shelter of the bigger building.

Della Torre rubbed his arm. And then it dawned on him. The neat circle with a small star-shaped pucker of peeled paint around it in the middle of the Golf's door hadn't been there before.

"What the—?" he said. "There's a hole in my car door."

"I tried to tell the captain," said the policeman who'd approached him before.

"Somebody shot my wife's car."

"I mean, I was about to ask the captain to move—" the young policeman stammered to Boban.

"You shouldn't have let him pull into the space," Boban said.

"I mean, I know there's no love for people from Zagreb around here, or for the UDBA," della Torre continued, ignoring the others, "but this is absolutely—"

"UDBA?" The young policeman blanched.

"Calm down, Captain," Boban said to della Torre. "There's a shooter on the other side of the river, which is why we've got a little post here. To keep track of him and find out what's going on over there. He shoots at us to keep us from looking."

"Fuck," della Torre said, turning angrily to Boban and adding, as if by way of explanation, "That's my wife's car."

"I'm sorry, Captain. I should have warned you. We'll get the people in the police garage to have a look at your wife's car. I'm sure they can sort it pretty quickly. Bring it tomorrow and we'll fix it," Boban said, an edge of exasperation in his tone.

"What the hell's going on around here?"

"Around here, Captain, people shoot at each other, because around here people want to start a war and the only thing stopping them is us, the police. Captain," Boban said, his anger building to match della Torre's, "you wanted to see what's going on around here. Well, that's what's going on around here."

But della Torre wasn't listening. Irena would have his nuts sliced and fed to the cats. How could he go back and say, "Darling, here's your car. Doesn't smell of cigarette smoke, but it does have extra ventilation."

Boban turned to the three policemen. "Have you fellows been watching behind yourselves as well?"

A dark-haired man, about Boban's age and with the same solid build, said, "No, sir. We've just been told to keep our eyes on the Serbs across the river. Why?"

"Why? Because somebody's been watching you from out there," Boban said, pointing back to the field.

"Over there? Where?" asked the policeman. "There's nowhere for anyone to watch from."

"Oh? I think you'll find that there are a few dips in the ground, if you have a little wander along the road. When there was wheat in the field, somebody spent a bit of time out there watching you. There's a pile of cigarette butts and a couple of bottles and an old crap or two. So unless you guys head out there to do your business, somebody was making you their business," Boban said.

"Who do you think it was, sir?"

"It wasn't my grandmother. Who do you think it might have been? If it had been a friend, he'd have come over to share a drink and a dirty joke, don't you think?"

"I suppose so, sir."

"Fuck," Boban said. "Well, any of you want to make a report?"

"Sorry, sir," said the dark-haired one, who seemed to be the most senior of the three. "There's not much, except Damir here—" He pointed at the tall, sandy-haired boy beside him, the youngest of the three. "—thinks he might have seen something this morning."

"If you follow me, sir," Damir said, leading them into the bigger of the two buildings.

Boban and Damir sheltered behind a wall as they looked out of a large opening left for a window fronting the river. The youth pointed to a spot across the river, his arm stretched into the empty space, while Boban held a pair of binoculars to his eyes. Then they heard the sound of another crack from across the river, followed by the crunch of burst tile, along with yet another crack immediately after.

"Ow." Damir jerked his arm back into the building, holding it between his thighs. "Ow, ow, ow."

"What happened? What's the matter?" Boban asked.

"I think I've been shot," the young man said, his voice rising, tearful. "In my arm."

"Let's have a look," Boban said.

Damir held out his right arm. The fleshy part at the top of his forearm, just below the elbow, had been sliced open at a diagonal to the depth of three centimetres. The flesh pulled back cleanly, showing a white-pink gash. There was no blood.

"Listen, boy, just a flesh wound. That's not been made by a bullet. Probably a tile shard," Boban said and then turned to the other two. "Boys, get me the first-aid kit. Double-quick time."

Damir sat on the floor, holding his arm out in front of him. It still hadn't started to bleed, the open wound looking like a pork cutlet in a butcher's window. Della Torre watched, fascinated.

The dark-haired cop came running with a green tin box with a red cross on a white field on the lid. Boban worked quickly, applying a thick wadding to the wound and then wrapping it tightly in a long spiral of bandage up and down the arm, so that the young policeman couldn't bend his elbow.

"This, my boy, is going to need a few stitches. The captain here will drive us to the hospital. You'll be there in ten minutes, and I promise you, the minute you start feeling proper pain, the doctors will give you a very nice little injection," Boban said, helping the young man to his feet while keeping out of sight of the shooter across the river. "Ready, Captain?" he asked.

All della Torre could think was that the newly shot Golf would soon also be covered in blood. But he nodded and led them to the car.

Boban and the boy sat in the back. Della Torre drove as fast as he safely could, Boban directing him the whole way. It took less than a quarter of an hour to get to the hospital. Della Torre dropped them in front of the building and then went to park the car. For a moment he thought he might as well just leave, go to his hotel, get a nice tall beer, and then line up a row of shot glasses full of slivovitz. Shot glasses. He hated getting shot at.

An admissions nurse pointed him to the emergency room, where he found Boban talking to a doctor in the corridor.

"I have your briefcase, Lieutenant. And your radio is in the car," della Torre said.

Boban nodded at him.

"Thank you, Captain, and thank you for driving us here. I can promise you that Damir didn't leave a drop of blood in the back of your car." And then he added: "Your wife's car."

The doctor looked at della Torre with a slightly bemused expression. She had a thin and careworn face and plenty of grey in her hair, though della Torre guessed she was around his age.

"Oh, excuse me," Boban said. "Miljenka, this gentleman has come all the way from Zagreb to learn how to get shot at. Captain..." Boban paused. Had he really forgotten della Torre's name?

"Della Torre," he said, forcing a smile.

"Dr. Miljenka Boštrić. Dr. Boštrić runs emergency admissions," Boban continued.

"Della Torre, did you say? That's an unusual name," she said. "I have a friend who's a della Torre. Irena della Torre. Do you know her?"

"Irena? She's my wife. Her car's just been shot."

"Your wife." Dr. Boštrić beamed at him. "She's a wonderful friend. Oh, I am pleased to meet you." She embraced him, kissing him on both cheeks. "We're so excited about her coming. It won't be a moment too soon."

It was hard to tell who looked more puzzled, della Torre or Boban.

"Irena, coming here?" della Torre asked. "I didn't know she was coming for a visit."

"Well, it'll be some visit. She said she'd cover for six weeks."

"Cover?" della Torre asked.

"Yes. She's filling in for some colleagues. We're very short-staffed, and she very kindly said she'd lend a hand." A shadow of doubt crept into Dr. Boštrić's eyes. Della Torre's jaw moved up and down, as if he were miming language. "To help out. Until October..." Dr. Boštrić's voice trailed off but then revived again. "She'll be bringing an eminent surgeon from London. Not right away, but I think he'll come in early September. A specialist in bullet wounds. We can use as many spare hands as we can."

"Irena's coming here?" della Torre said again.

"I'm sorry. Didn't you know?" Dr. Boštrić looked both embarrassed and uncertain.

"No. I'm sure...I mean, we are so busy and have our own lives. Dr. Cohen is coming, right?"

"Yes, yes, Dr. Cohen from London," Dr. Boštrić said, worried about what damage she might be causing Irena.

Della Torre took a deep breath and pulled out the smile he'd often used to get reluctant witnesses to remember things, to not be afraid of the UDBA man asking questions.

"I'm sorry, the shock of being shot at made me forget," he said. "Yes, of course I remember Irena telling me. With everything that's happening, we don't see much of each other these days. I've been on the road pretty constantly and she's, well, you know what it's like. She sleeps and eats at the hospital."

Dr. Boštrić looked thankful and relieved.

"Oh, we know very well what it's like," said Boban, smiling at della Torre for the first time. "I didn't realize you were the husband of the marvellous Dr. Irena. I haven't met her, but I've heard so much from Miljenka. You should have said. But of course you wouldn't have known to say." Boban took della Torre's hand and shook it with feeling. "We need doctors here. Many of the ones in the hospital have gone, disappeared. Some because they were Serb and life wasn't nice for them, with the Croat nationalists coming from Zagreb. Others because they don't want their families to be caught up in any fighting. They're smart because they're doctors; they know there'll be plenty of blood spilled around here. It's good to find friends. There are so few honest, real ones..."

Della Torre acknowledged the half-apology with a half-shrug.

"I'm sorry I didn't introduce myself properly," he said. "I seldom think to mention that I'm Dr. Irena della Torre's husband. I suppose I should more often."

"Definitely." Both Boban and Dr. Boštrić nodded vigorously, oblivious to della Torre's sarcasm.

"If you'll excuse us, Captain," said Boban. "Maybe you'd like to have a cigarette outside. I'll meet you out front in five minutes. Just to see how Damir's stitching is coming along. It's a clean wound, apparently."

"Yes, of course," della Torre said. He held out a hand to Dr. Boštrić, but she put her arms around him and gave him a squeeze and a kiss on the cheek instead, as if they were old friends.

.     .     .

Della Torre was on his second Lucky when Boban reappeared.

"I'm sorry for not being...more welcoming, Captain," he said. "It's just that Zagreb keeps sending us people who take up our time and do their utmost to complicate our lives."

"No, I understand perfectly. And I'm sorry about your officer being wounded," he said, flexing his arm. "I know what it's like."

Della Torre was wearing a short-sleeved shirt, no jacket. Boban took a long look at the scar on the inside of della Torre's arm.

"Bullet?" he asked.

"Nine-millimetre, probably."

"Ouch. Made a bit of a mess, eh?"

"Only because it hit square on the funny bone."

"Not much of a laugh."

"No."

"Serbs?"

"Bosnians," della Torre said, ignoring the policeman's surprised expression. Boban didn't push it.

"Listen, Captain." Boban's tone had become considerably friendlier — conciliatory, even. "I'll have to stick around until they're done with Damir. I'll get somebody else to drive me to Osijek."

"No problem. I'm staying in Vukovar anyway."

"Great, so except for the hole in your car, I haven't inconvenienced you too much," Boban said with a wry smile. "I'd like to buy you a drink, but I ought to stay at the hospital. There'll be forms to fill out and I'll have to talk to Damir's parents and whatnot."

"No problem," della Torre said again.

"I'll tell you what, if you still want to talk to the boss I'll sort something out."

"Love to," della Torre said, surprised.

"We normally try to keep him insulated from Zagreb types. Time wasters, we call them. No offence."

"None taken."

"He's pretty busy during the days, but he tries to keep an hour clear in the morning for admin, usually between nine and ten. We make sure he only gets interrupted for emergencies, but I can bend the rule for you."

"That's very kind of you," della Torre said.

"Come to the Osijek station for nine and ask for me. You can bring the radio then. I promise not to report it stolen," he laughed.

They parted with a handshake.

Della Torre decided to leave the car where it was and walk into the centre of town, along the river. The Danube, now dark in the shadows of the fading evening light, flashed between the buildings to his left. He'd never seen it blue. Sometimes it was milky white. And sometimes it took on a gunmetal hue. Usually it was the colour of faded asphalt, and as smooth as a newly paved road. It was indolent, except in the spring, following the rains and the winter melt, when it churned and elbowed its way beyond the banks, reminding everyone that it was one of the great rivers of the world.

That night it was placid under the wall of clouds, which hung over the Serbian side, brooding and purple. They had warned of a storm to come even before he arrived in Osijek. Della Torre wondered when they'd break.

10

**I**T **MIGHT HAVE** been a shitty day, but at least it was over as far as della Torre was concerned. His meeting with Horvat wasn't due until the following afternoon. He was to stick around his hotel after lunch, and Horvat would come round and say hello. That's how his people had put it. Maybe it wouldn't be so bad. He'd get his meeting with Rejkart over with in the morning, come back to Vukovar for the requisite chat and rigor mortis smile with Horvat, and then be the hell out of this dead end and back to Zagreb by dinnertime. And this free evening he'd use to catch up on his drinking with a mindlessly trashy novel—both of them lifting him out of this world, this existence, for an hour or two. He was looking forward to it.

He stood at the bar of a café that was empty except for a couple of old men playing cards at an outdoor table. Vukovar was a pretty Austro-Hungarian town with low architecture dominated by rusticated stucco buildings and pavements sheltered by stone and brick arcades, a remnant of the empire at its greatest bloom.

A solid young woman in a blue waitress uniform and white apron stood in the corner by the bar. She appeared to be wiping the counter without putting any effort into it. Della Torre looked her over, wondering whether she'd noticed him. She wore a pair of white wedge-soled sandals with ankle straps. They were the sort of shoes that just about every shopgirl in the country seemed to wear, and looked like something designed by a social realist with a foot fetish.

He rapped on the bar.

"Excuse me, can I order a drink?"

She looked at him with utter indifference.

The Yugoslav government had regulations for the oddest things; anyone who wanted to wait on tables had to enrol in a special high school course and be awarded a special diploma before they could serve drinks. It might have been better if the students had been taught something useful, like how to smile. And be polite. But maybe there were regulations forbidding that too.

"A beer and a coffee, please. Short coffee, long beer," he said.

He was relieved to find the espresso drinkable. She waited for him to pay before getting him the beer, and then came back slowly with the change. Maybe she'd heard foreigners tipped. People from Zagreb were considered foreign here. He massaged his sore arm after pocketing the change and then lit a Lucky Strike. The old woman who ran the kiosk at one end of Zagreb's main square kept a few untaxed packets under the counter for favoured customers. And made them pay through the nose.

Della Torre was only halfway through the bottle of Karlovačka when he saw the man in the tight black T-shirt and combat trousers from the Osijek police station.

Outside, by the door, he could see another couple of men, similarly dressed, though looking less like bodybuilders than ex-bodybuilders. Their arms bulged, but so did their guts.

The man came over to him and prodded a thumb behind him towards the door. "This way," he said.

Della Torre looked up, tired, shaken, and now irritated.

"The door? Sure. You might want to use it."

"If you got a gun, you'll want to give it to me," the man said, holding out his hand.

He had neatly combed dirty-blond hair. Della Torre couldn't remember the last time he'd combed his own hair. His wedding day, he figured. The man had the sleepy eyes of somebody used to getting his way.

"I'd love to give it to you," della Torre said. "I've got to remember to carry one. Just for times like these."

"Let's go, then."

"I didn't realize the café was shutting."

"Boss wants to see you."

"Does he, now? And which boss might that be?"

"Gentleman you're here to see. Otherwise you've wasted a trip from Zagreb."

"I'm afraid my appointment is for tomorrow."

"Was. Isn't now. Now it's now."

It took della Torre a moment to process what the man had just said. He stubbed out his cigarette and followed him out the door. It looked like his date with a bottle of slivovitz would have to wait.

The bodybuilder headed away from the river. The two men loitering at the door followed behind.

"I thought the Hotel Danube was in that direction," della Torre said, pointing back towards the river.

"It is," said the man.

"My meeting's meant to be at the Danube. Tomorrow."

"Maybe it was. Isn't now."

"So would you mind telling me where we're going instead?" he asked, straining to stay polite.

"Ribar."

"And that's a restaurant, I take it." Della Torre found himself slightly out of breath, trying to keep pace with the man. Any quicker and they'd be jogging. "So there was no point in setting up the appointment. How did you find me, by the way, or did you follow me all the way from Osijek?"

"The gentleman stays well informed. And he doesn't like to be predictable. Doesn't want to make it easy for the Serbs," the man said.

Della Torre could understand why. Especially around these parts. Horvat had been agitating against Serbs living in Croatia ever since he'd come back to the country, about a year before. He was a hero to the nationalists in the Croat government. Not least because he was rich, having built up a pizza empire in Canada.

A few months earlier, Horvat had taken a more direct approach to local politics, after growing tired of the local police's efforts at keeping peace between the two nationalities. Together with a couple of like-minded friends, he'd fired a clutch of rocket-propelled grenades into a Serb village on the outskirts of Vukovar. They'd damaged a garden wall and, it was claimed, slaughtered a coop full of chickens. But, more importantly, Horvat had made plain his political intentions. For him, nothing short of war would do, and he was doing a fine job of paving the way.

In a part of the country where Serbs and Croats were so heavily integrated, neighbour turned against neighbour. Enmity and fear replaced the accommodations of everyday life. But rather than being prosecuted for the assault, Horvat had been feted by Croatia's ruling party. Before, he'd had the leadership's ear. Afterwards, it was said, Horvat had them by the balls.

The Ribar was in the vaulted ground-level cellar of a thick-walled nineteenth-century farmhouse located in Vukovar's suburbs. The restaurant smelled of cooking cabbage, damp, and saltpetre. The walls were panelled in dark wood. Somebody had made an effort at lifting the atmosphere with amateur copies of Old Master landscapes done in pastel, together with a soft-focus tropical beach print, which showed a setting sun lighting up a religious sky. It made della Torre think of bloodstains.

Horvat was standing at the bar in amiable conversation with what looked to be the owner. Other than a few paramilitary types like della Torre's newly acquired friend, the restaurant was empty. Horvat spotted him, said something to the man behind the bar, and they both laughed.

"Ah, the gentleman from Zagreb who's come all this way just to have dinner with an old, insignificant guy," Horvat said with a show of bonhomie. Della Torre affected the most insincere smile he could without being outright rude.

Horvat was based in Zagreb. He could have seen della Torre there any minute of any day of the week. But by demanding that della Torre drive to the far end of the country for the meeting, Horvat was making a point. What the point was or why he was making it, della Torre had no idea. Maybe he was sending a message to the rest of military intelligence.

"Marko della Torre," he introduced himself, taking Horvat's hand.

Horvat was a little above average height for a Croat, and they tended to be tall. He was thin, with the wrinkled, yellowy face of a heavy smoker. He had white hair, dark eyebrows, and a mouth that was permanently turned down in one corner — the residual effects of a stroke from years before — giving his speech a slight slur.

"What will you have to drink?"

"A Karlovačka," della Torre said, naming the pale beer he always drank.

"A Karlovačka it is, then," said Horvat, holding a pack of Sobranies towards della Torre. Della Torre declined the pastel-coloured cigarettes, the only brand he couldn't bring himself to smoke. Horvat shrugged and lit one for himself. He held the cigarette between the index and middle fingers of his right hand, between the palm and the knuckle, so that when he came to draw on it, his hand covered the bottom of his face.

"So you've quit since this afternoon?" Horvat asked. It seemed his spies had briefed him well.

"I'm trying to cut back. Figure I might live longer."

Horvat laughed. "My boy, it's not smoking that's going to kill you," he said, pointing at the fresh scar on della Torre's arm.

"I can only hope I've changed my ways early enough," della Torre said, surprised that Horvat seemed to know about his wound. He wondered if Horvat's mercenaries were very different from the hired assassins who'd almost done away with him.

"Here, let's sit," Horvat said. They moved to a table lit by a faint spotlight near the opposite wall. He didn't introduce della Torre to any of the paramilitaries, nor did any join them.

"We can speak English," Horvat said with a strong accent. "Twenty years in Winnipeg. The language is good for something: nobody else speaks it around here."

That was true. Yugoslavs learned German or Russian at school. Only academics and people who worked in the tourist industry, mostly on the coast, spoke English.

"Fine," della Torre replied.

"We can order some food. Or is it too early for you?" Horvat asked.

"I could eat now," della Torre said. "Think their baking is any good here?"

"Sure," Horvat said, uncertain as to why della Torre had asked.

"Then I'll have one of those...what's it called? You know, the flat bread with tomato sauce and cheese sprinkled on top, cooked in an oven?" della Torre said.

Horvat looked at him for a long moment before allowing a little smile to break on the working half of his mouth.

"You like pizza. I had pizzerias all over Manitoba and Saskatchewan, some in Alberta, Ontario; one even in Montreal. Excellent pizza," Horvat said.

He was mocked among the anti-nationalist intellectuals in Zagreb, who called him the pizza man. But if it bothered Horvat, he never showed it. Pizza had made him rich.

"They don't do pizza at Ribar," Horvat said, calling their host over with a look and a flick of the fingers. "I will order for both of us, something traditional."

He got quick revenge by ordering cabbage leaves stuffed with pork in a heavy sauce for della Torre. Traditional winter food. Horvat chose grilled fish for himself.

"So, maybe I should explain why I asked to meet you. Or maybe not. You are investigator. It will give you mystery to solve." Horvat laughed a granular smoker's laugh, punctuated with a cough. "You are very interesting man for me, very interesting," he said, dropping articles the way Yugoslavs who learned English later in life usually did. Even ones who'd lived in English-speaking countries for twenty years. "I know you were investigator for UDBA. When I was in Canada, I had to move to Winnipeg because of UDBA. We political activists were always in danger."

Della Torre nodded. The UDBA had been notorious for its attacks on dissidents and whoever the government called terrorists. Their assassins had struck in almost every western European country, as well as the U.S., Canada, Australia, and even South Africa and South America. Della Torre had never heard about any attempts on Horvat. Then again, he wouldn't have unless they'd been successful.

The dishes arrived promptly. Horvat's whole fish had been grilled and covered with an oily sauce of garlic and parsley and was served with boiled, cubed potatoes and chard. It looked edible. Nice, even. Della Torre's was two fist-sized lumps of ground meat wrapped in boiled cabbage leaves and covered in an anemic cream sauce that tasted of stock cubes. For a while he vacillated between hunger and apathy. He tried to console himself with beer and slices of chewy white bread. But hunger eventually won. The food went down like rubble.

"Before UDBA you were lawyer," Horvat said.

"You're well informed."

"Ah, I like interesting people. Before you were lawyer you were commando, no?"

"Yes."

"Tell me about commandos."

"What's there to tell? After university I did my national service, and while I was in basic training, I got pulled out because some people heard that I spoke American English."

"Yes, you speak English like American."

"I guess the years I grew up there were formative enough for me to keep my accent."

"Your father writes very good English. I don't like . . . always what he writes, but he writes well. He writes Italian too. You speak it?" Horvat said with a curious smile.

"Yes, I guess most Istrians speak it. Italian TV is more entertaining than the local offering. Frankly, it's amazing any of them speak Serbo-Croat," della Torre said.

He was slow to notice the change in Horvat. The older man's expression went from benign to closed, and was filled with fury in the space of four syllables.

"Serbo-Croat? These are two different languages," Horvat said, switching back to Croatian, his voice rising so that it stilled whatever other conversation there was in the restaurant. "It is a subversion created by the Communists to destroy our Croatian language. And it is an affectation of Istrians to speak Italian. They are as Croatian as I am."

Della Torre looked down at his stuffed cabbage, pulling some meat from the wilted white leaf with the tip of his fork.

"But we were talking about your time in commandos," Horvat said in English, the storm passing as quickly as it had built.

"They wanted somebody who spoke American English so

that when the Americans invaded, they could drop me behind the enemy lines, where my job would be to commit sabotage while blending in. Or something like that." The Yugoslav government kept its people in line by keeping alive the threat of an invasion by the Russians or Americans. As a country that was Communist and yet had broken with the Soviet bloc, positioned right between the East and the West, it balanced on a geopolitical tightrope. To be sure, there were plenty of advantages. Russians and Americans could be played off against each other so that concessions could be squeezed from both — finance, cheap oil, a blind eye to Yugoslavia's vendetta against its dissident émigrés. But it also made the country a prime candidate to host the start of the next world war. Then again, maybe Yugoslav waiters were just the people to serve canapés at Armageddon.

"And would you have? If America invaded?"

"No," della Torre said. "I'd have welcomed them."

"Good," Horvat burst out. "Good for you. Give those Yugoslav bastards poke in eye. And how did you find it in commandos?"

"Hard. I barely scraped through basic training. I think they made it easier for me, and then when I got my lieutenancy, my men carried me. I was without question the worst officer in the whole of the commandos since the Second World War."

Horvat laughed. "Oh, it wasn't so bad, from what I hear. Your men were quite fond of you."

"They get sentimental about their mascots."

"Is that what you were, Gringo?" Horvat said, enjoying della Torre's surprise that he knew the nickname.

"Yes," he said.

"You married Jew," Horvat said. Della Torre's face must have registered shock, because Horvat immediately held up his hand. "Is okay, is okay. I understand. Every young man makes mistakes. You are now looking for divorce. I know. You don't want children with this woman. I understand. You become more mature. Maybe is time to find nice Croat girl, have children with her," Horvat said, talking over della Torre's horror. Until then, he'd felt merely distaste for the man opposite him. Now it was disgust. Loathing.

How did he know so much about him? And why?

And yet whatever Horvat did know he didn't really seem to understand. Della Torre wasn't leaving Irena. It was the other way around. And no, he didn't want children. Not with anyone. But if he did have children he could only imagine having them with Irena.

"I was friend of Svjet's," Horvat said, watching della Torre. Svjet was constantly being dug up out of della Torre's past, an unhealed wound. The deepest form of unhealed wound: shame.

"Oh?" Della Torre's fork hung in the air for a brief moment and then, with huge effort, he ate. He could taste only gristle in the ground meat; vinegar in the salad; flat, bitter water in the beer.

Svjet. Another Croat dissident. Another old man.

A painful memory from the first time della Torre had gone to London, more than a dozen years before. He had taken a postgraduate law course paid for by the Zagreb prosecutor's office. He hadn't been there long when he'd been approached by the Montenegrin, one of UDBA's most notorious operatives.

He'd been at his shared flat, studying after breakfast on a Saturday morning, when the doorbell rang. He'd answered. The man standing there was almost as tall as him, more solidly built, wearing an unmistakably east European suit. He'd asked to see della Torre's passport before identifying himself with an UDBA ID.

He came in but wouldn't accept a coffee or anything. He just stood there and said, "I have a job for you. You are to get to know a man called Svjet. He goes to the Croat Sunday service at the Brompton Oratory. Introduce yourself. Become familiar with him. Don't tell him you were sent. Let him believe it's because you're lonely for Croat company. In everything else be honest with him. Tell him who you work for and what you're doing in London. He'll understand."

That was it. And della Torre did as he was told. Who was he to refuse an order from the UDBA? And such an innocuous one. But there was nothing innocuous about the UDBA. Even then he knew it.

When his law course had ended and he was about to leave London, the Montenegrin visited della Torre again. He'd handed della Torre a file and told him to deliver it to Svjet. The Montenegrin said it contained details about the UDBA assassination of another dissident in Paris a couple of years earlier. Again, della Torre did as he was told, dropping the file with Svjet before returning to Zagreb, telling him, truthfully, that it had come to him by way of someone he knew in the UDBA. Soon after, Svjet told his wife and daughter he was off to Trieste to meet someone about the file. He was never heard from again.

"Yes. Well, when I say 'friend,' I don't mean we agreed on everything," Horvat continued. "We had differences, of course." Croatian dissidents were notorious for never being able to agree on any one position. There were as many firmly held beliefs, unshakable convictions, as there were émigrés, each one at war with the next over who was the biggest patriot, who had the purest notion of a true Croat future, who'd suffered more for their faith. None would compromise. "But I used to visit him in London. Or we met in Munich. Many Croats in Munich. Before, I think, you met him. Croatian exiles everywhere, we were like brothers. We had common enemy."

Della Torre forced himself to look up from the food, to hold Horvat's eyes. His breathing was shallow and he felt the prickle of sweat on his palms.

"Then he disappeared. You were in London. You knew him there before he disappeared."

"Yes. I was studying international law," della Torre said, in a slow monotone. "Then I was with the prosecutor's office."

There was a long silence. The first of the evening.

"Lost your appetite?" Horvat asked with amusement.

"No. It's just that I guess I wasn't in the mood . . . for stuffed cabbage."

"My fault. I'm so sorry for having chosen badly," Horvat said, pleased with himself. "So you met Svjet in church?"

"Through the Croatian mass at the Brompton Oratory," della Torre said. "They have a chapel where they do an early Sunday morning service in—" He paused. "—in Croat."

"Bravo. But you don't seem to me to be a very religious man. Nothing to be ashamed of. Religion is mostly for women. You were student. You didn't get up early on Sunday for body of Christ, blood of Christ, eh?" Horvat said.

No, thought della Torre, it wasn't religion that got him up and across town at that early hour. It was fear.

"I know why you did," Horvat said.

Della Torre looked around the restaurant. He counted at least seven paramilitaries and remembered seeing another three at the door.

"Excuse me," he said, standing up and walking towards the back of the room.

One of the paramilitaries caught Horvat's eye and followed della Torre to the toilets, watched while he tried to force out a dribble of urine. He'd dried up. Evaporated. His mouth. His piss. He thought he could feel the blood in his veins turn to dust. *Svjet*, he thought to himself. Svjet. Would the man's ghost never leave him alone?

He washed his hands and walked back to the table as though he were following a procession of tumbrels.

"We were talking about Svjet, I think," Horvat said.

"Yes." Della Torre lit a cigarette.

"I think I know why you went to mass. To meet Svjet, no?"

He blew smoke through his nose. "Yes."

"I knew it," Horvat laughed with glee. "You see. I knew it. I caught you. An old pizza man caught the UDBA lawyer. You see?"

Della Torre rolled the end of his cigarette around the ashtray, shaping the ember into a cone.

"Admit it, you didn't go to church to pray." Horvat made a show of putting his hands together and looking heavenward.

Della Torre shrugged.

Horvat pointed his fork at della Torre's wounded arm. "You got into scrape with some Bosnians. Some deep undercover work they didn't much care for."

"Something like that," della Torre said. It had been nothing like that at all. He'd been selling UDBA files to a crooked cop and somebody hadn't liked it. And when he'd run away to London, they'd sent a couple of hired guns to hunt him down.

"You see, I think I know what it is," Horvat said, the tiny twist of a smile playing on the side of his mouth.

"Oh?"

Horvat threw up his hands in mock frustration at having to explain himself, but he was enjoying his game.

"Obvious, isn't it? You are true Croatian. You didn't go to oratory to pray but to be part of Croat community. And when you finished with London, you were going to be Svjet's man in Zagreb, weren't you? Svjet told me about you. He had plans for you." For a man who'd suffered Tito's prisons and exile, Svjet was somehow hopelessly naive, vulnerable to flattery, to being given—handed by the gods—a handsome young acolyte whom he could mould in his image. Della Torre found it embarrassingly easy to be adopted by the old dissident. "You were in prosecutor's office. From there a short step to Interior Ministry, where we needed eyes to see what UDBA were up to.

Except Svjet got caught. And eventually they discovered what you were doing too, didn't they? They found out you were a sleeper for Croatian cause and they tried to kill you, didn't they?"

Della Torre stared at Horvat with incredulity. The émigré had built up some fantasy about him, a complicated fantasy that fitted della Torre into his nationalist imaginings. Horvat had convinced himself that the Bosnians who'd shot him had been UDBA agents sent to eliminate the Croat nationalist double agent in their midst. Della Torre knew these people spent too much time watching spy movies, reading spy novels. But now they wove their own plots too?

Horvat looked at the younger man with satisfaction, tapping the side of his nose with his index finger.

"I got you, didn't I? I knew when they told me about you. I remembered my conversation with Svjet, his boy in prosecutor's office." Horvat nodded. "I asked about you. Forgot your name, but they found it for me. I got background on you. Istrian? Yugoslav secret policeman? Nonsense. You're one of us."

The man had called him to Vukovar to show him what they were fighting for and how. To Horvat, della Torre was another of his fanatical nationalists.

He held out his hand over the table. Della Torre took it reluctantly and let Horvat pump it until beer bottles fell onto the floor. The half of Horvat's face that worked was beaming. The other half remained frozen — cold, turned down, cruel.

## 11

HE SAT IN the car for a little while before starting it up. He was pretty sure his blood alcohol level was finally close to legal. He could have slept another few hours. His shoes were still damp, and the inside of his head was a ball of fuzz pierced with razor blades. As long as he didn't make any sudden moves, he would feel no pain. He swallowed. At least his mouth was somewhere back to normal again. He'd had to clean his teeth three times and then down a long espresso and smoke a cigarette, but he finally got the oily paint-thinner taste of home-distilled slivovitz out of his mouth.

Della Torre had left the Ribar not long after that handshake, turning down the offer to stay for a few drinks with Horvat and the boys. The weather had just broken, and those black, threatening clouds had opened themselves up on the land-scape. The rain, mixed with hail, was Biblical. He'd started to sprint but was soaked through before he'd gone half a block. In a moment, the street became a stream, a tendril of the Danube sending its shoots up through the town. He breathed water, was pelted by ice until he stung. Even after he reached the ar-cades on the main street, the rain sprang back up at him from the force with which it had hurtled to earth.

He'd thought he'd wait it out, but why? He could get no wetter. His clothes could absorb no more water. So he might as well try to enjoy it, like Gene Kelly in *Singin' in the Rain*. Anzulović had made him watch the movie once. All della Torre remembered was the guy getting drenched.

As he'd checked into the hotel, they'd mopped the floors around him. The bellboy had delivered the bottle of slivovitz, compliments of the hotel. Best quality, he said. He had also offered to find someone della Torre could share it with. Della Torre declined, in favour of a hot bath and his novel. The slivovitz was just anaesthetic.

As he pulled away from the hotel, he noticed one of Horvat's militiamen watching him. Camouflage trousers, black T-shirt, thick arms and neck.

It took him the best part of an hour to get to the Osijek police station. Because he'd driven slowly, unsure of his reflexes. And because he took a couple of wrong turns. So it was after nine by the time he parked and got to the booking sergeant's desk. The same one as the previous afternoon.

"You're back."

"Lieutenant Boban, please."

"He told me you might come looking for him. He's in. Up those stairs, second floor to the right. I'll call to tell him."

He let della Torre through.

The door to Boban's office was open, but he was on the phone. He gave della Torre an apologetic look and pointed to the office next door, miming that he should knock.

Rejkart opened it. Della Torre was surprised by what he saw.

The police chief was a young man, younger even than della Torre. He wasn't yet in his mid-thirties and looked younger still. He was about della Torre's height, but thinner, with hollow eyes from lack of sleep and months of worry. His thick black hair sat high on his head, but the feature that really stood out was his luxuriant black moustache, which harked back to an imperial age. For years della Torre had had one too, but he'd shaved it off during his ill-fated trip to London this past spring. His had been a weak effort by comparison.

"I'm told you're a friend, even though you come from Zagreb," Rejkart said, holding della Torre by the shoulder as he shook his hand.

"It took a while to convince the lieutenant."

Rejkart waved della Torre in and shrugged sympathetically when della Torre refused a drink. Della Torre sat in a slightly reclined padded office chair facing Rejkart's plain wooden desk. The desk was mostly tidy, with two telephones and, in one corner, a small stack of papers. Rejkart sat in a chair next to della Torre.

"My men are overprotective of me sometimes," Rejkart said, smiling apologetically. "Especially when it has to do with Zagreb. All we seem to get from there these days is trouble-makers. Thank you for taking Damir to the hospital."

"How is he?"

"He'll be fine. A clean, simple-to-repair wound, I'm told. A sharp piece of tile sliced through muscle. Lieutenant Boban tells me the doctors think he'll be fit for work in a week's time."

There was a pause. Rejkart gave della Torre an encouraging smile. He sat back in his chair as if he had all morning to chat about football or the weather, but his eyes danced back towards his desk. Della Torre realized the police chief had sat away from it to avoid succumbing to the temptation of looking at his papers while entertaining his guest. Nothing about Rejkart, from the pallor of his skin to his fatigued eyes, suggested he gave himself over to any leisure.

"I won't play games," della Torre said. "Anzulović sent me to see how you were doing, but he didn't want me to tell you because he thought you'd varnish the truth, paint me a pretty picture, and I'd leave not knowing any more than if I'd read *Vjesnik* at a café in Zagreb this morning."

Rejkart laughed.

"Anzulović..." he said, shaking his head at the name. "He's been at it since the start of the year, trying to get me transferred out of here." He smiled when he saw the look of guilt on della Torre's face. "Ah, I see he told you."

"He might have mentioned something along those lines. But that you've been...ah...reticent with him."

"Well, I shouldn't keep him hanging on. Tell him I'm accepting the latest offer. They're making me head of training at the Zagreb Academy. I haven't told anyone here yet, so if you could make sure it doesn't go beyond Anzulović I'd be grateful. It won't become official until next week. I've got some things to finish up here first. Between my wife, my officers, and Anzulović, everyone wants to get me the hell out of here. So I said yes to the academy job. It'll be dull, but I could use a bit of dullness after this place. If that's what he sent you here for, to find out whether I'd finally given in, then you can tell him I have."

"I'll tell him," della Torre said.

The phone rang. Rejkart asked della Torre to excuse him and picked up the receiver. He listened and then said, "Let me know if anything more comes up."

"So how is the old man?" Rejkart said, turning back to della Torre.

"Getting older. He's looking tired," said della Torre.

"Aren't we all. I hear they've shut down Department VI."

"We're owned by military intelligence now. Run by a man called Kakav."

"I know Kakav. He was with the Zagreb police when I worked there. A sort of commissar, if I remember. Not very intelligent but somehow manages to worm his way up to the top of the shitpile, if you'll excuse the expression."

"That's the man."

"Not someone to get on the bad side of. Venomous, if I remember well," Rejkart said.

"Thanks for the advice."

"Sounds like it's something you might have already found out for yourself."

"Yup," said della Torre.

Rejkart smiled. There was a wisdom to his young face, warmth and concern. Della Torre was getting an inkling of why his men liked him so much.

"Has he changed?" Rejkart asked. "Is the first thing he asks whether you've seen any good movies lately?"

"Anzulović? He used to, but he's given up. I don't go to any good movies. Or bad ones, for that matter," della Torre said.

"Neither do I. Not anymore. But whenever we talk, he still asks," Rejkart said. He pulled out a pack of Lord cigarettes and peeled back a corner, pushing one out slightly and offering it to della Torre.

"Thanks." Della Torre leaned forward to light the police chief's cigarette and then his own.

"He was head detective when I was starting out on the Zagreb detective squad. After a while, I noticed he was bunking off Thursday afternoons," Rejkart continued. "I wondered what he was up to, so one day I followed him. I thought he might have a mistress. I'm not sure what I would have done if I'd found out he did. Anyway, I was pretty disappointed to discover he was going to the university cinema club. I thought I was being clever and subtle, but he knew straight away I'd followed him. In fact, I think it was that afternoon or the next day in the office that he asked me whether I liked movies. I thought, boy, that's me back on the traffic beat. But I managed to say yes. And then he asked whether I'd like to go with him the following Thursday."

"The movie club shut down," della Torre said. "He takes videos into the office now. He's got a TV and a machine. Locks his door and tells his secretary to take his calls."

Rejkart laughed.

"Sometimes it was just us there, me and him. In the cinema," Rejkart said. "I didn't go often, and after a while I'd only go to the Hollywood movies and maybe a Japanese sword movie. What killed me was when he took me to a four-hour-long Russian film. I'd fallen asleep and Anzulović just left me there. When I finally got back to the office, I got it in the neck from my immediate superior. Anzulović refused to back me up when I said I'd been with him. He told my boss that he thought I'd bunked off to spend the afternoon with some woman. When I admitted I'd fallen asleep at the movies, nobody believed me. For a while I had a reputation as a ladies' man just on the strength of that story. That was before I got married..."

"He's still a funny guy."

The telephone rang again. Rejkart answered, moving back behind his desk. He spoke little. His head was bowed as he listened. When he looked back up at the end of the one-sided conversation, his cheeks were slightly more sunken and his face was a little more pale. He forced a smile.

"Sure I can't get you a drink?" Rejkart asked after he hung up. "I can order you a coffee, but I'm trying to cut back myself. I'm jittery enough as it is, and I spend most of my days having coffee with discontented Serb or Croat villagers."

"If you've got something soft, that'd be great."

"Coca-Cola?"

"Sure," della Torre said. He decided he wouldn't point out that Coke was full of caffeine.

Rejkart got up and appraised some drinking glasses he found in a cupboard.

"I'm not sure how clean they are," he said.

"I'll take my chances."

As he was pouring, something caught Rejkart's eye outside the window. The glass overflowed.

"Sorry," he said, finding some paper towels. "I saw someone I'd rather not outside."

"Girlfriend's husband?"

There was a hollowness to Rejkart's laugh. "A fellow by the name of Zdenko. He's one of the paramilitaries who've descended on us from parts unknown, somewhere in Herzegovina. He seems to be the fixer when Horvat's not around."

Della Torre stood up to take the glass from Rejkart. He could see a man standing in the shade of a tree. The same paramilitary who'd found della Torre in the café, who'd been standing there the previous day.

"Anzulović's wife still have that poodle?" Rejkart asked.

"Yup. It's older, yellower, and Anzulović hates it even more."

"He still afraid it'll outlive him?"

"Says he knows it will."

The telephone rang again. Rejkart picked up the phone and listened. His smile evaporated.

"Yes, yes, I'll be there." He looked up at della Torre. "I'm sorry. I have to go. Something's come up. You're welcome to wait for me here, but it might take a little while."

"Maybe I could go with you?"

"Yes, yes, of course. It could be uncomfortable, though. I don't think dangerous. Well, that's not true, everything's dangerous here. But no more dangerous than usual."

"That's okay. I've already had someone shoot my car—I mean, my wife's car—yesterday."

"Yes, I heard. I'm sorry about that. I'm sure if you take it round to our mechanics, they'll fix it, though it might be a bit of a wait. We've got cars stacked up there. Can't get the parts. Belgrade stopped sending them to us, for some reason," he said. "We'll take my car."

.    .    .

They headed back towards Vukovar. The place was proving to be a magnet for della Torre. Boban, Horvat, and now Rejkart.

Rejkart asked if della Torre was carrying a weapon. Della Torre said he wasn't.

"Good," he said. "The Serbs have been setting up roadblocks. They're worried about some of the Croat nationalists who have been coming through, so they blockade their local roads. I can usually talk them out of it, but only because I ask them nicely and don't carry a gun. It wouldn't do if they found you with one."

About twenty minutes to the south of Osijek, they slowed down. A small group of Serbs had rolled oil barrels onto the road and were guarding the spot, armed with shotguns. Rejkart stopped the car a good forty metres short.

"Stay here," Rejkart said to della Torre. "Don't do anything sudden and make sure they can see your hands. Hang your right arm out the window and put your left hand on the dashboard."

Rejkart stepped out of the car and opened up his sport coat so that the Serbs could see he wasn't hiding anything. For a while they kept their shotguns trained on him but had lowered them by the time he'd strolled over. Della Torre couldn't hear what was being said, but it looked like an impassioned conversation on the part of the Serbs, while Rejkart calmed the situation with modest gestures. Finally, after a good half-hour, they put their shotguns on the ground and, with Rejkart's help, rolled the barrels out of the road. He shook their hands and returned to the car.

"Takes some courage to go up to vigilantes like that," della Torre said as Rejkart turned the car back towards Osijek.

"Oh, they're just frightened. All they want is to be reminded that the neighbours they grew up with, used to go drinking with, and played backgammon with on a Sunday afternoon won't kill them in their sleep. I spend most of my days going from one roadblock to another trying to calm them down. But it's getting harder with the nationalists around. They don't want Serbs and Croats living together peacefully."

"Horvat's people?"

"Both stripes. But around here it's mostly our lot, Croats. They want Serbs out of Croatia, doesn't matter that they've been living here as long as we have. Anyway, no one's terribly trusting since Borovo Selo."

Borovo Selo was the Serb village near Vukovar. Four local cops had taken it into their heads to go into the village one night to pull down the Yugoslav flag and replace it with the Croatian one. They denied they'd been drinking. Two were wounded and captured. The next day Zagreb, full of bravado, went over Rejkart's head and best advice and sent busloads of police, around 150 of them, into the village to free the two hostages, as they called the captured policemen. During the raid, a dozen cops were killed and another twenty were injured in the firefight. Probably half a dozen villagers died too.

"Anzulović tells me you've had some death threats."

Rejkart laughed bitterly. "If it was only some, it wouldn't feel so bad. It's hard to find the bills among all the letters telling my wife how many ways I'm going to die."

"Is that why you're finally willing to go back to Zagreb?"

"It gets tiring being hated. Being called a traitor for trying to remind people that they aren't enemies, that they've got far more in common with each other than they do with some of these strangers who have come from god knows where. I'd be able to cope with that. Most of the death threats are from cranks anyway. Old men or students who have been whipped up into a froth. They're usually drunk when they write. You can almost smell it on the paper. But it's become different lately."

"How?"

"How? Horvat has made it plain he wants me buried."

"I met him last night."

"Did you?" Rejkart turned to look at della Torre.

"He seems to have convinced himself I'm a friend."

"For goodness sake, let him believe it. A worse enemy you couldn't imagine."

"What about the Serb nationalists?"

"Oh, they're bad too. But they're not the ones doing most of the stirring here. It's the Croats. The Serbs don't need to. They've got a huge army just across the river." Rejkart pointed across the flat land to where, in the distance, a line of trees marked out the Danube. "They're waiting to be provoked into using it. And for some reason Horvat wants to accommodate them."

"And you're doing your best to be the peacekeeper."

"I feel like I'm trying to plant carrots in the middle of the O.K. Corral. I'm a coward for wanting to get out. But if I stay, I know I'm a dead man. If I go, maybe they'll forget about me. Maybe the next guy won't be hated so much."

"Only because he won't work as hard to keep the peace."

"Because the peace can't be kept."

.    .    .

They drove back to the office without incident and then sat in the car in the police parking lot, under the half-shade of a withered tree, the engine off. The day's heat was already stifling, the open windows offering little solace.

Rejkart closed his eyes and leaned back against the headrest. "I hate going into the office. I hate the telephone. I hate how it rings. How every time I pick it up, the only alternative to bad news is worse news."

"Was this worse? I mean earlier. It didn't look like a pleasant conversation."

"It wasn't a pleasant conversation."

Della Torre stayed quiet, not wishing to rush the youthful chief of police.

"Anzulović said he wanted to know what was happening.

The unvarnished truth," Rejkart began.

"Yes."

"He trained me at the Zagreb force. Always took an interest in me. Helped me out here whenever he could."

"Yes, I owe him one too. Or maybe a dozen," della Torre said.

"That call was from the other side."

"Other side?"

"Other side of the river. Serbia. A friend of mine is a senior police officer there. Officially, I can't speak to him. But the phone line is still open."

"Do you think no one else is listening in?" della Torre asked, incredulous at the risk Rejkart was taking. He'd have been surprised if the policeman's office wasn't bugged by the Croat nationalists, but it was a nailed-on certainty that any calls he received from Serbia were being monitored.

"Of course other people are listening in. People on our side and on theirs. What can I do? Nothing. But we keep in touch because people have been going missing and sometimes we know something about it."

"Somebody's gone missing?"

Rejkart put his head in his hands.

"Ten days ago, about twenty of our police and thirty or forty civilians we know about, but probably more, all Croats, disappeared from a Serb pocket on this side of the river."

"And your friend knows what happened to them."

"No. But his officers found the bodies of four of our policemen and as many civilians in a ditch. Not far from where you were with Boban yesterday evening, on the opposite side of the river."

"A house or something in a copse by the river, on the Serb side?"

"That's it."

"Shot?"

"Through the eye."

"And the others?"

"He doesn't know, but I'd be surprised if they don't turn up in the same condition. There's a Serb paramilitary called Gorki, Darko Gorki, who's said to be operating there. Ever heard of him?"

Della Torre nodded. "Yes. He's a criminal. Has a long record. Did time in Belgium and Sweden, I think. Maybe France. Wanted in Switzerland for armed robbery. Suspected of murder too. Fitting name." The root of *Gorki* meant "bitter gift."

"How have you run across him?" Rejkart asked.

"The UDBA used him. When the UDBA had dirty jobs in other countries, they tended to use Yugoslav criminals, organized crime or mafia, professionals rather than just amateur know-nothings. He's one of the criminals the UDBA found handy."

"He killed people for the UDBA?"

"Not that I know of, but he's well liked by people in Belgrade."

"Seems that he's being given free rein," said Rejkart.

"Like Horvat."

"No. As far as I know, Horvat isn't operating death squads. He's running guns out of Hungary, supplying them to Croatia out of a sense of patriotism, he says. Though if you ask me, he's pretty patriotic to his wallet. His people have been involved in the occasional shooting, but we haven't any reason to believe they're doing the systematic killing."

"Maybe that's coming." Della Torre offered Rejkart one of his Luckys. "What do you do about the bodies your friend found on the other side of the river, and the other missing people?"

"Nothing. I can't do anything yet. I see the families every day and I tell them I'm doing everything I can. I don't know what to tell them. We won't be able to recover the bodies. Officially, the Serbs won't help us. They'll deny everything. And if our nationalists find out, they'll want retribution."

"So you sit on the news."

"Yes. For now. I don't know." He was silent for a long while and then he sighed, opening the car door with the deliberate movements of a man more than twice his age.

They stepped out of the baking car. Della Torre walked the police chief back to the front of the station, where their cigarette butts joined an army of yellow filters in a waist-high planter that might once have held a rose bush. They shook hands, Rejkart finding a smile from somewhere, sending his warmest regards to Anzulović. On the way back to the Golf, della Torre noticed Horvat's man, the same one, Zdenko, loitering in the shade in sight of the police station.

**D**ELLA TORRE STOPPED for gas at a lonely station in the middle of the plains, halfway along the highway. He bought only enough to get back to Zagreb. He'd have filled up the tank, but when he pulled out his UDBA petrol card, the attendant sucked his teeth and said, "Sorry, we don't take cards."

"It's not a credit card," della Torre explained. "The police will pay you back."

"No, they won't."

"Yes, they will."

"Nope. Bunch of Serbs came through a couple of months ago. Tried the same thing on me. Haven't seen a dinar yet."

"But it's an UDBA card," della Torre said with frustration.

"Well, I can see it's not American Express."

"Don't you know what this card means?" Della Torre used to hate it when UDBA officers threw their weight around. But that was when they hadn't needed to.

"Means you got to pay for your gas like anybody else."

He ostentatiously wrote down the man's details, the name of the gas station, the time. He even demanded the man sign it. The attendant obliged while chewing on a bit of straw. Maybe there was something in della Torre's manner that told the man the sheet of paper would just be filed in a wastebasket.

Faced with spending his own cash, he asked for the minimum. Besides, gas stations in Zagreb were still honouring the UDBA card. But he was so irritated with the man that he didn't buy a drink at the station shop. He suffered with thirst until he found a roadside shop that sold him a couple of Capri Sun juice bags and a box of pretzel sticks.

He was glad to get away from those benighted lands in the east. He was glad that Rejkart was moving back to Zagreb. He'd liked the man from the start. Then again, he wouldn't have wished Rejkart's impossible job on anyone. At least not anyone with a soul and a conscience.

He thought about dropping the car off at Irena's apartment but then remembered about fixing the bullet hole first. Somebody in Zagreb would be able to do it. He drove over to his apartment, pulling up on the wide pavement. The one-way street had three lanes and parking spots herringboned on either side. Not for the first time, he felt grateful for the Austro-Hungarians' foresight in planting trees along the road. Now giants, the horse chestnuts gave enough shade to ensure the summer heat didn't cook his brain while he walked around town. Or even just crossed the pavement to his building.

There was no sign of Rebecca. He called out into the empty apartment and then wandered from room to room. She'd taken all her things. He went through the dirty laundry basket, where he kept his precious documents hidden. They'd been undisturbed. His service Beretta was there too.

His buzzer rang. The automatic unlocking system no longer worked, so he had to go down the high, echoing stairwell to answer it himself. The front door was missing its glass. Irena was standing behind the wrought-iron grille work.

"Hi," he said, opening the door. "I only just got back."

"I know." She didn't look happy. "What happened to my car?"

"Umm, there was a little accident."

"I'm listening."

"Want to come in?"

He smiled at her. Irena's anger expressed itself in cold blankness. Most people wouldn't have noticed, but della Torre had come to know the look well. In one sense it was a relief that she wasn't one to cause scenes in public. Or in private, even. But he hated that look, which reminded him of an empty white Venetian carnival mask. It kept from him her warm humour, the gentle irony in her eyes, everything that had made him fall in love with her nearly half a lifetime before.

"I have no desire to join your ménage. What happened to my car?"

"I'm alone. Promise."

"Your strumpet already gone?"

"She's not my strumpet."

"Ah, so you admit she's a strumpet."

"No, I meant she doesn't have anything to do with me."

"Which is why she wanders around your apartment naked."

Where most Yugoslav women he'd ever met used emotional levers freely — weeping histrionics or outright rage — Irena limited herself to cutting sarcasm.

"I'll explain, Irena. But not on the pavement…" And then, trying to turn things back at her: "Maybe you ought to justify a thing or two as well."

He walked back up the stairs to his apartment. The thick walls and terrazzo of the hallway made the building cool, even in the heat of the afternoon. Irena followed him.

"Would you like a coffee?" he asked when she sat down at the little oilcloth-covered table in his narrow kitchen. The window was shuttered against the sun, though enough hazy light filtered through the slats.

She didn't answer, nor did he wait for her to before putting a pan of water onto the ancient gas burner.

"What happened to my car?" There was still that ice-cold anger.

"Someone shot it."

"Someone shot it?"

"That's why it has a hole. How did you know I was back?"

"Who shot it? Why?"

"Some Serb. In Vukovar. Actually, he was in Serbia and I was parked by the Danube on our side near Vukovar. And he shot at me."

"So why does the car have a hole in it, and not you?"

"Maybe he doesn't like Volkswagens."

"Some Serb just randomly decides to take a shot at you and hits my car instead?"

"It might not have been random."

She stared at him. Her eyes were green like jade. There was a little high colour in her cheeks. He hoped it was the heat.

"Do tell."

"I was with some policemen from the Osijek force and, well, it seems that the Serb's been shooting at them for a while."

She nodded. "So you thought you might like to stick my car in the way."

"They didn't tell me not to park in front of a bullet."

"Marko, why is it always you?"

"A combination of suave self-assurance, good looks, and intelligence? Look, they were very apologetic and assured me they'll fix it."

"They who?"

"The Osijek police. Not the Serb. All you need to do is drop the car off at their garage and they'll sort it out. Make it look like a brand new Zastava." He paused. "Why didn't you tell me?"

"You had company. Remember?" she said.

Her tone had softened a little. But only a little.

He got up to make the coffees. Three big teaspoons of instant into each cup, then half-fill each with boiling water.

"Irena, why do you have to go to Vukovar? I mean, it's not safe and it's just going to get worse."

"They need doctors. They need doctors who don't have families to worry about."

"You mean if we'd had children, you wouldn't be going?"

She didn't answer.

"Irena, it's a lost cause," he said. "When the Yugoslav army decides it's had enough with this whole Croat independence thing, it'll take them fifteen minutes to flatten Vukovar on their way to Zagreb. The place has forlorn hope written all over it. And it's full of idiots trying to provoke the army into doing something sooner rather than later. You're going to be needed here."

"I'm only covering for six weeks. That's it. They're getting bullet-wound cases and I need to develop some skills if I'm going to be of use to anyone."

"Is that the only reason David's coming? To teach you how to deal with bullet wounds?"

"He's coming to help train some of us."

"Bit of entry and exit, eh?"

"Don't be vulgar," she said, sharply. "You of all people have no right to be saying anything in that respect. What happened to your redhead? You know, the one who only wears clothes to cover up her shoulders. I never figured you for being partial to redheads."

"I don't know."

"You don't know you're partial to them?"

"I'm not. I don't know what happened to her. She disappeared."

"Had her fill, did she?"

"Now who's being vulgar? Besides, we were talking about Vukovar and you."

"How did you find out?"

"I have my ways. Remember, I'm a secret policeman."

"How could I forget? How did you accidentally stumble on

this information? Or was one of your friends snooping through my apartment?"

"Of course not." He hated the implication that he'd spied on her. He had no doubt that the UDBA had spied on her. Had spied on them both. But not at his instigation. "Your friend at the hospital told me. A boy, a young cop I was with, was injured, and she heard my name. Though I can't remember hers. I think she ran the emergency room."

"Miljenka Boštrić?"

"That's right. She heard my name and, well, it wasn't hard to put two and two together. So how long's David going to be there?"

"Not long."

"He can't get there through Belgrade. I don't think they'd let him across the border."

"He's flying to Zagreb. I'll pick him up."

"Long round trip."

"We might stay in Zagreb. But frankly, that's none of your business."

"Well, you're still my wife."

"I thought you said ex-wife."

"Slip of the tongue," della Torre said, sipping his coffee. "He staying long?"

"Until he leaves."

"None of my business?"

"Nope."

"I'm sorry about the car. I'll pay to get it fixed. I mean, if the Osijek cops don't."

"You will pay," she said with finality. She finished her coffee and stood up to leave. "Can I have the keys." He fished them out of his pocket. "But at least I'll find the tank's full." She caught the expression on della Torre's face. "Won't I?"

"Umm. I meant to. They wouldn't take my card and I didn't have much cash..." he stammered.

Irritation forced Irena's eyes shut. She put her hand on her forehead and then looked at him. "You'll pay for that too."

He walked her down the stairs to the front door.

"I can't convince you not to go to Vukovar, can I?"

"No. I'm committed."

"Then will you at least be careful?"

"Only because you asked nicely."

"Irena, you know I mean it. We may have our…difficulties…"

"Only in actually managing to get divorced."

"I still love you," he said.

"I know," she said, and gave him a little peck on the lips.

She walked towards the car, stopping to contemplate the driver's-side door before unlocking it. She was about to get in when he called to her through the ironwork grille.

"I forgot to ask," he shouted to her.

"What?"

"How did you know I was back? I'd only just arrived."

"You were waiting at the traffic light. I was just heading up to the hospital from the university and saw you there. Made an idiot of myself trying to catch your attention," she said and then, after a pause and not bothering to lower her voice, as she might have done once upon a time: "You know, Marko, for a secret policeman, you seem pretty oblivious most of the time."

**13**

HE WOKE EARLY and couldn't get back to sleep. So he showered, shaved, got dressed, and headed off to the UDBA offices. Maybe he'd try to track down what happened to Rebecca. If only to get his spare key back. The sun was still low and cool, though the clear sky meant it'd be another scorching day.

He hadn't expected there to be many people at the UDBA building at that hour of the morning. But he had expected there to be furniture.

The offices had been stripped of anything movable. All the boxes stacked up along the walls were gone, highlighting a pale green whitewash paint. The colour of fear. Strangers had always found the UDBA building terrifying. Irena refused to walk through its doors. Della Torre supposed he must have felt a twinge or two when he'd started working there—anything associated with the UDBA was unsettling. But that feeling had gradually faded. Until now. Now he felt the building's brooding menace, from its terrazzo floors to its five-metre-high ceilings, its massive internal walls and tall windows that forever invited people to jump.

He went up to his office. It too had been completely cleared out.

He was at a loss to think of where everything had gone, but then remembered that Anzulović had mentioned the lingerie shop on the ground-floor level of the new military intelligence building on Ilica, where, he guessed, he'd find his colleagues. And a chair to sit on.

He was heading back down the abandoned corridor when a sliver of light under Anzulović's door made him look in.

Anzulović's desk was there. It had a telephone on it, and a lamp. And in the chair behind the desk was Anzulović. He looked tired, even more tired than usual, and slightly dishevelled. He was leaning back, staring ahead. Della Torre had to knock on the door to draw attention to himself.

"You been sleeping in that chair?" della Torre asked. "What's the matter? Wife throw you out for snoring?"

Anzulović ran his hand over the stubble on his face. "Been a long night."

"What happened, they forget to move you?"

"Most of my stuff is gone, but I needed the desk and the phone," Anzulović said, reaching into a drawer and pulling out an unlabelled bottle of clear liquid and two small shot glasses etched with flowers. He poured the homemade slivovitz into both.

"Met your friend Rejkart yesterday. Seemed a very nice guy," della Torre said, raising his glass and knocking it back. He exhaled pure alcohol. "Said not to worry about him. He's given in and taken a job running the police academy here."

Anzulović gave della Torre a hollow stare.

"His friends there have a funny sense of humour, but—"

Anzulović cut him off. "Haven't you heard?"

"Heard what?"

"Rejkart was killed last night."

"What? Impossible. He was fine when I left him yesterday afternoon."

Anzulović had spent the night piecing the story together,

using every ounce of pull he had to get whatever information he could. One of the witnesses was in intensive care under police guard, though he'd managed to tell the emergency crews something of what had happened. Others contributed fragments, contradictions, unreliable bits.

"As far as I've been able to work out, this is what happened," Anzulović said, staring at the confusion in front of him, sheets of paper with scraps of writing, some circled, much crossed out, arrows linking bubbles, winding, overlapping, nothing like the methodical notes he normally put together. "Seems he got a call in the office about a roadblock," he started.

"He spent a lot of time going from one group of vigilantes to another, calming them down. He took me on one of his little trips," della Torre said, still in shock over the news.

"Well, he was heading off to a community meeting. A few local politicians were with him, two Serb worthies and a Croat. Apparently he spent a lot of his evenings at these things. As he was leaving, a call came through about a roadblock. So he took a detour." Anzulović sighed heavily.

Rejkart and his companions were on a straight stretch of road when they came upon a man standing in the middle, on the broken white median line, a couple of hundred metres in front of the roadblock.

The man was holding a gun. Not a single-bore shotgun like the farmers carried, but a military weapon. The car slowed. The man raised the gun, pointing it at the car.

Before the Zastava had come to a complete stop, the Kalashnikov's muzzle vomited orange-red bursts. In the same instant, holes opened in the windscreen, perfect round holes in the centre of crazed glass, holes made by the bullets that had killed Josip Rejkart and two of his companions. The third, grievously wounded, only just survived that still, calm summer evening.

Anzulović's eyes showed ugly, brutal pain. "I should have

pushed him harder to leave. He was stubborn. And now his wife's a widow. Thank god he didn't have kids. They'd still be infants."

"Do they know who did it?"

"The local cops think they've got a name. Zdenko. Probably some farmer. They always pin it on some unlucky slob. Saves them from having to do proper detective work."

"One of Horvat's men is called Zdenko. I met him. I mean, I met them both," della Torre said.

"Horvat's man?"

"Yes. Horvat knew the minute I showed up in Vukovar, and Zdenko was the fellow who took me to him. He's a paramilitary. Or dressed like one. "

"They all dress like paramilitaries. Even the pansies do," Anzulović said.

"Well, that's what he looked like to me. And he'd been keeping a watch on Rejkart's office. Both of us noticed him."

"Not very discreet."

"Maybe Horvat wanted to send a message. That there's no compromise. He wants the Serbs out," della Torre said. Momentarily he wondered if somehow his presence in Vukovar had given Horvat a sense of security about ordering the killing. But he quickly dismissed the thought. "I'm sorry. Rejkart was a nice guy. A really nice guy. His men seemed to be very fond of him, even if the nationalists weren't."

The words were like dry leaves in della Torre's mouth. They crumbled as he spoke, crushed under the weight of what had happened. Rejkart had been a young man with a gentle authority. It horrified della Torre to know that someone so real could be no more. And to think that della Torre could have been one of the car's passengers.

"Whoever it was, he got away," Anzulović said. He spoke so quietly, in such leaden tones, that della Torre wondered whether he might be speaking to himself. "The militia and the cops have put roadblocks on every major road from Osijek. All the way up to Zagreb. But he disappeared." Anzulović shrugged. "Horvat's man, you say?"

"Horvat's man."

Anzulović nodded. He'd dismissed Horvat as a well-connected nuisance, a dangerous buffoon who thought himself a hero, a rich man playing games. Now he was an enemy.

"A shame. We need people like Josip. Reliable people with a sense of decency. I have a feeling they'll be in short supply," Anzulović said.

It was clear to della Torre that the pain Anzulović felt was for himself rather than for the country.

"Why do you think they did it?"

"Why? Because they didn't like him," Anzulović said.

He didn't elaborate. Della Torre didn't need him to. Nationalists on both sides of the border were straining, frothing for a fight. Though a half-formed Croatia, mewling in its newness against the might of the Yugoslav army, would be like a terrier pup against a Rottweiler. A terrier pup that thought itself a lion.

"Come. You've been here all night, haven't you? Let's get a coffee," della Torre said, still standing.

"I suppose I could use one," Anzulović said in an even tone. "I've got to let the movers take my desk. Everything else is at the new offices. Or should be."

.    .    .

Anzulović and della Torre headed north and west along Zagreb's grand avenues. On mornings like this, the city was especially beautiful. The heat was only just rising, and the pale blue sky set off the mustard yellows and ochres of the imperial Austro-Hungarian buildings. Giant plane trees stood along its green, open squares.

Cafés had spread their tables and chairs throughout the pedestrianized centre, making it look as if whole streets were preparing for a banquet. Anzulović and della Torre sat at one and ordered coffees and the dense rolls that passed for croissants. Anzulović talked. He talked about movies and then he talked about Rejkart, and about the movies they'd seen together when they'd both been on the Zagreb force, bunking off on a Thursday afternoon or sometimes going to a Saturday matinee, telling their wives they were off to see the Dinamo match.

"I once read about some English guy, a mountain climber or something, who faced down a charging rhinoceros by opening a pink umbrella in its face," Anzulović said. "Rejkart was like that. Stupidly brave. And determined to do things his own gentle way. I don't think he'd have given up. He told you he'd taken the academy job, but they said they were still waiting to hear."

Della Torre nodded. Rejkart had sounded sincere about wanting to leave. But the commitment he'd showed to his job was, in retrospect, more convincing.

"Rejkart told me some of what's going on over there," della Torre said.

"Like?"

"Like Horvat is smuggling guns..."

"Of course he's smuggling guns. We don't have any, and he's getting them to us."

"Sure, but hear me out. He's raising funds from ordinary Croats."

"Heirlooms, postage stamps, jewellery, Deutschmarks from under their mattresses," Anzulović said, reeling off the propagandized news reports.

Della Torre held up his hand, demanding his right to finish. Anzulović rarely ever interrupted. He'd normally listen until whoever was speaking ran out of steam and then stay quiet long enough for them to fill in the silence. Sometimes with things they might not have wanted to tell. Della Torre took Anzulović's impatience as a sign of his exhaustion.

"Rejkart thinks...thought that Horvat was taking a very fat cut off the top."

"He's profiteering?" Anzulović said.

"Something like that."

"What else did he tell you?"

"Not much about Horvat, but while I was there he took a phone call from a cop on the Serb side."

"On his office line?" Anzulović's hands crumpled the table-cloth in agitation.

"Yes."

"Stupid boy."

Della Torre shrugged. "Too late now. Anyway, the Serb cop said they'd found a bunch of bodies on their side. Croats. Some policemen, but a few civilians as well. Executed. They were found opposite Vukovar, on a patch being run by one Darko Gorki. Remember him?"

"Gorki. Criminal. Ties to the UDBA. Quasi-official," Anzulović said.

"Yes. He did some bank robbing and gun running around northern Europe. Did jail time in just about every country — as far as I can remember, France in the '70s, Belgium in the early '80s, Sweden in the mid-'80s."

"I know the jail time they hand out. Sentenced to twelve years for bank robbery but they get out after eighteen months." It was an old subject they'd deliberated over the years, the extraordin-ary laxness of northern European justice. "And while they're in, they have their own televisions, drugs on the room service menu, and buggery on tap. For those that like that sort of stuff," Anzulović said. There had long been rumours about Gorki. "So Gorki's what? A regular with a unit? A paramilitary?"

"Actually, he sounds more like an old-fashioned warlord. He's to the Serbs what Horvat is to the Croats. Though as far as I can tell, Horvat's not as violent. Gorki's a soldier, while Horvat's a politician."

Anzulović nodded. "I think you're right. People like him and Horvat will do what they like. They will act with impunity until... well, until we learn to be civilized again." Anzulović drew forward. His eyes were bright with a sort of inner fever. "Gringo, I get a sense our Colonel Kakav is going to have you spinning like God gave you wheels instead of legs. Maybe he just wants to make your life difficult. That's the feeling I get. Unless he can nail you for shooting Strumbić, which is still a possibility, though not a big one. But as you go tearing around the countryside, I want you to do something for me."

"What?" Della Torre was willing but cautious. Who knew what Anzulović would ask, given the state he was in?

"As you go around, I want you to keep a tally. I want you to keep a record of all the murders you encounter, anything that doesn't fit in with an honestly conducted war. If you can investigate straightaway, do so, but discreetly. Anyone prying too much is unlikely to get a lot of support from the people who run our lives. If you can't investigate, note it down and somebody will look into it later."

Della Torre nodded. Not that he wanted the grim duty. But it was a duty someone had to do.

·    ·    ·

It was mid-morning by the time they made their way to the new offices in the high-rise, one of the only ones in central Zagreb, over the lingerie shop on Ilica, at the corner of the city's main square. Anzulović's face sagged with exhaustion and the burdens of life to come, but he seemed a little less distraught. He showed a pass and signed in della Torre at the front desk, which was manned by a couple of conscripts.

The elevator door opened to a scene of general disorder.

Boxes were stacked along a central corridor. People wandered around, some with a purposeful look, a few of the old-timers vague and lost. Most had complaint written on their faces, but when they approached Anzulović, della Torre gave a shake of the head that couldn't be misinterpreted. The boss wasn't to be bothered right now.

So Anzulović remained unmolested as he led della Torre to his new office, where they parted. Anzulović's took up a corner on the same floor, opposite their communal secretary. His desk wouldn't be moved until later in the day, but that didn't matter. The new office had a sofa and Anzulović planned on giving it a test drive.

The first thing della Torre noticed was the rubber plant. Mostly because he nearly tripped over it. His eyes had been on the ceiling, which was about half the height of the old office and of his apartment, so that it felt like it was bearing down on him.

He should have unpacked or written up the notes from his Istria and Vukovar trips, but instead he sat by the window, one which, mercifully, he could open, even if the office was nominally air-conditioned. He'd never really warmed to the old UDBA offices, but they had a certain elegance. This place was functional and drab, characterless. Socialist modern. And he didn't like the fact that once the Yugoslav jets started attacking, this would be a tempting target. A high building in an otherwise low-rise city.

He was wondering what had happened to Rebecca, when Anzulović walked in.

"It's like there's nobody else in military intelligence," Anzulović said.

"What?"

"It's you again."

"Where is it this time?" della Torre asked, resigned to his new role as dogsbody.

"Hotel Esplanade. Tomorrow. A meeting."

"Who with?"

"You, me, and some other people — including our new lord and master, Colonel Kakav. And Croatia's new deputy minister of defence, announced this morning."

"And who might that be?"

Anzulović heaved a big sigh. "Horvat."

"Shit."

"And do you want to know what his portfolio is?"

"No, but you're going to tell me anyway."

"Procurement. And intelligence."

"Double shit. So what the hell does he want with me? Us."

"That we find out tomorrow," Anzulović said. Stopping in the doorway on the way out, he added: "Oh, and just to make your day perfect, I won't make you guess who's joining our happy little ship here in military intelligence. I'll tell you." He paused theatrically, smiling with more than a drop of *schadenfreude*. "Your old friend: Julius Strumbić."

**14**

**T**HEY WALKED THROUGH the morning's rising mugginess to the Hotel Esplanade, near the main rail station, passing on the way the statue of a mounted King Tomislav, Croatia's king when the country was first, briefly, independent. Heroic as he looked in bronze, there was a melancholy to him too. A young man, younger than della Torre, he'd disappeared into the night a thousand years ago.

The Esplanade was the city's only truly grand hotel. It had been built between the wars, and there was a time when passengers on the Orient Express would overnight there on the way from Venice to Istanbul. It was where the gentry from Vienna based themselves when handling their affairs in the empire's former southern provinces. For a while the Communists kept it as their hotel of choice. But ultimately it proved too redolent of Croatia's bourgeois past for the hard-liners, so they built a soulless concrete tower farther west.

Now the Esplanade was tired, drab like much of the city, its spacious, well-proportioned main rooms let down by flaking paint and cheap fabrics in dull earth tones. And Communist-era service. But the new Croat administration favoured it, if only because they could offer its decline as evidence of the brutal lack of culture of the Serb-dominated Yugoslav Communists.

But when he passed through the main doors, the decor wasn't what della Torre noticed. Sitting side by side in a far corner of the lobby, where they could watch all who entered, were Horvat and an old man. The old man was shrunken into himself. He was bald but for a thinning fringe of grey hair, and he wore glasses with solid square frames. Engrossed in conversation, he toyed with a wooden walking stick. Neither man seemed to see Anzulović and della Torre.

"Fuck," said Anzulović, pulling della Torre to the side so they were out of sight.

Della Torre nodded. "Horvat. Who's the old man with him?"

"That, my dear Gringo, is the Dispatcher."

Della Torre felt his legs and chest grow heavy and his tongue thicken. "The Dispatcher?" Tito's henchman, who'd come out of retirement earlier in the year to organize the Bosnian hitmen who'd made a mess of della Torre's elbow — a reprise of his job from the old days. Tito would say what he wanted and the Dispatcher would figure out how to do it. Often it included jailing or killing people. "But I thought he was . . . I thought he'd be . . ."

"Scared to show himself? Because he's Belgrade's man?"

"Yes. What the hell is he doing here? What's he doing with Horvat? Fuck, somebody's got a rope around my neck."

"I suppose we'll find out. But never underestimate the Dispatcher's power of reinvention or his ability to survive. Remember, not only did he make it back from Goli Otok alive, but Tito gave him his job back. Some snakes just won't die."

The old man had been suspected of spying on Tito and was packed off to Yugoslavia's infamous penal island in the 1960s. And then when the Croatian independence movement of the 1970s threatened to destabilize the country, Tito pulled the Dispatcher out of prison to help put down the revolt. Somehow he always survived. Not least because he was good at figuring out which way the wind was going to blow. Maybe that's what he was doing now.

Della Torre nodded. Anzulović looked worried. But they didn't have time to fret about what they'd just seen. Colonel Kakav had tracked them down.

"No time to take in the sights," Kakav said, waving them towards a grouping of sofas and armchairs around a low table by a plate-glass window overlooking the square. "We have people to talk to."

Kakav wore a new double-breasted navy-blue suit. But because he was on the short side and carrying too much weight around the middle, with a neck to match, it looked borrowed. He had on a pewter-coloured tie, which he wore loose. He'd undone the top button of his shirt, an off-white Communist-era number with shiny vertical stripes woven in. Any effort at looking professional was undone by a polyester slobbishness. With an odd combination of smug self-satisfaction and nervous anticipation, he bounced on the balls of his feet as he herded the men to the chairs.

"Wait here while I tell the deputy minister that you've arrived," he said, intending to exert authority but instead sounding wheedling.

Della Torre caught Anzulović's eye. The thought passed between them: how had this man ever managed to rise above traffic warden? Then again, Kakav was utterly convinced of his own competence and abilities. So while smarter people laughed, his bosses kept giving him more responsibility, and then promoted him elsewhere when they discovered their mistake.

They didn't wait long before Horvat strode over with Kakav in tow. The Dispatcher hadn't accompanied them.

Anzulović and della Torre stood up in unison.

"Gentlemen." Horvat gave della Torre half a warm smile and all but ignored Anzulović.

"Congratulations on your appointment, sir," della Torre said. Anzulović kept his peace.

"A duty. But real congratulations are in order to you, Major." Horvat took della Torre's hand and gave it an effusive shake.

"I'm sorry, sir, but you're mistaken. My rank's captain," della Torre said.

"Oh, but—" Kakav started with what he might have supposed to be an expression of munificence, arms opened out like a priest's.

"There's no mistake." Horvat cut him off, smiling that half smile. "One of the first things I did this morning was promote you. Congratulations, Major della Torre. We need good senior officers in our new army. I'm never mistaken about my people."

"Yes, congratulations, Major," Kakav interjected, ignored by the others as if he were just another piece of social-realist sculpture.

Della Torre wasn't sure what to say. The promotion was so unexpected and so irrelevant that all he could do was stammer a half-hearted thanks. Anzulović, whom Horvat still hadn't acknowledged, was a major. Whatever rank della Torre was given, he knew his place relative to Anzulović. And it wasn't that of an equal.

"Besides, we couldn't have a junior officer carrying out a mission of the importance we'll be handing to you," Horvat said, his eyes flickering behind della Torre. "Ah, here he is. Our American friend, Mr. Dawes."

Della Torre looked over his shoulder to see a tall man approaching. He was roughly della Torre's age, maybe a year or two younger. He wore chinos and brown loafers and had on a white button-down shirt and a blue blazer with shiny brass buttons. The man was even taller than della Torre, though he was much more well padded. His shoulders were too narrow for his broad hips, making him slightly pear-shaped and giving his legs the appearance of tree trunks.

Unlike the three men from military intelligence, neither Dawes nor Horvat wore ties.

"Forgive me for being early," Dawes said in American English, coloured by a faint Southern accent. He had a broad smile and white teeth. "One of the disadvantages of staying in the hotel where you're holding meetings is that you haven't got an excuse for being late."

Horvat laughed with Dawes. Della Torre managed to smile politely. Anzulović, whose English was rudimentary, struggled. Kakav wore the rictus grin of ignorance.

"I'm afraid the lieutenant colonel doesn't speak much English. And I don't think Major Anzulović is very proficient either," Horvat said.

"That's okay, because I don't speak much Serbo-Croat," Dawes said.

"Croat," Horvat corrected.

"My apologies—Croat." Dawes smiled indulgently. "All I can say is *da, ne*. And *piva*. I find wherever I go that once I can order myself a beer, everything else becomes infinitely easier and more pleasurable."

He sat down, taking over most of a sofa. The others sat too.

"We will have coffee." Horvat looked over to reception, where a stationed waiter caught his eye and came over. Behind the waiter was a photographer wearing a pair of Japanese SLRs around his neck as if they were Olympic medals. Horvat made a show of surprised annoyance.

"My apologies, gentlemen," he said in English. "Only an hour ago my appointment is made, and press have found me already. What I can say?" He shrugged elaborately. "We will do quick photograph and then they will leave us alone. No?"

Dawes looked bemused and then slightly alarmed when Horvat put his arm over the American's shoulders as the photographer snapped away. A stunned della Torre found his way into one of the pictures. Anzulović, who'd withdrawn into a corner of the room, found it hard to hide his disgust.

"Sit, sit, please," said Horvat, abruptly shooing the photographer away. "Some coffees, yes?" He turned to the waiter and ordered in Croat.

"I would appreciate it if you could have a word with your photographer there," Dawes said. "I would find it most uncomfortable to find my picture in a newspaper. I told my wife I was spending the weekend golfing in Florida."

Della Torre smiled politely as both Dawes and Horvat laughed elaborately at the weak joke.

"Of course not. Of course not," Horvat said, putting his hand on the American's forearm in emphasis. "Now, about coffee..."

"Would you mind asking if they do American-style? I find your espressos disappear too quickly," Dawes said. He'd held his smile throughout, though his eyes suggested he'd been as amused by the photo shoot as Anzulović.

Della Torre had taken the last chair, the one with its back to the room. He offered around his Luckys, which only Dawes refused. It was hard to turn down American cigarettes.

Anzulović and Kakav sat like a pair of lemons in a fruit bowl while Horvat and Dawes talked about the weather. Della Torre watched the American. Dawes had big hands, his index finger constantly tapping out an unknown rhythm on the arm of the sofa. Smoke curled around the rest of them; Dawes didn't seem to mind.

Della Torre didn't contribute anything. He just sat there joining threads, spinning a story full of holes for himself. The Dispatcher knew things, knew about plenty of skeletons from the Communist times. It would make sense for Horvat to want to know him. For his part, the Dispatcher would want the world—no, della Torre—to know that he was under a powerful man's protection. This made sense. The American? He couldn't have looked more government if he'd been an eagle holding a clutch of arrows, right off the cover of della Torre's secret passport. Croatia wanted American friends. Hell, everybody wanted American friends. And here was an American friend. Della Torre struggled to figure out his own part in it. Other than having grown up in Ohio, he couldn't think of what might tie him to Mr. Dawes. Showing Americans that there were people in Zagreb who spoke their language just like they did? It seemed too far-fetched.

He was lost in thought when he suddenly noticed the silence. What conversation there was had stopped and the others were looking in his direction. Not at him, but rather somewhere over his left shoulder. He followed their gaze, turning in his chair to see a striking redhead.

Rebecca.

She stood there smiling like a diplomat at a reception. She wore a well-tailored business suit with a linen blouse cut low enough to subtly show off her breasts. Her hair was pinned back in a bun, though a few strands had come loose to frame her face. She wore a vermilion lipstick that gave her lips a seductive glow. Somehow it heightened the girlishness of the freckles across the bridge of her nose, which had been brought out by the Istrian sun.

"Rebecca," he said, jumping to his feet, embarrassed and taken by surprise. "It's great to see you. I thought you'd disappeared completely. I'm afraid I'm in a meeting right now. Maybe I can see you later?"

She touched her cheek to his, blowing a kiss just past his ear.

"Marko," she said, and then walked past him to Dawes.

"Would you make the introductions, John?" she said. "I hope I'm not too late. My run was longer than I'd expected. I got a little lost."

"Not at all," Dawes said. "We were just discussing how the heat's not too bad so long as it doesn't get humid. Anyway, you know the major already. This is Deputy Defence Minister Horvat. And this is Lieutenant Colonel Kakav, and Major Anz..."

"Anzulović," Anzulović said, bowing slightly to disguise the faintly amused look in his eyes.

"And this is my colleague Rebecca Vees. Now that she's here, maybe we can start," Dawes said.

Della Torre made an effort to keep his mouth shut so that he wouldn't gawp like the fish he was. It was the third time she'd caught him completely off guard. Rebecca made herself comfortable on the sofa, next to Dawes. The waiter brought their coffees and a bottle of clear spirit and five shot glasses. Rebecca ordered a glass of mineral water.

"Our American friends wish for some help," Horvat started, "and we would like to help them." He turned to Dawes. "What you ask for, we will try to do. And if we cannot do it, we will try harder."

"That is very kind of you, Minister," Dawes said, smiling. "First, I'd just like to make clear that we are here informally. We don't represent anyone. But to the extent that we have the ears of Washington, we will let people know how helpful you've been. And make every effort to ensure that they do something for you in return."

Della Torre drew on his cigarette until the ash threatened to fall onto his lap, and then crushed the butt in a cut-glass ashtray. His attention was focused on Rebecca, his mind forcing together bits of two different puzzles. Nothing quite fitted, though he knew that somewhere among all the scattered pieces was the picture of a man drowning in his own ignorance. A man who looked an awful lot like della Torre.

He looked over to Kakav and felt a ripple of sympathy for the apparatchik, sitting there in his blue suit with his pasted-on grin, fathoms below the surface of any understanding.

"As you can appreciate, we won't go into detail here," Dawes continued. "But if the major is happy to take on the assignment, my colleague here will brief him separately."

All eyes turned to della Torre. For a moment he couldn't

understand why. Anzulović was the major. But then he remembered his promotion.

"I have complete confidence Major della Torre will do everything he can," Horvat said, breaking the silence.

"Yes. Yes, of course," della Torre said.

"Then it is agreed." Horvat filled the shot glasses from the clear bottle. They were one glass short, and Horvat made sure Anzulović was the one left out. "So we drink to this friendship. The major and the beautiful miss."

He laughed, then raised his glass and threw back the slivovitz. Della Torre saw that the Americans barely touched their lips to the liquid, leaving full glasses on the table. If Horvat noticed, he didn't betray it.

As they rose to leave, Rebecca stepped towards della Torre and rested her fingers on his forearm, holding him back.

"Let's go upstairs," she said. "I have a nice suite. We can talk."

Della Torre nodded. He was starting to realize that he was little more than an automaton, there to be programmed and then set into motion. It was like being back in the commandos. Of course it was. He was in the army now.

As they passed the front desk on the way to the elevators, della Torre caught sight of the Dispatcher sitting in a large winged chair, contemplating him with a beatific smile.

**D**ELLA TORRE AND Rebecca took the elevator up to her suite in silence. Its sitting room was tired, like much of the hotel, but nevertheless it was spacious and had extravagant views of Zagreb Cathedral's double spire and, far beyond it, the low, forested ridge of mountains to the north. Della Torre took the armchair by the window.

"Can I get you a drink?" she asked.

"No. Care to explain yourself?"

"You're a smart guy. What explanation do you need?"

"They sent me to my father's so that you could inspect me. I suppose I passed."

"You passed."

"Couldn't you do that in Zagreb? Why did you need to involve Dad?"

"Why do you think?"

"Because you wanted as much background as possible before meeting me."

"We like to be thorough."

"Who's 'we'?" He knew. Or close enough. Whether it was the CIA or a branch of U.S. military intelligence hardly mattered. It made no difference to him. Croatia was desperate to do what it could for the Americans, and hopeful of favours in return.

She moved off her perch on the arm of her chair and helped herself to a bottle of clear soda from the mini-bar, examining the label before opening it. "Inka...What is it?"

"Tonic water," he said.

"Oh. Maybe not."

"I'll have some, then."

"Thought you weren't thirsty," she said.

"Maybe it'll get the bitter taste out of my mouth."

She gave him a sideways glance and opened the bottle. She poured him the drink, helping herself to a diet Coke instead.

The Inka was tepid.

"What we need is to talk to someone called Petar Djilas. He worked for the UDBA but is retired now."

Della Torre paused. Djilas. The Montenegrin.

"You want his phone number?" della Torre asked, taking out a cigarette.

"I wish you wouldn't smoke in here," she said.

He lit it anyway.

"We've got his phone number," she continued, not pressing the issue. "And his address too. We'd like to see him and have a little chat."

"Call him up and make an appointment."

"We'd love to do that, but we have it on good authority he wouldn't be interested in talking to strangers."

"And what do you want to talk to him about?"

"Some of the people he killed. In the States."

"I don't think he actually killed anyone in the U.S. He ran some teams that did, but he never pulled the trigger."

"We're interested anyway."

"Well, in that case, I can tell you for nothing that Djilas only ever did what he was ordered to do. I've investigated him a few times. Now, the American government may not like what he was doing—I don't like what he was doing—but he was doing what the Yugoslav presidency told him to do. Take it up with Belgrade, not Mr. Djilas, who executed his job exactly within the limits of Yugoslav law."

She watched him with a patient smile. Her lips were slightly parted and her eyes told him she was something other than just amused by him.

"Marko, all we want to do is ask him a few questions about what went on."

"There's a good chance I've got my notes on those operations. You probably know that my job was to investigate old UDBA assassinations. I kept my notes. Against the rules, but I've got them. Why don't I give you what I've got, and then you don't need to bother the Montenegrin."

"The Montenegrin?"

"It's what we called—call—Mr. Djilas," he said. "Montenegro is where he's from. The black mountains, down south. Where he lives now. In a place that's like a fortress."

"We'd like to talk to him because what we want won't be on file."

File. It made della Torre think of the tangle he'd tied himself into. It had started with the Pilgrim file, something about nuclear centrifuges that had involved the Montenegrin. The file that had somehow led the Dispatcher to send the Bosnian killers after him. And now for some reason the Montenegrin had entangled della Torre with these Americans. Did this have something to do with Pilgrim too?

There wouldn't be any budging her. Somebody further up the chain had presented her and her friend Dawes with a job, and she was doing it. He understood that.

"He won't fly up to Zagreb to see you. I can guarantee that. Even if you ask pretty please."

"We're not going to be asking. You are. He knows you and trusts you. That's why we need you."

"You seem well informed."

"We are. And we know he's not going to come to us. So we're going to go to him."

"To Montenegro?"

"Unless he'll meet us in Dubrovnik." Croatia's ancient walled city — as given over to tourists as Venice, and even more beautiful — was a short drive from the Montenegrin's haven.

"I doubt it. He won't cross the border. He's too sensible for that. In fact, he won't go to Serbia either. Old UDBA wetworks agents don't tend to have long life expectancies. He's got himself a very nice, very safe arrangement where he is," della Torre said.

"Which is why you're going to help us plan it all out. So that we have a nice, comfortable chat with Mr. Djilas." That smile again.

"What if I said no?"

"Well, I think your minister was pretty keen that you do what you can. But if that's not convincing enough, the U.S. government isn't very happy about its citizens working for foreign governments. Especially foreign intelligence services. And especially when they're Communist."

Della Torre nodded. His face betrayed no emotion. Rebecca gave him a sympathetic smile. He looked out at the view of the city.

"But really, that isn't meant to be a threat," she continued. "I heard you have enough trouble here without having to worry about what the U.S. government thinks. Something about shooting a police officer."

There had been a time when della Torre fantasized about running away to America; he'd wondered whether he might not quietly disappear once the war started in earnest. Not back to Ohio. But maybe California. The UDBA would no longer take an interest in him. And the Zagreb police, well, their reach barely made it to the city's streets.

"What do you want from me?"

She smiled a broad, slow, lazy smile that made it clear she'd always known she'd win.

"I need a bit of organization. First I need a secluded location near here with a three-hundred-yard clearing. For tomorrow or the day after. Then I need a house near Dubrovnik that's very, very private..."

"At this time of year? Even with the political situation like it is, Dubrovnik has more than a few tourists around. I mean, it's one of the biggest attractions in the Mediterranean."

"You'll have to be clever, then. But I'll make it easy for you. It can be half an hour, maybe forty minutes away from the city."

"How big?"

"It doesn't have to be huge. But it's got to be able to sleep... let's see, make it five or six people."

"Who else is involved?"

"That comes later."

"Anything else?" he asked.

"I need as much background on Mr. Djilas as you can get. A nice briefing note."

"I thought you already had that."

"I do. But I want one from you."

"When do we go?"

"We? You're just helping us to fix things so that they won't go wrong." She emptied the can into a glass and threw it into a bedside bin. "How long do you think it'll take to drive down the coast?"

"Drive? What's wrong with flying?"

"People watch airports. Driving draws less attention."

"Well, you see, that's a little problem. The Krajina Serbs have blocked the main road. The only other way is to take a ferry or to drive the coast road. But that'll be busy."

"I'm sure you'll think of something."

He finished his Inka. The warm bubbles scoured his mouth.

He got up to go.

"Should I get in touch with you here?" he asked.

"I'm registered under my name."

I'm sure you are, he thought.

"You have my keys," he said.

"I do, don't I." She made no move to return them.

"My father will be disappointed."

Her eyebrows rose in amused puzzlement.

"That I've got your keys?" she asked.

"You know what I mean."

"I'm sorry. Piero's a very nice man, but he shouldn't feel too hurt. Not as hurt as innocent people sometimes get."

He didn't bother to shut the door behind him.

. . .

On the way back to the office, he smoked a couple of Luckys. Lucky Strike. The irony that it was his favourite brand never escaped him. He couldn't remember the last time he'd been lucky. Overhead, the filigree of tram wires held the city in a web. He was oblivious to the old man walking on the other pavement, barking orders like a drill sergeant and then pausing to whimper like a dog. Or the young nun in a wimple and green mirrored sunglasses, the top buttons of her grey shirt undone and a cigarette hanging off her bottom lip.

He'd been stitched up. He'd been sent from one end of the country to the other so that the Americans and Horvat could inspect him. A piece of military chattel. The Croat government would do everything it could to get the Americans involved in its affairs, though he was sure Horvat was playing another angle. He just didn't know what.

Whatever it was, Horvat was a dangerous man. Even more dangerous was the fact that he had dealings with somebody who only a few months before had tried to have della Torre killed. What the hell did the Dispatcher have to do with this?

And what did the Americans want with the Montenegrin? To talk to him? The thought made della Torre laugh out loud, so that the woman walking beside him gave a little skip of surprise and then sidled away.

Della Torre wouldn't have noticed the black Toyota Hilux with tinted windows parked opposite the military intelligence building, had it not been involved in a standoff with a Zagreb tram. The Hilux was pulled halfway up onto the pavement, making itself an obstacle to pedestrian traffic, though this wasn't particularly unusual. Yugoslav drivers were notoriously inconsiderate, especially ones who had the sort of money to afford expensive Japanese trucks. But it also blocked the road enough to keep the tram from passing. The tram driver kept ringing his bell, but the Hilux wouldn't move. Only when a traffic cop took an interest did it finally pull away.

Della Torre showed his old UDBA ID to the uniformed soldiers at the entrance to his new office building.

"I'm sorry, sir, but who are you visiting?"

"I'm not visiting anyone. I'm going to my office."

The soldier looked blank.

"We've moved upstairs," della Torre said.

"I've been told that only people with military ID are allowed through. They're on our sheet."

"I haven't got mine yet. It's coming," della Torre said, folding his arms over the top of the high reception desk.

"I'm afraid, sir, you'll need someone to get you, then. We've been told only military ID."

"Look, my whole office, my whole department, has moved upstairs. As far as I know, none of us has military ID," della Torre said.

The soldier continued to stare blankly.

"Have other people come through with UDBA IDs?" he asked, exasperated.

"Yes, sir."

"Did you let them in?"

"Yes, sir."

"So let me in too."

"But they had someone come down to collect them."

"All of them? How did the first one get in?"

"Well, we haven't been on duty all day..."

"If I get one of my UDBA colleagues to come down to vouch for me, will you let me in?"

"Yes, sir, if your name's on the list."

"You mean you have a list?"

"Yes, sir."

"Why don't you check my name against the list?"

"Sorry, sir. We need to see military ID. Lieutenant Colonel Kakav—" the soldier started to say but then caught himself as della Torre dropped his head onto the high reception desk. "Are you all right, sir? It's just that your forehead might smudge the forms."

Della Torre was rescued from the fit of impotent pique he usually reserved for Yugoslav bank tellers, clerks at the gas board, and post office officials, by a colleague who was just leaving the building. He vouched for della Torre on condition that della Torre came down to collect him later.

He went in search of Anzulović to fill him in about his meeting with Rebecca and to talk over the morning more generally, but Anzulović was out. The secretary didn't know where. He figured he might as well start writing up the report on the Montenegrin that Rebecca had asked for. But when he got to his office, a man was sitting in his chair, smoking a cigarette and gazing out the window.

"Julius," della Torre said. "As if my day wasn't awful enough already."

16

"**YOU KNOW, GRINGO,** I once felt bad for myself that I didn't have any shoes that fit. My feet were sore. But then I saw a man with one leg. And you know what I thought to myself?" Strumbić asked. "I said, there's a man who's only got half my troubles." He laughed uproariously at his own joke. "I wanted to congratulate you, Major."

"News travels."

"Take a seat, colleague."

"Thanks," della Torre said, not sounding the least grateful, as he found a chair under a stack of files.

Strumbić sat there, grinning. He was half a head shorter than della Torre and about five years older, powerfully built, though gone to fat. He'd taken some colour over the summer during his enforced absence from work, though della Torre knew it was a farmer's tan. Even so, there was an underlying unhealthiness to Strumbić. His close-cropped hair had mostly gone grey. Jaundiced and bloodshot eyes. His teeth a mix of gunmetal and yellow. It made the grin that much more gruesome.

"I've been transferred to military intelligence."

"I'd heard."

"Thought you might be a bit more pleased about it, Gringo."

"When are you going to sign the affidavit, Julius?"

"Affidavit?"

"The one that says I didn't shoot you."

"But you did."

"Julius..."

"All right, all right. I'll think about it."

Strumbić had that look about him, like a waiter hovering for a tip.

"How much is it going to cost me?" della Torre asked.

"Life isn't just about money, Gringo."

"Julius, you've..." Della Torre didn't know what to say. Strumbić was the most corrupt cop in Zagreb. He always had been. He was without a doubt the richest person della Torre had ever met, though he hid his money well. But not so well as to stop della Torre from stealing a considerable amount of it. Had Strumbić forgiven him for stealing his money, his leather jacket, his cigarettes? For shooting him and locking him in his own wine cellar? They had a complicated relationship.

"Listen, Gringo, I'll let bygones be bygones. I'll sign the form, though we'll have to think about how you might pay back what you owe me. But really, all I want is a little friendliness, a little understanding, now that we're going to be working together."

"Friendliness and understanding?"

"I understand you've been talking to some Americans. I'd like to be friends with them too. That's all."

Della Torre bent back to look at the ceiling and then out the window. He didn't know how Strumbić had come by the information. Possibly Kakav. It didn't matter. Anything worth knowing, he'd find out about eventually.

"Julius, they don't want to know you. Take it from me."

"Course they don't. But that's because they aren't yet aware of how helpful I can be. What a good friend I can be. That's where you come in."

"You're not the sort of friend they need or want. You're the sort of friend exactly nobody needs."

"And this from a man whose life I saved."

"Only after doing everything you possibly could to get me killed."

"Let's leave old arguments to lie, eh? These are new times. Era of the Americans. Gringo, wherever Americans go, they're the people to know. I'm sure you'll find a way."

Strumbić was right. Americans meant money. Endless amounts of it. And Strumbić could smell money no matter how much shit it was buried in. All that mattered was finding directions to the pipeline and figuring out how to tap it.

Outside, the heat shimmered off Zagreb's red-tiled roofs like ripples of lava. There was another city famous for its ancient ochre, orange, and red roof tiles. Dubrovnik.

"Julius, tell me. That weekend place of yours near Samobor. How private is it?"

"How private? If you want somewhere to hide a herd of elephants, it's pretty useful," Strumbić said.

"Have you got a three-hundred-metre clearing there?"

"Three hundred? The meadow at the top of the hill's probably that. Maybe a bit less. I never measured. Why?"

"What about your place near Dubrovnik?"

"Šipan?"

"Yes. How quiet is that?"

"What do you mean, 'how quiet'? You can hear the fucking birds and the waves. Sometimes an airplane passes overhead."

"That's not what I meant. Are there many tourists?"

"You get the occasional yacht in Šipan harbour and sometimes you get a few Germans on a day trip from Dubrovnik, but the island's too far for most tourists and there aren't many attractions."

"How far is it by ferry?"

"About an hour."

"Oh," della Torre said. A near miss, but too far.

"But the right way to do it is to take a boat across the strait to a village on the mainland and then drive down."

"How long's that take?"

"My motorboat and car and I'm driving? Then it's ten minutes for the crossing and a quarter of an hour down to Dubrovnik. You can usually get a fisherman to run you over from either side of the channel, takes about fifteen minutes that way. I hope your sudden interest in my affairs means that you've had a change of heart about me."

"How big's the place? How many does it sleep?"

"Are we negotiating a summer rental? It's not a palace, if that's what you're looking for. It's one of those old sea captain's houses, but done up. Four bedrooms in the main house and another couple in the courtyard."

Della Torre looked in wonder at the cop. It wasn't just luck that Strumbić had something handy in the countryside near Zagreb and something off the Dubrovnik coast. He had properties scattered across the whole of Croatia and as far afield as London. And not a penny of them mortgaged. It wasn't ordinary corruption that had made Strumbić rich. Otherwise half the police force would be doing as well. It was the sort of entrepreneurial corruption that would have made Strumbić a rich man anywhere, in any age.

"Can I have use of your weekend cottage?" della Torre said. "Tomorrow or the day after? And maybe the Šipan house? I'm sure our American friends will come to some financial arrangement."

"Always money with you, Gringo. Tell you what. Why don't I come out to Samobor with you. I'll have a chat with our American friends. See what they think. Maybe I'll go down to Šipan with you. You know, show you how things work. In case there are problems with the boiler. And maybe along the way, I'll do a bit of affidavit signing."

Della Torre almost admitted he wasn't going anywhere. That he was just making arrangements on behalf of the Americans. A dogsbody. But he didn't.

"I'll see what I can do."

Strumbić got out of the chair by the window and headed for the door.

"Gringo, I think I'm going to enjoy working with you."

**A**NZULOVIĆ DIDN'T COME back until late in the day. Anyone else gone that long without explanation, and della Torre would have figured him for an alcoholic. Not Anzulović.

"Good movie?" della Torre asked when his former boss popped his head into the room.

"Escapist crap. I find Hollywood most depressing when they give me what I think I want."

"I won't ask what you saw. Won't mean anything to me."

"Never mind, it's only playing for another week. As if the movie was't bad enough, I had to tear a strip off those cretins downstairs to get in."

"You managed?"

"Course I managed. Threatened to shoot them. Try it."

Anzulović sat down on a plastic chair next to della Torre.

"I'm sorry," della Torre said.

"About what?"

"About getting promoted. I don't know why. I don't know what I've done and I don't want it. I don't want to have the same rank as you. Frankly, I prefer the buck to stop with you."

"Well, you've got it. And don't be sorry. I have a feeling I'll need friends with a bit of clout around here as long as Horvat's around."

"Not to mention Kakav," said della Torre.

"Forget about Kakav. He may be a reptile, but he also has a reptile's brain. As long as you grab him just behind the head, he can't bite. Smack his forehead down hard on the edge of a table and he's quiet for a while," Anzulović said. "No, Horvat's the dangerous one. Funny thing is, more to you than me. He has high hopes for you, whereas I know he doesn't like me much. Probably because I was a friend of Rejkart's. But maybe because of the Dispatcher."

The name chilled della Torre's blood.

"I thought the old man had crawled back into his hole."

"So did I. But when all the rest of life is wiped out, he and the cockroaches will be left."

"I don't understand it. Is he friends with Horvat? Does he still want me dead?" Della Torre rested his chin on his hand and contemplated the indestructible rubber plant in the corner of the room.

"I don't know, Gringo. Though I'll tell you what I think. I think the Dispatcher was doing tricks for Belgrade. And now he's doing them for the Croat government. He doesn't know any more than we do how this whole thing is going to turn out, and he wants to make sure he's covered on both sides."

"But why make the public appearance?"

"It wasn't too public. Just enough to show us that he has friends in high places, in case we get ideas. He'll have been talking to Horvat anyway. He may be ancient and he may be poison, but he knows a lot. Politicians value his survival skills. Maybe Horvat talked to him about getting to know the Americans. The old man knew plenty about Tito's diplomatic shenanigans, playing one side against the other. Half the time Tito didn't trust his own foreign ministry people, thought they were all spies for somebody else, had his translator run the show for him. I'm sure the Dispatcher helped out as well."

"You seem to know a lot about it."

"Of course I know a lot about it. When you disappeared to London, I was the one who dug around. And I was the one who went to ask the old man why he wanted my friend dead."

"I didn't know that," della Torre said, surprised and grateful for Anzulović and feeling even more miserable that he was losing some of the older man's protection now that he was no longer his junior.

"Well, you do now. A thank-you and a Lucky Strike might be in order."

"Thank you," della Torre said, handing his pack over to Anzulović. "Now what?"

"I suggest you do what the Americans want. Horvat might be running things now and the Dispatcher might be pulling the strings, but the Dispatcher's old. And Horvat ... well, Horvats come and go. Americans are forever." Anzulović gave della Torre a wry smile. "Fetching, that redhead of yours. How is it that you keep landing them? Irena, Grace Kelly in London, and now Rita Hayworth."

"Who?"

"Never mind. What did she want?"

"Djilas. The Montenegrin."

Anzulović sat up. "And what does she want with the Montenegrin?"

"She says she wants to talk to him. About UDBA wetworks operations in the States."

"Just to talk?"

"That's what she says."

"But you don't think so."

"No. I mean, not that he'd take a phone call from her. He won't take one from me. He's sensitive that way."

"So she wants to see him. For a chat."

"That's what she says. To clarify some things not in their files."

"He won't come here." Anzulović blew smoke through his thatch of nostril hair. He was clean-shaven otherwise, though he could have woven himself a fine moustache and sideburns from the foliage growing out of his nose and ears.

"That's what I told her. Wants to meet him in Dubrovnik."

"Will he go there?"

"I doubt it."

"So what do you think our new-found American friends want with him?"

"I don't know," della Torre said with a shrug. "Maybe it is just to talk to him. But in Washington."

"Or Aviano," Anzulović said, referring to the American air force base north of Venice.

"Or there."

Both men had smoked their cigarettes down to the filter and dropped them into a cracked tea saucer.

"Whatever they want, I'm going with them," della Torre said. "Djilas may have done unmentionable things, but as far as I know he did them within the letter of Yugoslav law. If the Americans have a beef with anyone, it's with the presidency."

"The hangman's friend."

"No, but I'm not going to let him stand as some sort of sacrificial lamb to win the hand of American friendship."

"Forever the lawyer," Anzulović said. "Anything else new?"

"Strumbić wants to be involved."

Anzulović let out a laugh from deep in the diaphragm, an honest, infectious laugh that della Torre hadn't heard in what seemed like a lifetime.

"The Americans are welcome to him. Let him loose on them. He'll give them a real taste of the Balkans."

"You're not serious."

"Why not? Strumbić is the most honest crook any of us will ever meet. And he's a smart guy. It would do you good to have somebody that canny by your side. And we now know that in a pinch he's not going to shoot you in the back. Had plenty of opportunity to do that already. Might not step in to save you, but at least he's not going to be standing on your head when you're under water."

"That's encouraging. I'm going to be shot and drowned. Only not by Strumbić."

"You've already been shot."

"Thanks. That cheers me up."

"I'm serious, Gringo. He may not be your closest friend, but he can be a useful ally. So if you can, let him play along. And who knows, you might be able to get him to sign the affidavit."

**18**

HE CALLED REBECCA after Anzulović left. She seemed pleased by the description of the field at Strumbić's weekend house and even more so about his villa on Šipan; both fit the requirements she'd laid out. It didn't take long to convince her that he wouldn't be able to arrange a meeting with the Montenegrin in Dubrovnik. He'd have one shot, he said. And the only way it would be effective would be to meet the Montenegrin on his terms, on his choice of ground. And della Torre, because he knew the man well, would have to go along.

She agreed to it as if she'd known all along and had merely been looking for him to come to the same conclusion. For him to propose it. Maybe as an act of goodwill. But it took a lot of persuading for her to take Strumbić as part of the deal. The quiet place in the country and the ideal location near Dubrovnik finally convinced her.

On Friday morning, della Torre and Strumbić arrived at the Esplanade early. They waited on the hotel's raised terrace and had a cigarette and a coffee. Della Torre thought he saw a black Hilux parked at the end of the square, but he wasn't sure. Strumbić was distracted by something else.

"Get a load of that," he said to della Torre. And then, louder:

"Hey, Red, where's the fire? Between your legs?"

The woman had passed below the corner of the terrace and was out of sight by the time della Torre turned to look. But he already had a bad feeling.

Rebecca strode up to their table, dressed in tight running gear, her hair tied back under a damp baseball cap. It was still early, but the morning was hot and she glistened.

"Hello, Marko."

"Rebecca Vees, this is Julius Strumbić."

Strumbić beamed, and said, "Please to meet you," in the clearest English he could conjure. He spoke the language reasonably well, though he sounded like a cross between Dracula and a Viennese psychiatrist.

In a lower tone he asked della Torre in Croat, "Does she speak the language?"

Rebecca replied, in Russian-accented Croat, "*Da*. I know what *legs* and *fire* mean." And then in English: "I can work out the rest."

Strumbić froze for half a beat and then burst out laughing.

"Is good. We will be friends in English," he said, putting his hand flat against the small of her back.

Rebecca gave Strumbić a warm smile in return. She's generous with those smiles, della Torre thought.

"If you fellows don't mind, I need to shower. I'll be quick. Promise. Why don't you come up, and then once I'm sorted you can help take some of my bags down."

They went up with her and sat in the suite's sitting room while she showered and dressed. Strumbić grinned knowingly at della Torre but didn't say anything. Rebecca came out wearing shorts, walking boots, and a vest under a thin, flowery shirt.

"Maybe you can each carry one of these bags, and I'll take this one."

They each took one of the identical suitcases, metal covered in hard plastic with ribbed sides. They weren't particularly heavy.

"I have car near," said Strumbić. "BMW."

He'd gotten back the car that della Torre had once stolen, though della Torre wasn't quite sure how. Strumbić had never mentioned it, so maybe it hadn't cost him.

"That's nice of you, but how about if I drive? I've picked up a new car and I'd like to give it a test run," Rebecca said.

As it happened, her car was parked just down from the BMW. It was a two-door Mercedes coupe as big as a saloon.

"I thought this might be a bit more comfortable than the Volkswagen for long drives."

"Is good idea. Volkswagen is okay, but this is Mercedes," said Strumbić approvingly. "Very, very nice Mercedes."

Della Torre considered the motor with mixed emotions. The last time he'd been in such a high-spec vehicle, he was being kidnapped by three Bosnians who'd been paid to kill him.

They loaded the suitcases in the boot. Strumbić sat in the back. Before della Torre got into the car, curiosity made him look around for the Hilux. He thought he saw it on the opposite corner, but again he couldn't be sure.

Rebecca started the car, but just before pulling away she turned to Strumbić and said, "Honey, I suggest you buckle up. Seat belt."

"Is no problem. In Yugoslavia seat belt is for child and woman."

"Well, this woman isn't taking you anywhere unless you buckle up." She fluttered her eyelashes at him, but there was no give in her voice.

Strumbić grumbled but gave way. Money before scruples about his manliness. Della Torre was a rare Yugoslav. He had no problem wearing a belt, not least because he remembered all too well how one had saved his life only a few months earlier.

Rebecca drove the car even more aggressively than she had the Golf. She said she was testing the machine's responses, accelerating hard so that the eight-cylinder, 5.6-litre engine bellowed, and then braking even faster, until della Torre thought each manoeuvre would end in an accident.

"If we get pulled over, you might have to talk to the nice policeman for me," she said, not taking her eyes off the road.

Once they were off the motorway, Strumbić guided her through Samobor's tight streets. It was a pretty town at the foot of the steep hills that rose up at the Croat and Slovene border. They went through to the other side and up a narrow road that wound its way along a hillside ridge, deep into the countryside. Rebecca took the corners fast.

"I'd take it a bit easy," della Torre said. "I was in a wreck not far from here in a car a lot like this one."

"Were you driving?" Rebecca asked.

"No. I was a passenger," della Torre said. Somewhere deep in his memory he could almost smell the Bosnian peasants he'd been squeezed between in the back of that Merc as they drove him to his grave.

"Well, whoever was driving, I'm better," she said, decelerating into a bend and then accelerating hard through it.

"I see why you wear seat belt," Strumbić said, cackling as the wheels threw off gravel that edged the rutted road, flinging it into a deep ravine with a stream at the bottom. "You slow down now. Is little road in hundred metres."

She swung the car onto the rough track as if she'd driven the route every day of her life. They bumped over protruding roots and potholes until the track twisted right, stopping on a levelled area cut into the edge of a steep meadow.

"Nice place you got here," Rebecca said.

She was looking over the clearing cut from the otherwise heavily wooded hill. There was a little two-storey house halfway up the slope, where the land flattened like a step before rising again. The house had a steep-pitched red-tiled roof and looked over a deep, pretty green valley and higher hills beyond. A village straggled along the valley floor.

They could hear distant cockerel calls and barking dogs.

The meadow, a couple of hundred metres square, was bounded by woodland. Rows of vines ran below the house and some above it, and to one side an orchard had been planted on the hill. A giant cherry tree shaded the house, and under it stood a wooden table and a pair of rough benches made from halved logs. The last time della Torre saw the place had been at night. After he'd locked Strumbić in the wine cellar, having just shot him in the shin.

"Marko told me that there was a three-hundred-metre clearing. This can't be it."

"Up there, is two hundred fifty metres maybe. Come, is this way," Strumbić said, pointing up the hill.

He led Rebecca and della Torre to the top of the meadow at the crest of the hill, where the land once again levelled off. There was indeed a long and straight, if narrow, clearing, cut deep into the forest, much deeper than the main part of the meadow.

The grass had been mown to a hard stubble. Where the forest would have started were low stumps, cut not long ago. The trees had been cleared and piled to the side, chopped into neat lengths.

"I making little road here up to main road," Strumbić explained, pointing at the long, straight stretch. "Not now but maybe next year. Cutting trees and then I put asphalt. Make garage up here too. Maybe swimming pool."

"Looks perfect," Rebecca said. "Is there anybody else up here? Anybody who'd notice a bit of noise?"

"What kind of noise? Sexy noise nobody care..."

Rebecca cocked her right eyebrow, neutralizing Strumbić's leering grin with an indulgent smile. Della Torre chose to ignore the comment. Anyone who spent time with Strumbić became inured to his innuendoes.

They walked back to the car, where they unpacked the

metal cases, a wicker basket, and a couple of picnic blankets. She was wearing a wide-brimmed sunhat and big square sunglasses. It was midmorning and already a heat haze was rising off the ground.

They carried the cases to the near end of the field, where she unrolled the blankets and laid them on the ground.

"Bit early for a picnic, isn't it?" della Torre asked.

"Not for the sort I've got planned," she said.

She pulled a litre bottle of water from the basket and took a long drink, then passed it to the men.

Strumbić declined. "Water is like poison for me," he said.

Then she pulled out a couple of spray cans and marched off, marking one metre after another with deliberate strides along the full length of the clearing.

Strumbić whistled.

"Gringo, I've got to hand it to you with the women. A wife like yours would keep most men happy. But then you get yourself that bird in London—most men would give their left arm and right nut for one quick spin. And now this one. Never had a thing for redheads before, but she's got me converted."

Della Torre shook his head. "You've got it wrong."

"The hell I do. I don't know much about the finer points of international law, but men and women—that I do know something about," Strumbić said.

Rebecca had stopped at a tree in the far distance, on which she spray-painted at head height a white circle and within it a red cross.

"What do you think she's up to?" Strumbić asked.

"Tagging."

"What?"

"That's what they call it when kids graffiti their nicknames or initials."

"Smurfs?" For some strange reason, people had been spray-painting the word around Zagreb.

"I'm not sure that counts. That's just a lack of imagination and not enough decent television," della Torre said, watching Rebecca making her way back towards them.

Still silent, she took one of the suitcases, turned the combination code on the lock, and popped it open. From inside the padded compartment she withdrew a long metal tube. With the remaining pieces, including an ingenious folding stock and an attached bi-pod stand, she assembled a rifle. She attached a silencer to the barrel and finished off with a high-powered scope. Both men stared at her, incredulous.

She stood up, raised the rifle to her shoulder, and pointed it at the target. "Very nice scope," she said. "There's a night vision one too." She handed the rifle to Strumbić, who took it admiringly.

"I have a few other toys," she said, opening the biggest case flat like a butterfly. On one side it held a Heckler & Koch submachine gun with a light detachable stock and four magazines in its cushioned mould; on the other were two Beretta handguns, with a row of magazines and several boxes of nine-millimetre ammunition.

Strumbić whistled, pointing to the third case. "And there you have M75?"

"A what?" Rebecca said.

"It's one of our anti-aircraft guns," della Torre said. "A cannon."

"Oh," she laughed. "I suppose you can't be too prepared. No, it's a comms set. Radios. I guess you're pretty used to the Berettas. They're standard here, aren't they? Have you tried the Heckler & Koch?" Strumbić shook his head, but della Torre had been trained on a version of the machine pistol in the army. "Well, we'll have to have a go."

She fixed the stock onto the submachine gun, loaded it with a long, curving magazine, and then showed them how it was operated. There was something disconcerting about having a deadly weapon explained by a pretty young woman dressed in summer hiking gear, a big straw hat, and beach sunglasses. Although both men paid close attention, they were uneasy.

She flipped off the safety, moved the setting to semi-automatic, and fired off a few rounds. She then flipped it to automatic and let off a burst.

Strumbić gave it a go after her. He grinned with pleasure.

"Is loud," he said.

"Yes. Normally I wear ear protectors or plugs, but today I wanted to spend some time calibrating that," she said, pointing to the rifle.

She spread a rug on the ground. The men watched, fascinated, as she fixed a tripod on the rifle and then the big scope and lay prone.

"You've done this before," della Torre said. "I'm assuming this isn't something you learned at college."

"You know, Marko, you are a very perceptive man," she said, mocking him gently. "Now, I don't mind you boys watching. In fact I rather like boys watching. But you mustn't talk. Not while I'm getting it just right."

Rebecca took steady shot after steady shot, making small adjustments to the sight and the gun after each. At first della Torre and Strumbić focused on her, how her upper body wrapped itself around the rifle, how her hamstrings and buttocks flexed and became taut with each round and then relaxed until the next one. Her legs were smooth, unblemished, with the lightest bit of colour, stretched open in an inverted V to brace herself.

Della Torre noticed that Strumbić was crouching a metre behind Rebecca, as if he were sighting along her rifle to the target, though he suspected the cop was looking no farther than her ass. He could hardly blame Strumbić. Della Torre would also have liked to run his hands up those legs from where the short socks ended just above the tops of her boots, up her calves and the back of her knees, along the toned hamstrings to the cuffs of the shorts, and beyond. If her finger hadn't been on the trigger of a sniper's rifle.

After a while, della Torre turned his attention to the weapon. He was surprised at how well the silencer worked. There was a metallic clunk, more like a heavy steel spring being released, followed by the clink of the spent shell casing hitting other casings.

Eventually she sat up. Strumbić had disappeared down the hill to get out of the blazing sun.

"Want a go?"

As she spoke, a deep roar built through the valley like summer thunder, except it came out of a clear sky. Rebecca stood up, rifle raised. And then, at exactly their eye level, a Yugoslav air force fighter jet flew past. The pilot turned his head towards them. Della Torre resisted an urge to wave. Rebecca tracked the jet with her rifle, eyes on the scope.

"He needed a shave," she said as the roar of the jet filled the air and then faded with a long finish, the plane disappearing from sight.

"MiG-21. Balalaika," della Torre said. "The Yugoslavs are testing approaches to Zagreb. He'll probably set off the air-raid alerts, but if he's carrying bombs they're going to be too late."

"Think he's carrying bombs?"

"Probably. But I don't think he's going to be using them. Not yet. They've been flying over to warn the Croat government what's in store for them."

"He was going slow enough that I'm pretty sure I could have knocked the visor off his helmet. He was exactly in range. I put it at around 250 metres. If I'd pulled the trigger he'd have made a pretty big hole in the hillside. They'd have chalked it down to an accident."

"You should have pulled the trigger, then."

"Unfortunately, I'm not allowed to. Other people's wars and all that."

"You know, I really do believe you wanted to do it."

"I've never brought down a MiG-21," she said. "You going to give the rifle a go, or do you think there are more Balalaikas heading our way?"

"I doubt it. They'll be coming from all corners. Testing Zagreb's reflexes, I think. But they don't want to test so much that they run into somebody with their finger on a trigger, if you know what I mean."

"I know exactly what you mean. Here," she said lowering the rifle back to the ground.

"Sure. It's been a while since I played with one of these. See if I still can."

"I won't bother to tell you to squeeze the trigger as gently and smoothly as you would a nipple."

"Thanks for that."

"Though not everybody likes their nipples squeezed gently." She smiled before adding, "I'm told."

He lay down on the rug, smelling the hot earth and dried grass underneath. Grasshoppers sprang madly around him, distracting him as they bounced off his arm and head. Rebecca refilled the magazine for him.

"It's a semi, so you have to squeeze off each shot. There isn't any wind, so you don't need to adjust the flight. I've calibrated it to 260 metres. The focus dials are on the right side."

He was surprised at how well the kick was absorbed by the stock. He didn't know the calibre, but it was clearly more than nine millimetres. A .338, he guessed.

"Nice rifle."

"Isn't it. I'll take a few more shots just to make sure before I pack this up. If you want to join our friend, take the other two cases down for me, will you. Put the big one in the car and take the smaller one to the house. Maybe we can play with the radios. They're a new system and I'd like to see how well they work."

The cases put a strain on his weak left arm, but he managed. He did as he'd been asked and joined Strumbić, who was sitting under the cherry tree. The cherries were long gone, the blackened and dried remains of the ones that had escaped Strumbić and the birds scattered across the ground. Lumps of dried yellow resin clung to the tree's ancient black bark.

Strumbić took a tumbler, grown opaque with age, and poured it half full with deep yellow wine out of a plastic jerry can, topping it up with soapy mineral water out of a tall bottle.

"I cooled it in the cistern." A big concrete cistern to catch rainwater was dug into the ground on the other side of the house. Strumbić kept water bottles in it, attached by their necks to nylon ropes that were anchored to a steel ring at the top, guaranteeing himself a cool drink even on the hottest days when the power failed. Della Torre could see a new metal shutter to the wine cellar's window, and a patched-up frame. So that was how Strumbić had got out.

They could hear the steady clank of the rifle shots higher up the hill.

"She's something, this one," said Strumbić, shaking his head. "If you haven't got your sights on her, mind if I give her a go? Actually, what am I saying? I'll give her a go anyway."

"Be my guest. But she'll wear you down to a toothpick."

"You say that like you know what you're talking about."

"What about your girlfriend? I won't even mention your wife," della Torre said, ignoring Strumbić's comment.

"Fuck the wife. As for the girlfriend, fuck her too. Gone, and good riddance. Stupid little cow. She was screwing one of my men and didn't think I'd notice."

"What happened to your man?"

"He's doing traffic. On an island in the middle of the highway."

"A promotion, then."

"He's staying there until a bus hits him."

"Nice to know you're not someone to bear a grudge."

Strumbić laughed, offering della Torre a cigarette.

"You know, I've always loved coming up here," della Torre said wistfully.

"Always liked having you up. Always considered you a friend, Gringo."

"Till you set those killers on me."

"We're not getting into that again, are we? You know very well I had to. Didn't want to do it, but the people you were playing games with weren't the sort I felt like fucking with."

"Maybe." Della Torre knew Strumbić hadn't had much choice. The Bosnians had come to him for help to set up della Torre. And Strumbić, seeing which way the wind was blowing, had made the phone call. There hadn't been any real way out of it. Sure, Strumbić had been offered inducements. Like a few thousand Deutschmarks. And being allowed to live. But della Torre could hardly blame Strumbić; he'd been as much at fault for selling Strumbić the files in the first place. Stupid. Was he being stupid again, getting sucked into this American adventure? Or could you really call it stupidity if you had no say in the matter?

They smoked and drank the potent wine mixed with water. Della Torre contemplated a fat spider working her way around her web, which glistened in the crook of the cherry tree. The spider was using a long leg to test the integrity of each anchoring strand: busy, quick, but efficient. When a small fly flew into the web only to break through, he watched her run to the spot and mend the damage.

Strumbić was slicing some homemade dried sausage when Rebecca joined them. Tiny drops of sweat were beaded on her forehead and her upper lip. Della Torre could almost taste the hot saltiness of her skin. Her blouse clung to her breasts. The big square sunglasses shaded her eyes, but she clearly knew exactly what both men were thinking.

"Somebody going to pour me a drink? Unless there's a mint julep on offer, I'll have exactly what you gentlemen are having." She took a long drink of the watered-down wine and then poured herself a glass of mineral water on its own. "Tastes like somebody had a bath in it."

"Is water from tap also," said Strumbić.

"That's all right, I'll hide the flavour with a bit more of that yellow wine there," she said, helping herself to a slice of dried sausage.

"I thought you just wanted to talk to the Montenegrin," della Torre said. "That's a lot of artillery we're taking just to talk to someone."

"Sometimes people need to know you're serious in case they start to worry you're wasting their time."

"And what happens when they come armed too?"

"We'll have bulletproof vests," she laughed. "Nobody's going to be doing any shooting. All we're doing is bringing some insurance."

"And the people who are going to meet us down there?"

"Just some communications backup. We Americans like to do things properly. Don't we, Marko?"

"Relax, Gringo. Is like holiday," Strumbić intervened.

"Gringo?" Rebecca was amused.

"Nickname. I don't like it very much, but it stuck."

"I like it. Gringo," she said, smiling. "Like you stepped right out of a cowboy movie."

She turned her head towards Strumbić, though her eyes momentarily stayed on della Torre.

"So, Mr. Strumbić, I hear you know a little about Dubrovnik," she said.

"Please. Julius," he said, making like he was offended at her show of formality.

"Julius," she said, correcting herself.

"Is very beautiful. Pearl of Adriatic is called."

"I've always wanted to go. I hear it's lovely all around there."

"Is very beautiful. Most beautiful island is Šipan. My island."

"You have an island?" she asked innocently, barely masking her disbelief.

"No island. House, little house on island. Is very nice. Very quiet," Strumbić said getting into his stride. "Nobody near, on beach. But very quiet island. But not so far from Dubrovnik. Half-hour, a little by boat, a little by car."

"No one lives there?"

"Not many people. Old people only. Young people go to work in Dubrovnik or go to America. Two small villages and much old buildings. Old palaces falling down from time of Dubrovnik nobles. Not so much tourists. Sometimes come on yacht." He pronounced the word as it was written. "Not many come on ferry. So is all peace and quiet."

"Sounds divine. Maybe we can go swimming there. In privacy, for a day or two. We can have a little break maybe. I love skinny-dipping."

"Skinny-dip?" Strumbić was puzzled.

"She means swimming naked," della Torre said, breaking his silence. He'd been admiring how she reeled Strumbić in.

Strumbić gave a broad, satisfied leer. "Yes, I like naked swim, *naturische*."

"Maybe it would be nice to stay on your island. For a few days, because I need to be in Dubrovnik . . ." she said.

"Yes. Of course. You and me." He paused for a while and eventually added: "And Gringo."

Once they'd finished their wine, they tested out the radios, small units that buckled onto a belt with a forked wire, one end leading to an earpiece and the other to a tiny microphone that could be clipped onto a collar. The radios were voice-activated, with precedence between the units so that they could all talk. Della Torre and Strumbić marvelled at this technology even more enthusiastically than they'd admired the weapons.

Before they left, Rebecca went back to the target and dug all the slugs out of the tree, dropping them into a Ziploc bag. Della Torre noticed she'd already picked up all the bullet casings.

Rebecca, Strumbić, and della Torre were damp with the heat when they got back into the car, and she turned the air conditioning on full blast for the trip back to Zagreb. The day had felt almost like a holiday. Except that della Torre was troubled by this woman who lied shamelessly and shot guns like a professional. And by the black Hilux they passed in Samobor.

**19**

## SWEDEN, FEBRUARY/MARCH 1986

THE BOY WAS curled up in the passenger seat. He'd wrapped himself in the red and green tartan blanket. It had taken a long while to get the chill out of the car, even though the Montenegrin had turned the heat on full.

At first the boy had complained about being dragged out of the warm apartment, but the hot air and the sound of tires on gritted road sent him into a doped-up slumber. The Montenegrin knew he wouldn't wake easily. Most nights he'd fall asleep on the floor of the flat, not responding even when the Montenegrin lifted him onto the sofa and tucked the blanket around him.

He was a strange boy. Efficient. Useful. Yet a dopehead. Pretty, in a hungry, pinched way, but never seemed to have any company or any friends. In fact, the Montenegrin had never seen him with anyone else. The boy didn't talk about himself, or about anyone else, really.

The post, mostly circulars, that came to the apartment was in somebody else's name, a Turkish name, it seemed to the Montenegrin. The boy threw all the letters away. All the bills, he said, were automatically covered by the welfare office. There was no telephone.

The Montenegrin asked the boy where he usually lived, but the boy was noncommittal. He seemed mostly to live in Malmo, though he wasn't clear about whether he lived there alone or with others. All he knew was that the boy was a Serb with an Albanian surname from a village in Kosovo, where his parents now lived. The Montenegrin didn't know whether the boy had any brothers or sisters.

The boy seemed to have plenty of money, but spent little. He said he did some low-key dealing to students at the university, but only ever carried enough on himself for his own use. He was keeping a watch on things in Stockholm for the Serb. But what that entailed, the Montenegrin never figured out, and in the end he guessed the boy was an opportunist who had found an opportunity to sell dope in the city and live for free.

Other than that, the boy didn't seem to do much. He played pool in a couple of local pool halls, mostly against Kurds or Sudanese immigrants, never gambling more than a couple of kronor at a time and usually winning. He watched television. And he did math puzzles. Pages of them.

The boy washed his clothes in the building's basement laundrette, but he didn't seem to have much in the way of a wardrobe. A couple of pairs of jeans. T-shirts and brushed cotton shirts, and some wool sweaters. He had a sleeping bag he seldom used and a towel that he dried over a radiator. He had barely any toiletries and never cooked, restricting himself to sandwiches made from white processed bread and salami, and milk drunk straight from a red carton. Hot meals he took at Turkish or Kurdish restaurants. Kebabs with spicy sauce.

The boy's contacts, probably made through the Serb, clearly trusted him. He'd got the gun on consignment and then let the Montenegrin choose his commission after agreeing to the weapon. The Montenegrin, not expecting to use the Smith & Wesson, had considered asking the boy to find him a hunting rifle with a scope and a silencer. The boy had made getting a gun surprisingly easy.

The boy said he'd never been arrested, though the Montenegrin was skeptical — the boy seemed to know a lot about the Swedish police and how they operated.

The boy puzzled him. He was like an inexplicable gift from the gods. The Montenegrin knew he'd have had a much harder time without him.

The Montenegrin had city maps and guidebooks. But being led around by the boy had allowed him to ignore the inconsequential and irrelevant. Best of all, the boy had helped him to become anonymous in Stockholm's immigrant community.

He switched on the car radio. It was tuned to a pop station, which the Montenegrin figured would be as good as any other. The music didn't matter to him. He was waiting for an announcer's grave tones signalling that the prime minister's assassination had become public knowledge.

Though he didn't understand Swedish, the jokey, light-hearted chat between songs told him the news hadn't yet broken.

He drove within the speed limit. The roads were well gritted and the sky was clear, but he wasn't used to driving in that sort of cold and was especially cautious about doing so at night. It took about half an hour to get past the suburbs and into the country. From there he'd have another hour or slightly more to get to the place where the boy had taken him to test-fire the Smith & Wesson. He wasn't sure about finding it in the dark, but left that worry for later.

It was a quiet spot, down a rough track about twenty minutes from the main road, in the heart of deep woodland. Hunters and loggers, heading farther into the forest towards a big lake, kept it passable. But the area the boy had led him to was undisturbed. He said no one came there, even in the summer. It was a logging plantation, but the trees were too small and wouldn't be taken down for another ten years. Until then, there was no reason for anyone to go there.

When the Montenegrin had asked him how he knew of the place, that he was worried it was somewhere the mafia went routinely to test out their guns, the boy said they never went that far out of Stockholm, even to bury bodies. He just happened to know the place, he said.

The Montenegrin navigated by the clock. The highway looked all the same to him, but he remembered the road interchange before the one that was his exit and he watched carefully for it, allowing a few big trucks to pass him along the way. Otherwise there was little traffic.

He focused his mind as he drove, focused on the radio, focused on the signposts in the dark, making sure he didn't slow so much that he risked an accident.

The Montenegrin's thoughts drifted to his own three girls. Two big ones, grown up. One married and the other one working in Dubrovnik. The youngest...

There was nothing to be done for her but to put her in a home, the doctors said. Maybe he'd do as they advised when he got back. They said she'd never walk or be able to do much for herself or even talk beyond rudimentary language. Her brain and body didn't function properly, and there was nothing he could do for her.

Why then did he doubt them? When he'd sat with the little girl on his lap, in the warmth of the autumn sun, she'd spoken to him. She was four years old and could barely make herself understood. Maybe he was mistaken. No, what he'd heard was language. She'd spoken to him about the light on the water, how it sparkled like the glass in the rose bowl on the dining-room table. He found it hard to believe, yet she kept talking, slowly, laboriously, but he understood what she was saying. Insights that seemed impossible from a crippled, retarded child, and yet he was sure of it. Could a child who had thoughts like that really be mentally defective? A child who saw things, could speak of them, at an age when his eldest girls, the normal ones, could only blab nonsense.

The sign for the intersection came up. The Montenegrin looked in the rear-view mirror to ensure no one was coming up fast behind him. There wasn't anyone, so he slowed down and took the next couple of kilometres at half the speed limit until he reached the turning, where he left the highway. He was pretty sure he had it right, but at night all these small Swedish forest roads looked alike.

He drove on the dirt road's compacted snow and gravel. The tires had a good grip and the car was four-wheel drive, so he had no problem controlling it. Once again, he measured distance by time. He was driving at about two-thirds of the speed he'd gone during daylight, so he gave himself half an hour to get to the right place.

The trees were forbidding in the beams of his headlights. Twice he caught the demonic red reflection of a small animal's eyes in the distance, but he couldn't tell what it was, fox or small deer or something native to these parts that he didn't know about. Did they have wolves?

When he reached a couple of landmarks he'd seen before — a big boulder that seemed to come from nowhere, and beyond it a tall fir tree that apparently had two trunks — he slowed right down. Beyond that he found the track, little more than a gap in the woods, barely enough space to squeeze between the trees, their needles scraping along the sides of the car. He didn't want to drive too far off the loggers' road for fear of getting stuck. He'd spun the wheels when they came here before, so he stopped well short of the narrow clearing where he'd done his target practice.

The boy had said you could fire machine guns here and no one would notice.

He left the car idling and got out. From the boot, he got out a good torch, a big Maglite that could double as a truncheon, and grabbed an empty rubbish bag made from heavy plastic, the sort that was advertised never to split. Carefully, he put the torch on the roof of the car and opened the passenger door. The boy was still sleeping; he'd barely shifted from the moment he'd shut his eyes.

In a smooth motion the Montenegrin pulled the plastic bag over the boy's head, twisting him around so that his hands were pinned under him, and then knelt on his back. The boy woke with a start and then thrashed as he panicked. Fear gave him strength, but he was no match for the Montenegrin, who was nearly twice the boy's weight and still powerful despite his middle age. The boy tried to bite through the bag, but his shrieking inflated it away from his mouth.

The struggle lasted for three minutes before the boy fell limp. But the Montenegrin held his position for an additional full five, tracking the seconds on his watch, before he pulled the boy out of the car. He took the plastic bag off only when the boy was lying on the snow. People who died of suffocation sometimes bled from the nose, and he didn't want blood in the car. He aimed the torch down and with some difficulty stripped the corpse; the boy wore tight-fitting clothes. He stuffed them into the garbage bag.

He reached back in the car for the two cans of cat food and then, having wrapped the boy in the tartan blanket, carried him into the thick of the woods, pacing off fifty metres. The going was difficult—carrying the body over his shoulder, pushing through low pine branches, snow falling on him in lumps. The snow was deeper on the ground than he'd expected, given how thick the forest cover was.

Finally he lay the body on the ground, face down. He took a folding knife from his pocket and then counted the ribs up the left side of the boy's back. Finding the spot, he pointed the knife straight down and stabbed once. Barely any blood came out of the wound. It was insurance. Whether the boy had suffocated or not, he was without question dead now.

He wiped the blade with some snow and dried it on his trousers. He opened the cat food and squeezed it onto the body. The food was still warm, so its scent would carry to any scavengers living in the woods. The corpse wouldn't last long if the foxes found it. But he knew that if the body froze, it would stay preserved until the spring.

He made his way back to the car, inspecting his tracks closely and looking around the car for anything of his or the boy's that might have dropped. He assured himself the woods were too thick for hunters, but if somebody did find the body he wanted as little as possible to be traced back to him.

He shoved the bag with the boy's clothes into the boot and then slid back into the driver's seat. He sat there shivering, the heater on full. When finally he was in control of his muscles again, he shifted into reverse and then looked back over his shoulder. The wheels spun. He cursed. He pressed the gas again. They kept spinning.

There was plenty of fuel in the car; he'd kept the tank full, just in case. But he hadn't figured the snow would pose any difficulty for a four-wheel drive. That's why he'd picked the car in the first place. This would be a bad place to get stuck. He guessed it would be more than a twenty-kilometre walk back to the main road. The boy had said that truckers always picked up hitchhikers, especially in the winter. If it came to that, the car was unlikely to be discovered for some time. But on the night of Palme's death, everyone travelling away from Stockholm would be regarded with suspicion.

It was known to snow heavily in the Yugoslav mountains, and the Montenegrin was familiar with winter driving, but stupidly he hadn't bought chains for the Opel. Swedish roads were kept pristinely clear, especially the motorways. He tried again, tried some tricks he knew, such as accelerating while pressing on the brakes and turning the steering wheel. But the car kept spinning ice.

He took his foot off the accelerator, forcing himself not to panic. He got out and tried to rock the car off the slick patches the spinning tires had made, but he was finding it hard to get a grip under his shoes. He should have bought those Korean boots with the felt insoles; his toes were freezing. He got back in the car and ran the engine to get warm; he was worried the sweat he'd worked up would give him hypothermia if he stayed in the cold.

He stared along the tunnel of brightness his headlights made through the conifers growing on either side of the track. The quiet stillness of the night, apart from the sound of the engine, was unnerving.

"Think," he said to himself.

He'd gather branches and wedge them hard against the tires. That might give him a little purchase. He could jack up the car and put the floor mats, and maybe the boy's clothes or the bedding, under the wheels to make a ramp. Then he remembered the rubbish bag full of things he'd emptied from the kitchen. There was a full kilo bag of salt in it. He'd bought it on his first shopping expedition because it was cheaper than a salt grinder or the gourmet crystals. He had never even opened it, because they'd never cooked in the flat.

He got the bag out and spread its contents under the two rear wheels. He waited for it to seep into the ice and then he tried again.

At first the wheels continued to spin, but then he felt them grip. The car jerked a little to one side. He rocked the steering wheel, alternately pumping the brake and accelerator.

And then he was moving, reversing down the track. He didn't dare stop to turn the car around but kept reversing, using the pale red glow of the rear lights to guide him, as if he were backing into the mouth of hell. He drove that way for . . .

how far was it? Two kilometres? Longer? His back and shoulder ached with the effort of sitting in the twisted position, until at long last he reached the gravel road that would take him back to the motorway.

It was only when he saw the ramp to the highway that he dared stop to relieve himself by the side of the road, making sure he was on the crest of a small rise so that he could coast out of any trouble. Then he sat in the parked car, breathing hard for a few minutes as the past hour caught up with him.

He turned the radio back on as he pulled away, the car swaying through the gravel and snowy ruts of the rough road. He'd not been able to listen while he concentrated on driving out of that endless forest. Still there was no news. Could they really not have made the announcement about Palme's death? The lively disc jockeys had been replaced by one with a soporific voice who played odd, jangly music that grated on the Montenegrin's nerves. He tuned in to another station that seemed to be just talk. But here too there was no excitement.

He shrugged, though a little, nagging uncertainty tugged at him. What if it hadn't been his target? What if he'd killed someone other than Pilgrim, someone who'd looked like him? He pushed it all out of his mind—Pilgrim...Palme...the boy.

He drove. He was at least five hours from the Helsingborg ferry, assuming all went well. Assuming the Swedish police hadn't set roadblocks this far from Stockholm. Assuming his luck held.

**20**

## CROATIA, AUGUST 1991

**THEY STOPPED AT** a police roadblock on the northern part of the coast road, where it cut along the Velebit mountain range that divides inland Croatia from the Adriatic Sea.

Rebecca had called after their return from Strumbić's weekend cottage, interrupting della Torre's desultory unpacking at the office. He'd given up on the forms sent to him by Kakav, which had to be filled in triplicate and stamped by six separate departments before he could hope to get his military ID.

The call wasn't so much a conversation as a series of nicely worded orders. Pack lightly for a trip that could last up to two weeks. Leave in two days' time. And tell Strumbić he's coming, but only for the first few days, just long enough for them to get settled into Šipan. Any fair bill he presented for use of the property would be paid in cash.

That was good enough for Strumbić. He took the news, churlishly delivered by della Torre, with a certain smug satisfaction. When della Torre said it would only be for the trip down and then a couple of days in Šipan, Strumbić shrugged and said, "We'll see."

Della Torre could tell the Zagreb cop's enthusiasm wasn't just down to his eagerness for a few days in the sun. He was straining to get away from Mrs. Strumbić, who wore away at her husband with her cheese-grater nagging. Della Torre, on the other hand, felt deeply uneasy about Irena leaving to go to Vukovar. He didn't want her there. In fact, he'd rather she went back to London and her lover's arms than waltz into a Danube tragedy. Because that's where it was headed. He was sure of it. And he felt guilty about abandoning her for sunny safety.

He'd spent the whole drive from Zagreb ruminating on Irena, his irritation made worse by the fact that Rebecca wouldn't let him or Strumbić smoke. It was going to be a long trip to Dubrovnik.

The Velebit police, proudly displaying the Croatian insignia, the red and white checkerboard shield that so incensed the Serbs, were waving traffic off the Zadar highway onto a smaller road to the coast. Della Torre asked Rebecca to pull over. The cops didn't like it.

"Keep going," the one nearest shouted. "Go down to Senj and take the old coast road."

Della Torre got out of the car. The policeman raised his rifle a little, eyeing him warily. "If you need to take a piss you can take one somewhere else. There's no stopping here."

Della Torre showed his UDBA ID. "What's going on?"

The cop looked carefully at the ID and then up at della Torre and then back down at the ID, which he showed to his colleague, who was sitting inside the police car they'd parked across both lanes of the highway. Della Torre followed him and leaned against the squad car.

"I thought they shut down the UDBA," the cop said.

"They did." The cop regarded him skeptically, so della Torre continued: "But all us former UDBA people still exist, and now we're working for Croat intelligence. I'm military. You can call me Major."

"It says captain here."

"Well, it's major now. In the military."

"You have any proof—" The cop spat on the ground. "—Major?"

Only a few weeks before, the whole country had cowered before that bit of laminated card. But UDBA, it seemed, no longer spelled fear.

"Are you sure you know what you're doing, officer?" della Torre asked.

"I figure I do...Major." He stared with a practised emptiness at della Torre. "The Serbs cut off the road down towards Gospić, and my colleagues and I are here to tell folks to take the coast road down by Senj...Major."

"I thought the Serbs were on the other side of Gospić."

The cop tilted his head at della Torre as if he couldn't believe somebody could be so stupid. "I don't know where you've been, but this road's been blocked more or less since the start of the year. Last year we could shift some of the logs they dropped across it, but nothing doing now. Nowadays you try that and they shoot at you. They've got the road cut off on both sides of Gospić. You've got to go down to Senj, along the coast road, and then up."

"What about the small roads?"

"You mean get off the highway before where those Serb lumberjacks have set up camp?"

"Yes."

"You sure are desperate to get to Gospić quick."

"No. I just know that if we follow the coast road it'll take us a week just to get to Zadar."

"You're not kidding. But go this way and the only place you're going to get to is a funeral. Your own. And as much as I'd like that..."

Della Torre ignored him. "What about the locals?"

"What about the locals?"

"Well, do you let them take this road?" Della Torre asked, enunciating each word to show his irritation.

"Yes."

"How far?"

"Most of the way to Gospić."

"And you can turn off onto the little roads before then, can't you?"

"Yes," the cop said, giving della Torre a dull-eyed stare.

"And are those little roads blocked by Serbs?"

"Not that I know of."

"There been a police patrol to Gospić today on the little roads?"

"This morning."

"Any problems?"

"No."

"What about past Gospić?"

"The Serbs have trees down there too."

"On the main road or the little roads?"

"Main road."

"So you're telling me that if we take the main road and turn off just before the Gospić exit and follow the little roads through Gospić and then on past it, we should avoid the Serbs and avoid having to go down to Senj and the coast road, which to my understanding is a fifty-kilometre traffic jam," della Torre said, using incremental lawyerly logic to make his point blindingly clear.

The cop shrugged. "Except I'm not letting you on the main road. You're just going to have to follow everyone else down to Senj. Major."

He dropped della Torre's ID on the ground. Della Torre stared at it and then up at the cop, whose eyes were emotionless and, somewhere deep down in the blackness of the pupils, contemptuous. After the shock came the rage. With difficulty, della Torre contained himself. There was nothing he could do against this man. He bent over, picked up the ID, thinking revenge but knowing that searing hatred of the UDBA was everywhere. And with the fear gone, they could show it.

Perhaps the cop had good reason to loathe the UDBA. Many people did.

Della Torre walked back to the car. He leaned into the window. "The pricks aren't letting us past. Serb roadblocks on the highway are pretty permanent now. Everything's got to go through Senj and along the very slow coastal road. But it seems Julius was right when he said it was only the main highway that's a problem."

Rebecca had been keen to drive down as quickly as possible. None of them was looking forward to the single-lane road that wound its way along the coast. Even though foreign tourists were thin on the ground, refugee traffic had been growing; displaced people were being put up in otherwise empty seafront hotels. Add the military traffic and some domestic tourism—it would take more than the prospect of a civil war to keep Yugoslavs from their seaside cottages in August—and all it took was a broken-down bus or a tractor pulling along a family's possessions, and traffic could be snarled for most of a day. A coastal ferry was a possibility, but Rebecca was reluctant to use it. The ones that took cars from Rijeka to Dubrovnik were exceptionally slow, slower even than the coast road, and worse still, were subject to snap inspections by the Yugoslav navy, looking for gun smugglers.

"If we could just get past the cops, we'd be able to turn off before the Serb roadblocks and onto small roads. They seem to be clear. Though I suppose if Serbs saw people using them they'd block those as well. We could do that, go through Gospić and along small roads on the other side until we can join the highway beyond the roadblocks again. Which would mean getting to Zadar in a couple of hours if all went well. As it is, we're going to have to go down the coast road and be in Zadar in, oh—" Della Torre looked skyward as though he were doing a difficult sum. "—sometime tomorrow."

Strumbić grinned at him.

Della Torre went back to the cop. "We're going this way. But thanks for taking an interest in our safety."

"You try that and we'll shoot your car out from under you," said the cop.

He stood there, making no move.

Della Torre rubbed his hand over his face. He should have stopped noticing he no longer had a moustache by now, but it still came as a surprise to him. He was wondering what sort of threat to launch at the recalcitrant cop. In the old days he could have had the man in an UDBA jail within the hour. Things were different now, and this cop knew it.

Strumbić appeared in the corner of his eye.

"What seems to be the problem?" Strumbić asked pleasantly.

He looked like an older version of the Velebit cop, his belly hanging slightly more over his belt, his jowls a little looser, his hairline slightly higher up the forehead. But they'd been stamped from the same mould.

"There's a certain reluctance to let us through," della Torre said.

Strumbić took the roadmap from della Torre and went over to the cop. They shook hands and the cop lowered his rifle to the ground stock first while Strumbić put an arm over the man's shoulder. They walked away from della Torre over to the verge on the other side of the highway. Another cop had taken the first one's place to wave traffic onto the smaller road, dealing with the almost inevitable complaints and questions but at the same time looking over his shoulder to see what was happening to his colleague. The cop in the car had got out and had his hand on the holster of the gun on his hip.

After a long five minutes, Strumbić and his younger doppelgänger came walking back, all smiles.

"What are you waiting for, Gringo? Let's go."

"Go where?"

"Where do you think?" Strumbić said, pointing to the empty

highway beyond the roadblock.

When they got to the car, Strumbić thumbed for della Torre to get into the back seat. "I have map. He show me where road-block is. I sit front, show Rebecca."

Della Torre did as he was told.

The cops waved them through. Rebecca steered around the policemen's Zastava, driving over the grass verge. Another police car was parked at the side of the road a little farther along, but they were quickly past, driving along a highway cut through mountain forests. With an open road, Rebecca quick-ly worked her way up the gears, pushing the big Mercedes to autobahn speeds.

"What the hell happened there?" della Torre demanded.

"We have nice talk. I ask him how much, and he say fifty Deutschmarks. I give him one hundred and he happy to shut up." Della Torre could see Rebecca grinning in the rear-view mirror. Strumbić turned around to look at him, as pleased with himself as a dog that had got the steak. "He show me road, best way to Gospić, and then after Gospić back to highway. No Serbs. No problem."

"Looks like we were smart to take you along, Julius," Rebecca said.

"Of course. You see. I help in Dubrovnik also. You see," Strumbić said.

Della Torre sat deep into the leather of the rear seat. He watched the countryside pass, high, dark hills covered in a mixture of giant pines and oak that even the summer sun failed to penetrate. Somewhere to the left, thirty or forty kilometres, was Plitvice, a fairyland of turquoise lakes, each one tumbling into the next in a series of waterfalls made to be photographed for tourist calendars. A fairyland until six months ago, when the Serbs started shooting at Croat police and the Croat police fired back, a busload of Italians caught in the middle the whole while.

It was astonishing more people hadn't been killed, della Torre thought.

·    ·    ·

The Merc's smooth, quiet ride made him oblivious to the fact that it was eating distance like a glutton. There was a cooler box on the floor space in front of the empty seat. The hotel had organized drinks, snacks, and sandwiches for them. The seat itself held one of the black metal cases, the one with the sniper rifle, along with a heavy shoulder bag.

They were most of the way to their turning when Strumbić developed an unspoken gratitude for Rebecca's insistence that he wear his seat belt. It was either a feral dog or a black fox. Whatever it was, it darted in front of the car from the shrubbery which, untended by maintenance crews, had grown wild at the side of the road. Rebecca braked hard, manoeuvring to avoid hitting the animal. The tires squealed, scorching across the hot road, threatening to fishtail the Merc, though Rebecca kept deft control.

"Close," she said. The creature had disappeared just as quickly. "Guess they're not used to cars around here anymore."

She pulled over, though they hadn't seen any traffic at all.

For a long moment they sat still.

"If me driving, I hit," said Strumbić, though he didn't make it clear whether he'd have done so intentionally or that he was admitting to not being as good a driver as Rebecca.

"Oh, I'd have hated to. I'm an animal person," she said.

"That's nice," said della Torre, waiting for his pulse to slow.

"You're not?" she asked, noting the sarcasm in his voice.

"Not what?" he asked.

"An animal person."

"Only when they're on a plate," he said flippantly. "Except for cats."

"Oh, you're a cat lover then?"

"No. They taste too much like rodent," he said.

She screwed up her face at him in the rear-view mirror, as if he was a drunk who'd soiled himself in public.

"Or so I'm told," he added hastily.

She paused for a while and then asked, "Rodent? What sort of rodent?"

"Oh, I don't know, squirrel...or rat." He squirmed at the memory. Being in the commandos had been an unpleasant way to spend more than two years of military training. Unpleasant in many, many respects. "I imagine most rodents taste alike."

There was another long moment of silence. A faint smile played on the edge of her lips.

"She saying pussy taste like beaver," Strumbić said.

"Are beavers rodents?" della Torre asked.

"Some are. Though not the ones you eat," Rebecca said, deadpan.

After a pause, Strumbić guffawed.

"What?" della Torre asked.

Strumbić explained the joke to him in Croat. Trust Strumbić to have an imperfect grasp of English except for the vulgarities, della Torre thought.

Strumbić got out to piss in the bushes and Rebecca stretched her legs. Della Torre handed her a chilled Capri Sun. He noticed how, when she'd finished, she didn't throw it onto the verge but rolled up the package and stuck it in a paper bag she kept in the compartment at the bottom of the driver-side door. She was neat, besides being an animal lover.

Midway through a stretch, she stopped and stared along the road behind them.

"Marko, what do you make of that?" she asked, pointing.

In the distance, near the crest of a hill they'd descended and where the road reappeared after a bend, della Torre saw a faint glint.

"Looks like a car," he said.

"Yes. And what about that car?"

"It's not moving."

"Do you remember passing a car back there?"

"No."

"Neither do I."

She pulled out a pair of field glasses from the canvas bag, portable but powerful Zeiss binoculars. When she'd had a good look, she passed them over to della Torre. The resolution was astonishing, as good as the big, heavyweight glasses he'd had to use when he was in the military. It wasn't a car but a truck. A black truck. Its doors were open and he could make out two figures standing next to it.

"Black Hilux," Rebecca said.

He lowered the binoculars and looked over towards her. She'd braced herself against the Merc and was resting her elbow on its roof, using it to stabilize her arm as she focused the big telescopic sight from her rifle. It was considerably more powerful than the Zeiss. Strumbić was standing behind her, taking it all in.

"Friends of yours?" Rebecca asked generally.

"Black Hilux, you say?" della Torre asked.

"Yup."

"I saw one in Zagreb a couple of times."

"There was one that tried to follow us to Julius's cottage. It picked us up when we were driving back, as we passed through...what's it called...Samobor," Rebecca said. "And they were following us this morning from Zagreb, though they're a bit slower than us. We'd have lost them if it hadn't been for the traffic jam at the police roadblock."

Della Torre considered the woman, making a mental note not to underestimate her. About anything.

"Know anything about it, Julius?" della Torre asked.

Strumbić shook his head. "Not my friends. Maybe UDBA. Serbian UDBA. Maybe interested in Americans. Maybe Croatian

UDBA. Maybe mafia. Is much smuggling from Bosnia. Drugs to boats in Zadar, Split, and to Italy."

"Even though the Serbs have closed the roads?" della Torre asked.

"Smugglers know different ways. Pay money to go."

"If they're mafia, what do they want from us?"

Strumbić shrugged. "Mercedes?"

Della Torre nodded. "Maybe they're just lost tourists."

"Maybe." Rebecca's look suggested she didn't believe it.

She took one of the metal cases from the boot, unlocked the combination, and put it on top of the one next to della Torre. She didn't say anything about it. She didn't need to.

They set off again, though at a more measured pace now. Their turning wasn't far off and they didn't want to go racing into a Serb roadblock. Rebecca kept her eyes on the rear-view mirror.

They turned off the main road without seeing any signs of Serbs or anyone else. The single-lane byroad was tarmacked but rough at the edges. The forest flashed past, Strumbić continually having to remind Rebecca to slow down as he tried to locate where they were on the map. At one point they raced past a unit of irregulars lounging by their cars in a little clearing.

"What do you think?" della Torre asked Strumbić. "Theirs or ours?"

"Whoever they are, they'll end up doing more damage to their own side. It was like they were out for a picnic," Strumbić replied in Croat. "But that's probably the last we see of that Hilux."

The mountain forest gave way to a broad valley of rolling hills. More hedges and flat fields of maize and wheat were scattered among red-tiled houses and hamlets. The fields were broken by single trees and sheep meadows.

Before long they hit a cluster of hamlets, and not far past the hamlets, Gospić.

They stopped at a roadblock made up of a couple of saw-horses put up by a unit of the Croat militia, the half-police, half-army that provided what security it could to these parts.

A tall soldier wearing a loose shirt and a slack expression bade Rebecca lower her window.

"You took a wrong turn. You want to go to the seashore. No tourism here. *Kein Tourist, verstehen?*" And then, turning to his friends, who were eyeing the car, he said in the broad, slow accent of a boy from the hills: "Get a load of this redhead, boys. How long you think she spent on her back to buy this motor?"

"Ask her how much and I'll tell you how long," one of his fellow militiamen called back.

The soldier turned back to Rebecca. "You get to the coast down that road," he said, pointing to a side road. "Down that way a kilometre, and you get to the coast road. But first there's a tax. A Gospić tax." He paused in thought. "A hundred Deutschmarks. *Hundert Deutschmark*," he translated helpfully.

"Listen, son." Strumbić talked across Rebecca from the passenger seat. "Why don't you keep your trap shut and the road open. We're driving into Gospić, where we're going to stop for a little break, and then we're driving onto the highway once we find somebody who can direct us past the Serb roadblocks."

Della Torre was surprised, thinking that Strumbić might pay his way out of this like he had earlier. But on reflection, he knew Strumbić was right. The police were professionals and they knew that there were rules about successful bribe-taking. These were stupid farm boys. Show a willingness to pay them a hundred Deutschmarks and they'd ask for two hundred.

"I wasn't talking to you," the boy said in a slow, leisurely way. His disregard for the passengers of the Mercedes spoke of a dangerous combination of stupidity and bravado.

"Julius," Rebecca said, "let me handle this."

She smiled apologetically to the soldier and fiddled with the gearshift. The soldier sauntered to the front of the car and started waving Rebecca backwards. Rebecca looked over her shoulder as if to reverse, revved the engine, and then popped the clutch. But rather than going backwards, the car jumped forward, knocking the soldier flat on his back in the middle of the road. The car didn't hit him hard enough to do much damage, and Rebecca braked the same instant. Della Torre was shocked into silence. Strumbić hooted with laughter, while half a dozen irate militiamen surrounded the Merc, their rifles raised.

Rebecca rushed out of the car and went straight for the fallen soldier, bending over him. He'd raised himself up onto his elbows. His immediate outrage cooled. From where he sat, della Torre could see the militiaman wasn't looking into Rebecca's face but rather somewhere lower. The magic of a low-cut blouse.

She cooed over him and stroked his head, making apologetic gestures to show that she'd meant to reverse rather than go forward, until the group of militiamen relaxed and started to laugh at their fallen comrade, who hadn't suffered anything more than a couple of bruises.

Della Torre joined her, showing his ID to the men. Unlike the cop at the roadblock, these boys didn't realize that the UDBA was no longer a force. One of the militiamen hurried down the road to a nondescript restaurant in an unfinished two-storey red and white cinder-block building, from which a flustered and reluctant senior officer followed. He was a middle-aged man, thinning up top and fat around the middle, his green shirt untucked and open down the chest.

"You run the militia here?" della Torre asked, having informed the officer of his rank and who he was.

Apprehension flickered across the officer's face. "I'm told that you tried to run over one of my men."

"An accident," della Torre said dryly. "I suggest you discourage them from demanding bribes and from being insubordinate. Because pretty soon you'll have some professional officers coming this way. And a few of those professional officers would be happy to summarily execute soldiers they consider to be in a state of mutiny. That's just a friendly word of warning.

"Now I need you to show me on this map how we can get back to the main road where we won't bump into any tree trunks your Serb neighbours might have left lying around. And where we might get an edible lunch in Gospić."

**21**

**G**OSPIĆ WAS A typical small Croat town. It had a big square, a church with a tall baroque steeple, and an entirely forgettable restaurant.

They had an indifferent lunch, fried schnitzels for the men and an omelette for Rebecca. They sat on a pleasant shaded terrace next to the main road and within sight of the little river that passed through the town. Strumbić spent much of the time recounting the looks on the soldiers' faces when Rebecca hit their friend.

"Clutch slipped," Rebecca said nonchalantly. Della Torre tried not to think about how the boy's finger had been on the trigger of his rifle. But all of the militiamen had had their safeties on, and they had all ducked out of the way when the car jumped. They hadn't looked like they were up for much of a fight.

After a quick round of black coffees, during which Strumbić and della Torre desperately puffed down a last cigarette, they left Gospić, following a small, dusty road, long lines of cracks running along its asphalt so that its edges more or less crumbled into the verges. The landscape gave way to another set of long fields, with isolated low hills breaking up the valley floor, while to their right the mountains piled up into the blue distance beyond.

The way out of town was much like the way in, though in this direction the militiamen hadn't bothered to block the road, content to merely eye the passing Merc from the shade of a giant mulberry tree.

They drove through a smattering of hamlets, each little more than a few houses strung along the road. Della Torre suspected it wasn't just the heat of the afternoon that made this feel like a newly abandoned landscape. There were no animals; no sheep, cows, or horses. No dogs sleeping in the shade of shuttered houses. There was no other traffic on the road, and inside the Mercedes there was no sound other than the hum of the air conditioner and the rumble of tires on the aged road. It reminded della Torre of the countryside around Vukovar. Silent and seized with fear.

He watched Rebecca in the rear-view mirror, her eyes frequently flicking to read the road behind them. He could see the consternation behind the half-tint of her big sunglasses. He turned to look back. In the middle distance, a cloud of dust was being kicked up by a black car.

"Hold on, boys," she said, accelerating the Mercedes. The road twisted. For long patches it was paved, only to give way to gravel for a few hundred metres and then revert to rough asphalt. The ground rolled, and fields were broken by copses.

Rebecca spotted a farmer's track between a clump of shrubs and a cornfield. Barely braking, she turned off the road like a rally driver and bounced the car into the tall, ripe corn.

"Wait here, I'm having a look," she said, getting out of the car, but first helping herself to a Beretta from the aluminium case next to della Torre. "Try not to have a party while I'm gone."

Not long after, they heard a heavy car pass fast along the road, scattering gravel behind it. Rebecca strolled back.

"The Hilux?" della Torre asked when she'd slid into the car.

"Yup." He noticed that she put the handgun on the floor under her seat. "What do you fellows suggest?"

"Maybe he going to Zadar too," Strumbić said.

"Maybe," della Torre echoed. "Though I'd guess they were probably looking for us."

"Funny, I was thinking the same thing," said Rebecca. "The question is whether they're just following us to see where we're going or if they want something from us."

"You mean if they want to talk to us?"

"Or something."

"But they could stop us in Zagreb, no?" asked Strumbić.

"Zagreb's a busy place," della Torre said. "People who drive cars with tinted windows tend to like their privacy."

"What do you think? Wait a little while and let them think we're long gone? Go back?" Rebecca asked.

"I've got a feeling you already know what you want to do," della Torre said.

"Why don't you boys have a cigarette? We'll have a drink and then carry on. The way they were moving, it looked like they thought they'd lost us. I don't think they'll stop."

They sat smoking in the cornfield while Rebecca scouted the road again before pushing off. The route through the country was quicker than the coast road, but della Torre couldn't help but wonder what the eventual cost of speed might be.

They were back on the half-paved road, driving between wheat and cornfields and vineyards broken up by the occasional copse. The farther they drove, the more the landscape became lumpy with rocky escarpments, the white stone of the Velebit Mountains rising up through the reddish brown earth like rows of cracked teeth from bleeding gums.

"*Winnetou* is film here," Strumbić said as they passed a narrow green valley in between two ranges of high rock.

"Winnie what?" Rebecca asked.

"*Winnetou*. Film from book. Is made here."

"Uh-huh," she said, unconvinced.

"Is about famous Indian Winnetou and cowboy friend Old Shatterhand. Cowboy and Indians, you know."

"I know cowboys and Indians, but I've never heard of either of those people."

Strumbić was dumbfounded. Everybody had heard of *Winnetou*. Even if they hadn't read the books, they'd seen the films. They were famous.

"German movies made with the Yugoslavs," della Torre said, remembering something Anzulović must have told him once. "They're based on books by Karl May. May was a German who wrote a bunch of adventures about exotic places. Had a hell of an imagination. I don't think he ever left Germany, and most of what he wrote was from a prison cell."

"A bad guy, was he?" Rebecca asked.

"I think it was debtor's prison. Anyway, he's famous in Germany and here. And everybody in Germany and Yugoslavia loves cowboys and Indians. Mostly because of him, I think. He was Hitler's favourite writer. "

"German and Yugoslav cowboys and Indians?" She laughed.

To Strumbić, nothing hitherto had emphasized Rebecca's strangeness quite as much as the fact that she didn't know about *Winnetou*. Sure, it was odd finding a woman who could handle a rifle like she did. But not to have heard of *Winnetou*? He'd once arrested a middle-aged farmer for killing his father with a potato. Shoved it raw down the old man's throat because he'd turned the television off during a broadcast of one of the *Winnetou* films.

They were driving between a cornfield on one side and a vineyard on the other, and approaching a wooded hillside crowned with bare white rock, when the front of the car erupted. It sounded like they'd hit a dog or burst a tire. Rebecca swerved instinctively and slammed her full weight on the brake, not even coming to a full stop before throwing the Merc into reverse. Another thud. The car bellowed as she opened the throttle fully, clouds of dust rising in front of them, obscuring the road.

"What the fuck?" della Torre said, pinned to his seatbelt by the backwards acceleration.

"Is not tire?" Strumbić shouted over the car's roar.

Another thud, and steam burst out of the hood and the car stopped dead.

"Out. Out fast. Get into the corn. Grab the bags," Rebecca yelled.

They were scrambling out of their seats when a round hole punched through the windshield a little to the right of centre. Another hole appeared, lower and to the right. Della Torre felt air on the back of his neck, and from the corner of his eye he saw that the back windshield had disappeared. They spilled onto the tarmac, crouching behind the false protection of the open car doors, della Torre managing to grab one of the hard cases and the canvas bag. He'd left the other case in the back seat. There was no sign of Rebecca.

"Fucking Gringo. Why is it that whenever I'm with you, somebody ends up shooting at me?" Strumbić said as they threw themselves into the cornfield.

"Rebecca?" della Torre called.

"I'm here," she replied from the vineyard on the other side of the road.

"Can you see where they are?" della Torre asked.

"The trees in front, where the road curves," Rebecca called back.

Della Torre waddled in a squat back to the edge of the cornfield, where he could see down the road and smell the dripping petrol and hot oil pouring out of the car. Rebecca was opposite him, crouching between two rows of vines across the line of fire.

"Not a very good shot, is he?" She spoke to him across the asphalt killing zone, her voice even, controlled.

"Gives us hope," della Torre called back in a hoarse croak, trying to make himself heard without calling attention to himself.

Steam boiled furiously from the Merc's punctured radiator, spreading a little cloud over its dented hood. As the other two talked, Strumbić crawled, head down, deeper into the corn. Now and again a metallic thud hit the car or the sound of rending plants resounded through the cornfield, causing both men to flinch.

"Have you got the rifle?" she called over to them.

Della Torre crept back to the case, which Strumbić had dragged with him, and opened it.

"No. I've got the machine gun and the other Beretta," della Torre said.

"Can you load up and give them a spray or two so I can get to the car?" Rebecca asked.

"Don't be crazy."

"Just do it."

Della Torre slid a long, curved magazine into the Heckler & Koch and handed it to Strumbić, taking the Beretta for himself.

"On three," he called to her. "One. Two—"

Strumbić was up before della Torre finished counting, his arm raised, pumping bullets in the general direction of the woods. Della Torre did the same. A cob of corn exploded somewhere beside della Torre's head; he couldn't be sure whether it had been hit by a bullet from the woods or Strumbić's wild firing.

"I ever mention I don't like being shot at?" della Torre said, wiping flecks of green and yellow pulp off his face.

"Okay, I got it," she shouted. "Throw me a box of bullets from the canvas bag. Wrap it up in plastic so they don't end up scattering everywhere. They're the big ones."

Della Torre found them, the biggest calibre in the bag. The square box was heavy and he squat-ran back to the edge of the cornfield, where he could see Rebecca crouching on the other side. With a heave, he got the box over to her just as a bullet ploughed a furrow in the old tarmac in front of him.

"What you think? Wait until they tired and they look for us?" Strumbić asked.

Rebecca ignored them as she assembled the rifle and scope. "Julius, you stay there and fire the occasional round into the woods just to keep them occupied. Marko and I are going in a bit closer."

Della Torre wasn't feeling enthusiastic about her plan. But neither was Strumbić.

"That's great. I get to stay here for some crazy shooter to use as target practice," Strumbić complained in Croat, but he let off a quick buzz-saw burst of bullets in the direction of the woods.

"Julius, if you don't mind, see if you can avoid hitting me in the back. At least not until you intend to," della Torre said.

"Gringo, if I want to shoot you, first I'll shoot off your dick, and only then will I turn you around and shoot you in the back."

"Okay. So if I lose my dick, I'll know it wasn't an accident."

"Julius, shoot high so you don't hit us," Rebecca shouted from the vineyard. "I don't want to be on the wrong end of that spray gun. Marko, only fire when you know it's them. All right. Let's go."

Both della Torre and Rebecca moved away from the dead Mercedes and each other—he, deeper into the corn rows, while she walked along the vines. He could hear the angry bark of a powerful rifle and the tall cornstalks ripple and shred as though lashed by a metal-tipped bullwhip.

Now and again he heard the woodpecker hammer of Strumbić's machine gun—three, four sudden bursts, and then silence.

Once he'd got far enough away from the car, a good fifty metres from the road, della Torre hazarded a look through the plants' tasselled tops. At a quick estimate, he figured three hundred metres separated him and the shooter. He continued his reluctant walk towards the wood, stooped and cautious as he moved through the corn, trying not to ripple the stalks for fear of alerting the gunman. But the shooter seemed to be concentrating on Strumbić, who was returning fire from farther back in the cornfield.

The road ran between him and Rebecca, straight towards the hill, before curving sharply to the left on Rebecca's side, following the contour of the land. Eventually she'd have to leave herself exposed if she wanted to cross into the wood. Not that it would be much easier for della Torre. The cornfield ended about twenty metres before the wood; in between was a strip of weeds and piles of white stone shifted from the field by generations of farmers.

He was already near the edge of the cornfield. Farther to the right was a mown meadow. If he tried crossing there, the shooter would have a clear view of him. Worse still, there seemed to be heavy brambles in that direction, and bushes with long, ugly thorns. He'd have to take his chances here.

The heavy rifle hidden in the wood barked regularly. From the delay between shots, della Torre guessed it was bolt-action. From the damage the Merc had sustained and the raw, throaty sound the gun made, he figured it was around .50 calibre.

He wondered whether this was a Serb ambush. But why hadn't they given the Hilux the same treatment?

For a long few minutes he squatted at the edge of the cornfield, building up the courage to launch himself into the woods. He breathed deeply and steadily, willing his heart to beat less frantically. He held the Beretta hip-high, gripping two spare magazines in his other hand.

Strumbić was still shooting from somewhere behind him.

Ahead and a little to the right was the gunman. Sweat plastered della Torre's cotton shirt to his skin. He wished he was wearing his sunglasses or a hat. The sun was relentlessly bright and high.

The gunman fired three or four rounds a minute, sometimes in rapid succession and sometimes as if he was waiting. Strumbić fired mostly during those quiet periods. Was the shooter alone? No other gun was heard, but that might not mean much. If he wasn't alone, how many of them were there? What other weapons did they have? Was the shooter there just as a distraction while his companions stalked them, much as della Torre and Rebecca were trying to do in turn?

He paused to listen. Silence. And then the rifle's bark.

He ran. Hard, fast, and low, stumbling over the rocks of the nettle-choked strip of no-man's land. He caught a glimpse in the distance, where the road curved away from him, of a black truck. The Hilux.

A SMALL-GAUGE AUTOMATIC opened fire from the woods. Until then, there'd only been evidence of the big rifle. It meant they'd spotted him.

He heard an angry buzz of bullets whipping through the corn behind him. The run was the longest twenty metres of his life.

Strumbić's machine gun coughed out its reply. Della Torre didn't envy him. The corn offered decent cover, but no protection. Strumbić would have been unlucky to catch a bullet from the big rifle, but it was going to be harder to hide from a spray of automatic fire. The light-calibre gun might not be as accurate over that distance, but those scattered bullets could wound or kill just as effectively.

Then again, della Torre wasn't too happy about his own circumstances either.

Thorny shrubs tore at him before he made it to the safety of a big oak. He wished he had more firepower than the Beretta. He didn't really know what he ought to be doing. He didn't want to get too close to the shooters, not least because he didn't want to risk being hit by Strumbić's occasional wild salvo. But if he could somehow flank them, he might be able to draw a bead on one of them.

The big gun kept up its regular delivery, always aimed towards Strumbić. The smaller automatic ripped through the foliage, but nothing much seemed to be coming his way. As far as he could tell, all the noise was coming from the same direction. The shooters were sticking together. Whoever had followed them from Zagreb to the wilds of the Dalmatian hinterland seemed to be amateurs at this game.

During a brief break in the firing, della Torre thought he heard a familiar metallic clank in the distance, though he couldn't be sure. He listened for it again, but it was pointless— Strumbić and the rifleman had gone back to trading volleys.

He edged deeper into the woods, where there were fewer low shrubs. The big beeches and chestnuts kept the ground clear, giving him passage. He noticed plenty of ankle-high blueberry bushes and could smell the forest mushrooms amid the decomposing leaf litter. His arms stung with tiny rips from the thorn shrubs he'd charged through. They'd pricked through his trousers as well. He could feel the heat of the afternoon even in the shade of the trees. At a guess, he figured he was within a hundred metres of the shooters. There was still no sign of them separating.

He scrambled uphill, hugging the profile of the landscape, careful of twigs and loose stones, hoping to make his approach from behind and to the side. He turned towards the sound of the rifle once he got about forty metres into the woods.

He used every skill he could remember from the commandos to move silently, but each one of his steps filled his ears with a dry explosion, a starburst of noise.

He was wary of the smooth rock that frequently broke the surface of the earth here. He moved patiently. High overhead he heard the tearing of leaves and the thud of bullets against branches. Strumbić's fire.

And then, there they were. At first he could only hear them; they were dressed in camouflage, including their baseball caps.

"Kill him yet?"

"He's still firing, isn't he?"

"Well, give me a go, then."

"You had your go. You barely hit the car."

"Think they're all there?"

"Course not. There's the one who made it to the trees."

"I told you to let them get closer before you started shooting."

"I got it, didn't I?"

"You got the car, dimwit. I didn't see you hit anyone."

"Think we hit the redhead?"

"Must have done."

"Shame."

"There's the one in the cornfield still shooting and the one in the woods."

"What do you think he's doing in the woods?"

"Taking a piss. How the hell do I know?"

"Think he's going to try to get to us?"

"With what?"

"He had a gun."

"I didn't see a gun. Had a good sight of him and he didn't have a gun. Nothing serious, anyway."

"If you had such a good sight of him, why didn't you get him?"

"'Cause my fucking machine gun jammed."

"It didn't jam, you just forgot to take the safety off."

"Same fucking thing."

"That's not a jam."

"Will you shut up? I can't think to shoot straight."

One had a deep voice. The other's was as high as a woman's. They both had lugubrious Bosnian accents.

Bosnians...

Why was it always Bosnians?

Della Torre finally sighted on them, but he did not have a clear enough line to be sure of hitting them with a pistol at that distance. There was a big fallen tree in the way, which they were using as cover. He estimated he was about sixty metres away. Too far to be reliable with an unfamiliar handgun and precious little practice.

He'd have to get to within thirty metres before risking a shot. He didn't want to miss. Given the damage it had done to the Mercedes, the rifle could probably shoot through trees. He kept low, moving smoothly.

He was close, almost close enough to be sure of hitting them, when he slipped. He was on slightly higher ground and was heading down when the leaf litter fooled him. It hid one of those flat, smooth white rocks. His leg shot out from under him, dropping him on his back as if he'd stepped on ice wearing hobnailed shoes. He tried to catch himself with his weak left arm but it buckled under him, and all he managed to do was lose the spare magazines he'd been holding, hammering his right elbow in the process. He'd switched the safety off and the impact fired the Beretta, only just missing his own foot.

The Bosnians reacted immediately. The one closest to della Torre turned his machine gun on him, but he aimed too low. The spew of bullets took chunks off the trunk of the mighty fallen oak, sending bits of bark flying.

Della Torre scrambled backwards, desperately trying to get behind a nearby tree, firing the Beretta more in an effort to distract them than out of any hope of hitting anything.

Then he saw the rifleman shift the big gun in his direction. It was long and ugly with its disproportionate telescopic sight. At that distance, the shooter couldn't miss. Della Torre, despite moving all the while, was mesmerized. The rifleman's preparatory sequence singed itself into his mind. Bolt pulled back. Released. Hand down towards the trigger. Rifle up, level with the man's ribs, its bipod legs spread open, hanging in the air. The cavernous barrel aligned with the stock, marking an invisible line straight to della Torre's midriff.

The other Bosnian, the one with the submachine gun, had stopped to change magazines; della Torre could hear the click as it went in.

The rifleman wore aviator sunglasses and a baseball cap backwards. But what struck della Torre was the man's satisfied grin. Instinctively, della Torre braced his muscles against the coming impact of the gunshot. He winced in anticipation, though he suspected he wouldn't feel much for long.

But the muzzle flash never came. Instead, the shooter's forehead bloomed open like a red and white rose and then disgorged a pale blue-grey mass. The shooter fell forward, smashing face-first into the fallen tree with the hollow sound of a dropped watermelon. And then he disappeared from della Torre's sight.

The other Bosnian dropped the submachine gun and crouched down to his fallen comrade. "Elvis. Elvis. Shit, holy mother of God and Mohammed's angels."

Then the submachine-gunner, small and thin, popped up from under the tree trunk and bolted, full of panic and noise, heading straight at della Torre.

"Gringo." It was Rebecca, from somewhere in the trees. "Get him. Go."

But the man shot past della Torre before he could aim the Beretta.

Della Torre got up, the pain of his fall deadened by adrenaline, and chased after the Bosnian through the undergrowth. The Bosnian was small and skinny and fast, quickly pulling away from della Torre, who gulped air into his tobacco-dulled lungs, his thighs aching as he climbed the hill.

The ground underneath became rougher and harder, and the trees ended in a low, rough cliff of white stone. The shooter had started to climb but hadn't gotten far. Della Torre couldn't have asked for a clearer target. The sun was reflecting on the stone around the man so that he looked nothing more than an insect on white paper. He'd lost his hat, and his brown hair was almost as long as a girl's. He struggled to find handholds, clawing the stone in desperation. He was unarmed.

Della Torre chambered a bullet, raised the Beretta, and took a shooting stance, as he'd been taught all those years ago. With his thumb he ensured the safety was off.

"Halt," he called out.

The Bosnian kept trying to climb but turned to look down at della Torre. It wasn't a man he was chasing. It was a boy. He had a little fuzz on his top lip, and eyes like a deer's, full of fear, self-pity, horror.

"Halt," della Torre shouted again. But the boy continued to scramble like a drowning man struggling for air.

Della Torre fired. Once. Twice. Scoring the stone above the boy's head.

"I said halt."

The boy finally stopped. He was shaking, tears streaking his face.

Della Torre stared at him. He couldn't have been more than fifteen or sixteen. "Why were you shooting at us?"

"I don't know." The boy spoke in that drawling, undulating accent of the deep Bosnian valleys.

"Tell me now or I'll shoot you off that rock."

"I don't know," came the panicked voice, high-pitched with fear. "Elvis got the job. He said we were after a cop. Dad just drove. I wasn't shooting, I swear. I was just there to hand them the ammunition. I swear I wasn't shooting. Ask Dad, he's at the car. Ask him."

"What cop? Who paid Elvis?"

"I don't know. I don't know."

"Were you in Zagreb waiting for us?"

"Yes, but I don't know anything."

"Whose car was it?"

"I don't know, Dad got it. Dad gets cars. Please don't shoot me. Please don't shoot me."

He didn't doubt that the boy knew nothing.

Maybe Elvis knew something. Had known something. But he'd looked pretty dead when della Torre saw him last.

Somebody'd paid the Bosnians to follow them and to shoot them. They'd even fixed them up with a nice car.

A gloom settled on della Torre. What to do with the boy?

They couldn't take him to the police station back in Gospić. It'd be difficult to cover up the gunfight, and once it got out that an American woman had been involved, he knew the pandemonium it would cause.

"What's the name of the cop you're after?" della Torre asked again. "Who's the cop? Why did you want to shoot him?"

"I don't know." The boy was frightened, tearful. "Elvis's cousins paid him because the cop owed them money and caused problems. Dad knows them. Ask him. He'll tell you. He'll tell you who they are."

"Get down here," della Torre said. "Quick, if you want to live."

The boy scrambled down. He was even more pitiable on close inspection. His camouflage gear hung loosely on his thin frame; his pimpled face was blotchy with tears.

"Boy, I'll tell you this once, and then I'm not responsible for you. You run in that direction; follow the cliff, don't try to go up it. When you find a track, follow it to a village. Tell them what you like, but don't tell them about this."

"What about Dad?"

"Forget about Dad. Dad's going to jail," della Torre lied. "You find a bus to take you to Zadar and you call your people to fetch you. You understand?"

The boy nodded, though he might just have been trembling.

"You got money?"

The boy shook his head.

Della Torre pulled a couple of notes out of his wallet and handed them over.

"You tell nobody nothing, understand? Anybody asks, you don't know, because that's the truth. Go. I'm going to fire a couple of shots after you. Don't stop and don't turn around, because if you do, boy, you're dead."

The boy nodded. And then he ran, sobbing, while Della Torre fired twice into the trees.

23

**H**E WAS CLOSE enough to touch the rifle's muzzle. He hadn't been as cautious as he should have been. The shooting had stopped and the woods were quiet, dappled pale green with spots of sunlight. Insects, like motes of dust, danced in the light. He'd stepped between two trees only to see death's small round eye staring at him.

Rebecca lowered the gun before he had a chance to react.

"You should be more careful when going out for a stroll in the woods. I heard the shots and came to see if it was you or him," she said.

"I was the one doing the shooting."

"So you couldn't run him down?" she laughed.

Della Torre shrugged noncommittally. "I smoke too much."

"It'll kill you."

"So they say. Thanks for getting the shooter."

"It was a snatched shot. You were lucky I got him the first time. Quite something, a Krönlein shot. I'd only ever heard about them," she said.

"A what?"

"Krönlein. A high-velocity bullet at close range. Blows the top of the head right open and pops the brain out in one whole piece. They're rare."

"Oh," he said, remembering the instant of the man's demise. He hadn't even had time to register surprise. "His name was Elvis."

"Was it?"

"That's what the boy called him," he said. "I mean, when they were talking and just before he was about to shoot me."

"Did he?" Rebecca smiled. "Well, I guess there's no longer any doubt that Elvis is well and truly dead."

Della Torre couldn't share the joke.

"Were there any others?" he asked, pushing his thoughts away from the bloody image.

"There's the one by the Hilux. He's not going anywhere fast. I don't think there's anyone else, but I'll take a look around. Why don't you go tell Julius that he can put the gun away."

Della Torre nodded, though he wasn't feeling very hopeful about catching Strumbić's attention without getting shot.

He edged gingerly to the edge of the wood by the road, sheltering behind a tree.

"Julius," he shouted. No response. "Julius."

"Gringo?" came the faint reply.

"Don't shoot. Do not shoot. Understand?"

"Yes."

He made his way around the tree and into the light. Immediately he heard the rip of Strumbić's machine gun.

"Stop shooting," he yelled, his face pressed against gravel, tasting the dusty road. He shouted until he thought he'd stripped his throat raw.

From across the cornfield he heard Strumbić laugh hard and loud. And then, just as suddenly, he stopped.

Della Torre got up warily, ready to duck again, but Strumbić was quiet. He ran down the road in a semi-crouch, ready to dive onto the verge at any moment, his heart beating hard from the effort. He stopped at the still-smoking Mercedes, furious, gripping the Beretta hard, sore with temptation to fire it into the corn.

"What the fuck were you doing, Julius?" he said.

Strumbić remained crouched at the edge of the cornfield. "Sorry, didn't realize it was you."

"The fuck you didn't. Liar," della Torre said. "Come on. Get out of there. The shooter's dead and we don't have to worry about the others."

"Can't."

"What do you mean you can't?"

"Do me a favour, Gringo. Grab my bag out from the trunk and throw it over to me. And a bottle of water from the car."

"Why don't you just come and get them yourself?" Della Torre wasn't having any of Strumbić's games.

"Because I shat myself and I'd like to freshen up, if you don't mind."

"You what?"

"You heard me."

Della Torre hooted. It came as a blessed relief after the terror of those minutes in the woods. "You got so scared that you shat yourself?"

"No. It only just happened. I was laughing so hard at you eating asphalt that, I don't know, must have been the fucking lunch in Gospić, poisoning bastards."

Della Torre couldn't stop laughing.

"Okay, so it's funny," Strumbić allowed. "I thought I just needed to fart."

Della Torre did as Strumbić asked, passing him the chamois cloth from the boot as well.

"I would be much obliged if you didn't make this general knowledge," Strumbić said.

"What's it worth to you?"

"It's worth me not murdering you in your sleep. And I'll let you off the hook for those three cartons of Luckys you stole off me in the spring."

"And your leather jacket?"

"I got that back. That and the Beemer. It's just the money you owe me. But we won't talk about that now."

Della Torre gave Strumbić some privacy to clean himself up and change. Once Strumbić was decent again, they strolled to the Hilux, kicking up white dust along the broken asphalt and gravel road.

"So what happened?" Strumbić asked.

"Shooter got shot."

"You?"

"No. Rebecca."

"Any others?"

"Some guy by the Hilux I haven't seen yet, and a boy."

"Dead?"

"Not the boy."

"You shoot the guy by the Hilux?"

"No."

"But you let the boy go."

"Good guess."

Strumbić tapped his nose. "Never had you down for a killer. The redhead, on the other hand...Seems she doesn't just eat men."

Della Torre nodded. He'd met plenty of killers before, but never one like Rebecca.

There was a body slumped in the driver's seat of the Hilux, head hanging out the window and black blood pooling on the dusty white ground.

Strumbić was the first to see it. "Shit. He moved."

They ran, closing the distance fast. They pulled the man out of the car and lay him flat on the ground. He'd been shot in the head. The bullet had mashed his left cheek, destroying his eye and crushing part of the forehead, but the man was still breathing. They couldn't tell if he was conscious, though he might have been talking. He was making a grumbling, moaning sound. It had a rhythm to it. Maybe he was praying. He was almost blue, he was so pale—where he wasn't caked with blood.

"Can you hear us?" della Torre asked.

The man didn't respond. Just kept making that small, regular moan.

"He's not long for it," said Strumbić.

"Unless we get him to a hospital."

They heard a rustling in the wood. Both men crouched down behind the Hilux, guns at the ready.

"It's just me," Rebecca called.

"This one here's still alive," della Torre shouted back to her.

She rushed over to them. "He saying anything?"

"No."

"Nothing?"

"I don't think so. Nothing I can understand. We need to get him to a hospital, fast. Otherwise he isn't going to make it."

She stood over them, silently surveying the man on the ground.

"He's not going to make it," Rebecca said with finality.

"You don't know. You've made a mess of his head, but he's breathing and the bleeding seems to have slowed. If he's lasted till now..." Della Torre, knee on the ground next to the man, turned to Strumbić. "How long to Zadar, do you think?"

"Hour. Drive fast, maybe less."

"We'll have to take him back to Gospić, then. They have a country hospital there."

"No, he's not going to make it. Can he talk now? Can we get something out of him?" Rebecca asked.

"I don't think so. Medical attention and a month in hospital, and we might start getting some sense out of him. But not in the state he's in now."

"I'm afraid he's not going to a hospital."

Della Torre stood to confront her, but she just smiled, pulled out the Beretta that she'd tucked into the back of her shorts, the one from the car, under the driver's seat, and operated the slide so that he could hear a bullet click into place. She bent down and shot the man through his open mouth. The man jerked, and fresh scarlet blood spread from under his head into the white dust.

"He didn't make it."

Both della Torre and Strumbić stood still, shocked at the execution. For a moment della Torre's ears buzzed and he felt oddly light-headed, but he willed himself not to faint. And then he felt his back pocket to make sure his passport was there. His secret American passport, which he always travelled with, keeping it like a talisman against...against what, exactly? Against becoming an unidentified, abandoned corpse? At least the Americans always took an interest in their citizens. Especially dead ones in foreign countries.

"Let's get the one from the woods," Rebecca said.

She left her rifle in the Hilux and led the men back to where the shooter had been. Della Torre and Strumbić stumbled in her wake.

Rebecca carried the shooter's equipment as well as his rifle and the machine gun back to the truck, while della Torre and Strumbić dragged the corpse by its feet, looking away from the mangled head, which was churning the dry leaves into a painted trail of blood and soil. They left the brain where it was.

When they had the two corpses lined up on the side of the road, they went through the vehicle. There were clothes in a couple of holdalls in the back of the Hilux, along with a handgun and boxes of ammunition. A bag of snack food was in the back seat: boxes of pretzel sticks, a loaf of bread, half a salami, and a block of cheese, along with a couple of boxes of biscuits. Strumbić found an unlabelled three-quarters-full glass bottle in the front.

"Slivovitz," he said, having unscrewed the lid and sniffed. "Want some?"

Della Torre shook his head. Strumbić took a long pull from the bottle.

They wiped the blood off the front seat with one of the Bosnians' shirts soaked with slivovitz, but otherwise the truck had been spared damage. Della Torre puzzled over the bullet's exit path and then realized what Rebecca had done. She'd shot him through the open window. He'd been sitting on the other side of the truck. The impact of the bullet had pushed the man's head out of the driver's-side window so that almost none of his blood, other than a bit of fine spray from the initial wound, stained the interior. It left the truck all but unmarked. Was that intentional?

Whether it was or not, they needed another vehicle after the Merc's demise. It looked like the Hilux would have to do.

The keys were in the ignition.

"Guess they correctly figured we'd pulled off somewhere earlier, and found themselves a nice ambush spot," Rebecca said. She kicked the ground, raising a little cloud of white. "Must have been looking for our dust."

She and Strumbić went through the men's pockets. The driver's licences confirmed they were from Bosnia, from the hills around Bihać, an hour's drive northeast. Between them, they had a couple of hundred Deutschmarks and a fair stack of dinars. There were some photographs of women and babies and various slips of paper, stamps, and business cards. Nothing terribly meaningful. Elvis's name really was Elvis. He'd been in his late twenties. The driver had been pushing forty.

"So what we do now?" Strumbić asked.

"Now we load them into the back of the Hilux and take them back to the Merc. See if you can find something to cover the floor so that they don't make a mess of the truck."

There were a couple of sleeping bags, which della Torre and Strumbić spread out over the truck bed. They shifted a couple of army surplus duffel bags to the side and lifted the men in, heads hanging out the door, as Rebecca wanted.

Strumbić looked over the sniper rifle that had destroyed the Merc and against which he'd been duelling. It was a heavy, brutal weapon. Della Torre had been right: .50-calibre bolt action with an attached duopod and a big scope.

"Some cannon," Strumbić said. "Thank fucking god they didn't know how to use it, or right now I'd be spread over three fields. Thank god it wasn't Rebecca pulling the trigger."

"We'll drive these fellows to the Merc and give them a Viking funeral," Rebecca said.

They all climbed into the Hilux, Rebecca taking the wheel. She drove carefully so that the bodies wouldn't roll out.

When they got to the shot-up Merc, they shifted the corpses into the seats. It was surprisingly hard to fold them to fit, especially the driver. Harder still doing it without making a bloody mess of themselves. But they managed, and then shoved in the Bosnians' possessions and wallets after della Torre wrote out their details in the small black notebook he always carried. Strumbić held on to the Bosnians' Deutschmarks. The massive .50-calibre rifle they wedged into the Merc's trunk.

They loaded the Hilux with their own bags. Strumbić suggested keeping the Bosnians' food, but both della Torre and Rebecca vetoed him.

The Merc looked forlorn, the men awkwardly slumped in its interior. Rebecca borrowed Strumbić's cigarette lighter and damped the rag della Torre had used to wipe the blood off the Hilux with another splash of slivovitz. Having stuffed it into the carburettor and fixed down the accelerator on the car, she lit the rag. They drove off just as the fire was building in the engine. They were around the bend before they heard the first small explosion. The second and its fireball followed soon after, releasing another billowing black plume into the clear blue sky.

Della Torre knew it wouldn't take much investigation to figure out the Bosnians hadn't been killed in the car, even after this inferno. But he doubted the police would make the effort. They'd stick to their first impressions. Separatist Serb gangsters killed some people foolish enough to be driving through this no man's land. UDBA types who'd bullied their way through Gospić earlier in the day. The woman with them? Must have disappeared. Slovene whore, probably.

As long as the boy got through to Bihać, there'd be no reason for the cops to challenge their prejudices. Even if they found him, they'd be inclined to put the blame on the Serbs, probably attributing it to in-fighting.

Would the boy get back? Della Torre was hopeful. He'd got away and Bihać wasn't far. He'd have to cross Serb lines to get there, but these Bosnians from the hill country learned to live in the woods from a young age. He'd manage, especially with some money in his pocket.

"You know much about car," Strumbić said to Rebecca, having put on his seat belt without needing a reminder.

"Honey," Rebecca said, looking ahead, alert, "there's not a lot I don't know about cars. Or guns...Or one or two other things."

They didn't talk. They drove with the windows open and the air conditioner running, the thick afternoon air cut by a steady cool blast, mitigating the abattoir smells of death, home-brewed slivovitz, other men's sweat and fear that clung to the truck. They didn't pass another car until they got to the main road, and even there, traffic was impossibly light for a summer's day. Croatian cops were rerouting traffic at both ends. It was hard to believe this had once been — should still have been — Dalmatia's main north–south road. The Serb rebels had put a ligature on Croatia, hoping the infant republic would die away.

It wasn't long before they were deep into the last chain of mountains in the Velebit range. Stark, sharp high rocks like bleached bone erupted from the dense forest, so that the vista was reduced to a primitive painting of blue, green, and white.

They crossed high over the watershed. The forest was replaced by scrub and a dry, stony landscape as they descended the other side of the mountains. The air was redolent of lavender and thyme and the thick resin smell of summer pine.

Another half-hour and they were within sight of Zadar's walls. They had planned to stop for the night farther south, but Rebecca drove straight towards the ancient port city, with both men's unspoken consent. It was still high afternoon. Della Torre could trace in his mind the whole of the shooting. It felt as if it had lasted for days, and yet, he realized, from the first shot to the funeral pyre, it couldn't have taken more than three-quarters of an hour.

All he wanted now was to shower. Cleanse the horror of the afternoon off his skin. His lawyer's mind spun. He hadn't been complicit in the execution of the older man. The man had anyway been fatally wounded and the final shot had no significance. There was a risk in keeping him alive because . . . But his mental gears kept slipping back to Anzulović's command. That he keep a tally of corpses so one day there could be a reckoning. In the kingdom of man, not just of heaven.

.   .   .

Rebecca pulled the car into a parking spot under a spreading palm tree in Zadar's old town, one of a row separating the road from the long stretch of the seaside promenade.

They carried their bags and Rebecca's hard cases to a tall, Italianate hotel. Strumbić sorted out the rooms. One with a balcony for Rebecca, an adjoining twin for him and della Torre, all on the American woman's credit card.

They showered, changed, and met at the hotel terrace. Rebecca's eyes were still shiny and bright, though della Torre could see the tiredness in their corners. The adrenaline had long run out, but the experience of death remained sharp.

"A toast to Rebecca. She is great hunter. *Živeli*," Strumbić said, raising his second glass.

Della Torre lifted his half-heartedly. He knew he'd have had a hole in him big enough to put beer bottles through were it not for Rebecca's reflexes and instinct. And yet she horrified him. Maybe because he knew Yugoslavia was at the dawn of an era of Rebeccas, a time when it wouldn't be unusual even for women to kill in cold blood.

They drank and then ordered food.

"Anybody have any ideas why those fellows wanted to shoot us?" Rebecca asked. They'd talked a little about it in the truck. Speculated. But the way she asked, she seemed to know they were hiding something from her.

Della Torre didn't say anything. Rebecca kept her eyes on him. Strumbić shrugged.

Della Torre hadn't told them what the boy had said, that the Bosnians had been after a cop. Strumbić? Or him?

"Think maybe somebody doesn't want us to go to Dubrovnik?" she asked.

Again, no answer.

He was thinking of the other Bosnians, the ones who'd tried to kill him and Strumbić in the spring, whom he'd run from and who'd tracked him down in London. He'd call Anzulović later, give him the names of these dead Bosnians, find out whether they had anything to do with the first ones.

The sun flattened itself against the horizon, throwing a sparkling blade across the Adriatic so that they had to turn their eyes from its orange light.

Strong coffees were followed by stronger drink. Eventually the waitress left the bottle of slivovitz at their table.

"*Živeli*," Strumbić said, thick-tongued, raising his glass.

Della Torre flagged, not quite keeping pace. For a while, he'd kept his eye on Rebecca, seeing whether she'd play the same trick she had at the Esplanade, of only touching the liquor to her lips. But she was drinking. She dropped the Bosnians and took up smiling broadly at Strumbić, encouraging his bold, wolfish looks as they drank to each other. And then it was as though della Torre wasn't even there.

A folk combo—fiddle, three tambours, guitar, and accordion—dressed in the traditional national costume, pitched up on the waterfront promenade, playing and singing for themselves, it seemed.

"Sounds like something halfway between 'Cielito Lindo' and 'Zorba,'" said Rebecca.

"Dance?" Strumbić said, rising unsteadily. He bowed with his hand held open before him in an unintentional parody of a nineteenth-century dandy.

"Dance? I'm not sure I can even stand," Rebecca said, throwing her head back and laughing, but putting her palm into Strumbić's waiting hand.

Della Torre excused himself, though neither of them was listening. His legs threatened to rebel against his upper body, carrying him under protest into the hotel and to the elevator, where he stood, leaning hard against the wall for a long time, trying to remember what floor he was on and what that number looked like.

Somehow he got back to the room without mishap. He threw himself heavily on the bed, only to see that he'd left the door wide open. With Herculean effort, he rose and shut it and lay back down. He wanted to talk to Irena. He knew he should call Anzulović to tell him what had happened, but it was really Irena that he wanted. It took him three attempts before he dialled correctly. The phone rang for a long time, but there was no answer. She couldn't have gone to Vukovar already, could she? She was probably at work. Working the night through. Her absence from his life had become a growing wound. It was his stupidity, his selfishness, his fault.

He fell asleep in his clothes. Sometime in the night he heard

Strumbić come back, stumble around the room, and turn on the bedside lamp. Theatrically hushed conversation went on around him, and then the light went off again. When he went to the toilet in the night, the other bed seemed empty, though della Torre wasn't sure. He woke in the morning to the sound of a small animal in his head banging pipes with a hammer. There was no sign of Strumbić.

Della Torre decided to go for an early-morning swim. He found his swimsuit, borrowed a hotel towel, and walked across the road, under the line of palm trees, to the broad steps that descended to the sea. He swam as hard as he could, parallel to the white stone promenade, until the morning sun warmed him in the water.

When he got back, he saw Rebecca and Strumbić breakfasting on the terrace. Rebecca looked composed—a little tired, but as serene as she'd been on the first day he'd met her. Strumbić was dissolution personified. Pasty except for the rings under his eyes, overweight, cigarette in hand, a man who looked so far beyond redemption there wasn't a map in heaven or hell that could lead him back.

"Good swim?" Rebecca asked.

"Yes," he answered, not knowing how to tell her that it hadn't washed him of his sins but had only made him feel them all the more sharply, through the tiny cuts where his skin had been scored by thorns.

"I'm tempted, but maybe we ought to get going. It's a long drive. We'll share it today," she said. "Though I think Julius is likely to sleep most of the way."

"I'll do some driving," della Torre agreed.

He shuddered to think of travelling at Rebecca's speed on some of the roads farther south, the single lane in each direction with a hard cliff face on one side and a sharp drop into the sea on the other.

But the trip was uneventful. Strumbić snored from the back

seat much of the way. Della Torre and Rebecca alternated every few hours. He insisted on it and she didn't argue. The Hilux was easy to drive; it didn't have quite the Merc's luxury or naked power, but it was fast enough.

They stopped at a roadside place for lunch and took a good break every two hours. The previous day had affected them all. When she drove, they listened to Rebecca's music. Tapes of Michael Jackson and Prince and people he'd never heard of. He'd brought only a single tape of his own, Glenn Gould playing Bach's *Goldberg Variations*. They listened to that twice and then turned off the stereo. The tight, winding road demanded the driver's attention. The hard landscape of scrub and mountain, falling away to the blue-green sea below them, at once mesmerized and sharpened the senses. They didn't talk about the previous day. Or about what they were going to do in Dubrovnik.

They didn't need to. He knew now, without a doubt, that they weren't going there to talk to the Montenegrin. They were going there to kill him.

**F**ROM THE ROAD, high up the steep mountainside, the island of
Šipan appeared like a jade dragon rising out of a sapphire
sea. Signs pointed to Dubrovnik ahead, but on Strumbić's
command they pulled off the road and followed a narrow tarmacked track down the hillside to a village in a cove. Strumbić
pointed out a house on the beach and had Rebecca drive behind
its high wall to a hard standing under a bougainvillea-covered
trellis. The house was owned by an absent fisherman who'd
made the parking spot available for Strumbić's use.

Given the village's tiny size, it was guarded by a surprisingly
substantial concrete harbour wall, with various motor cruis-
ers tied up alongside the breakwater. Strumbić sauntered over
the mole's wide white flagstones to one of the smaller boats
and peeled back its sun-faded blue canvas tarpaulin. The vessel
rocked under his weight as he rolled the cover onto the bottom
of the boat. The engine started at the first attempt. Strumbić
explained that the fisherman kept the launch fuelled up and
tuned. They loaded the boat, and—after Strumbić passed
around life jackets, much to della Torre's surprise and relief—
they set off across the channel.

Šipan's verdant lushness had surprised them after the harsh, stony scrub of the mainland. A ridge of high hills stretched the length of the island, while the green was separated from the sea by a white band of rocky shore.

There were two harbours and two villages at either end of the island, about six kilometres apart. Some houses were scattered between, along with the ruins of dozens of summer palaces from Dubrovnik's Renaissance. These days there remained only a couple of hundred islanders—old people and a handful of fishermen. There wasn't anything for the young. A few people like Strumbić had holiday houses on the island and sometimes tourists came to stay, spending a night or two in rooms let out by the locals. Mostly, though, it was day trippers, and not many of them either. Ferries weren't frequent, and Šipan was just far enough from Dubrovnik, and sufficiently devoid of attractions, that only adventurous travellers bothered to visit, a few young Germans or wealthy Italians on their yachts.

Strumbić's house was about half a kilometre from the southern village. It had been built in the early nineteenth century by a rich sea captain, for his retirement. It looked like a child's drawing, a stretched cube two storeys high, white stone with a red-tiled roof, green shuttered windows, and not much ornamentation. Situated a little way up the hill, it overlooked the sea and had a clear view of the mainland and the islands farther south. Strumbić took the crossing at a gentle speed, sparing them sea spray. When they landed, he tied the boat to a concrete jetty, where he left them waiting while he walked briskly up the hill towards the house. He was back a few minutes later in a beat-up Yugoslav version of a Fiat 500. They piled the luggage into it, and della Torre and Rebecca walked behind it the hundred metres or so to the house.

From Zagreb Strumbić had arranged for a local woman to open up the villa and stock it with necessities from the tiny shop that doubled as a post office, about a kilometre up the road from the village. There were only two telephones on the

island, his and the one at the shop. The government had intended to make the villagers pay to bring the line from the
mainland, but no one could afford it. So except for emergencies
and special occasions, the islanders did without. Strumbić said
he'd thought of undercutting the post office by offering the locals cheaper calls from his phone, but had decided against it.
His privacy was worth more than the money.

Della Torre took his bag and one of Rebecca's cases into the
cool interior of the house. It had a cantilevered stone staircase,
and the floor's black and white marble tiles formed the pattern
of a compass rose, cracked and worn with age. The high ceiling
was crossed with heavy oak beams and plastered in between.
Della Torre stepped into the sitting room to the right of the
hall. The kitchen and dining room were on the other side. Two
big windows offered a splendid view of the sea to the south,
and two sets of French doors opened onto a cobbled courtyard
in the back, where he could see a pair of old lemon trees in
broad stone planters that had once been wellheads. The room
was furnished simply, with wooden benches covered in big, lin-
en-covered cushions. On one wall was a large speckled mirror
in an ornate rococo frame, and on another a large nineteenth-
century painting of the Battle of Lepanto.

The elegance of the decor astonished him. There was
plenty boorish about Strumbić. He was crude and vulgar with
women. His education was truncated and his tastes narrow. He
only ever seemed to read the cheap pocket paperback graphic
novels sold from kiosks. The films he watched were shoot-'em-
ups, westerns, war, or crime. He was contemptuous of artists
and writers, and his dress sense was no better than that of a
typical Yugoslav functionary.

And yet...he was smart. One of the cleverest people della
Torre knew, though his brains were fully devoted to corruption. He was tone deaf to classical music but had a resonant,
melodious voice when he sang folk songs late at night in bars.

He'd long gone to fat but could dance a waltz or a polka better than a boy half his weight and age.

Most of all, he had exquisite taste in real estate. His marital flat in Zagreb was grand and elegant. The garret in which he put up his current mistress was charming. He'd designed his country weekend retreat near Samobor himself. The apartment in London was a cool, expensive space. Even so, none of them matched this villa.

For some reason a fat, well-thumbed coffee-table book sitting on a waist-high stand caught della Torre's eye. He flipped through it. It opened onto a creased page with a photo spread that showed a similar floor to the one in Strumbić's entrance hall.

"Bought the place as a ruin. Cheap until I started doing it up," Strumbić said wryly, as he stepped into the room. "You get some people on the island who can do things, but if you want craftsmen, you need to get them from the mainland. Materials too. It's a pain shipping stuff by fisherman's boat, let me tell you. Then there's the fittings. What you get in this country is crap. Had to bring them in from France and Germany, tiles from northern Italy." He shook his head at the effort.

"But it doesn't look done up. I mean it's lovely, but it doesn't look brand new," della Torre said, puzzled.

"Made it all the more expensive."

"I guess you had some clever people do some good copies."

"Copies?"

"I mean from this book. Your floor looks like an exact replica of one of the pages."

"What do you mean replica? That is my floor."

"Your house is in the book?"

"Don't be stupid. You think I'd let somebody photograph the inside of my house and put it in a book?" Strumbić looked appalled. "So that some wise guy can say, 'I want that floor,' and strip it out? Not on your life."

Della Torre looked at Strumbić, stunned, only slowly comprehending what he was hearing. "You stole somebody's floor?"

"I bought it. Somebody else stole it."

"You saw the floor in the book and you had somebody steal it?" della Torre asked again, a string of questions lining up in his head.

"Sure. Nice floor, eh?"

"You used an interior design book as a catalogue? You stole somebody's floor?"

"So you keep saying," Strumbić said in irritation. "Don't get too worked up about it. They probably stole it from somebody else in the first place."

Della Torre's eyes opened in wonder. "What else did you steal?" he asked, following Strumbić back into the hall.

Strumbić ran his hand up a delicately wrought cast-iron upright on the banister.

"You stole the banister?"

"Only because it was attached to the stairs. Two for one, you might say."

Della Torre shook his head at the scale of Strumbić's larceny. There, for one, was a man who dreamed big.

They walked into the back courtyard, where they sat at a shaded marble table.

"What does Mrs. Strumbić think of the villa?"

"Mrs. Strumbić won't get on a boat. Why do you think I bought a place on an island? I'd have bought something in the centre of Dubrovnik otherwise," he said, taking a drag of a cigarette. "It's nice here, but it's not perfect. You want a woman under the age of seventy, you got to bring her yourself. And even though we're isolated, people tend to know your business. As of twenty minutes ago, not a person on the island doesn't know I'm here with two guests, one of them a redhead with nice tits. Then again, they're all pig-ignorant and don't know a soul who matters, so who the hell cares what they say about me. And they haven't a clue as to who I am. Just that I'm rich and that I'm from Zagreb. They call me Mr. Julius."

Rebecca came to the door, a signal for Strumbić to show them around the house. Della Torre said he'd been given the tour and took the opportunity instead to call Anzulović. He gave him the names of the Bosnians, though not too many details about the events outside Gospić. Even if Strumbić's line wasn't tapped, Anzulović's was. Anzulović promised to dig around for anything he could find on the men and whether they might be tied to della Torre's other Bosnian friends. Della Torre then tried to call Irena, but she wasn't answering, either at home or at the hospital. The news was full of small-scale fighting around Vukovar. Was she there already? He tried the number she'd given him. Without success.

.    .    .

Over the days, they developed a routine. They woke early, swam, and breakfasted on bread and cheese and ham. Strumbić made traditional Turkish coffee on the stove. They idled for an hour, and then they'd pile into Strumbić's tiny, clapped-out car and head to the island's deserted west side, with its rough, low limestone cliffs. And there they'd test Rebecca's weapons.

"Not that you're likely to need to fire these, but we've seen now that things come up, haven't we," Rebecca said.

Della Torre was rusty. Strumbić was good with the Beretta, indifferent with the submachine gun, and inept with the rifle. Lying on the ground and firing didn't suit him. He could never find a position where he didn't jerk the trigger. He was much better the day they set the rifle on an old wall and brought a folding chair from the house. Rebecca joked about building a stool onto the rifle for Strumbić.

In the evenings they went to the little restaurant in the village. People knew Strumbić but were wary of him. He didn't go out of his way to endear himself to the locals, but he didn't antagonize them either. They respected his privacy. At Rebecca's request, he asked the people at the shop and at a little guest house on the harbour to keep an eye out for any strangers, especially if they were Bosnian.

Mid-week they took Strumbić's motorboat back across the channel and got into the Hilux. It took them a little more than twenty leisurely minutes to reach Dubrovnik's northern suburbs, an unexceptional collection of late nineteenth-century Austro-Hungarian architecture and bits of 1930s Italian design, together with a few relics from earlier centuries and ribbons of bland modern hacienda-style houses and tower blocks. The road and dockside to their right were lined with palms, while the plots had luxurious green gardens.

"So, this is Dubrovnik," said Rebecca.

She might have been on the verge of saying "big deal," but they'd come around the shoulder of a mountain rising up from the sea and suddenly, in front and below, they saw the fortress city. Even della Torre, who knew it well, felt his breath catch.

The citadel's massive, high walls were bone white, almost blinding against the blue sky and sea, as if they'd been chalked onto the landscape by a fairy-tale artist. Their enormous mass was hard to square with their precise, beautiful lines. It was the home of every imagined troubadour, knight, princess, unicorn, and Templar.

"My god," Rebecca said.

"Of course, the way you're meant to approach Dubrovnik is by water," della Torre said. "We're taking the servants' entrance here."

"I'd seen photographs—" she started.

"Pah. Photographs. Is never tell truth. You must kiss walls, then you know Dubrovnik," said Strumbić.

They spent the morning exploring the old city, climbing the huge curtain wall that held in the Renaissance city, with its tapestry of tightly woven, faded red tile rooftops interspersed with tall, narrow church towers. A rugged mountain crowded Dubrovnik against the sea, which sparkled blue.

Rebecca spent much of her time up high, taking photographs from odd angles with a small camera she'd dug out of her bag. She had della Torre stand for half an hour at a particular spot on the Stradun, the broad pedestrian road that ran along the old city's spine. He could see her on the wall over the entrance gate, surveying the area.

As they wandered up one of the city's cobbled alleys, they came to a dead end. Instead of turning back, Rebecca stood at the base of the wall, launched herself up an ancient walnut tree that had grown into it, and then scrambled over the inner parapet onto the wall walk. An angry guard remonstrated with her, complaining that she needed a ticket. She showed him the one she'd bought earlier and then looked over the side, grinning at the two men below.

Throughout the morning Rebecca marched, following some internal map, some unspoken agenda, largely ignoring the interiors of historic buildings to focus on the ramparts, and dragging the two men in her wake like reluctant children.

When the sun rose high enough to rob the city of shade, they finally called an end to Rebecca's adventure. Della Torre and Strumbić were all for lunching at a well-known harbourside restaurant in the old town, but Rebecca insisted on driving the little way down the coast to the Hotel Argentina, where they ate on a terrace above the sea, with spectacular views of Dubrovnik.

Their conversation was desultory. Rebecca never spoke about herself, and if she asked questions, her curiosity always seemed to have an end in mind. Strumbić seemed content with the past few days. He hadn't been very enthusiastic about being made to rise early or the physical regimen Rebecca had imposed on them, but he liked shooting in the woods and eating and drinking in the afternoon. Enforced indolence suited him, as long as it didn't last too long and he felt that there'd be a pay-off at the end. Besides, it sounded like Rebecca was keeping him more than entertained at night.

But della Torre was finding the time spent with Strumbić and Rebecca awkward. He felt as if he was in limbo, powerless over his own future. The killings had affected him.

Mostly he was worried about Irena. She was on his mind as he looked over the serene waters of the Adriatic towards the city. She'd be in Vukovar by now. Television news reported an increase in Yugoslav military activity along the Danube, though mostly mortar and rocket-propelled grenade attacks on surrounding villages. But there was talk of heavier artillery being drawn up on the opposite bank. Casualty numbers were growing and people were fleeing deeper into Croatia.

They'd finished their meal when a man approached them. He'd been sitting alone at a neighbouring table and stood up to ask della Torre for a light, ignoring the book of hotel matches on his own table.

"Thanks," he said, inhaling. "I couldn't help hearing that you're American."

"I live in Zagreb," said della Torre noncommittally. "You?"

"I'm trying to get a measure of what's happening around here," he said. "Steve Higgins."

Della Torre shook Higgins's extended hand. "Marko. This here is Julius and that's Rebecca."

"Mind if I join you? Not too many people other than wait-ers speak English around here. I don't speak Croat, and my German's not up to conversation."

"By all means," della Torre said.

A cloud of irritation passed over Rebecca's eyes, but then she gave Steve Higgins one of her well-toothed smiles.

"If you gentlemen don't mind, I'll duck out of the cigarette smoke for a little bit and have a look around," she said.

"Oh, I'm terribly sorry," said Higgins, slightly flustered and half rising out of the seat he'd just taken.

"Never mind, these two will be smoking like chimneys anyway," Rebecca said airily as she left.

"I'm sorry for driving your companion away," Higgins said.

"Think nothing of it," della Torre replied.

Strumbić pulled his chair further into the shade and leaned back in it. He wasn't interested in conversations with tourists. "I am not so good conversation after lunch, Mr. Higgins," he said. "Too much hot sun and wine."

"Looks like I'm chasing everybody away," Higgins said uncomfortably.

"Don't worry about it. You're on your own in one of the most beautiful cities in the world and thirsting for conversation. Happens to all of us," della Torre said.

"Yes, also because I heard you speaking American English and Croat. I was hoping I might be able to pick your brain a little."

"Pick away, though I'm not sure what I can tell you."

"I'm a reporter, a stringer for the wires and some newspapers in the U.K. and Canada. I'm working on the States, but you know how it is. It's tough making them interested in the world, even when there are revolutions and civil wars happening."

"Well, I'm afraid you're not going to get much of a story out of me, Mr. Higgins. I don't know anything and I'd rather not be quoted."

"Oh, it's nothing like that. I'm not writing anything right now. Just working on some background."

"You certainly found a nice place to do it. But the story isn't here. Unless you want to write about how badly the tourist trade is doing."

"I've written that story a couple of times already. My editors aren't interested. I'll probably head up to Krajina in the next few days to report on the Serb separatists. Crossed my mind to go up to Zagreb and then east. Things seem to be heating up there."

"Sounds like you'll be busy."

"Sort of. Not many of us Western journalists in Yugoslavia, and it's a nice patch to stakeout, especially if things start happening when the ceasefire ends."

The internationally brokered truce would expire in a week or so. The whole country was on tenterhooks about what would happen after.

"You're right. But you're in the wrong corner of the country for excitement," della Torre said.

"You think so? I'm not so sure," Higgins said. "So how is it that you speak Croat so well? And English?"

"I grew up in the States, but I live here now. Have lived here for a while."

"And what do you do, if you don't mind my asking?"

"I'm a lawyer."

"Here with clients? Or friends?"

"A mixture of business and pleasure. What about you, Mr. Higgins? I assume you haven't been here long."

"No," he laughed. "I've been circulating around eastern Europe for the past couple of years, the revolution trail. I was in Romania last."

"And you're American?"

"To tell you the truth, I'm both American and Canadian. Usually I stick to Canadian because it makes people less inclined to argue about what a terrible thing Vietnam was or ask me to sign their green card application form." He laughed again.

"I'll bear that in mind when I'm filling mine in," della Torre said. Other than his father and Irena, and his friend Harry in London, no one knew he was American. And Rebecca. "Where in Canada, or the States?"

"I grew up in a little place you've never heard of, called Lethbridge. It's in Alberta. My dad's an oil geologist. He's from Texas, but they've got gas in Alberta and that's why I grew up there."

"You're right, I've never heard of it."

"What about you?"

"I grew up in Ohio."

"Never been."

"I think you're missing about as much as I am never having gone to Lethbridge."

"You're probably right."

"They must pay well, your employers, for you to take a room here," della Torre said.

Higgins smiled apologetically. "Seemed like a nice place to stay."

He was in his early thirties, sandy-haired and tall. Della Torre didn't know what journalists were supposed to look like, but this one looked more like a cowboy. There was a rangy boniness to him that spoke of outdoor living, skin that looked like it had been buffeted by strong wind.

"So what have you found out in your time in Dubrovnik, Mr. Higgins? Other than that most of the tourists are gone."

"Well, if you go over to the other side of that mountain a little way—" He waved his hand inland. "—you will find a surprising amount of military activity, given that there's nothing on this side except for a very old walled city that has no strategic significance to anyone."

Della Torre sat up straight. "Is that so?"

"Really, that's what I wanted to ask you about. I've been asking everybody, but nobody seems to believe it."

"I have to say it sounds unlikely. Did you hear this or did you see it for yourself?"

"Oh, I saw it for myself. Hard getting over that way. They don't like people crossing the border."

"But you managed."

"I managed."

"Even though you don't speak the language."

"I found a waiter who speaks decent English to help me out. Very useful translator, and happens to know people who know people. The right amount of cash can sort out most difficulties."

"Expensive business, this reporting."

"Yup."

Strumbić was reclined as if he might be sleeping, but della Torre could tell from how he shifted his head now and again that from behind his mirrored sunglasses he'd been tracking a couple of girls in skimpy bikinis going down to the hotel's swimming pool on the lower terrace.

"So you crossed over with the help of a waiter and found out stuff that nobody here believes," della Torre said.

"Something like that. Though I also met a couple of British mercenaries. They're training soldiers on the other side of the mountain. Friendly fellows, until they get drunk. And then they're a couple of teddy bears. Anyway, if you hear of anything that might be interesting..."

"If I do I'll let you know."

Della Torre turned away slightly, as if to end the conversation. Higgins didn't take the hint.

"Since I'm here, can I get you a glass of wine?"

"I'm okay," della Torre said. "But I've never known Julius to turn down a drink. Even when he's unconscious he manages to nod."

"Thank you," Strumbić said, though it sounded more like "Sank you."

"My pleasure," Higgins said, calling over a waiter.

"Not that I've been of much help, but I've got a question for you," della Torre said. "Have you ever heard of a guy called Horvat? Owns a pizza chain in Canada?"

"The guy who's been made Croatia's defence minister."

"Deputy defence minister," della Torre corrected him. "Anyway, I was just wondering if he ever made the news in Canada."

"He used to talk about Croatia, but he mostly stayed away from the hard-line nationalists. I had an editor look up a clippings file on him after he got the government job. Really, it looked like his main preoccupation was making money rather than liberating his people. His pizza places were mostly across the prairie provinces, though he had a couple in Toronto and Montreal. Excuses to spend time in the big city."

"Oh." Della Torre wasn't surprised but was still disappointed. The UDBA had a file on Horvat and it said more or less the same thing. Liked to posture, but really just a businessman. In fact, not much more than a year earlier he'd been in very quiet discussions with the Yugoslav consulate in Toronto about bringing his pizza chain to the Dalmatian coast.

Higgins put out his cigarette, exhaling through his nose. He wore a funny grin. "Course, there are the rumours," he said.

"Rumours?"

"Not even rumours. I mean, just a bit of two plus two equals a very shady character."

"And what might those two be?"

Higgins paused and smiled. "This is so frivolous, so speculative that it's probably nothing," he began.

"Try me."

"Well, Horvat's pizza shops get supplied from the States. His trucks go up from the Midwest to the prairie provinces, loaded with whatever supplies he needs. They go west to east across Canada. And east to west. Big country. Lots of transport."

Della Torre watched Higgins light up another cigarette.

"I don't normally smoke much, but it's hard not to in this country," Higgins said, looking at the cigarette. "Anyway, Horvat has quite a logistical operation. One of his trucks got stopped in Nebraska or somewhere like that. Couple of handguns in the back. The driver was fined for not having a permit, and the case dropped right off the map. Except that a reporter friend noticed the story. Then there was the story that one of his trucks going from B.C.—"

"B.C.?"

"British Columbia. Our west coast. Anyway, it was pulled over for speeding, and the cops found that the back smelled funny. The truck was empty, but they found some dust in the corners that was clearly crumbs of dried pot. The driver said that when he was on break, he'd sometimes smoke a joint. But the way my friend tells it, there was more than a couple of roaches' worth back there."

"So you think he employs criminals."

"I think he makes money in ways other than just pizza."

"Seems a stretch on the basis of a couple of guns and some dusty marijuana."

"A friend of my journalist friend, a crime statistician at the University of Toronto, noticed some interesting correlations between a rise in gun crime and a drop in pot and cocaine prices, associated with Horvat's pizzerias opening up locally."

"Correlation?"

"That's math."

Della Torre shot Higgins a sharp look. "I know what *correlation* means."

Higgins shrugged. "Not everybody does. Anyway, as far as I can tell, nobody's looked into it much. But when I was a kid and we wanted to buy some dope, we could order some from Horvat's. The pizza was average. Cheap, but nothing special. But the delivery guy always seemed to know how to get some grass."

"You think Horvat's a drug trafficker?"

"I think making money is what he does, however he can. I think he made it easy for the people who worked for him to do stuff that wasn't maybe legit, and he seemed to profit from it."

"Thanks," Della Torre nodded. "Maybe it's my turn to buy you a glass of wine."

"Love to, but it'll have to be next time. I've got a man to talk to about getting over the border," he said. "I'd be awfully grateful if you passed along anything interesting you've heard about anything going on around here."

"I'm not really the sort of person who knows much," della Torre said, thinking that was truer than it sounded. "But I'll let you know. Good luck." Della Torre watched the journalist disappear. A funny, perceptive, and indiscreet fellow. He liked him.

Strumbić really had fallen asleep by the time Rebecca came back.

"You gentlemen ready to go?" she asked.

"Wherever you demand," della Torre said. "Though I think Julius is settled in for the afternoon. Interesting fellow, that Mr. Higgins. A journalist."

"Oh?" Rebecca said, though she didn't seem interested.

"At least that's what he claims to be."

"I'm sure he is. This is where journalists stay," she said. "See if you can get Julius up."

"Thought that was your speciality."

She flashed him a look of irritation.

"Let's go," she said.

When they got back to the villa, Rebecca spelled out her plans. "Julius, tomorrow I'd like you to leave Šipan by the regular ferry and check into a room I've reserved for you at the Argentina. I'd like you to spend a couple of days finding out what you can about Mr. Djilas. Marko and I are going to be getting in touch with him to see whether we might be able to arrange a visit."

Della Torre nodded. Strumbić didn't seem troubled about being turfed out of his own house.

"Is nice hotel. I like," he said.

## SWEDEN, MARCH 1986

IT WAS GETTING on for four in the morning when the music on the radio was replaced by frequent news bulletins. At first the Montenegrin couldn't make out much, but when he'd listened hard enough, a name became distinct: Olof Palme.

The ripple of relief that ran over him was quickly replaced by a nervous prickle. The Swedes may have been slow to react, but they'd be hunting him now.

They'd be more alert at the Helsingborg ferry crossing to Denmark than they had been when he'd come over. When he had driven from Copenhagen in the stolen Opel with Swedish licence plates, no one had stopped him on either side of the narrow channel between the two countries. He'd been surprised at how short the ferry crossing was. Once upon a time the entire area must have bristled with Vikings. The Vikings of the modern age, criminal gangs like the Yugoslav mafia, still used the route.

But most of the traffic was local, commuters between Sweden and Denmark going to work or shop. Flights out of Sweden or ferries directly from Stockholm to, say, Hamburg would have been too dangerous. Police cordons and inspections would become ever looser the farther he got from the capital. He just had to hope he didn't have to explain to the border guards why he was driving a Swedish-registered car while travelling on a German passport.

He had found the vehicle in a covered long-stay car park. He'd heard that Swedes from Malmo who worked on long-term contracts abroad, often on engineering projects in the Middle East, tended to leave their cars there for months at a time. He was hoping it was true. That no one would have reported it stolen.

But his biggest concern was the gun. He kept the heavy revolver tucked under his seat. He'd thought about leaving it with the boy's body, but there was a chance it would be found and traced back to him. And, he admitted to himself, he wanted it as insurance, in case he needed to get through a one-man police roadblock. It'd buy him a little time at least.

A sign appeared up ahead, indicating a town a kilometre down the road. He turned off at the exit and drove slowly down the main road until he spotted a phone booth. He took a bag of Swedish coins out of the glove compartment and then braced himself for the cold. The shock of icy air on his face and eyes made him gasp and blink.

He piled the coins into the machine and then dialled a number for Cologne. The line rang and rang. Eventually the call was disconnected, so he repeated the performance until someone answered on his fourth attempt.

"What?" There was a tired, impatient voice on the other end, speaking in rough German.

"Pilgrim," the Montenegrin said.

"Could you repeat that, please." The speaker was more alert now.

"Pilgrim," the Montenegrin said again and hung up.

He hurried back to the car. He felt the creeping tiredness as the adrenaline of the evening wore off. He was tempted to stop somewhere for a cup of coffee but knew that would be a mistake. He had to press on. It was a long drive and he didn't want anyone to see or notice or remember him. He took one of the small triangular orange pills he kept in a little round tin in the inside pocket of his coat, washing it down with a swallow of bottled water. From experience, he knew it would keep him going for another four hours, after which he'd have to take another pill. Three running was his maximum. Any more and, he'd learned, he could no longer trust his reactions or judgement. With just a little luck, he wouldn't need more than two.

He pulled back onto the motorway, cranking up the radio and turning the heat down to keep him awake and focused. There was more about Palme, none of which he understood. He tried to get a German or English station on the shorter wavelength, but heard nothing but static and Swedish.

Had he chosen to, he might have allowed himself the luxury of thinking about his dead wife or about the burden of raising a crippled child. He might have reflected that his wife's and daughter's fates were a punishment for the work he did. But he knew that line of thinking led nowhere. There was luck, and there were things one could influence. It was crucial never to confuse the two. The danger with luck was that it led to complacency. Or to despair. He hadn't allowed his good fortune with the Palme job to dull his thinking. Just as he'd refused to allow his wife's death and his child's tragedy to defeat him.

He drove through the night, focused on the smooth road and the trees sliding by. Traffic picked up in the morning. He was feeling light-headed, and it was still dark. He'd driven past a handful of small towns and settlements, seen their streetlights battle feebly against the endless blackness of the Swedish night. And now, it seemed, he had returned to the land of the living.

From the fringes of Helsingborg, he followed the signs to the ferry terminal. The Swedes were good at signs, clearly marked with pictures to prevent any confusion. He made his way around a set of switchback roads to the modern port, set apart from the heart of the old city.

He drove through docklands framed by big, shed-like warehouses or older, neat brick buildings, and then pulled up in a big parking lot. His back and legs complained as he got out of the car. For the first few steps, he walked like a cardboard cutout. The cold air on his face was bracing, telling him how tired he was. He was reminded of his bladder as well; he'd driven five hours non-stop.

There were public toilets in the ferry terminal. The lighting was harsh, white fluorescence. He was momentarily disoriented looking at himself in the mirror. The man who stared back at him was worn, the sallow, almost bleached face heavily lined. There was more grey in his hair than he remembered. But what affected him most was the blankness of the eyes. Hollow, to the ends of the universe, so that he could barely look into them. He ran hot water over his hands until some warmth crept into him, and then he went out to buy a ticket.

"Terrible news." The man at the counter spoke no German but had good English.

"Oh?" the Montenegrin asked.

"Yes. Olof Palme, our prime minister, was killed last night."

"Killed? An accident?"

"No. Murdered. Assassinated," the man said, his voice shaking. "We only heard on the radio this morning. One or two newspapers have the story, but they don't say anything."

"That is terrible. I'm sorry."

"To think, in Sweden. Maybe in Africa or Greece or America. But in Sweden?"

"Have they caught the murderer?"

"No. They don't even have a good description. One of the local police was around this morning, and he said they weren't told anything by Stockholm."

"So how will they check at the border? How will they know at passport control what to look for?"

"There is no passport control here. We have open borders between Sweden and Denmark and Norway."

"But surely the police will be checking people leaving the country?"

"Yes, of course. But in Stockholm. They've not been told what to do in Helsingborg."

"So they won't do any inspections? That is very strange."

The man shrugged, holding his hands up. "In Sweden, we are not used to these things. We have no plans for them." He paused as he slid a printed card towards the Montenegrin. "I have given you a ticket for the next ferry. But you must hurry, otherwise you will have to wait for the one after."

A queue had formed behind the Montenegrin, so he paid the ticket and walked quickly back to the car. He pulled off as soon as the Opel started. The quicker he caught the ferry, the sooner he'd be out of Sweden.

But the ticket seller had been mistaken. Police were at the docks stopping traffic, seemingly at random. The Montenegrin slowed to a crawl. The pill had worn off, and he was at once tired and agitated. But this was no time to take another.

One of the policemen stepped in front of the vehicle, holding up his hand. The Montenegrin rolled down the window, but he understood nothing of what the officer was saying.

"I'm sorry," he said in English. "I speak no Swedish. English or *Deutsch*?"

"*Ja*, English," said the officer. "You go over there and stop."

26

## DUBROVNIK, AUGUST 1991

**D**ELLA TORRE MADE the call to the Montenegrin first thing in the morning, two days after Strumbić had left for Dubrovnik. He used a satellite telephone Rebecca had set up on Strumbić's front terrace. He didn't know where it'd come from, only that when she parked the Hilux by the fisherman's cottage, there were a couple of bags in the back. One was a canvas holdall full of ammunition. The other was a hard case that proved to contain the phone and its folded dish antenna.

There was a series of beeps and clicks before he got a dial tone. But the phone was answered quickly.

"Mr. Djilas?" he said.

"Yes."

"This is Marko della Torre."

Pause.

"Gringo? Where are you? You sound like you're calling from the moon."

There was an odd echo and delay on the phone, making conversation sound tinny and distant.

"Sorry, it must be the line. Mr. Djilas, I was wondering whether I might be able to visit you for a conversation."

"A conversation?"

"About your work."

"I'm retired."

"I know that, but I still have investigations to run."

"For whom? I thought Zagreb had shut down the firm, or are you working for Belgrade now?"

"You're right, Zagreb's down. But I have a couple of investigations to complete."

"About what?"

"About a couple of American jobs."

"During my time or before?"

"Your time, sir."

"You know I've always been open to you before, but things are changing. It's dangerous to have been in my line of business."

"I know, sir."

"I don't have much inclination to travel to Zagreb or Belgrade these days."

"I know, that's why I offered to travel to you."

"I don't go to Dubrovnik either."

"If you'd like I can travel to your home."

"I think that might be wisest for me. You'll be alone?"

"There is a woman."

"Oh?"

"She's an investigator. An American one."

"An American investigator? Now what might you be doing with an American investigator?" The Montenegrin sounded both amused and wary.

"The Americans are thinking of putting out an international warrant on the man who ordered the jobs."

"So why should I want to talk to someone who wishes to prosecute me?"

"She doesn't, sir. She wants the men who pulled the triggers and the men who ordered the jobs. Not the people in between."

The Montenegrin laughed. A distant, hollow laugh. Maybe it was just the connection.

"Well, if they want to place a warrant on me, they will anyway. Bring her. Does she speak Serbo-Croat?"

"No. She knows you speak English."

"And this American woman, what is her job?"

"She's just a diplomat, a lawyer," della Torre said, hesitating.

"Then I shall sit with you as a friend and her as a prosecutor. How soon do you wish to see me?"

"As soon as you can be available, sir."

"You are already in Dubrovnik, aren't you?"

"Yes."

The Montenegrin didn't sound surprised. "Well, timing will be difficult. I am away from this afternoon to tomorrow afternoon, and then again from early Sunday morning for some days."

"You're a busy man."

"Fishing is demanding of a man's time."

"Could we see you tomorrow, then?"

"Tomorrow afternoon. We will feed you here. You like grilled fish?"

"But of course. That would be most generous."

"Then we shall see you tomorrow afternoon. If you are driving from Dubrovnik, may I recommend you come unarmed. You will find it uncomfortable enough crossing the new borders even without having to explain weapons to the militia. I will make an effort to ensure that you are welcomed cordially. Do you know where to cross the border?"

"Inland from Cavtat, I'm told."

"That's right. It will be a pleasure to see you, Gringo. Not spending time with interesting people like you is one of the regrets of my retirement."

"It will be a pleasure to see you too, sir. Is there anything I can bring for you from Dubrovnik?"

"I want for nothing. Come with your American, that's enough."

Rebecca was pleased with the result of the conversation, though she didn't look as though she'd had much doubt about how it would go.

"Sounds like he likes you," she said.

"Yes. I've always treated him fairly. The government tried to use him as a scapegoat when an assassination attempt in Scotland went wrong. I helped with the evidence supporting his defence. He retired not long after."

"Well, it's nice to know we found the right man for the job."

"What job might that be?" della Torre asked, lighting a cigarette.

"I meant you being the right man to get us to Mr. Djilas, of course."

"Of course. Oh, before I forget. No guns. Even if you were to get one past the border police, his people would find it. And they wouldn't be happy about it."

"Who said anything about guns? We're just going for a chat."

.    .    .

They went for a swim in the afternoon after talking to Strumbić, who seemed to be enjoying the Argentina. He'd also had some success digging up information on the Montenegrin.

Rebecca wore her loose cotton shift down to the quay. The material was translucent, patterned with bleached red and white vertical stripes. Which was why della Torre saw she was naked underneath, even before she stripped it off and dove into the sparkling water.

Della Torre sat on the stone and watched Rebecca for a long while, until she gave him a quizzical look and swam up to the jetty. She held onto the hard edge, resting her chin on the back of her hands, lazily kicking her legs behind so that he could see the small of her back and the firm white roundness of her ass.

"What?"

"You know, I don't know anything about you," he said.

"So what do you want to know about me?"

"Anything. I don't know if you're married. Come to think of it, I'm not even sure of your name."

"My name's Rebecca. And I'm not married. I was, but it didn't last long."

"Who do you work for?"

"The U.S. government."

"Which part?"

"Does it matter? It doesn't matter what my boss's first name is or the size of my office or the address of the building I'm based at. None of that matters. I work for the U.S. government, just like you work for the Croatian government now and used to work for the Yugoslav government."

"I suppose so. What do you do for them?"

"What you see me doing."

"You hunt and kill men."

"I'm given a job and I do it."

"Those Bosnians weren't the first men you've killed, were they."

"That a question or a statement?"

"A statement."

"So what's the question?"

"Do you like it?"

"Do I like it? I do it. You ever ask Djilas that question?"

"No. But what makes you do it?"

"I'm American and I love my country. I'm from a military family. Not one of those fucked up military families but one that works. My parents are still married and nobody's an alcoholic. I'm the first woman in my family to have been in the military. I was taught to shoot by my grandfather, who bought me my first gun when I was six. It was a .22 rifle with a shortened barrel and a pink stock. My grandfather died a couple of years ago. He was eighty-six and hunting alligators the week before he died. He had an annual bag limit, 160 alligators, and every year he filled it with 160 shots.

"My father was in the Marines and stayed with the Marines even after he retired. My mother was a Marine's daughter, a Marine's granddaughter, and a Marine's wife, and she never complained about the life she was given. She had three children. The two boys died when they were little, one drowned and another got meningitis, both before I was born, so you can feel sorry for my parents but not for me.

"When I went into the Marines, my mother knew it was something I had to do. Because it was what she'd have done when she was young if her parents had allowed her to. The Marines sent me to university and they told me they wanted me to learn engineering and Russian, and that's exactly what I learned. And then the Marines told me that they wanted me to work for another part of government, and that's what I did too. Understand, Major Gringo?" She said it in a matter-of-fact way, but with a smile that left him unsure of what to believe. Maybe it was true.

"I understand," he said. "What's your rank?"

"I don't have a rank."

"When you left?"

"Well, I happened to be a major too," she said. There was a levity to her tone, an irony. Maybe it was because she knew she could control men and enjoyed doing it. She stared at him with a gently ironic look until he had to turn his eyes south across the water and then towards the mainland.

"We'll be wishing Mr. Strumbić a fond farewell," she said eventually.

"Oh?"

"Yes. I think it's time he went back to Zagreb. We'll see what he happened to find for us first though."

"You don't seem too sad about it."

"About not seeing Julius again? Why should I be sad?"

"You seemed to have developed quite a . . . rapport."

"Sex, you mean?" She laughed. "He's half man, half pig, and all dog. I won't miss him."

Della Torre's look of disquiet at her cruel description stayed her.

"That's just Strumbić. Don't worry, I don't say the same about you."

"No?" he asked.

"No. You're a lot like your father. A lot."

His shock at what she'd said was palpable. She laughed and dove under the water, surfacing next to him, grabbing him by the leg, her breast brushing against his foot. "That's not a bad thing, by the way. It's a good thing."

"Thanks," he said, not the least mollified.

He pushed himself off the edge, pushing past her brusquely, sliding into the water, where he stayed under for long strokes, plunging so deep that he risked running his belly across the black sea urchins, their needles pulsing as they moved across the stony sea floor. He surfaced, slightly dizzy from holding his breath.

"Bravo," she called. "Must be some kind of record there. Thought I'd be fishing you out with a hook." She swam over to him. "I'm a little bit curious about something."

"What?" he asked coldly.

"Those shooters. Strumbić told me those weren't the first Bosnians out to get you. A man with a hard-on can't keep secrets. A couple followed you to London."

"Did he tell you why?"

"Said you upset somebody, stealing files from your employer. But it wasn't your employer that put the hit on you. Somebody else did. Who was it?"

"You don't know?"

"No."

"Neither do I. I'm not sure they were just after me. They probably didn't like Strumbić either."

"But it had nothing to do with the Montenegrin?"

"No. I doubt it," della Torre said. He was being truthful, if evasive. There was no need to tell her about Pilgrim, about the Bosnians who'd been after him earlier in the year, or that these Bosnians almost certainly had been trying to finish the job on Strumbić, if not him. She might know already. She seemed well informed about everything. But he didn't feel like discussing it with her.

"Good. That was why we've been hanging out here for the past week. I wanted to make sure nobody else was following us. A little island like this is a good place to keep an eye out for enemies. As long as you're well prepared," she said, treading water.

"In that case it looks like we're in the clear."

They pulled themselves back onto the stone jetty, where they let the warm morning sun dry them—her naked, him in his small, tight swimming shorts from when he'd been a teenager, which felt even more constricting than they normally did. The sea shimmered like a sequined dress. The mainland looked bare, the white and grey stone mottled with drab greens and burnt yellow browns. It had been a dry summer. He tried to avoid looking at her, but couldn't. Knowing she was a killer and a practised whore, however she justified herself, made no difference.

"But the real thing I wondered about was that boy. The Bosnian boy," she said.

Della Torre froze. "What Bosnian boy?"

"One of the ones who was shooting at us, the one you chased. Why did you let him go?"

She knew.

"He got away. Too fast for me. I smoke too much," he said. He could feel his heart hammering in his throat.

"For a smoker, you seem to have some decent lung capacity."

"Good genes, I suppose."

"You see, when I went back to the woods, I found where you'd had him. Up by the cliffs. There were some bloody hand-prints on the stone. Must have cut himself trying to climb."

Della Torre listened, not moving a muscle.

"He seemed to get up to a certain height and then come down. There was what looked like a couple of bullet marks in the stone, but it's always hard to tell. He must have passed you when he came down."

Della Torre didn't answer.

"I tracked him through the woods. Wasn't hard. Got to a hay-field after that. Very easy to follow a path through a hayfield. I didn't chase after him. But you know what? He'd stopped. Must have been sick. He was bent over. More than half a mile away, probably closer to three-quarters. The range on these rifles is only half a mile. If I'd started running after him, he'd have heard and bolted, and you don't want to have been run-ning if you're going to be doing long-range shooting. Be lucky to hit anything farther than a hundred yards."

The hollowness he'd begun to feel dissipated, and della Torre breathed a bit more easily. She dressed, pulling the shift over her head. She put on her broad-brimmed sun hat and her big sunglasses so he couldn't see her eyes.

"So you came back then," he asked, trying to sound disinterested.

"There was a useful rock, perfect height above the ground, and I thought it would be a real shame not to try. I mean, what the hell, eh?"

"Yes?" Della Torre shuddered involuntarily, though the air was still and warm and the water had mostly evaporated off his skin. She sat next to him, naked under the gossamer-thin shift, which clung to her skin as it dried.

"I missed," she said.

Della Torre's elbows trembled behind him, almost giving way with relief.

"I missed twice," she said. "But then he stood up and looked back. Bullets probably passed close to him and he must have heard them. That's when I got him. There was no wind, but even then it was a lucky shot. Middle of the belly. Once he was down it was easier for me to get another bullet into him. He'd fallen on a little rise. Took me a few tries to range it properly. But it's a terrific scope. I thought about walking over to make sure, but even if he wasn't dead straight away, there was no way he was going to last, and I thought it best to get out of there. It was too far for us to drag him back, so I guess it'll be a mystery for the local cops to solve."

Della Torre got up, numb and unsteady, the stone hot underfoot. Without a word he turned and walked back up the hill to the house, feeling like Jason fleeing the horror of Medea.

**T**HEY ARRIVED AT the Hotel Argentina just before lunch. A large pink stuffed toy bear sat at one end of the reception counter, where any other hotel might have had a vase of flowers. Shaking off Communism was one thing, but eliminating Communist kitsch was going to be a higher order of struggle. Della Torre and Rebecca checked into separate rooms, after which he went down to the terrace and found Strumbić attached to a bottle of beer.

"Julius, you seem a contented man."

"Gringo, I am, I am. Rebecca not with you?"

"She's unpacking or something."

"It's been a thoroughly satisfying couple of days. Found a friend from Zagreb to keep me entertained."

"A retired cop?"

Strumbić laughed. "A working girl. She's on the game in Zagreb except during the holidays, when she comes down here. I get professional courtesy rates."

"Is that better than wholesale? Thought that part of your life had been happily organized in Šipan."

Strumbić looked around before continuing. "Tell you the truth, our redhead scares me."

"I don't want details."

"Performance flags when you feel that from one minute to the next somebody might shove a loaded gun up your ass."

"And I thought you were having fun."

"Well, you know, I had to make a stand for the masculine gender, but truth be told, I felt like I was the woman in that particular relationship. Nice to be reminded of how things ought to be over the past couple of days."

"Good hotel?"

"I could get used to it. Menu's got a bit of variety too, so you aren't stuck with either meat on a stick or squid that's come frozen on a slow boat from the South Atlantic. I don't know why more places don't just do fish out of our sea."

"That's because there aren't any left."

"You might be right. Still, it's been good. Found out some interesting stuff. Could be lucrative interesting stuff. Your Canadian friend Higgins isn't the dumb cowboy he looks."

"Shame you'll be on the next plane back to Zagreb."

"The fuck I will."

"It's not me saying it."

"Ah, Rebecca," Strumbić said, looking over della Torre's shoulder.

"Julius," Rebecca said. "Looks like a couple of days in a luxury hotel suits you."

"Is good," Strumbić said.

"So, what have you found out about our Mr. Djilas?" she asked, joining them at the table.

"Interesting things."

"And you're going to tell us?"

"Gringo says I going back to Zagreb."

"I'm afraid so." Rebecca unpeeled a stick of Wrigley's gum and folded it into her mouth.

"I take some holiday, I stay."

"I'm sorry, Julius. But my budget doesn't stretch to any more time in the Argentina, and Marko and I will be too busy to have roommates."

"Is okay. I pay."

"Sorry. There's a plane ticket for Zagreb with your name on it. You'll be leaving early tomorrow morning. Your Colonel Kakav is expecting you back. We've locked up Šipan for you. I'll send the keys back with Marko, in case we discover we've forgotten something there. We'll make sure your motorboat is sorted out," she said. "So, tell me about Djilas."

Strumbić gave Rebecca a look that would have bled her dry if it'd had a handle and blade. "I'm sorry, I find so little out. I stay. I think I take holiday here."

"Oh, shame, really," she said, chewing her gum. "It'll be awfully hard to unfreeze that British bank account you have."

Strumbić flashed della Torre an angry look, but della Torre gave an almost invisible shrug and shake of the head. He hadn't told her anything.

Rebecca looked at a printed roll of fax paper she had pulled out from her leather case.

"Oh, sorry, I'm mistaken. This can't be your account. It's in the name of Mr. Julius Smirnoff. Forgive me, Julius. There's an awful lot more money here than a policeman would ever be able to earn, even a policeman with a villa on the sea and a country house and a couple of apartments in Zagreb. I guess then there's nothing I can do to stop you from staying. Have a great holiday."

Strumbić knew he'd been cornered. Smirnoff was the name he used to hold his English account. Only della Torre and Harry Martingale knew. Only della Torre could have told Rebecca.

Strumbić lit a cigarette and pulled a little notebook bound in creased dark blue leather out of his back pocket. "He have nice house in village on Bay of Kotor, big ground. He always have two or three men at house." His words were hard and cold.

"Even when he's away?"

"Always. Cousins of him, live in village. All village is cousins of him, four hundred cousins. He pay for *ambulant*...how say..."

"Clinic," della Torre intervened.

"Yes, doctor clinic in village, have good school, is rich village. He have twenty men from village work for him and twenty or thirty more men from other villages. Not work for him all time, but do little jobs and have guns. He afraid of Belgrade government. He have many friends in different militias in Montenegro, but Yugoslav National Army not so much. They mostly from Belgrade."

"So he has a big, strong network," she said, though none of it seemed to surprise her.

"Yes."

"What does he do with all these men?"

"Many around Kotor Bay watching. Like army, Montenegrin's army. They also go fishing. He have one big, one little fishing boat and village have ten more small and medium fishing boat."

"Fishing?"

"Fishing. They go to Adriatic, find big boat, take drugs, go and take drugs to Italy. Or they get drugs from Albanian mafia and take to Italy. Bari and near Bari. Get paid, lira and Deutschmarks. Good money for business."

"Do they sell drugs here too?"

"Maybe little in Dubrovnik, but most go to Italy."

"Anything else?"

"They get guns from Yugoslav army or big boats from China and sell to people in Italy. To people in Croatia and Montenegro too."

"Sounds like a good living."

"Is better than work for police," Strumbić said with a shrug.

Rebecca cocked her eye at him. "So what is his home life like?"

"He have two daughter. One live in village and one in Vienna. Grown."

"Three," said della Torre.

"Three?" Strumbić said, caught off guard by this gap in his knowledge.

"There's a young one too. Lives with him. She has problems; her mother had complications at birth and died. The girl is…" Della Torre shrugged. How many years had it been since he'd seen the little girl? He'd brought her a soft toy, but it had been painful watching her trying to grip it. She had little control of her movement. She made sounds. Her father said she spoke to him; he said her mind was clear, that she was funny and a good conversationalist if you had patience. Della Torre wondered if it was true or if the Montenegrin was deluding himself, wishing something into reality.

"Is true?" Strumbić seemed doubtful.

"She stays at home. That's why he invested so much in the local clinic. A nurse does therapy with her, but she doesn't leave the house much. He doesn't usually let people see her."

"Shame," Rebecca said.

"Are you saying it's a shame or that he's ashamed?"

"Course it's a shame," said Rebecca. "I was saying he's probably ashamed to let people see her."

"I don't think so. I think he doesn't want her to hear and be hurt by what people say. People in this country aren't always delicate, especially about the handicapped. Before they learned better, the villagers used to ask why he bothered to let her live. In fact, that's probably why she's not more common knowledge. She's officially registered as his housemaid's daughter, in case something happens to him."

Rebecca nodded. "So another daughter is in the house too?"

"No, other daughter live in village, is married," Strumbić continued. "Old lady live in house too. She Djilas cousin, do cooking and cleaning. And woman comes from village to help cleaning."

"The old lady is the housemaid," della Torre said.

"What other security do they have?"

"You mean besides thirty armed men plus the local militia and police force?" Della Torre laughed.

"Yes."

"Have two dogs on chain. Big dogs," Strumbić said.

"So no burglar alarms or surveillance systems?"

Della Torre and Strumbić caught each other's eyes.

"I think you might be confusing Montenegro with Washington, D.C.," della Torre said. "They rely on people and relationships around here rather than technology. I bet he never locks his front door."

"Do his guards live on site?"

"Is little house next to big house for when men stay there, but not same men all time, change. Mostly from village, but always two men stay during night and one more at day," Strumbić said.

"He sounds like he's worried about something."

"Most men in his line of business have short lifespans. And it's not because the work causes cancer," said della Torre.

"I can imagine."

"That's why he moved back to the village. It offered him the best buffer. Strangers don't often just show up, and when they do, they're outnumbered and outgunned. He's well connected to the Montenegrin power base. He keeps the local militias equipped and makes sure the local politicians drive German cars."

"Sounds like a godfather."

"A reasonable description. He put in the years in civil service, and these are his fringe benefits."

"How old?"

"Fifty-four," della Torre said. "But he looks younger than Strumbić here."

Strumbić, who was barely forty, gave della Torre a baleful look and straightened.

"What about getting from here to there?"

"Militia at border crossing. Smugglers cross inland from Cavtat," said Strumbić. "But problem is now also paramilitary from Belgrade there."

Della Torre sat up. "Not just the Yugoslav National Army?"

"No, paramilitary come. Gorki wolfs. Is not very nice."

"Gorki? I thought he was in Vukovar," della Torre said.

"He here now."

"Shit," said della Torre. Gorki's Serbian paramilitaries were spreading across the country like a poison. Hitherto, the Yugoslav government in Belgrade could argue that it represented the Yugoslav ideal, a single state formed of a number of nationalities for the wider socialist good of the southern Slavs. But as Gorki's men became ever more prevalent and powerful, the Yugoslav fiction would fade and naked Serb hegemony would surface. The Serbs had a lot of long-lasting grievances against the Croats. Gorki here, in Vukovar, wherever, could mean only one thing. A return to the ancient blood feud.

"What?" Rebecca asked.

"Gorki is a very nasty piece of work. A criminal the Yugoslav secret service used to use in other countries."

"You mean like the hit squads?"

"Something like that. Anyway, he's got a band of paramilitaries. They're Serb ultra-nationalists. Last I heard they were killing civilians near Vukovar. Maybe they've got plans for here. Not a nice bunch of people. They are best to be avoided. The name fits the man. *Gorki* means 'bitter gift.'"

"It does in Russian too," Rebecca said, indulging him with a brief smile.

"Sorry. Forgot you'd know that," della Torre said. For a moment, he was tempted to tell her about Gorki's grudge against the Montenegrin. The personal vendetta. Not that he was certain about much of it himself. But then, he thought, why complicate matters?

Rebecca looked at her watch. "I'm afraid, gentlemen, I have a prior engagement. Please don't stand, I'm sure you have plenty to talk about."

After Rebecca left, there was a long silence between the two men.

"It wasn't me, Julius."

"I should have killed you when I had the chance, Gringo. Both times."

"Look, I don't know where she gets her information, but she does. She probably didn't need the stuff you got on the Montenegrin. Somebody's kept her incredibly well informed. And it's not me. She knew all about London and the Bosnians, the first Bosnians sent to kill me. I hadn't told her a thing." Della Torre tried to catch Strumbić's eyes, but the cop had put on his mirrored sunglasses.

Long silence. And then Strumbić grudgingly said, "I might have mentioned something about it. She was curious after those pricks shot at us. Kept pestering me to tell her. Must have caught me at a weak moment."

"I can imagine how weak that moment must have been. You were drunk and she was on top of you. Metaphorically speaking, of course."

"Naturally."

"Look, Julius. She is well plugged in and she isn't a person to fuck with. She executed one of the Bosnians. Maybe two of them. Hell, maybe all three. Only one of them was an immediate danger to either of us. And it didn't seem to me that she'd only just discovered killing doesn't disagree with her."

"She got her first rifle, a .22, when she was six."

"Story sounds familiar," della Torre said.

"Shortened barrel with a pink stock? I think she mentioned it as a warning, just in case I hadn't noticed how good she is with a rifle," Strumbić said.

"I guess she's got a spiel. Sorry, Julius. If it's any consolation, she's got me by the short and curlies too."

"Only thing to do is what you have to do when you get crabs. Shave 'em off and burn everything you touched. Including the mattress."

"I'll try to remember that."

.     .     .

Strumbić disappeared immediately after lunch to put his interesting business enterprise on ice until he could get back from Zagreb.

Della Torre was smoking on his own, drinking a Karlovačka beer, considering Rebecca, when a familiar face popped up.

"Marko." It was the Canadian from the previous day.

"Hello..." della Torre said.

"Steve."

"Steve," he echoed, having forgotten the name.

"So you're back."

"For a couple of days only. How's your hunt going?"

"Oh, it goes," Higgins said. "I went up into the hills with my waiter friend. Scary. There are lots of militiamen around, irregular army types. It smells like they're getting ready for something."

"War, you mean."

"I guess so."

"How did you get across the border?"

"The usual. Showed my passport with a hundred-dollar bill inside."

"They give you trouble?"

"Not too much. My waiter talked to them, told them I was a journalist and that he was a translator."

"Did you have a visa?"

"You mean other than the one with Ben Franklin's picture on it?" Higgins said. "Sure, but they didn't bother to look. Just the cover of my passport and the colour of my money."

Della Torre nodded. He was convinced that if the right people could be found and the right bribe offered, the whole war could be called off.

"You going across yourself?" Higgins asked.

"Maybe. I thought it might be pretty difficult."

"Not if you've got a good guide and adequate paperwork. Dollars. Or Deutschmarks, probably. I'm not sure Canadian bills would have worked. My waiter told me that they're mostly just a bunch of country boys. Everyone's heavily armed, but they're not professional border guards."

"Which post did you go through?"

"The one near the airport."

"Cavtat."

"Yes, though I'm not sure I'd recommend it for most. My waiter seems to think they shoot at strangers, though they seemed to know him and his car pretty well."

"They check his car documents?"

"I don't think they even noticed him. Just my passport. And the cash."

"Any other impressions?"

"My impression is that there are a lot of soldiers on that side, mostly paramilitaries, though they also seem to be mobilizing regular army in this direction. You could see some heavy artillery parked up. But it was a weird feeling. Not really threatening. But dangerous."

"Strange. There's nothing militarily strategic for the Serbs down here. Dubrovnik does tourists and nothing else. There aren't any Serbs on this side either, so that's not much of an excuse. Maybe they're just collecting some Montenegrin and Bosnian troops with a view to advancing them north," della Torre said, more to himself than the other man.

"Maybe. But I think I'll stick around anyway. Like I say, it smells like there might be a story here. Besides, I feel like a holiday. It's pretty nice here, especially now that all the tourists have been scared away. And there's not much competition around. I've sold a couple of stories over the past week."

"A couple of stories will cover your costs at the Argentina?"

Higgins shrugged. "Money isn't everything."

"Handy to know, thanks. You writing anything now?"

"Not yet. You know anything interesting?"

"Ever hear of a guy called Gorki?"

"Can't say that I have."

"You will. He's a Serb paramilitary with a criminal record across the whole of western Europe. Last week the rumour was that he was killing civilians by the Danube, up near Belgrade on the Croat border. This week it's said he's here."

"In Dubrovnik?"

"The other side. Maybe some of the people you talked to were his."

"Gorki, you say?"

"Gorki. It's said he has a wolf, a real wolf, not a dog that looks like one. Keeps it on a chain and takes it with him wherever he goes."

Higgins looked skeptical. "Wolves don't much like being on a leash. You hear of people up in northern B.C. or Alaska who try to domesticate wolf pups. They don't tend to stick around. But I'll keep the name in mind."

"Anything else new?" della Torre asked.

"Oh, nothing really. Except that your friend Horvat is here," Higgins said.

"Horvat?"

"Saw him last night, he came to the hotel for dinner. Private room. Business."

"Oh?"

"Yeah. My waiter friend said there were some discussions about imports."

"Like?"

"Guns, among other things."

"Guns? He's a deputy defence minister. Of course he's looking to import guns."

"I know. But like I say, he's got a reputation for being canny. Plenty of smuggling goes on up this coast. I don't know why a defence minister would want to be smuggling guns, unless he can get them at a low price and then sell them on to the government at a higher one. But that's just a guess. A lot of that sort of stuff seems to go on around here. Turkish, Chinese, Egyptian, Lebanese boats go up the Adriatic, stop in international waters, then a fishing boat pulls up at night. That friend of yours who looks like a cop seems to know something about it."

"Strumbić?" Della Torre bit his tongue. He paused for a beat. "What does he know about it?"

Higgins shrugged. "Ask him...Anyway, a colleague in Toronto says Horvat's got a rep."

"Rep?"

"Reputation. Raised money from the Croatian expats in the States and Canada. The U.S. State Department doesn't like it because there's an unofficial embargo on selling weapons to Croatia. They figure if Croats can't get guns, there won't be war. So everything's got to be black market. And Horvat seems to be good at gun smuggling. You might ask around if the price is commensurate with the quality, though."

"How the hell do your guys in Canada know this?"

"Because he told them."

"Horvat told them?"

"Yes."

"You're pulling my leg."

"Nope. Told a reporter in Toronto when he was there on a fundraiser recently. Off the record. Said he was done buying Bulgarian crap. Even the criminals didn't want it anymore. And that he's getting good Chinese Kalashnikovs and Hungarian machine guns."

"Mr. Higgins, it has been an enormous pleasure to get to know you."

"Marko..."

"Della Torre."

"Marko della Torre, the feeling is mutual. And I hope one day it's as rewarding for me as it seems to be for you."

"You are an exceptionally perceptive person, Mr. Higgins. I'm sure you will always know more than us mere plodders."

"Mr. della Torre, in my line of business you starve if you're stupid. Actually, you don't starve. You go home and get a job selling insurance. Even so, we hacks can only ever write a tenth of what we know."

"And the other ninety percent?"

"We trade for food."

"In that case, it would be my pleasure to buy you dinner sometime."

"I'll hold you to that."

"**I**RENA?"

"Marko, is that you?"

Della Torre was standing, staring out of the hotel window as he held the phone, surprised to hear her voice.

"You're a hard woman to get hold of. How's Vukovar?"

"It's been busy."

"Nobody seems to know you there, or if they do they never know where you are."

"The doctors share the ambulance rotation, so I'm often out. And I hadn't realized that this office is in the teaching wing and there's not a lot of teaching going on."

"Where are you living?"

"In the hospital. Honestly, it doesn't make sense for me to spend time coming and going, so I've just made a little home for myself in the nurses' dorm."

"You'll burn yourself out."

"Oh, don't worry about me. Besides, I'm going to be in Zagreb for a few days next week."

"Oh." Della Torre felt something sink inside him. David really was coming. He'd been hoping the start of the war might have put off the British doctor.

"Look, Marko, I'm sorry. It's not like you'll ever stop meaning a lot to me. It's not like I ever fell out of love with you. But you don't want the life I do."

"You mean operating on bullet wounds while you're being shelled by Serb guns?"

"We're fine. Vukovar's fine. They've been shelling the villages but we're okay."

"He going to go out there with you?"

"I told you, he's coming out to train some of the doctors here."

David Cohen had pulled the bullet out of della Torre's elbow. Maybe he should be more grateful.

"He's going to spend his holiday operating on people?"

Irena laughed. "Funny thing is, he's not allowed to work here. He's restricted to lecturing."

"You mean gunshot wounds in Croatia are different from ones in London?"

"Blame the bureaucrats."

"He must be pretty keen to see you if he's willing to go to a war zone."

"He says that he might do a bit of research while he's here."

"I can just imagine the sort of research he'll be doing." Della Torre tried to say it with a certain levity, but it sounded more bitter than funny.

"Don't be like that, Marko."

"I might be back in Zagreb then. Maybe I'll look you up."

"Come for dinner."

"Do you remember last time?" he said, hopeful of igniting some small longing in her, hoping that stumbling night of painkillers and booze and exhaustion not so many weeks before had meant something to her. Even if nothing had happened between them. Had it? He sat back on the bed.

She ignored him. "How's Dubrovnik?"

"The way down was a bit rough."

"I heard the traffic jams have been awful."

"Deadly, you could say."

"Oh?"

"Nothing. But the rest has been a holiday. It's strange. I've been made almost entirely redundant. Just waiting to be told what to do." He stared out the window, watching the black clouds build, reminded of that day he'd met Horvat in Vukovar. When the heavens opened on him. How long ago had it been? A lifetime squeezed into a couple of weeks. The rough polyester bedcover scratched the backs of his thighs.

"Isn't that what the army's meant to be like?"

"I suppose it is. I keep forgetting I'm back in the army," he said.

"The boys here say it's ninety percent boredom and irritation, and ten percent sheer, mind-freezing terror."

"Sounds about right."

"Well, I hope it's all nice, sunny boredom for you."

"Thanks."

"By the way, I forgive you for the bullet hole."

"The what?"

"In the car. Captain Boban was very apologetic and one of his mechanics has patched it inside and out. All it needs now is a paint job."

"Oh yeah, and I'll bring you some petrol from Dubrovnik. Do you want the drinkable sort as well, or just the stuff you stick in the fuel tank?"

She laughed. "I forgive you that too. Just don't ask to borrow my car again." He heard a voice in the background. "Listen, I've got to run, I've been away longer than I'd intended. Maybe I'll see you next week."

"Maybe."

"I'd like that."

"I would too. Take care of yourself. Don't do anything dangerous."

"No chance," she said and then paused. "You neither."

"I'll try not to dive into the shallow end of the pool," he said.

"What? Oh, well, enjoy your holiday then."

They rang off. The skies had been crystal clear all week, and now they were as leaden, as troubled, as he felt. He mulled calling London, to hear Harry's voice again. The only woman he knew who could soften the pain of losing Irena. But he didn't.

Once, in anger, Irena had said that he missed her only because Balkan men were so incompetent they needed mothering all their lives. Later she apologized, because he'd lost his mother when he was young. She was right, of course. He could barely boil an egg. His father was only a little better. Growing up, there was always a female relative or friend who'd taken pity on them, made sure they were properly fed and that their clothes were cleaned. It was what women did there.

Was that all Irena had meant to him? A cooked meal and ironed shirts? No, even at his most self-hating, he knew he'd loved her for herself. Even now, after years apart, the sting of her absence was the hand that no longer brushed his. It hurt not to have the easy laughter of shared jokes, the stolen kiss after lunch, the Bach concert.

He sat naked on the bed until the wind caused the unsecured balcony door to bang against the little desk in the room, its rusty hinge braying like a donkey. He shut it and called Anzulović.

"Gringo, I'd almost forgotten what your voice sounds like. Enjoying your holiday?"

"Once, the bar ran out of ice. And I stubbed a toe on the rocks getting into the sea."

"I love hearing how you suffer. In Zagreb we're discovering the joys of a post-socialist summer. It's still hot and sweaty. Except now the reason you can't have ice cream isn't because they've run out, but because you can't afford it. It's called progress."

"I'll mail you some."

"Thanks. Get them to deliver it to Colonel Kakav."

"Happy families, is it?"

"More pleasant than you think. He's working from the sea-side. Calls twice a day to make sure the phone lines still work."

"Did you get anything on our Bosnian friends?"

"Yes, they're dead. Found in a burnt-out Mercedes near Gospić. Murdered by renegade Serb terrorists. Found a kid in the field nearby too. But you weren't calling about their welfare. Our records show that the older of the two adult males had a criminal conviction for smuggling, while one was wanted in Šibenik on an attempted rape from last summer. Who the hell calls their kid Elvis? Oh, and he'd also been questioned by the police in relation to a couple of murders that go back a few years. The kid was clean, as far as we know."

"So, generally, not nice people."

"Even worse than not nice. Cousins and known associates of the fellows you left in London. Who, by the way, are only being charged with gun possession by the Brits. The prosecution decided it wouldn't be able to get any of the shooting charges to stick." The Bosnian assassins who'd shot him had come off the worst in their gunfight with him and Strumbić. Well, Strumbić, really. Della Torre had been in no shape to pull a trigger even if he'd had the presence of mind to know where to point a gun. The Bosnians had been arrested as Dr. Cohen plugged their wounds in the London hospital.

None of this was news della Torre wanted to hear. "So Strumbić and I have somehow earned the Bosnian mafia's undying love."

"And one day they're going to run out of incompetents and start using people who know what they're doing."

"So what's the bad news, then?"

"The bad news is that Horvat is a really, really close friend of the Americans and has mentioned you a number of times to senior people in government. I'm told. He doesn't talk to me."

"I always wanted to be a celebrity," della Torre said.

"Enjoy it. One day you'll slip into anonymity like the rest of us." Anzulović paused and della Torre heard conversation on the other end of the line. "Listen, Gringo, I've got to go. Some emergency about the paper clip order."

Della Torre hung up but kept hold of the phone. He had half a mind to call his father, but then figured it would just depress him more. The old man would ask about Rebecca in a round-about way, and he'd have to lie.

.  .  .

He had fallen asleep reading in bed when a knock on the door made him stir.

"Thought you might be in here," Rebecca said, walking into the room without waiting for an answer. "Get some clothes on, I'd like you to meet a couple of people. And bring your passport. The American one." She smiled at his look of surprise, adding: "There are better ways of hiding it than wrapping it in your underwear."

She waited, watching while he dressed. Then she walked him down the hall and opened the door to a large suite.

There were three men, the big American from Zagreb and two others.

"Gentlemen, this is Marko della Torre. You've met John Dawes. And these are Rob and Bill."

Della Torre shook hands with them all, Bill and Rob repeating their names for him.

"John is just down to say hello. He'll be accompanying Julius back to Zagreb tomorrow," she said. "And the other two gentlemen are our backup. Just in case. They've been based here, but I thought it would be just as well for you to meet them in case we happen to need them later on. Though we won't."

"Well, I hope you've managed to enjoy Dubrovnik," della Torre said generally.

"It's a very nice town, Marko," Dawes said. The other two remained silent. "I'm sure that when things settle down there'll be many, many American tourists enjoying its refinements."

Della Torre hadn't noticed the other two at the hotel before, though they looked well established in the suite. They must have stayed out of the public areas. They couldn't have looked more American. Like Dawes, they had big white smiles and large builds, like college athletes who'd long since graduated to desk jobs, not quite fat but heading that way. Their hair was neat and well cut, in contrast to della Torre's. But mostly it was the clothes that did it. Polo shirts, tan chinos without belts, and deck shoes, no socks.

Rebecca put her hand on della Torre's forearm and guided him to the door.

"I thought it best for you to know we're not alone," she said, holding the door open for him. "And we'll need the passport. Don't worry, you'll get it back. Promise."

Della Torre looked around and then reluctantly handed over his American passport, his little blue key to freedom. It didn't matter. It had been forever compromised.

"It's been fascinating," della Torre said to the men. "We'll have to have a longer chat next time."

"You can count on that, Marko," Dawes said. "By the way, your Mr. Strumbić might want some company tonight, to keep him from having too good a time, if you know what I mean. I understand he's done a good job of keeping himself occupied."

Della Torre headed back to his room. He felt like a dog taken for the occasional walk, allowed to sniff a crotch or two, and then left to lie lazily on a sunny terrace. He'd have resented the Americans if he hadn't already been conditioned by Yugoslav bureaucracy. Anyway, the Americans were more pleasant about bossing him around. Eventually he'd learn what aspects of life he could control and what weren't worth worrying about.

He wondered whether Higgins had run into Bill and Rob.

He wondered how Rebecca was planning on doing the job. Killing the Montenegrin. He had little doubt about her intentions. Or that she was an assassin. But whatever her methods, he wasn't going to help, he promised himself. He wasn't going to be an accomplice. And fuck Horvat for expecting otherwise.

He wasn't sure how to stop her, though. Would he really sacrifice himself for the Montenegrin, another professional killer? No. He couldn't back out either. But he wouldn't help. He couldn't not help. He grimaced.

Della Torre asked the hotel switchboard to ring Strumbić's number, but as he expected, the cop wasn't there. He took a chance on Steve Higgins and got lucky.

"Mr. della Torre, what a pleasure. I'm glad you caught me. I was just on my way out."

"I thought I might buy you that dinner."

"Sounds great. If you don't mind my mixing work and pleasure."

"I'd be disappointed if you didn't."

.    .    .

They met by the big pink teddy bear in reception and walked along the hillside coastal road towards Dubrovnik's old town.

"My waiter heard from a friend of his that somebody interesting booked a table in a nice restaurant in town," Higgins said.

"Interesting for me?"

"Maybe." Higgins didn't elaborate.

"Oh, good. I like surprises," della Torre said. "You know anything about a couple of Americans staying at the hotel?"

"There's a few. Which ones were you thinking about?" Higgins asked.

"A couple of guys named Bill and Rob."

"They look government?"

"Maybe."

"I've seen them. They've been around for as long as I have but make themselves pretty scarce. I tried to talk to them but they weren't interested."

The wind had picked up and the sky was darker, but the rain that had threatened most of the day continued to hold off. They entered through the old city's massive ramparts. The walls never failed to awe della Torre. The city had been largely re-built in the seventeenth century, after an earthquake destroyed much of the medieval fortress. It was hard to believe anything could dent the solidity of those walls.

There were few people in the city's narrow, straight streets. The smell of rain kept what tourists there were under cover. Higgins and della Torre found a bar built into the wine cellar of a grand house near one of Dubrovnik's best fish restaurants, and sat on high stools by the window. Both ordered beers. Della Torre lit up a Lucky Strike and offered one to the Canadian, who hesitated before taking it.

"I don't know if I'm trying to quit or to start," he said apologetically. "I took it up when I was nineteen to annoy a girl-friend and have been stopping ever since."

"You couldn't irritate her any other way?"

"She hated it, and I was trying to be a wounded romantic. Besides, we were in Spain. Everyone smokes in Spain."

"So what happened?"

"She went off with another guy. In fact that's why I start-ed smoking, because she kept getting friendly with this guy. I wanted to make a point, not thinking she'd ever dump me."

"And you were left with a habit and no girl."

"Exactly. One of the worst trips of my life, and I've spent most of my time since university in war zones or shitholes, if you pardon my language." He paused, catching sight of a man walking down the Dubrovnik alley. "Here they are, or one of them, anyway."

The lights in the bar were dimmed and the windows small, but even with the storm clouds they could see outside. A man in late middle age passed them. Horvat. He was with someone else. Someone della Torre recognized.

"Any idea who that is with Horvat? Or is it just a body-guard?" Higgins asked.

"He's a fellow who goes by the name of Zdenko. Killed the chief of police in eastern Slavonia a couple of weeks back."

Higgins' eyebrows jumped. Della Torre was strangely pleased to be able to surprise the journalist with this nugget.

"Heard about that. Can't remember the cop's name."

"Rejkart."

"I assume the police might like to talk to this fellow."

"You'd be assuming right. Though it looks like he's under Horvat's protection."

"So Horvat had something to do with the killing?"

"Maybe," della Torre said. Like an iceberg maybe had something to do with the *Titanic*.

"Shall we order another beer and see if anyone else comes along?" Higgins asked.

"I was just thinking how thirsty I am," della Torre said, but stopped short of calling the bartender over. John Dawes and Rebecca were passing in front of the bar on the way to the same restaurant.

"Isn't that your pretty American friend?"

"A coincidence, I'm sure."

"It is Dubrovnik's best restaurant. No reason she shouldn't be going, though it looks like a double date," Higgins said.

"Yes," della Torre said. "Shall we see if it's a coincidence?"

They ambled across the Stradun, its paving stones smoothed to a perfect sheen by generations of pedestrians.

They looked in the windows of the restaurant but saw no sign of Horvat or the Americans. Della Torre went in and spoke to the maitre d', who told them the guests were in a private dining room and he could leave them a message, hinting there might be a price for the service. Della Torre declined, saying he thought the woman looked like an actress he'd seen in a film.

Deciding not to loiter, della Torre and Higgins wandered over to another, cheaper place for dinner. Overhead, an enormous flock of starlings took over the heavy dusk, wheeling through the alleyways and down the Stradun.

"How'd you know Horvat was coming?"

"A waiter friend of my waiter friend."

"Sounds like you've got diligent spies."

"I pay well."

"And Horvat being in Dubrovnik was of interest?" della Torre asked.

"Horvat being in Dubrovnik when I know there are gun trades going on is of interest. For war reporters, gun running is an interesting business. Because it usually leads to gun shooting. And when two sides are doing the shooting, sounds an awful lot like war. And when Canadian citizens who happen to be ministers in foreign governments are involved, especially citizens who own well-known pizza chains? I can see the headlines now. 'Dough Bullets. Daily .45 Specials. Fully Loaded Pizzas. Kalashnikovs to Go.' That he's associating with a cop killer makes it all the more interesting."

"You know, I suspect you could do this for a living."

"Mighty kind of you to say. After dinner, what do you think about finding your friend Mr. Strumbić? He's entertaining. And informative."

"And I suppose you know where he is?"

"No," the Canadian cowboy said. "But I know where he will be."

29

THE RINGING WOKE him. It was persistent, refusing to stop even when he hid his head under the pillow. When he finally struggled into consciousness, the telephone made itself hard to find.

"You awake?" It was Rebecca.

"Not yet," he said. "What time is it?"

"Time to get up. I just put Julius and John on an airplane, and now we start dealing with today."

"What time did you wake up Julius?"

"About two hours ago."

"He must have been happy."

"You could have got drunk licking him," she said.

"Would have poisoned you first."

"Have a shower, get some breakfast, and then come up to my room."

Della Torre hung up. He winced at the pain in his head, at the foul taste in his mouth, and the memory of the previous evening. Sometimes he wished he was one of those people whose minds went blank.

It had been him and Higgins and Strumbić. They had found Strumbić at a cellar bar in one of the houses in the thick of

Dubrovnik's landward alleys. Dark lighting and red fabrics. Strumbić was happy to see them both. They drank to the loud music, mostly metal from the 1970s. Della Torre particularly remembered the Led Zeppelin and Deep Purple, songs to which the bar's patrons, long-haired types in leather, knew all the words. Half-hearted graffiti marked the stone walls. Someone had inked the words "Pink Rock."

He pointed it out to Higgins.

"Maybe they were thinking floral," Higgins said. "The Six Pistils. No, the colours would Clash. Maybe Dead-heading the Kennedy Roses. Or Big Black Dahlia, or the... shit, can't think of how to work the Ramones into this. I'm losing my touch."

"I can promise you that I haven't got the faintest clue as to what you're talking about," della Torre said.

"Never mind. They're bad puns about difficult-listening music of the '70s."

Strumbić introduced them to his girl from Zagreb. She was tall and young and slutty in the way Strumbić liked them, with lots of makeup, big breasts, pretty if strong features, and a low-cut blouse. Strumbić had arrested her twice in Zagreb on vice charges but had let her off with a warning. He said.

There were a few other girls like her in the bar, which was surprisingly full for how early in the evening it was. The three men drank shots of slivovitz. Higgins went to the other side of the room to talk to one of the patrons he'd recognized.

"How do you feel about having to go back to Zagreb tomorrow?" della Torre asked.

Strumbić gave an elaborate shrug and then grinned, tapping his nose. "Maybe it'll be a flying visit."

"Any idea why they want you out of here?"

"Don't know, other than they're pricks and they got what they wanted out of me."

"You mean about the Montenegrin?"

"That and a stay in Šipan."

"I don't get it. What did we do there?"

"I don't either. I don't believe the stuff about wanting to see if the Bosnians taking potshots at us had friends. Or not entirely. She hadn't lined the place up for that. Nothing about these people makes much sense to me."

"Higgins says you've got an interesting deal going on down here. Mind telling me what?"

"None of your fucking business, and Higgins shouldn't have been talking to you."

"Smart guy. He's been here for a couple of weeks and knows more than the whole local police force already," della Torre said. "So what's your deal? Women? Drugs? Guns?"

Strumbić laughed. "Gringo, what kind of criminal do you take me for?"

"One with a practised eye for a lucrative deal and an easy piece of ass. So what is it?"

"CDs."

"What?"

Strumbić pointed to the big floor speakers in the corner of the bar. "Shit we're listening to now."

"Compact discs?" The technology had only just started making modest inroads among Croatia's wealthy. Della Torre was surprised there was any market.

"Yup," Strumbić said. "Bloody expensive. But Higgins knows a man who runs a boat from Istanbul to Bari."

"And?"

"He's got these machines back in Turkey that copy CDs. Copies them, packs them up, and sells them to the Italians. Once he's in international waters off Dubrovnik, he'll drop them off with somebody who'll run them to shore for me."

"How the hell does Higgins know this Turk?"

"Met him in Bulgaria or somewhere. I don't know. How the hell does he know me or you?"

Della Torre thought about how easily and smoothly Higgins

had inveigled his way into their acquaintance. He was a man who seemed to know how to find informative people.

"So you talked to this Turk?" della Torre said.

"Sure did. He'll make a dry run. He'll get one of his usual smugglers to drop off some samples for me next week. If it's agreeable, we've got a business. He'll do whatever CDs I want. All I've got to do is figure out which ones are going to sell. I know some people in Zagreb who'll distribute them for me. Plenty of out-of-work pimps needing a bit of cash."

"Which is why our ears are bleeding now?" della Torre asked.

"Oh, it's not so bad. And it makes the girls hot. And when they're hot, they start jiggling."

"One day I'm going to have a word with Mrs. Strumbić."

"Gringo, I'd rather you just shot me in the leg."

They had a wary laugh. Both had grown hoarse talking over the music and so they just drank, played some pool, pretended to dance with the girls, and drank some more. Della Torre wasn't sure what time they'd made their way back to the hotel, but he remembered walking in the rain, singing "House of the Rising Sun," swapping Dubrovnik for New Orleans in the lyrics.

It wasn't until Rebecca woke him that he realized how much he'd drunk the previous night. A quick swim and a breakfast of black coffee brought him close enough to life to be able to face her.

She looked amused when she answered the door. "Heard you singing last night."

"Oh, sorry."

"Well, come in."

She had a big suite with a view to Lokrum, Dubrovnik's island. Bill and Rob were sitting on the balcony, drinking coffee. Rebecca handed della Torre his passport.

"See, I told you you'd get it back."

"Thanks," he said, flipping through it. He stopped at some newly stamped pages. On one was an endorsed Croatian visa. On another a visa to enter Yugoslavia. Della Torre looked up.

"Oh, we thought you might like to travel as an American. That way if something happens, the State Department can get you out." Rebecca said it in a chipper way, but della Torre understood. Whatever happened, the American government had made sure it could get hold of him. And keep hold of him.

"Gives me a warm and fuzzy feeling," he said.

"Maybe you can do something for me now?"

"As long as it doesn't involve bright lights or loud noises."

"That bad, eh? Well, we're not heading off until this afternoon, so you've got time to recover. But first I'd like you to go down to the hotel kitchen and get me a whole fillet steak, one of those long, thin cuts of meat. Think you can do that?"

"Developed a taste for beef?"

"You might say."

"How do you want it cooked?"

"Raw, please. Get it cut into four chunks. And see if you can get them to put it in a strong plastic bag with a good seal. I don't want it bleeding all over the place. Here's some cash, unless you can get them to charge it to your room." She handed over a sheaf of Deutschmarks.

He came back straightaway, the meat wrapped in newspaper and a couple of plastic shopping bags. It had taken a substantial bribe to get the catering people to give it to him. They demanded to know why he wanted it, seeing as they had an excellent chef and a very good kitchen that would prepare it any way he liked. He told them the American redhead staying on the top floor liked to rub raw meat on her breasts to keep them looking young. But it was the money that shut them up.

Bill and Rob had spread out photographs on a table, along with a detailed map of the Bay of Kotor. Della Torre was called over to have a look. There were pictures of the Montenegrin, of his house and his village from various vantage points, some on the water, some from higher up.

"If your people can get these, what do you need me for?" he asked.

"Oh, our people didn't. They're mostly from your people. They come from UDBA files. Though Bill and Rob filled in some gaps," Rebecca said.

Della Torre looked through the photographs. She was right. They'd have needed unusually good access.

"Recognize all this?" she asked.

"Yes." He'd been there not long after the Montenegrin had retired. Before that, the interviews had always been held in Zagreb or at the Montenegrin's offices in Belgrade.

"You've been there before, haven't you?"

"Once."

"Tell me how you approached the village and the house, and what you did with your car."

"Well, the usual way would be to follow the coast road until you get to the main border crossing. Then you go to Herceg Novi." Della Torre traced the main road south with his finger. He was pretty sure they'd be turned back. Politely but firmly. And that would be the end of that.

"What about this?" asked Rebecca, pointing to a little route through the mountains. It was the route the Montenegrin had recommended and the one Higgins used to cross the border. He should have figured she'd know about it.

"Smugglers who know the local cops use it, but it's the best bet. We'd be pretty unlucky to get shot at," he said.

Rebecca nodded but didn't say any more.

"Anyway, once we're across we just follow the main road in to the bay. There's not a lot of choice of how to get in," he said.

The Bay of Kotor was one of nature's wonders. The outer bay was shaped like a plumber's bend, leading from the Adriatic into a harbour ringed by rocky hills. On the north shore was the port town Herceg Novi, overlooked by its angular, thick-walled fourteenth-century castle. The inland end of the outer bay narrowed into a tight channel, guarded on either side by steep escarpments, that led into the inner bay. The inner bay looked like a fjord transplanted to the Mediterranean, completely surrounded by the sharp-edged black mountains for which Montenegro was named. It was nature's equivalent of Dubrovnik's walled harbour, but on a much grander scale. Its defensive attributes made it a natural home for the Yugoslav navy; the dark mouths of submarine pens opened into the bay's secret corners.

The ancient and pretty town of Kotor, still being rebuilt after the earthquake that had destroyed the area a dozen years before, sat at the far end. Opposite Kotor and across the water, in one of the bay's other small inlets was the Montenegrin's village. The navy dissuaded tourists from visiting much of the inner bay. The steepness of the mountains meant that nearly all traffic went by boat or along the meandering road that wound its way around the bay, only just above where water met raw limestone.

"As far as I know, the Yugoslav navy hasn't reinstated its travel restrictions. Up until the '70s you'd have to go through a checkpoint to get into the inner bay, and you'd have to have a pretty good reason to be there. But that's neither here nor there for us, because the Montenegrin has his own security.

"As defensive positions go, you don't get much better. His people will know about every car before it gets within ten kilometres of the house. You could come in by water, but the neck of the bay is so narrow you'd have to get past half the Yugoslav navy first. And anyway, he'll have his informants there too.

"It's too mountainous for planes or parachutists, and helicopters wouldn't have anywhere to land, never mind the weird thermals. Even if some enemy force did make it in, he's got lots of deep ravines to hide in. This is his house," della Torre said, shifting his attention to a high-resolution aerial photograph, "the highest one in the village. It has good views. It's not far up the hill, but the road to the house is steep. Most people park down at the bottom and walk up." He paused, sifting through some of the surveillance photographs of the Montenegrin's house. "These ones weren't taken by the UDBA."

"How can you tell?"

"Because they were taken with a telephoto. A very powerful telephoto. The UDBA wouldn't have needed to do that."

"You're right."

"They're recent as well."

"And how do you know that?"

"Banner," he said, pointing to a corner of the photograph.

"Well spotted. Yes, it was taken in the spring."

"Around the time you were organizing your visit to my father?"

"Bingo."

He nodded. They'd had it all planned out. Get to the Montenegrin through della Torre. And get to della Torre through his father.

Della Torre straightened, turning to look out over the Adriatic at the forbidding sky.

"So what normally happens when somebody arrives at Djilas's house? How does he welcome guests?" she asked.

"Like Strumbić said, he's got somebody at the gate."

"Day and night?"

"I was only there the one time."

One of the Americans spoke up. "Two men keep sentry during the day; they disappear at night. Then, as far as we know, one man stays at the little cottage at the entrance to the courtyard. It's sort of a gatehouse. The overnight security seems to be just the two dogs that they let loose in the courtyard. I suppose they're there to wake up the guy in the cottage."

"Thanks, Bill," Rebecca said.

"I guess you could park next to the house. But you'd want to be pretty sure of your parking brake. Like I said, the road is steep," della Torre said.

"Where does he have sentry points around the bay?" Rebecca asked.

"Who knows? He'll have people who live all around. The local cops will keep him posted. So will all the fishermen. He'll have military people on his side too; some of them are there to make sure the Yugoslav forces don't make a move against him. Shopkeepers, street-sweepers. It's like dealing with a mafia godfather. Everyone wants to stay on his good side."

"But not so much that they won't insult his kid," Rebecca said.

"You have to understand the mentality here. People would think they were doing him a favour. As if to say that they understood and wouldn't think badly of him if he put her away. It wouldn't cross their minds that he might want to do otherwise. This is still the sort of country where they either hide the handicapped or put them on a stool with a sign around their neck and a begging bowl in front."

Della Torre wasn't sure what sort of reply he'd expected from Rebecca, but her indifference to what he'd said unsettled him. "How long do you think it'll take us to get down there using this inland route?" she asked.

"Depends on the border. With a free run, an hour and a half, two maybe."

She nodded. And then, still staring at the photographs in front of her, she asked: "You getting along with that Canadian?"

The question caught della Torre off guard. But why should anything surprise him?

"Higgins? Seems a nice guy," he said and then, like an afterthought: "He is a journalist, isn't he? Or is he your competition?"

"What makes you think we'd know?" Rebecca said.

"Are we playing games now?"

"He's a journalist. Though how long he'll be a journalist in Croatia is another matter. Your deputy defence minister doesn't take kindly to people asking too many questions about him," she said.

Della Torre absorbed what she'd just said. He realized she'd mentioned Higgins as a way of slipping in the warning. Why? So that he could pass it on to the Canadian? Just how tied in with Horvat were these Americans?

"What time do you think we should show up at Mr. Djilas's?" she asked.

"He said he'd be back in the afternoon and that he'd feed us. Which means we should be there by around six. It'll be a drive back in the small hours. Dinner might start early, but if we want him to talk, it'll go on late."

"So we have lunch here and head off soon after."

"That's about right."

"What do you think, boys?" Rebecca asked the two Americans.

"Sounds like a plan to me," said Rob. Or Bill.

**D**ELLA TORRE COULDN'T help smelling blood when he stepped into the Hilux. Maybe it was just the steaks.

He was still thick-headed, but sleep, pills, and lunch had knocked the edges off the pain. Even so, he could have done without the tape Rebecca plugged into the sound system. It was a pop compilation; not as rough as the music in the bar the night before, but it wasn't Schubert either. The song titles written on the case, he saw, were in somebody else's handwriting. But when he asked her about it, she said nothing.

They followed the coast road south, past the small port town of Cavtat and Dubrovnik's airport, and then cut inland.

There were some Croat militiamen about who made half-hearted efforts to stop them and then watched the truck pass into no man's land. The small paved road ran up into the hills that framed the mountainous point where the southern tips of Bosnia and Croatia met Montenegro.

The road was clear into the hills, though they could see a manned post up on a ridge. They didn't encounter the Yugoslav border guards until they'd driven over the crest, which looked across limitless low brush and sun-bleached mountains. Green and white. At night, the vista would be an impenetrable blackness far inland.

A truck was parked across the track at the bottom of a stony valley, where it met a bigger road that stretched far into the uninhabited distance and, in the other direction, south into Montenegro. One lonely building stood at the crossroads, a wooden hut with a tin roof and an elevated water tank next to it.

Two men wearing army fatigues and sporting machine guns made their way from the building. Rebecca stopped the Hilux and della Torre got out. On the hillside he could see a stone-and-sandbag emplacement.

Della Torre handed his and Rebecca's American passports to the militiamen, each with a hundred-Deutschmark note on the picture page.

"What's this for?" said the militiaman, waving the money at him.

Only then did della Torre notice the strange flashes on the soldiers' shoulders. One patch was the Serb's white double-headed eagle with a sword. Della Torre couldn't read the writing on it. The other was an image of a wolf's head.

"That's for the various fees for crossing the border," della Torre said.

"It says here you were born in Yugoslavia. Why do you have an American passport? Are you a spy?"

"I was born here and I speak the language, but I'm an American."

"An American spy who wants to bribe us to cross the border." The man looked at him with dead eyes.

"If you look, both passports have visas."

"If you have visas, why do you put money in them?"

"I don't know how long you've worked the borders, but there are always fees to pay."

The soldier pocketed both banknotes. "Both of you out of

the truck. Put your hands on the hood. It'll make my corporal nervous if you start dancing around, so I suggest you stay still. I'll see what you've got in the back."

Della Torre and Rebecca did as they were told. They watched through the windscreen as the soldier opened up the back of the Hilux and picked through their things. He walked to the front of the truck with a bottle of slivovitz and a box of biscuits. He had the expression of somebody who had picked up a cup of hot coffee only to find he was drinking warm mud.

"There's import duty on these," he said.

"How much?" della Torre asked.

"Fifty," the soldier said.

"Dinars?"

"Deutschmarks," the soldier replied.

"They're not worth a fifth of that. I'll tell you what, they're presents for a friend. I'll give you ten Deutschmarks. Otherwise you can keep the stuff," della Torre said. He wasn't sure the soldier wouldn't keep the stuff anyway.

"Twenty. And only because I'm a nice guy," the soldier said.

Della Torre shrugged. It wasn't his money anyway.

"Pay the nice man twenty Deutschmarks," he said to Rebecca. "It's a tax."

She paid.

"What's this?" the soldier said, still picking through their things.

"Steak," said della Torre.

"What do you need to bring steak for?"

"In case we get hungry."

"It's raw."

"Tartare."

"What?"

"That's what they call raw chopped steak."

"I thought that was called ground beef."

"It's ground beef if you cook it. Tartare if you eat it raw."

He could see the soldier making a mental note. Americans were barbarians who didn't cook their meat and didn't bring with them anything worth stealing.

"The visas are irregular," he said. Della Torre doubted that the Americans had got anything wrong. More likely they were going to be "taxed" further. "You and the lady can get into the truck. You're going to drive to the border post. It's two kilometres along this road. My corporal will be following you. And don't think because you're American you can get away with any funny business."

Della Torre translated for Rebecca, adding, "I wouldn't try that trick of running anybody over this time. Just keep it nice and easy."

The other soldier backed the militia truck, a new-looking Land Rover with a spotless paint job, out of the way so that Rebecca could drive past. She drove slowly down the centre of the road, the Land Rover hard on their tail. They passed through the barren landscape; there were no buildings or signs, just road and rock. And then, from nowhere, a soldier sauntered onto the median line in front of them and signalled for them to turn off onto a dirt track. They followed into a little clearing, where they stopped at a tired farmhouse flying the Serb and Yugoslav flags.

Della Torre wondered how much effort the U.S. government would make on his behalf. As a native Yugoslav, he belonged to a diplomatic netherworld.

They parked and the soldier from the Land Rover took the keys from Rebecca. He was holding both of their passports. He walked them to the house, where they were made to wait on a dark-stained bench that was more a pew, in what had been someone's sitting room. There wasn't any other furniture. The only decoration was a framed picture of Mary, her radiant heart almost anatomical in its detail. Della Torre rubbed his hands on his trousers and made to stand up once or twice.

Rebecca sat patiently, unperturbed.

It couldn't have been more than ten minutes, though it had felt much longer, before the soldier returned.

"You." He pointed to della Torre. Rebecca stood up but the man told her to sit. Della Torre followed him to an upstairs room, what looked to have been a bedroom once, though now it was bare except for a desk and an old walnut wardrobe. And then he laughed out loud.

"Sergeant Major," della Torre said, exhaling relief. He hadn't seen his old sergeant major, the one who'd trained him in the commandos, for…he tried to remember. "How long has it been?" he said, taking the older man's hand.

The sergeant major was in his late fifties. His moustache and his short-cropped hair were more salt than pepper, though he looked fitter than della Torre.

"Lieutenant Gringo. Must be at least six years. Maribor, wasn't it?"

The sergeant major had long before retired from the army, but he'd never been good with money. Slipping into a senior position with the border police was a fine way of supplementing his meagre pension, what with the ad hoc taxes and fines he could levy, not to mention the occasional carton of cigarettes or soap powder that fell off the back of a truck.

"It's major now," della Torre said, smiling.

Of all the non-coms who'd kicked his ass during his army days, the sergeant major had been his favourite.

"Ah, forgive me, Major. Just goes to show how far brains will get you when you aren't good for anything else."

Della Torre shrugged good-naturedly.

"So, Gringo, what's this about you being a spy? This thing real?" He waved della Torre's American passport at him.

"Between you and me?" della Torre said, lowering his voice. The older man nodded. "It's as real as a can of Coke."

"Well, I always knew there was something funny about you.

You were as useful as a three-legged donkey. Never knew why the commandos took you. Always did figure they were training you for a spy. So who are you working for?"

Della Torre nodded at the passport and reached into his wallet, pulling out his UDBA ID card.

"Well, that tells me everything and nothing. Good thing for you I was here."

"You've been knocked down to guarding border posts at the arse end of the world," della Torre said.

"At least it's not Kosovo." The sergeant laughed. "Gringo, this here is a world of shit. I was sent here to set up a border station, now that we're different countries and all. Or I think we are, anyway." Like most of the army's professional classes, he was Serb. "And then suddenly these guys with the fancy shoulders drop in on us from hell knows where and decide to throw their weight around."

"Who are they?"

"They call themselves the Wolves. They belong to a fellow named Gorki."

"I know about him." *And power was given unto them over the fourth part of the earth, to kill with sword, and with hunger, and with death, and with the beasts of the earth.*

"They figure the Croats need a bit of sorting out around here. Who am I to tell them what to do when they've got Belgrade behind them? So they moved the border a bit farther up the valley and they tell everybody what to do. They made a little headquarters for themselves back there—" He pointed with his thumb behind him. "—and they play their games. Frankly I'm surprised they let you through without shooting you first."

Della Torre nodded. "Any idea why they're here? Last I heard they were pissing on Vukovar."

"They're there, they're here. They've got more volunteers than they know what to do with. They call themselves patriots. But from what I've seen, they go to wherever they can smell money. Belgrade says they're allowed to keep what they steal. And I guess he thinks there'll be plenty enough to steal around here."

"What? Rocks?"

"Rocks around here. Richer pickings in Dubrovnik."

"They're heading for Dubrovnik?"

"Who knows what happens when the ceasefire ends, eh? Between you and me and these four walls, the local militias have mobilized. They're in the mountains, but they're ready for something. The Yugoslav army is with them and they've got plenty of big guns. So your guess is as good as mine."

"You going to let us through, Sergeant?"

"What's your business, if you don't mind my asking?"

"I don't mind. To have dinner with an old UDBA colleague."

"No spying?"

"What do you think?"

"I think I'd like it to be none of my business and that if you get into trouble you don't mention the fact that you know me."

"Never saw you before in my life," della Torre said.

"In that case, here's your passports. No problem with the visas that I can see. Except the inking on them's too good. Nobody stamps this neatly in any of our embassies." He handed them over to della Torre, who smiled back. "I'm not being funny," the older man continued, "but you've just got to watch these militia guys. They're all amateurs, but some of them are vicious."

"Criminals."

"Exactly. Here, you can't go without having a drink first." The sergeant pulled out a bottle and a couple of glasses. "Maybe we should get your friend up here to join us."

"She's driving. Anyway, she's a waste of good slivovitz."

"Bottoms up." They knocked back the scorching home-brewed alcohol and shook hands.

"When you coming back through?"

"Sometime late tonight."

"Save it till the morning. Drive down this road at night, you're liable to get shot at."

"I'll bear that in mind."

.     .     .

Della Torre walked back down the stairs to the living room. Rebecca hadn't shifted from her seat. She was smiling at Gorki's militiaman. The soldier affected an air of cool detachment, but the blush on his neck gave him away.

Della Torre and Rebecca got back in the car and drove on, unimpeded. Della Torre explained what had happened.

"Stroke of luck my old sergeant is running the post."

Rebecca said nothing.

"The Wolves are dangerous. We shouldn't cross back over too late. We'll have to eat and run," he said. Surely the thought of being trapped on this side of the border would make her think twice about doing anything foolish.

"We'll figure it out," Rebecca said.

The road wound through the valley, and as they approached the coast they took the fork to Herceg Novi. Della Torre longingly watched the green sign pointing back towards Dubrovnik pass by. They drove unmolested. There was plenty of military traffic, though nothing like a general mobilization.

They skirted the port town, following the signs for Kotor. Once they got to the waterfront, all they had to do was go left. There was a single road, and that was the road they needed to be on. They crawled along for a while behind a horse-drawn wagon, its rubber wheels the only concession to the last decade of the twentieth century.

And then they reached the channel to the inner bay. Under leaden skies, the landscape was forbidding. Dark, cavernous mountain walls funnelled into what looked more like an alpine lake, belied only by the palms that lined the shore. A ceiling of cloud obscured the mountaintops, casting their slopes into black shadow, while tendrils of mist hung halfway between the peaks and the water. The late afternoon sun had broken below the cover, oozing bloody light.

"Montenegro. Black mountains," della Torre said.

"They're something. You feel hemmed in here, don't you."

"You can only get in or out of this bay along the shore road or on one that goes east, up across the mountains." Della Torre pointed towards the opposite corner of the bay. "But that inland road just takes you deeper into Montenegro."

"There's a track on the map, seems to go straight up the mountain, on this side. Little town or village at the bottom. Just where the channel opens into the bay. If you trace it all the way up, it joins with the road to the little border crossing we used, doesn't it," Rebecca said.

Della Torre opened the detailed survey map in front of him. "There's a track that goes up from this side of the mountain and another one that goes up the other side. It finishes up not too far from the border post we used, but they don't actually meet up."

"So what's in between?"

"Meadows? Fields? Pastureland? Something like that," della Torre said, wondering why Rebecca had committed the route to memory.

"Let's have a look."

"Those little mountain roads are terrible. If somebody doesn't run you off the road, you end up in some ditch or in a house-sized pothole. These maps ought to come with a health warning."

"We've got time to do a little exploring."

Della Torre shrugged, knowing better than to protest. He didn't particularly want to be at the mercy of a local farmer or militiaman if they got stuck. But better that than carry on to the Montenegrin's. So he used the map to guide them through the waterside village, counting off the little side streets and alleys until he found the unmarked turning to the track up the mountainside.

"Why do you ask me for advice if you already know what you're going to be doing?" della Torre asked.

"To make you feel useful."

"Thanks."

They left the road that wound its way around the bay and followed a series of alpine hairpins, always rising. The road was asphalted until they passed the last houses, and then it became a rutted gravel track. The Hilux bounced up to what proved to be a steep pass. They stopped at the top and pulled over on a rocky verge. Della Torre got out of the truck and lit a cigarette. The clouds had started to break up and the landscape opened below them, heady scenery of brush and rock ending in the bay's deep metallic blue waters.

"I think I like this road," Rebecca said, stretching.

She stood with her toes over the edge of the steep escarpment. Della Torre steered clear of precipices. People overestimate risks they have no control over and underestimate the ones they can do something about. Falling down a cliff face, he figured, was something worth avoiding.

They got back into the truck and reversed back onto the track, della Torre's heart in his mouth and his feet grinding hard into an imaginary brake and clutch as Rebecca cut the corner so fine that one of the back wheels seemed to spin in empty space.

Then they drove on up the mountain until they finally reached a meadow, where two flattened grooves marked a route through hip-high stalks of dried yellow grass. It would have been too much for most cars, but the Hilux managed. They drove through the fields until they once again reached track; the path they'd taken connected the two sides of the mountain.

"I can't see why everybody doesn't use this shortcut," Rebecca said, putting the Hilux through a five-point turn to head back in the direction they'd come from.

*Because most people worry about replacing their exhaust manifolds*, della Torre thought to himself.

They bounced their way back up through the high mountain meadow and down the hairpins, the track forever threatening to crumble into a cascade of rock at the bends. They reached the main road along the bay and continued their journey until they were at the far side of the inner bay. The road there had been carved out of rock, threading its way between mountain and water.

"The Montenegrin has a real fortress here. They'll have been watching us coming for the past half-hour, wondering what we were doing going up the mountainside."

"We'll have to tell him we got lost," Rebecca said.

Della Torre laughed.

"I'm sure we're not the first people who've gone up there to get a view of the bay," she said.

"I'm sure you're right."

She slowed down coming into the Montenegrin's little fishing village. Della Torre suggested she park just off the main road, next to a little pebble beach, but Rebecca turned left and drove up the slope, making the Hilux's engine whine as the grade steepened.

"This it?" she asked when they reached the end of the path, deftly balancing the truck, pointed skyward towards the mountain's high peak, with clutch and accelerator. A young man with black hair was standing by a low steel gate that opened onto a courtyard.

"This is it. Pull up to the side of the house and put the truck in gear. If it rolls backwards, you'd better hope the Hilux floats."

"Don't worry about the truck," she said, parking it next to a recent-model white Ford Bronco. It was the first American car they'd seen in Montenegro.

**31**

**D**ELLA TORRE TOOK the bag of biscuits and booze that the militia-man at the border had refrained from stealing. Rebecca carried a straw shoulder bag. The man at the gate gave their bags a cursory search and asked them if they were armed. He looked them over with a practised eye. From somewhere behind the house came the rattle of heavy chains and the deep, throaty sound of dogs baying at the visitors' strange scent.

The young man shut the gate behind them with a solid clang as the Montenegrin briskly took the stairs down from the house's raised terrace.

"Gringo, how good to see you," he said, gripping della Torre's hand and grasping his shoulder at the same time. "Apologies for my dogs, but you can never be too careful. They're being taken to the back barn. It'll shut them up. Fine truck you've got there."

"You too," della Torre said.

Ever since he'd first met the man, all those years ago in his student digs in London, the Montenegrin triggered a ripple of... was it fear?... in della Torre.

"Need them around here. They're good, the Broncos. I've got another one at my son-in-law's. The Mercedes I don't dare

308

drive up here anymore. I park that down in the village. Forgot
to leave it in gear one day and almost had to go fishing for it.
Can you imagine what the bill would have looked like getting that cleaned up?" Della Torre whistled appreciatively. The
Montenegrin had an S-Class saloon. "But I like those Hiluxes."

"They're not bad. We picked up ours on a whim, you might
say, but we've been happy with it," della Torre said, and then
switched to English. "Sorry. Mr. Djilas, this is Rebecca Vees."

"How do you do," the Montenegrin replied in accented but
clear English. He was as tall as della Torre, but more solidly built. His face was tanned and lined, his eyes dark, almost
black. A neat greying moustache covered his lip. "Shame about
the weather, but at least it's not raining. Was a real pig last
night. We were on the water, though it felt more like we were
under it," the Montenegrin said.

"I just caught the start of the storm," della Torre said.

"Well, you were up late, then. Pissed down around three
o'clock. Didn't last all that long, but it was damn wet," the
Montenegrin said in Serbo-Croat. "Excuse me, I will talk
English now. I forget sometimes," he said to Rebecca.

"That's fine. I brought my translator," she said, offering the
Montenegrin one of her most vibrant smiles. He was a good-
looking man and not unused to women's attention, but he still
took her smile with pleasure.

"I brought a few little things," della Torre said. "I know you
pensioners get thirsty lounging around in the sun, and here's
something for the lady of the house." Della Torre handed over
the bottle and the biscuits. "If I remember correctly, these are
the biscuits your daughter likes."

"You have an excellent memory, Gringo. She will be very
pleased. Very pleased. She doesn't often come to say hello
to guests, but she remembers you fondly. She still has that
German toy bear you brought her. But for me, you shouldn't
have. This is nice slivovitz, but you'll see the rakija we make

here is even more special," he said, with real warmth.

They went up the stairs to a shaded table on the terrace, laid with sliced ham, salami, and cheese with red pepper, radishes, and tomatoes that glowed with ripeness.

"Something to nibble on. It's early yet for dinner. Come, you'll have some wine and we'll try the slivovitz and rakija later."

They sat and exchanged pleasantries, della Torre and Rebecca admiring the dramatic view of the bay, its looming mountains and sparkling waters made fierce by the red evening light.

"It seems that troops are building up in the mountains," della Torre said.

The Montenegrin nodded and then shrugged. "What they want with Dubrovnik, I don't know."

"It's attracting some strange types. Gorki's paramilitaries are down here."

"Yes, I heard. They're not welcome," the older man said.

"I once heard a rumour that there was friction between the two of you," della Torre ventured. He tried to sound casual but heard the tension in his voice.

"I don't think we ever met, though he might say different. There was a time when I came into contact with any number of petty criminals," the Montenegrin said, dismissing della Torre's weak volley.

"Didn't you work with him?"

"No. He worked for people at the firm but not for me. Someone dear to him was once..." The Montenegrin paused, careful with his words. "Damaged. As part of a special operation I was involved in. Nothing we ever discussed. It wouldn't ever have been part of your investigative remit. And nothing that is relevant to our conversation this evening. Anyway, that is the source of his grievance."

"The UDBA always kept him at arm's length. They never used him on any big jobs, as far as I know. What was wrong with him?" della Torre asked.

"You mean besides being a psychotic? He was stupid. Took stupid risks. Even for a criminal he made unacceptable mistakes."

"And yet Belgrade now loves him."

"Ah...Cometh the hour, cometh the man. And the hour that's coming is a time of monsters. Even so..." The Montenegrin shrugged and smiled, staring off into the distance. Rebecca continued to listen quietly. Della Torre found it uncanny how unobtrusive she'd made herself, sitting back in her chair so that she was out of the Montenegrin's immediate line of sight, her expression mild.

"So you're not involving yourself?" della Torre said.

"As long as the war doesn't come to me, I am staying out of it. I am happy fishing."

"I hear you fish up some interesting things."

"I hear a Zagreb cop was in Dubrovnik asking about me. Anything to do with you?"

"Unfortunately."

"So what did he tell you?"

"That you fish Chinese guns from the Adriatic, among other things."

The Montenegrin smiled. "Your friend is a capable cop, then."

"Lucrative business, isn't it? The Croats need guns."

"Could be better. But I don't sell to Croats."

"Oh?"

"No. They're the enemy, I'm told. I'm a wholesaler. The people I deal with do retail. Who they then sell on to is none of my business."

"I see. So why's business poor? I thought it'd be booming."

"It was. But it seems somebody is trying to nudge his way into this little corner of the market."

"And who might that be?"

The Montenegrin laughed. "Gringo, I've never known you to be naive or ill-informed."

"He was in Dubrovnik last night." Della Torre looked at Rebecca, who was nibbling some bread. She smiled as if oblivious as to what they were talking about.

"Was he now? He's made a habit of spending holiday time down here," the Montenegrin said.

"And in Vukovar."

"Who?" Rebecca piped up. She spoke with that naive, cheerful ignorance that della Torre had seen briefly when he first met her at his father's, and then again when he introduced her to Strumbić. She liked it when men underestimated her.

"Croatia's new deputy defence minister. A Mr. Horvat," said the Montenegrin, in an accommodating way. "But we're not here to talk about my business. You have questions to ask of me."

"Oh, yes, that would be terrific. Get all the bureaucracy out of the way," Rebecca said in a bubbly tone, like a Hollywood ingenue. Della Torre noticed how effortlessly she vaulted from the background to the centre of the conversation. "It really is just filling in history. I'm sure you'll appreciate that U.S. government law enforcement doesn't like mysteries. And if we can clear them up, well, that gets me a promotion. As for what we'd do in return, we would be happy to talk about a plea deal in exchange for your testimony, if you ever happened to travel to the States..."

The Montenegrin laughed.

"And we wouldn't look to extradite you if you travelled to other European countries."

Here the Montenegrin held up a hand. "That's not necessary. Most European governments would be more than happy to put me on trial themselves without having to pay the price of a flight to New York. In my time, the UDBA was active across the continent. I will talk to you because sometimes it is useful that people should think I have friends."

She pulled a plastic file folder and a yellow legal pad out of her straw bag.

"Really I ought to be recording this, but Marko said not to bring any electronics, just in case."

Della Torre looked surprised but Rebecca just smiled at him.

"I've become too cautious in my old age. I guess I saw what happened to too many people who had senior positions in my department," the Montenegrin said soothingly. "But it doesn't matter. I will talk slowly and clearly. Ask away."

She went through the formalities, asking for his full name, date of birth, when he'd worked for the UDBA, and his rank and responsibility at each point.

"So we know now that since the late '70s you were an officer in the liquidation squad and that in 1985 you became head of the department and then retired in 1989. During that time were you directly involved in the deaths of American citizens or of anyone on American soil?"

"American citizens, no, I don't believe so. Though I can't be sure one or two of the people we will be discussing were not dual nationals. Because I speak good English, or maybe not so good but better than most Yugoslavs, I was from the start involved in directing operations in the English-language countries and in the Nordic countries, because they often speak English there and because we had no senior people fluent in Nordic languages. We had people who spoke Dutch and German, so those were not my responsibilities until I took over the department. In 1978 we had one operation in the United States. In 1979 we had two operations in Canada and two in the United States. I was involved in all of those, together with a liaison in the Yugoslav embassy who was an UDBA officer but not part of the black operations squad."

"Black operations?" Rebecca asked innocently.

"Liquidations. Killings. Internally we called it black operations and sometimes wetworks."

"Oh."

From memory, he listed names, locations, and dates; he gave

the code names of the assassination teams but wouldn't give the names of the people who had pulled the trigger.

"That you will not get from me. Most of these people are criminals, but they were acting under legal orders just as I was."

"You seem to remember these things well," she said.

"When you have a hand in death, you remember," he said.

"Who gave the orders?"

"They came from the presidency, down to my superiors in the UDBA—even when they renamed it the SDB, we called it UDBA—and then I helped to organize or supervise the operations. I arranged whatever equipment was necessary—guns, cars, money. Everything was accounted for."

"How did you come into the United States?"

"On a Yugoslav passport. Not my own, but an official one in different names. Usually with residency stamps for a western European country, so that I could say I was going to the United States on holiday. I would always be given a visa."

"Never turned down?"

"No. I had money and a ticket out of the country. Why would they refuse a tourist? Or someone going on a business trip?"

"What kind of business?"

"Bookbinding. I know a little bit about that. As a boy I was apprenticed into the trade. That's what I would tell them. I am going to such-and-such a library to look at their bindings. Or book preservation. Or something like that. Who would refuse entry to a bookbinder with a bit of money?"

"And then?"

"And then I would establish myself in the same town as the target or the nearest big city, rent an apartment in a big building, and organize the operations. Usually we would get any specialist equipment through the diplomatic pouch or I would buy a gun from an official gun dealer. In the United States this was very easy. No problem. In Canada, I would have to bring the gun from the United States or from the embassy in Ottawa.

In Europe it is a little more difficult to arrange, but not much."

"And?"

"Before the job, sometimes for months before, we would have someone in the target's community making trouble. Telling stories about the target so that there was confusion about his intentions, or even an idea that he was an agent pro-vocateur acting on behalf of the UDBA, or that he wanted to start another faction away from the consensus. Something like that. News would rise to the local police authorities and they would think, 'Oh, no, another quarrelsome émigré.'

"Then the team would be assembled. Usually no more than three or four, though sometimes it was a sole agent. We would use people with criminal backgrounds so that if they were caught, the Yugoslav government could distance itself from the operation. They would usually meet me or another agent for a detailed briefing of what we wanted and how and when it could be achieved. They would then do a little groundwork and then do the job.

"When the job was done, we'd all leave pretty quickly. The authorities almost always put the killing down to ordinary criminal activity or to rivalries within the émigré community. Sometimes it was made to look like an accident, but usually the presidency wanted to send a clear message so that there would be no mistaking why someone was killed, at least among the émigrés. That would serve a dual function. The local police would think the dissidents were paranoid and crazy, and the dissidents would be terrified and at odds with each other. It was a very good system."

"And when you ran the operations, how many killings?"

"There was one in the United States and one in Canada."

"Who ordered them?"

"Gringo here investigated both—he knows as much about them as I do, more even—but the order came down from the presidency."

"Directly to you?"

"No, through the UDBA hierarchy. I would be passed orders from the head of the UDBA, who would get them directly from the presidency. Things became more complicated when I took over; there was more supervision and the black operations involved more paperwork. The parliament took a more direct interest in what the UDBA was doing. That's why Gringo here had a job. To monitor us. But before 1986, when I was head of teams, operations were assigned mostly by verbal command. Much less would be written down, or only in codes where the cipher was in people's heads. The order then would also come from the presidency, but it would often go through the Dispatcher..."

"The Dispatcher?" Rebecca asked.

"He was Tito's man, and then after Tito's death the presidency kept him on because he was very efficient at what he did. Belgrade would issue vague orders and he would interpret them and put them into action; he'd organize things. He would say, 'This person needs to be arrested and put away for this long. It needs to be done quietly.' Or 'Do it so everybody knows.' Or 'This person needs to be liquidated. Make sure it stands as a lesson.' Sometimes—not that I have direct experience of this—he would say, 'This person needs help. Make sure he is successful in his endeavours,' and that would be done. The person would be given money, or paperwork would be made easier, or he would suddenly be able to hire a very good employee for not a big expense. But the Dispatcher retired in 1986."

Rebecca was busy taking notes. The Montenegrin spoke freely, but he refused to divulge any names.

"If you wish to use this against me in the international courts, my defence would be that I acted lawfully, according to the rules and laws of Yugoslavia and in the interest of the state. There were unlawful killings, those that were not determined by the whole of the presidency and with the approval of the supreme court, but done on behalf of a single member of the presidency to further his own interests. Those were usually domestic, but sometimes they were done abroad." He paused for a beat and then added: "But I only ever acted on direct legal orders."

For the first time, della Torre felt that the Montenegrin was...no, not lying, but more than just concealing the truth.

Rebecca had a list of other names—people of Yugoslav ancestry who'd died in the U.S., and U.S. citizens who had been killed abroad—but the Montenegrin couldn't help. Della Torre knew it was all for show, that the American didn't really care about the answers. She asked the questions mechanically, with intelligence but without interest. Exactly as a dispassionate bureaucrat might do it. The Montenegrin might not have realized any differently, but della Torre knew that Rebecca was anything but a dispassionate bureaucrat. The interview was a sideline, no more than a ruse. Rebecca didn't care about what the Montenegrin had done or who he'd done it to or where. Her interest was in the man himself.

As the conversation wound down, the Montenegrin sent a man who had been hovering in the background to tell the woman who cooked for him to start supper. Della Torre watched the man go into the house. In its shadows he saw the girl.

**32**

THE MONTENEGRIN FOLLOWED della Torre's eyes.

"Snezhana," he called across the table. "Come, it's your friend Mr. della Torre, who brought you the German bear."

The girl shuffled towards them. Her legs, never fully straightened, moved at odd angles. One arm was twisted like a claw in front of her, while the other seemed to act on its own orders. The girl's head was turned down to one side; her mouth and neck twitched. Her father sat forward in his chair but left her to her own effort, beaming at her progress.

"Isn't she a clever girl. The doctors said she would never walk, and look at her. Oh, she'll never win a hundred-metre race, but neither will I. Will I, darling?"

They watched as she made it over to her father and applauded with him when she got close enough for him to lift her on his lap.

"Well done, my angel. And now you can thank Mr. della Torre for the bear, which you've been meaning to do since you last saw him."

With huge effort she stammered out a comprehensible thanks and then went on to ask della Torre how he was. She was like a broken bird, tiny, much smaller than a normal ten-year-old. For a while her father fed her bits of cheese and helped her drink water from his glass and then, when the young man came back to say that their food was almost prepared, the Montenegrin sent his daughter back into the house, watching her the whole way, again fighting the urge to spring to her side.

"Her aunt, who's cooking for us tonight, will help put her to bed. Though when I'm home, it's something I like to do," said the Montenegrin. "She's named after her mother, who died when she was born. For a long time I used to think I was cursed, that she and her mother were paying for my sins. Maybe they were. But I know now I am blessed. Because this girl is more precious than even my two older daughters. They are normal and ordinary in every way, but this one here, she is exceptional. She never ceases to amaze me."

"Oh," Rebecca said politely, her warm smile belying the incredulity that della Torre could see in her eyes. Parents always find something to brag about in their children; they always drive their expectations low enough to find something notable.

"She is one of the cleverest people I've ever met," the Montenegrin said, not noticing Rebecca's skepticism. But before he could warm to his theme, the food was brought out.

They had fried fish with fried potatoes, boiled chard, and a salad of cucumber, tomatoes, onions, and a hard, salty cheese not unlike a Greek feta. Simple food, well made, that della Torre enjoyed. The clouds had broken up to fill the evening sky with dark reds and oranges and purples above the black mountains.

After they'd eaten, the Montenegrin brought out a couple of unlabelled bottles full of a clear liquid with a pale blue tint. He poured three shots, and with a salutation they knocked them back.

Della Torre found Rebecca puzzling. All evening she'd been drinking her wine ostentatiously; she giggled at the smallest jokes and, though she'd dressed soberly in a suit, he noticed the top of her blouse had fewer buttons done up than when they'd started. They talked some politics but mostly it was about travel, places the Montenegrin had been to that she'd also visited. They talked about London and Paris and Stockholm, New York and Toronto. When she spoke, she put her hand on the Montenegrin's arm and he returned her bright smiles.

"As fine as your booze is, I have something interesting too," she said, pulling a bottle of Maker's Mark out of her bag. "I thought maybe you gentlemen might not have had much experience of old bourbon."

"How did you get that past the militiaman at the border?" della Torre asked, surprised.

"My little secret," she giggled.

"Do you have any other secrets?" the Montenegrin asked lightly, though there was an edge to his voice.

"No other secrets. Or not ones I tell to strange men." Rebecca giggled again. She dipped her chin and looked up at the Montenegrin, that shy, abashed look della Torre had seen before. "It was in my bag all along. He just didn't look very carefully."

Della Torre was surprised at her. Except for the night after their firefight with the Bosnians, she'd always drunk moderately in his company. A glass of watered-down wine or two, and no more than a shot of slivovitz. But she'd already had a skinful and was looking like she'd dug in for an evening's worth.

"Well, in that case, thank you very much," said the Montenegrin. "I developed a taste for bourbon in America, but there is little opportunity to find it here. Shall we drink a toast?"

He was merry. The interview hadn't been confrontational; indeed, it had been less of a formality than when della Torre had questioned him in the past. The mugginess of the day had dissipated, and now the evening air was cool and clear. And he was enjoying the company.

"I had better be careful of drinking too much. I still have work to do. You're never so busy as when you've retired," the Montenegrin said. "But don't worry yourself, Gringo, we have time. My men won't be here until after midnight. I'll sleep on the boat."

Out of the corner of his eye, della Torre saw Rebecca straighten for a moment. A brief turbulence rippled over her face and then disappeared. When he looked at her, he saw that she was smiling in the relaxed, lazy way of some drunks.

"But you, you must stay," he said to them. "You cannot drive these mountains after what we've drunk, and there's no hotel in the bay that's as comfortable as my house. I have plenty of rooms." The Montenegrin flicked his hand towards the building.

"I couldn't possibly," Rebecca said, leaning over the table so that the top of her blouse opened up. "It would be impert—impertinent," she said. Her speech wasn't slurred but was a semiquaver slower than usual. Neither of them was fit to drive in these mountains.

"Rebecca's right," della Torre said.

"Of course she's not. I insist. My women will give you a fine breakfast, an American breakfast. Eggs and fried speck. And you'll have freshly baked bread to soothe your stomachs after tonight, eh?"

Rebecca was leaning back in her chair, eyes half shut, smiling contentedly. Her cheeks were slightly flushed and her hair had come loose.

"Maybe it would be best if she took herself off now," della Torre said, giving in, grateful not to have to risk the drive.

"Of course," the Montenegrin agreed. He called his man over and told him to fetch his sister-in-law from the house.

A matronly woman with black whiskers above her lip came out. She wore a dark calico print with small deep red flowers. She nodded at the Montenegrin's request and showed della

Torre, who was helping prop Rebecca up, to a room on the same level as the terrace. Della Torre was to have the room next door. He went back out once he saw that Rebecca was settled on the bed, fully clothed.

"My apologies," he said.

"Never mind," the Montenegrin said. "Young women weren't made to drink. It's a lovely evening, and easy for someone unused to the strength of the liquor to succumb."

"Yes," della Torre said uncertainly.

"She is very pretty. Are you sure you have only a professional relationship?" the Montenegrin asked slyly.

"Purely functional."

"Ah, well. Would that I were a younger man and you were here longer," he laughed. "My life is complicated enough as it is without having to deal with a lawyer who works for the American government. Just imagine what the divorce would be like."

Della Torre grinned. "Your offer of breakfast is generous, but I think we'll leave early, as soon as we wake. It's best we don't stay too long."

"You'll have to mind the dogs. They are let loose in the courtyard at night. The men need their rest. Besides, nobody comes or goes along this road without my knowing. They'll be chained up in the morning, even before you wake."

"You have yourself well organized here."

"I have to. Belgrade already sent somebody for me. The people who took over from the UDBA. They didn't get far. I think perhaps Gorki is here for the same reason."

"For you?"

"Maybe. Maybe not only for me. But he will be interested in my welfare. That it does poorly. As I mentioned, we have some bad blood. If he had the opportunity, he'd be quite content to put a bullet or two in me. I have to say, I wondered about you too."

"Me?"

"You work for the Croats now," he said. "The dissidents who sit in government in Zagreb have no reason to love me."

"No. But they have plenty else on their plate to worry about without settling old scores," della Torre said.

"And Horvat?"

"That I don't know about. I was asked to bring along Rebecca because she wanted to ask you some questions on behalf of the U.S. government." Della Torre shrugged, helping himself to a shot of rakija. "It's nice, this. Smooth."

"Mine. Made it myself."

"I just do what I'm told. Like you did. Except my line of work is a little different."

"Gringo, you say that as if blood doesn't flow from pens. Trust me, there's nothing more deadly than a writ signed by a lawyer."

"Not my pen."

"Don't worry, Gringo. I trust you. As much as I trust anyone."

The clouds had dissipated. In the depths of that walled-in bay, it was like looking at the sky from the bottom of a well. The stars were everywhere, though the moon tried hard to bleach them out.

"It's good how well Snezhana seems. I'm sorry I didn't bring her some picture books," della Torre said.

"Picture books? She reads the most complex novels. Jules Verne, Dumas. I have for her a whole library of them. It's difficult. She has problems holding her head still and it wearies her, but she makes great efforts and, with a patient nursemaid, reads and reads and reads."

"Is that so?" Della Torre was genuinely surprised.

"Yes, it is wholly surprising, but I don't lie when I say she has the finest mind I have ever encountered. She calculates in her brain enormous sums. Ask her eight to the power of three and it takes her longer to speak the answer than it does to figure it out. She doesn't go to school, but I have a teacher come here three or four days a week to give her lessons in history and geography and anything else that catches her fancy. You saw how she walked. The doctors said she never would. But she has superhuman powers of will. She writes on a computer I bought for her. She writes wonderful stories, really wonderful ones. She understands Italian, speaks it too. And English. I taught her a little, but most of it she learned from watching videos and cartoons. German too. Everything. She has a little Sony Walkman, and I have people send me tapes from Frankfurt and London and other places, and she listens. For hours. Everything sinks in. What she could achieve if her body worked better, it frightens me to think."

Della Torre smiled. "That's wonderful."

"You are skeptical, I know. So would I be too. It is difficult to see until you get to know her, but inside that broken machine is a miracle. The doctors said she would be mentally incompetent. She makes them look like fools. What she understands and observes is incomprehensible to me. She thinks and thinks and thinks. And never does she pity herself. Never." The Montenegrin said the last word with finality.

"Do you think perhaps she might get better attention somewhere else?" della Torre said gently.

"Yes. She has a sister in Vienna, where they have a very good clinic for children like Snezhana. But she tells me she loves it here. I take her swimming; she enjoys the water. She enjoys the sun. She has no real playmates, but she says she doesn't mind so long as she has books. What can I say? She is content. I can give to her whatever she demands, and she has aunts and people to help her with her needs."

"And if something happens to you?"

"Then she'll be provided for here or in Vienna, as she chooses. And it will be her choice. There's a lawyer in Belgrade who looks after her interests. He will ensure all goes well."

"I'm sure you'll live a long time."

"Oh, don't bet on it. I spent too long in the UDBA to have any illusions. Eventually somebody will want to be rid of me enough to take the necessary risks."

"Horvat?"

"Horvat?" The Montenegrin laughed. "Maybe. Though he's an amateur next to some of the creatures Belgrade has."

"Gorki."

"Gorki. Him too, though I'm safe enough from him here. And when I'm on the water, we have some protection from the navy. Not everyone loves his paramilitaries. But there are other ways, and sometimes I have to be on the road." He made an elaborate gesture of resignation.

"Why? Why Gorki?"

"He fascinates you, this man. Ah, well, the most dangerous, the most extreme criminals are fascinating," the Montenegrin said, smoothing his fingers though his thick hair as he sat back in the chair. "Why Gorki? For me it was a job. For him, personal. There was a boy who got in the way. I was sorry for it."

"His?"

"His son? No, not like that. I don't know what it was. There were rumours about him, of course. That he liked boys in a less than paternal way, if you understand my meaning. It is not unusual among people who spend long periods in prison," the Montenegrin said. "Gorki was in jail at the time that this happened. I hadn't realized there was any . . . relationship between them. The boy was useful for a job that needed doing and, unfortunately, was expendable. Though I'm not sure Gorki sees it that way."

They were silent for a while, smoking cigarettes. The older man seemed lost in introspection. Della Torre sensed a weakening. The Montenegrin couldn't defeat age. The skin on his forearms had become a little looser, the face lined and burnt brown by the sun. Had he started to regret a life of constant secret war?

"Tell me about Pilgrim."

"What?" The Montenegrin was startled into sudden vigilance, sitting up smartly, his eyes narrowed. "Where did you hear of Pilgrim?"

"It was in some files. Just a passing mention. Cross-referenced to you," della Torre said, taken aback by the other man's sudden intensity.

"It was nothing," he said abruptly and then softened. "When I first met you—"

"In London?"

"Yes, in London, I felt...how can I say...regretful to have engaged you in the operation."

"Svjet?"

"Yes. It had to be done. And I tried to keep you out of it as much as possible. You were never meant to be more than a messenger boy. But..." He raised his hands, palms upward, leaving the thought unspoken.

Della Torre finished it for him: "But the job needed doing."

Della Torre wondered whether his younger self had been very different from Gorki's boy. Another useful pawn in the game UDBA played. And the Montenegrin played the game professionally. Rare was the day when Svjet didn't sneak through della Torre's thoughts like a rat at a Christmas feast, making him shudder...Svjet had been in his late fifties, not much older than the Montenegrin was now, but had already slipped into decrepitude. Harmless. He'd taught della Torre to love late Beethoven. And in return, della Torre had helped to destroy him. Who had Gorki's boy helped the Montenegrin to destroy?

"It can be quiet here, especially in the winter." The Montenegrin spoke quietly. "There's snow at the tops of the mountains, and it's cold; the whole bowl of the bay here fills with mist. It's like an army of ghosts. It seeps into your skin. Long evenings you spend talking to your memories."

"Yes." Della Torre understood. However much he struggled with Svjet's memory, the Montenegrin would be torn at by legions.

"Gringo, I've had a soft spot for you since then. You've always been a man of conscience. And don't think I haven't been grateful for the times when those people in Belgrade wanted an excuse to use me as their sacrificial goat. You were a thin defence against their lies, but it was all I had, and it worked. So I thank you." One of the reasons the Montenegrin had retired was because the Yugoslav government had begun to cast around for someone to blame for its murderous programs. Della Torre investigated assassinations. Not all were clean, but the Montenegrin had been scrupulous.

Della Torre lit a cigarette and offered one to the other man, who declined.

The Montenegrin sat back in his chair and watched della Torre against the sounds of the night. In the house a washing machine had flipped into the spin cycle, and somewhere across the bay a 50 cc motorbike could be heard going through the gears. The Montenegrin drank back his spirit.

"It's important that you not ask too much about Pilgrim, Gringo. For your own good."

Della Torre didn't mention that someone had already tried to kill him over the file. That however much he might want it to go away, Pilgrim would nag at him.

"Gringo, believe me, if I could help, I would." The Montenegrin stood up, unaffected by the evening's drinking. "Now it's late. My men will be here soon and I have some things to prepare. Get some sleep and pity me while you enjoy your breakfast. Especially if it's raining. It was good to see you again." He took della Torre hard by the hand. "Come see me again when you can. I'm afraid there might not be much more opportunity. And give Horvat a bit of advice: tell him to steer clear unless he can swim strong and far. Oh, before

I forget—that American redhead of yours. Well, you're a young man. Take every chance you get while you can. The wife doesn't need to know everything." He laughed, though with a certain hollowness.

## HELSINGBORG, MARCH 1986

H E WAS A big young man with red cheeks and an irritated expression. He was bundled up in his practical police uniform parka and a hat that covered his ears.

"You go there," he said again after the Montenegrin had made it clear he didn't understand Swedish. "There to behind the car and wait. You show papers."

He spoke English with difficulty. The Montenegrin had grown so used to the Swedes' fluency with the language that the young cop's struggles surprised him.

The Montenegrin nodded and rolled up his window.

He'd started to make mistakes. He'd believed the man at the ticket office about the lack of police scrutiny at the entrance to the ferry. He should have taken a later boat, done reconnaissance on foot to confirm it. But he'd been in a rush to get on the ferry, to get to Denmark. He dug his heel back under the seat to nudge the revolver further out of sight.

In his youth, on weekends, through school and then when on leave from the army, he'd mountaineered with friends all over the Dinaric and Julian Alps, the many sharp limestone peaks. They'd had neither the equipment nor the experience to match professional climbers, though they still managed some dangerous routes. Yet the biggest risks were always coming back down, when they were tired and in a rush to get to their hostel to drink and sing into the small hours. Sometimes they took shortcuts, failed to check their equipment properly. Rope burns and sprains, crushed fingers and cuts from falling rocks were typical. But on one trip a boy had fallen badly, breaking his back. He lay there overnight, in a deep ravine, until a military alpine rescue team could be brought in. The Montenegrin remembered him crying in pain, hour after hour, begging for death. Had he carried a gun then, he might have...

The boy walked again, but only after a year in bed and then only stiffly, always in pain.

The Montenegrin's climbing stopped after that, but it was a lesson he'd always applied to his work: beware the exit.

He could have blamed his lack of attention on fatigue, on the aftermath of the previous night's adrenaline, on the long drive and the little pills he'd used to stay awake. It had been too long since he'd been an active operative; maybe it was the stress of having to both plan and act that had made him slip.

But he suspected it had been something else. Killing the boy had distracted him. From the first day, he'd thought hard about what he'd do with him. He hadn't wanted the boy involved at all, but, well, there he'd been from the start—useful, involved, a gift from the gods. And then one to be sacrificed back to them.

As discreet as he seemed, the boy would have eventually guessed what had happened, would have figured out the Montenegrin's involvement in Palme's death. The risk was too great, and it was a risk the Montenegrin wasn't permitted to take. It was a solo job, always had been.

Whatever the source of his error, he had to deal with the fact that the Smith & Wesson was under his seat.

Another policeman was searching a car farther ahead. The driver, a youngish woman, stood by her car door, remonstrating with him, pointing towards the ferry. The policeman shrugged and continued to poke around the car's boot, his breath steaming in the cold. Farther along, the Montenegrin saw another policeman holding a dog, an Alsatian, on a lead.

His heart sank. He remembered the scraps of hashish the boy had had. They were in the plastic bag in the back of the car.

The young policeman waved the Montenegrin on towards a space behind the woman's car. The policeman ahead didn't seem to be very methodical about how he was conducting the search. As far as the Montenegrin could tell, these looked like ordinary traffic cops, not border guards or specialists.

The Montenegrin put the car in gear and gently pressed on the accelerator while letting up on the clutch. The car juddered and stalled. He started again and the same thing happened.

The young policeman came over to him, speaking loudly in Swedish to make himself heard through the closed windows. The Montenegrin shrugged.

The car rattled and shook as he tried to drive forward. He hadn't stopped for fuel on the way, but the gauge told him he had nearly a quarter of a tank left. Yet the juddering wouldn't stop.

"I'm sorry, I don't know what's happening," the Montenegrin said, feeling another wave of cold air wash into the car as he rolled down the window.

A third policeman came over and joined the young one standing by the driver's-side door. By now most of the heat had leaked out of the car. The cold was even more biting here by the sea than inland. This policeman also started speaking Swedish, until the first policeman told him, "English."

"You have maybe low fuel?"

"No. There's still diesel in the tank."

"Ah, engine is maybe cold?" The policeman took his glove off and felt the car's bonnet, and then shrugged. "You stop engine."

The Montenegrin turned off the engine. Despite the cold he felt sweat run down along his spine; he felt it form patches on his chest and under his arms. His hand trembled, hovering over the gearshift.

"Now you start engine." The Montenegrin turned the ignition. The engine caught but ran unevenly, as if it wanted to stall. Ahead, the ferry's horn sounded, along with an announcement that he couldn't understand. The younger policeman waved a van around the Montenegrin's car towards the ferry and then another car, not stopping either of them.

The Swedish policemen spoke to each other and then the one with the dog went towards the back of the car. Had he locked the boot? Was the dog trained to detect drugs? Would there be enough scent in this cold?

The young policeman stood by the passenger-side door, making a motion for the Montenegrin to roll down his window completely. He put his head and one shoulder in through the window. The Montenegrin pushed his heel under the seat, keeping the gun wedged back.

"We push, you drive, soft on clutch. Much gas but soft on clutch. Okay?"

The Montenegrin nodded. He revved the engine and lifted up as gently as he could on the clutch. The engine heaved but the car still managed to move forward. He steered it towards the back of the woman's car just as she pulled away towards the ferry.

The young policeman ran alongside the car, his shoulder on the door frame.

"You not stop. Go fast now, just go, up into boat," he said.

The Montenegrin wasn't sure he'd heard correctly, but the policeman kept waving him on. Maybe the cop didn't want to organize a tow truck. Better to let the ferry company deal with a breakdown.

"Go now fast, up into boat," the policeman shouted at him.

A ferry official stood at the side of the boat, arms crossed, watching the events.

The Montenegrin managed to continue his shaky progress, pressing the accelerator until the engine whined, getting enough momentum going to get the car into the ferry's maw and into an easy spot, moments before the heavy chains started to rattle, lifting the ramp. He caught a glimpse of the policemen looking pink and pleased with themselves, waving him off. He waved his thanks back.

For a long time, the Montenegrin sat in the cold of the car as the ship's engines sent a deep tremor through him. He sat in awe and fear of his own luck.

Perhaps it would evaporate now. Perhaps the passport people would conduct a search en route, as they did on trains sometimes.

The ship set off.

It wouldn't be a long passage. Drivers generally stayed in their cars on the ferry, though there was seating up top for foot passengers. There were few vehicles in the hold; it seemed to be a quiet morning. The Montenegrin got out of the car, fished the gun out from under the seat, wrapped it in a chamois cloth, and inserted it into his jacket pocket. He shut the door, not bothering to lock it behind him, and climbed up to the passenger level and then out onto the open deck. The morning was drained of colour apart from a washed-out blueness. The passage of the ship across the strait made a cutting breeze across the deck.

He hadn't worn his gloves, and his hand stuck where he touched the steel gunwale. The cold burned and he jerked his hand back. He leaned over to where he could see the green-grey water, almost metallic and hard. Beyond the bows, he could see the castle that guarded Helsingborg's Danish twin, Helsingor, ghosts watching from its parapets. He huddled in his coat, regretting leaving his gloves and hat in the car. The breeze whipped tears from his eyes.

He stood at the rail on the side of the ship and fished a fresh packet of cigarettes from an inside pocket. He lit the cigarette, crumpled the cellophane wrapper and foil paper, and dropped them into the sea. With a cursory look around, he reached into his pocket and took out the chamois-covered gun.

An arm grabbed him, causing him to half-turn and, as he did, to drop the gun on the metal deck with a clank. Stupid of him not to have been more careful. How could he have missed the man in the steward's uniform?

The steward spoke angrily at him, though the Swedish cadences made it sound almost like a song. Once again the Montenegrin went through the explanation that he understood nothing. The man relented slightly.

"It is forbidden from throwing things off the boat. Forbidden," he said. "No rubbish in the sea."

The Montenegrin had trapped the Smith & Wesson under the ball of his foot. Gingerly, like a professional footballer, he got his toes under the gun. As he bent down as if to pick it up, he managed to flip it over the fifteen-centimetre gunwale.

The gun tumbled with a metallic clatter against the side of the ship before it disappeared.

"Oh, I'm sorry. I am very clumsy in this cold. The cigarette paper slipped out. And now I've also lost my Thermos. I must remember to wear gloves."

The man nodded, suddenly sympathetic. "Yes, it happens sometimes. Sometimes people drop cameras too. But usually it is because they are throwing rubbish over the side."

"No," the Montenegrin said regretfully. "Now I have no coffee."

"Come, it is too cold here. We have good coffee. But if you are in a car you must hurry to drink, because we will be in port in twenty minutes. It is too cold to be outside and the news is too terrible."

"Yes," the Montenegrin said. "I heard. I am very sorry."

"We are all very sorry. Many did not like Palme, but for him to be killed is a very bad thing. A very bad thing. Come, I will buy you coffee."

## DUBROVNIK, AUGUST 1991

**H**E WAS FAST asleep. It was a deep, hard sleep, the sleep of a drowned man. Someone was shaking him, but in his half-slumber he dreamed it was the storm waves battering him against the rocks.

"Come on, Sleeping Beauty," Rebecca whispered in his ear. "Wake up and wake up quietly."

"What? What time is it? Is it morning already?" Della Torre's tongue was thick and furry.

"It is for you. Now. Clothes on, quick. We haven't got much time."

He dressed, stumbling, half drunk, barely sensible. Why was this woman forever waking him?

"Not that way. Here, out the window."

"What?" Was this, he wondered, part of his dream? No, he was cold and irritated in the way he became when woken in the middle of the night.

"Out the window, and be quiet."

His memory, hard claws on stone, scrabbled for something. Dogs. "What about the dogs?"

"Don't worry about the dogs. The front door is locked but the window works fine, so out we go."

"They'll rip our throats out."

"The most they could do right now is dribble on you. Come on."

He followed Rebecca as quietly as he could, stumbling out the window onto the terrace and from there down the steps to the weathered stone courtyard. The gate was already open. It was dark, barely any moonlight left, so he moved gingerly to avoid stumbling. He could see dog-shaped shadows lying on the ground.

She led him to the passenger seat of the Hilux and then quietly shut the door. When she'd gone around the truck and taken her place behind the wheel, rather than starting the engine she released the handbrake and shifted into neutral, letting gravity take the Hilux backwards down the hill. Its tires crunched gravel, but otherwise the truck made no noise. She let it pick up speed, keeping one hand on the wheel and twisting back so that she could make out the little pool of illuminated road at the bottom of the hill. As they shot into the light, she steered hard, tugging down ferociously and braking at the same time. Della Torre could sense Rebecca's intense concentration as she strained to keep the truck from falling off the embankment into the water. He felt the driver's-side wheels come off the road onto a narrow gravel verge, but Rebecca steered back onto the road, where they slowed to a stop.

Only then did she turn the key to fire up the engine, sliding it into gear and pulling forward, still without lights. Almost instantly they were beyond the reach of the village's street lamps. Even in daylight, the road could be treacherous for the unwary. In the dark, della Torre was certain she'd crush them into a cliff face or drop them into the bay. She drove slowly, guided by little more than the reflection of a waning moon on the bay's waters, and a sixth sense.

Della Torre was by now fully awake, his senses sharpened by adrenaline. "Like to tell me what's going on?"

"We're leaving our host a little earlier than forecast."

"Is that because you managed to slit his throat, and now we're making a run for it before his people slit ours?"

"No such luck. He left after you went to bed. A car collected him."

"You watched?"

"Of course I did."

"I thought you were drunk and asleep."

"You were meant to."

"Oh. And I take it you had something to do with the dogs. Poisoned?"

"They're just having a little sleep."

"Hence the steak."

"Bingo."

"So why are we stealing away in the night like a pair of thieves?"

"Because that's exactly what we are."

"What?" he said, more in a desire not to believe than out of disbelief.

That's when he noticed the mewling sound from behind him. He turned in his seat to see something spread across the back, covered in a blanket.

"What?" he said. Fear of the truth was dawning on him. "Stop."

"Can't stop now. Got to keep moving, we don't have much time."

They'd gone around a bend in the mountain that dropped into the bay, and they couldn't see a trace of the fishing village behind them. She'd switched on the parking lights to allow her to speed up.

"Stop, goddamn it."

"Sorry, Gringo. We're going to have people looking for us before long, and I don't want to be found. Not yet, anyway."

Della Torre twisted around, pressing against her as he did.

"Hey, watch what you're doing," Rebecca said as he climbed with great difficulty over the gearshift and emergency brake into the truck's back seat. He pulled back the bundled blanket. Snezhana's mouth was sealed with electrical tape, which also bound her arms and legs.

"I'll take these tapes off you, Snezhana. Don't be afraid. It's Marko. I'm sorry this is happening. I'm sorry this happened. I had no idea. This may hurt your skin a little. Here we go."

She gulped air with harsh, rasping breaths, her eyes wild. He unbound her arms and legs, which shook jerkily. He sat the little girl up in the seat, held her, smoothed her hair, told her that she'd be fine, that he'd make sure she was fine, that she'd be returned to her father quickly, as quickly as he could manage.

She calmed a little, making sounds that he knew were language but that he couldn't understand.

"Snezhana," he said in Serbo-Croat in a low voice barely above a whisper. "Listen, Snezhana, this will be like an adventure. It will be like *The Three Musketeers*. You like *The Three Musketeers*, don't you? They had jolly adventures, d'Artagnan and Porthos and Athos and Aramis. That's what this is, an adventure like that. The woman driving the car is—" He thought hard, trying to remember the names of the book's villains. "—one of Richelieu's henchmen, and you can be, oh, I don't know? The Queen. This is just a little game. Don't be scared."

His words seemed to calm her, though now he felt the wetness of the seat where she'd lain. He mopped up the urine as best he could with a cloth from the back of the truck and kept the girl wrapped in the dry part of the blanket.

They'd reached the little road, the spur that went up the mountain and over the ridge, where they'd gone sightseeing the previous afternoon. He now understood Rebecca's interest in the route. Though unmarked on the map, it was the only other possible route out of the hemmed-in bay. Anyone watching for them would expect them to go out the way they'd come in, along the waterside road past the narrow inlet separating the inner from the outer bay, and then back through Herceg Novi before turning up towards Dubrovnik. This was also the most direct approach to the smugglers' border crossing.

Rebecca now had the lights on as she drove up the tight hairpins.

"You're mad," he said to her. "How do you propose getting the girl over the border? I assume you didn't manage to find her passport."

"You, Gringo, are going to get us all over the border. Children don't need passports in this country; they can travel on their parents'."

"They need to be registered on their parents' passport."

"Well, you'll just have to say that she needs a hospital badly and has to go to the one in Dubrovnik. Anyone looking at her will know you're not kidding. And it's not likely you'd be kidnapping a cripple for any reason, is it?"

"And what if I don't?"

"If you don't, well, you'll remember I am under the absolute protection of the United States government. As for you, maybe you are and maybe you aren't. I'll just tell them you kidnapped the girl and threatened me, forcing me to drive you to the border. How long do you think you'll live when your friend Mr. Djilas gets hold of you?"

He turned to the little girl again. "Snezhana, this will be like the story of..." He paused. He'd never told a children's story. What stories did they like? He scratched around his memory but only remembered fragments. Did Hansel and Gretel have a wolf? Then a tune crept into his head. "...the Ring. Do you know it?"

She stammered out a "No."

"Ah, you're in for a treat, because this story has giants and gods and a ring and dragons. Shall I tell it to you?"

This time she said, "Yes," with great effort.

He told her the story Wagner had turned into his epic. He embellished here and there and hummed some of the themes of the great opera cycle, the story of theft and revenge and broken vows.

Daylight broke. Rebecca kept to the small road along the ridge. A pale white light broke across the sky behind them, though the bowl of the bay below them remained dark. They drove past single houses and through woodland, the track becoming increasingly primitive, gouged from the high meadow, so that for almost a kilometre they bounced hard from rock to rut, Rebecca clinging to what path there was, until at long last they reached tarmac again.

And then they descended, not as steeply as they'd climbed, to a valley where they finally reached the road that would take them to the border. Only there did they encounter some traffic, a couple of green trucks with canvas. They were on a flat, open stretch, within sight of where the hills formed the border between Croatia and what was left of Yugoslavia, when a Land Rover with military markings turned from a farmer's ramshackle yard onto the road in front of them, cutting them off, and a car drew up behind.

Soldiers emerged, pointing their guns at the Hilux.

"Out," one of them shouted. "Everyone out."

"We need to get out of the car. Now's not a time to be funny, okay?" della Torre said to Rebecca.

Rebecca stepped out with her hands up. Della Torre held one up, the other supporting the little girl. Dawn was edging down the valley, though the air was still cool and damp with the night's dew. He could smell rosemary and pine resin and the faint traces of wood smoke and ash. The clouds made an uncertain sky.

A heavily armed soldier approached. He had the wolf flashings on his shoulder.

"Put the kid back in the truck."

The soldier motioned across della Torre with the weapon. He did as he was told.

Then the soldier prodded him forward to the camouflage-painted Land Rover and into the rear seat, next to another paramilitary. Unaccountably, it amused della Torre that the man had a mullet haircut, like a German footballer from the 1970s. He knew enough to keep his mouth shut. Not least because the man held a blunt-nosed submachine gun aimed at his side. The soldier who'd marched him to the car took his place next to the driver.

Della Torre watched as Rebecca was led more politely to the other truck. Another soldier got into the driver's seat of the Hilux and then all three vehicles headed off in convoy towards the farmhouse border post where he'd been entertained by his old sergeant the day before.

But this time around, his welcome was less cordial. They parked next to the outbuildings by the side of the farmhouse, and the soldier with the machine gun yanked him out of the car. Using the gun like a farmer might use a stick to steer a cow, he pushed della Torre into an ox shed. The heavy wooden door creaked shut and he heard it bolted behind him. He was alone, and for a moment he stood there contemplating the space.

A feeble naked bulb fixed high on a wall illuminated the disused barn. There were no windows and no other way out, though light glinted between the high beams and the tiled roof. It was roomy, square, with stone walls and a stone floor. He thought it wouldn't be too difficult to climb the rough-built wall and dislodge a couple of tiles from the roof. He'd be able to make an escape that way. But he suspected he wouldn't get far. He'd seen at least two dozen militiamen around the farmhouse. There'd be more in the surrounding countryside.

Chains were fixed into the wall at one end, with a rough wooden manger built in below them. The floor was stained in the corner there. A black stain like oil. Or dried blood.

He was fit to burst and pissed into a drain cut into the wall. It wasn't a terrible prison, though he'd have liked somewhere better to sit than a scrap of old straw.

He'd been there for maybe twenty minutes, squatting in the cool dark, comforted by the faded smells of cattle and wondering what would happen, when he heard the door bolt open. He stood nervously before it opened. It was his sergeant. For a moment relief washed over him, but the expression on the old soldier's face brought him back down.

"Gringo, I really don't know what you were thinking, but this is an enormous fuck-up. Kidnapping isn't taken lightly around here."

"Is the girl okay?"

"Who knows? Nobody can get any sense out of her. But she's being treated well."

"Good."

"No, not so good. Bad. I mean, I don't know whether she's okay or not, but you won't be. You've got a Montenegrin godfather called Djilas whose people are kicking like a field of mules being eaten by horseflies. But he's not your most pressing problem. Mr. Gorki is coming. Gringo, I will do all I can to keep you alive, but even though I'm regular army—maybe because I'm regular army—I don't carry any more weight than a peanut seller these days. I brought you a bit of paper and a pen. In case anything happens to you, write to your folks. I know your mother's dead, but your father's still around, isn't he? We sometimes read him in the paper. Gorki will be here in half an hour. Write to your father and your wife. I'll make sure your letters get to them."

The old soldier looked sad and puzzled at the seriousness of what had befallen them all. Even if della Torre escaped frontier justice, the law wouldn't be kind to him, wherever it might choose to weigh his guilt.

"What about the woman?" della Torre asked.

"The redhead? She's an American. A real American, not like you, Gringo. As long as America doesn't let the Croats buy weapons to shoot back at us, we're not going to step on any American toes. Even a dumb peasant like me knows that. But you, Gringo…" He shook his head as if in wonder. "Well, I'll do what I can, though I'll be in the shit for letting you through yesterday. Here—" The sergeant handed della Torre a pack of cigarettes and a lighter. "Just don't set yourself on fire. And don't try to climb out. They caught a smuggler the other day who tried to pay the import taxes with fake Deutschmarks—photocopies, if you can believe it. He thought he could get through the roof. He couldn't. Got stuck. Somebody had to shoot him down. Anyway, write, Gringo, write. It may be the last chance you have. Leave the letters in the manger. I'll find them later."

He shut and bolted the door behind him. Della Torre understood the catastrophic consequences of having been caught with the girl. He thought of Gorki's men near Vukovar—Rejkart had said Gorki'd killed how many? Forty civilians and Croat police, shot through the eye. Would Gorki dare to kill him, here, now? He was rabid, but not stupid.

Gorki would either deliver him to Belgrade or sell him to the Montenegrin. Wherever his best advantage lay. Della Torre took some comfort in the fact that he'd been treated well so far. Would the Americans intercede if he was sent to Belgrade? Or would they deny his citizenship? If Gorki delivered him to the Montenegrin, would he be able to convince the old man he'd had no part in his daughter's kidnapping?

Della Torre weighed the odds. They tilted heavily in the wrong direction.

He stared at the clean white paper, almost as thin as onion skin, held firmly by the clipboard's metal teeth, and took the lid off the cheap Biro. What could he write?

He scribbled out a tremulous note to his father, apologizing for the hurt he was bound to cause. For once, his neat, tiny, mechanical handwriting was fractured. He wrote to Irena to tell her that he loved her still and wished her love and luck and children. He wrote to Anzulović, explaining what had happened in as few words as he could, with a farewell to Strumbić. He'd always liked the rogue. And a few last lines to Harry, remembering most of the address in London. The British postal system would get it to her.

The letters seemed pathetic, insufficient even as a gesture. He'd tried to steer clear of platitudes but realized there was little else left. Small, empty scratchings of a life. He hid the pages under the hay when he heard the bolt being drawn back.

.　　.　　.

Della Torre recognized the warlord from old photographs. Gorki was a big man, not tall so much as massive, with a big, round head and strong shoulders, like a stevedore. He wore an ironic expression, one side of his mouth curled up in a half smile. He indicated for della Torre to sit.

"We will speak in English so this cretin here doesn't listen," he said, motioning towards the soldier in the room.

"You speak it well," della Torre said.

"And French and German and some Italian and more Swedish than I'll ever find useful again."

"I'm impressed."

"Don't be. Most of these languages I learned in jails."

"Yes, I heard you've enjoyed the hospitality of a number of countries."

"They were holiday camps. Here in Yugoslavia we do things differently. And here—" He pointed at his desk. "—we do things differently still. Here, I'm the jailer. And the judge. And the jury. And the executioner."

Della Torre felt his pulse race. It took effort to remain calm. He lit a cigarette. The soldier had allowed him to keep the half-pack of Lords. His Lucky Strikes were still in the Hilux.

"What is this I hear about Croat UDBA agents with American passports kidnapping Montenegrin children? It must be true that Croats drink our children's blood. Eh? Vampires."

Della Torre said nothing.

"The American woman said she was driving the girl to the hospital. The child certainly seems ill to me, but what do I know, I'm no doctor."

Gorki's eyes were wide-set on his broad face, but his mouth was small and disapproving above a strong chin. It wasn't an unpleasant face, but something about it suggested a casual violence. More generally, there seemed a certain fastidiousness to him. Della Torre could almost taste the other man's cologne.

"Are you a spy, Captain della Torre? An American spy?" He held up della Torre's American passport, an edge of anger rising in his voice. "Or a Croat spy using American papers? Eh? We hang spies."

Still della Torre remained quiet, not knowing what was expected of him. Gorki exhaled and sat back in his chair, playing with della Torre's passport.

"We had an alert this morning. It went to all police and border posts that Mr. Djilas's child had been kidnapped. The description matched that of the spastic in your car. But nobody can make any sense of what she's saying, so we can't confirm the name." He shrugged, his voice calm again. "The child needs a hospital. It's obvious. Eh? Needs a doctor. And Dubrovnik is just over there. I mean, she could go back to the hospital at Herceg Novi, but I think the Dubrovnik hospital is better. What do you think?"

Della Torre remained silent. His throat was dry and he struggled to swallow.

"So we have to make a judgement."

Gorki ran his hand over the top of his closely shaved head as if troubled by deep complications.

Della Torre watched with the hollow eyes of a slave. How many photographs had he seen in the UDBA files, portraits of condemned men in profile and directly facing the camera, knowing their fate, their eyes simultaneously pleading and full of despair, shorn of hope? That's what it was like, staring into dead men's eyes.

"Mr. Djilas is an unfortunate man. Unfortunate for not having taken better care of his daughter. But that's not something I can help with, is it? Eh? Poor Mr. Djilas."

Gorki lit his own cigarette and drew hard on it, letting the smoke curl out of his nostrils. He sipped from a small cup of coffee.

"My men were very excited when they saw you; they thought you must be the kidnappers of Mr. Djilas's daughter." He unrolled a long scroll of fax paper. "Same truck, same man, same red-headed woman. Crippled child. Such a close match, don't you think?" he said, looking up at della Torre. "How likely is it that there could be another? Eh? But the world is a mysterious place."

He paused, glancing at the window and smiling.

"I think they're mistaken. You and the American woman are humanitarians, taking a crippled girl to the hospital in Dubrovnik. If that's the case, you shouldn't be delayed. And I'll tell my men to keep a watch for a girl matching Mr. Djilas's daughter's description." Gorki yawned like a sated wolf. "Poor Mr. Djilas. Truly, he has chosen his enemies badly," he said, smiling. He drank down the coffee. "Once, a long time ago, he made a boy disappear. Poof. Into the Swedish night. Maybe he'll regret that now that his daughter has disappeared. Poof. Into the Montenegrin night. Eh?"

Della Torre had a hard time understanding what was happening. He heard Gorki's words but stumbled over their meaning.

"I don't know why you're sitting there. The American woman will be waiting in the truck and so is the girl. She looks so similar to the description of Djilas's daughter. The world is so full of these strange coincidences. Don't you think?" Gorki looked at his wristwatch, a chunky gold Rolex. "It is time the border post was opened."

He extended the blue-bound passport towards della Torre, his thumb on the American eagle crest, quiver of arrows in one talon, olive branch in the other. Della Torre reached to take it but Gorki wouldn't let go, gripping it tightly. Della Torre didn't dare pull hard. Maybe that was the message. Gorki's eyes mocked him, and then he released the document.

Della Torre left the room. Had the man not been an undying enemy of the Montenegrin's, he might have had him executed in the ox shed.

Della Torre climbed into the back seat of the Hilux, next to Snezhana, who twitched and trembled. He didn't say a word to Rebecca, but instead put an arm around the girl and said, in Serbo-Croat, "I'm sorry. We shall continue the story if you like, and then I will think of how to get you back to your father. Have faith in me."

**35**

THEY DROVE TO the coast, and then north. They drove under lidded skies, past the Hotel Argentina, past Dubrovnik's high white walls. They didn't stop until they reached the fishing village opposite Šipan. Strumbić's motorboat was at the dock. One of Rebecca's Americans was waiting to ferry them across to the island.

"Is Strumbić back, then?" della Torre asked, breaking his long silence.

"No."

"So you've taken over his house and his boat?"

"We thought we'd need a nice safe place. The Hotel Argentina is a little too public and accessible." She laughed and then stared at the girl sitting, small next to della Torre in the boat.

"How did he know?" della Torre asked, looking at Bill.

"I called. While you were indisposed back at the border."

Della Torre watched her. Had they planned things this way? Had it been one of a number of contingencies? Or were they merely infinitely adaptable, with their technology, their money, their unshakable confidence? They were Americans, after all.

"Did you know my old sergeant would be there?" he asked over the engine's motor.

"Hmm? Oh, no. *That* was a lucky accident," she said.

"But Gorki wasn't?"

She turned away from him to keep her hair from blowing in her face. "We should have blindfolded her," she said. "But the kid's probably too retarded to really understand what's going on, so I won't worry about it."

Della Torre held the girl. She was still wrapped in the blanket. He'd removed some of her wet clothes but knew he needed to give her a bath and get her properly dry. He'd gently fed her water from a bottle during the drive, spilling it into his hand, which he wiped on himself so as not to get her more wet. But now he was worried she'd get cold in the wind during the crossing.

"So what's going to happen now?"

"You're going to call Djilas and arrange to hand over the girl."

"What if he's not back yet?"

"In that case, you'll tell his people that he's to be back tomorrow evening and that we'll make arrangements for the following day. Otherwise we send the girl to an orphanage. We'll find somewhere in Romania." She laughed.

"She needs clothes. Her things are wet. Let me settle her down and go to Dubrovnik to buy her something to wear."

"You can take a ferry tomorrow morning. Rob and Bill brought your stuff from the hotel. She'll have to make do for today. All you've got to worry about is getting in touch with Djilas."

They docked against the concrete pier under the disapproving gaze of Strumbić's villa. Della Torre carried Snezhana to the house. Without discussing matters with the Americans, he took her upstairs and bathed her in Strumbić's ensuite bathroom. He dressed her in one of his T-shirts and then handwashed her wet clothes while she sat on the edge of the bed, keeping a watchful eye on him. At first he thought she was moaning to herself. But slowly he made out what she was saying.

She said not to worry. To be brave. He thought maybe she was talking to herself, but then realized she was talking to him. Telling him not to fear.

He carried the girl downstairs, where he found some bread and cheese. He sat her on a cushioned chair and tore off small bits of the food for her, as he'd seen her father do the previous night. The morning clouds had broken up, and in the hot sun a small-leafed tree cast scattered shadows across the courtyard.

He saw that she was less helpless than he'd thought. The right side of her body functioned poorly, but she had more control of the left. Slowly she fed herself. When he listened carefully, he could understand her. After they'd eaten, she spoke a little.

"Milady," Snezhana said, as if ruminating. For a moment he didn't think that he'd heard properly, and then realized she was laughing. The Milady in Dumas's novel had lost her head. Was she thinking of Rebecca?

"Yes?" he said.

"Daddy will find me. He leads a dangerous life and so must I. But he will get me."

"We'll get you back to your father. Don't you worry," della Torre said again. "Your father said you like to swim. Would you like to go now? I will hold you. And then I'll tell you some more stories, if you like. I haven't any books you can read, but I'll see if I can remember some stories from when I was your age. Tomorrow morning, early, I'll go to Dubrovnik to get you some clothes. I'll be back as quickly as I can, so that you're not alone for long."

"Yes, please, I would like to swim," she said, her tongue struggling to form the words. Each sentence ended in a sigh of relief.

One of the Americans tried to stop della Torre, but Rebecca

was there and she nodded her consent. It was an island, after all, and the child was incapable of making any escape.

The water was warm in the midday heat. Snezhana clung to his neck with her left hand, bobbing with him. She laboriously explained that her father was much more daring when they swam.

But once, as she thrashed on the little waves, she inhaled some water and coughed hard. He took her to the stone jetty until her lungs calmed and then carried her back up to the house, wrapped in a towel. He rinsed her of salt, dressed her back in his T-shirt, and kept her company in the room he'd taken for her, Strumbić's room. He watched over her, always poised to catch her, as she exercised by walking slowly around the bed, until finally she asked to lie down.

Rebecca called him before the little girl had fallen asleep.

"Time to make your phone call," she said, holding the satellite phone's handset towards him.

.    .    .

He was up before daybreak. He left the girl still sleeping, though he brought up a plastic glass of water and some crumbled bread and cheese for her to eat when she woke.

He took the early ferry, and one of the Americans, Rob, who'd already been up when della Torre came down, went with him. Della Torre smoked by the rail, watching the cold dawn rise and spread across the mountains high above the shoreline, while the American watched him.

They reached Dubrovnik's port in less than three-quarters of an hour. The shops were mostly still shut, so he found a bar open for a coffee and a breakfast roll. Rob sat with him.

He watched the news footage from Vukovar on a wall-mounted television. Sporadic fighting had broken out around the Serb villages that circled the town. The Serb militias were being supported by Yugoslav army regulars. The Croat national guard and police force seemed feeble by comparison, lightly armed and few in number. So far the violence had been contained. But della Torre wondered how long before the embers would be blown into a conflagration. His stomach sank at the thought of Irena caught in the middle of it all.

Rob tapped on his watch until della Torre got the hint. It didn't take much wandering around Dubrovnik's modern northern port before he found a shop selling children's clothes. It was shut but the proprietor was in, organizing stock. Della Torre spread a fan of Deutschmarks in front of the window. Business had been slow that summer, and the proprietor took the hint. Rob went in with him but quickly grew bored with della Torre's indecision. When the American had assured himself there was no other way out of the shop, he walked across the road and waited on a bench.

Della Torre didn't know how long Rebecca planned on keeping the girl, so he bought her enough underwear and shirts to last a week, along with some loose pyjamas, a couple of dresses, and some warm slippers. As he went to pay, he noticed that the till was out of sight of the American.

"Can I use your phone?" he asked the shopkeeper.

"Ah, no. That's not for customers."

"A quick call. I'll pay for it."

"There are pay phones outside."

"Ten Deutschmarks for a local call. You can watch me dial."

Once again, money swayed the shopkeeper.

He found the number in a local directory, and the hotel switchboard put him through to the room straightaway. The voice on the other end registered only the briefest sign of grogginess and then slipped into quick professionalism.

"It's Marko della Torre. I need a favour." He started without preamble, keenly aware that he had only seconds to make himself understood. It was a one-sided conversation. He hoped against hope that his threadbare plan would hold together.

Afterwards, he went to look for a bookstore. Rob was impatient to get back, but della Torre ignored him long enough to find some children's classics. They found a taxi to take them up the coast to the fishing village across from Šipan. Rob had radioed the house. The old women in the village, sitting on their shaded doorsteps, shelling beans into plastic tubs, watched them as they sat on the jetty wall, waiting for Strumbić's boat.

They'd been gone less than two hours. Snezhana had only just woken.

The little girl was pleased with his purchases. Della Torre gave her the breakfast she asked for, white bread dipped in warm milk. Then he took Snezhana swimming again, to escape the muggy warmth. When they got back, he fed her some of the biscuits she liked as a snack, and read from one of the books he'd bought, Robert Louis Stevenson's story about the adventures of young David Balfour.

The Americans left them alone, happy enough for della Torre to take responsibility for the handicapped child. The men, who were mostly stony-faced, avoided Snezhana, except when della Torre took her out of the house; then one followed behind. Rebecca also kept a detached watch on her, as if the girl were a strange animal.

Later, when Snezhana had fallen asleep in the cool of the thick-walled room, della Torre crept down the stairs to a quiet corner in the sitting room. He had the house phone in hand when Rebecca came into the room, shaking her head.

"Just calling my wife."

"'Fraid not."

"Why?"

"Because the phone's disconnected."

"Strumbić didn't pay the bill?"

"Bill didn't want Strumbić to pay for your calls."

"Oh. So do you mind if I use the satellite phone?"

"It can wait."

"In that case, you won't mind if I wander into the village."

"Phone there doesn't work either," Rebecca said.

"Bill?"

"Bill."

Della Torre nodded. It wouldn't have taken much skill to disconnect the island from the rest of the world. But surely they wouldn't interfere with the ferries?

"It'll be over in a day or two. So don't worry yourself too much," Rebecca said. "Just relax."

"Am I allowed to go to the village, or do I need a babysitter?"

"Feel free. Just make sure you stay in sight of us when the ferry leaves. Otherwise, Bill and Rob will get nervous."

"You don't trust me?"

"Oh, we trust you," she said. "But sometimes people do things they regret."

"I never asked you, what exactly did you think would happen to me when they took me away at the border post?"

"I thought there was a risk you'd be shot."

"You knew about Gorki?"

"Yes."

"Did you arrange for him to be there?"

"Our people let his people know that it might be in his interest to be around."

"You had always intended to take the girl?"

"No. But it was a possibility. I'd rather have done the job there, but..." She shrugged.

Suddenly, della Torre didn't know what to think. "You knew you could get the girl across the border?"

"After we crossed, I knew you had a friend at the border. And that Gorki's militia control that sector. And I heard Djilas mention how he and Gorki don't get along, for whatever reason. So yes, I thought there was a better than even chance of getting the girl across the border."

"What would have happened if we didn't?"

"Bill and Rob were monitoring the situation. They were there to get us out of trouble."

"Us or you?"

Later, it was the memory of her grin that stayed with him. Toothy, feline. "Us, of course," she said. He didn't believe her.

"What happens now?"

There was an ironic glint in her eye. "Djilas is a very rich man. And he's going to part with some of that money. Call it a commercial transaction."

"You kidnapped a crippled little girl for ransom?"

"Sure. Why not? Julius says Djilas has ready access to more than a million Deutschmarks and can raise more at short notice. Seeing him and his place, I can believe it. A million is enough. You're going to arrange for him to deliver it to us in Dubrovnik tomorrow morning, bright and early. And in exchange, he gets the girl."

"The American government kidnaps people for money? Or has this been a scam from the start?"

"Gringo, everybody in this country can be bought or sold. You. Strumbić. Him. He understands corruption, probably expects it. It'll be a relief for him, that Americans are no different from you people. It'll make sense, won't it?"

Della Torre understood. These Americans felt contempt for them all, for Strumbić, for the Montenegrin, for him. All open to bribery, to a backhander, to selling and buying anything and anyone. They thought that reducing the kidnapping to money would deceive the Montenegrin. Perhaps she was right.

"But it's not the money, is it?" he asked. "It's him."

She smiled. That was answer enough.

He was tempted to say he wouldn't be party to this any longer, but he was caught. However much he thrashed, he was on the hook and he couldn't escape. Not now. Because it wasn't just himself he had to worry about. It was the girl too.

"How does Horvat tie into this?"

"Horvat?"

"Yes. The man who introduced us at the Excelsior. The man you and your Mr. Dawes met up with in Dubrovnik the other night."

"Have you been playing spy, Gringo?"

"I was in town having a drink, and noticed you all going into the same restaurant."

"With your Canadian friend?"

"So what's the deal with Horvat?"

"No deal. He was just being polite. Keeping up with developments."

"Did you tell him about the Bosnians?"

"He was very interested in the .50-calibre they had."

"Should have been, since he smuggles them in."

"Not that one, apparently. It was a Chinese gun."

There was a sound overhead, on the landing, someone falling. Della Torre sprang up the stairs to find Snezhana on the floor near the top. He lifted her tiny, almost weightless frame and carried her back to the bedroom.

"Are you okay? Have you hurt yourself?"

The little girl struggled to make herself clear. "I'm fine. I was listening," she said. "The woman with red hair isn't Milady de Winter."

"No? Who is she, then?" he asked, smiling with relief.

"You'll see one day."

"Oh?" della Torre said, puzzled

"She's not Milady. My name comes from the word for snow," the little girl said. "I am."

She unsettled him. In that tiny, fragile, twisted frame there flickered a cool ferocity. What child imagined herself the villain, the vengeful Milady de Winter?

"So who," he asked, "am I?"

**36**

**I**T WASN'T DAWN yet when they took Strumbić's motorboat across the strait. Della Torre had had to wake Snezhana. She shook with the cold of the early morning, though he'd left her pyjamas on, pulling a dress over them and wrapping her up in a blanket to protect her from the night air.

The water was calm, but the three-kilometre-long passage was still tense. There were no dangerous rocks, but they went faster than della Torre would have liked. Strumbić's plastic-hulled motorboat bounced against the small waves, sending up spray. None of them was wearing a life jacket.

The forty-horsepower engine made it a quick trip, though they slowed sharply as they approached the other side, wary of the stone jetty. Rob sat on the covered bow, lighting their way with a powerful torch, while Rebecca steered, the motor chuntering leisurely. She manoeuvred the boat alongside the fenders that cushioned the mooring. Bill jumped out, and tied the boat fast. No one had spoken during the whole journey.

Rebecca and the two Americans carried the hard plastic and metal cases from the boat to the Hilux, which was parked in the shadow of the fisherman's house. The village was asleep, though a dog, picking up their scent on the faint breeze, sounded a warning.

Rebecca drove to Dubrovnik's walls, parking the truck within easy access of the citadel's northern gate. One of the Americans wired up della Torre to a radio, a discreet earpiece fixed onto his right ear. The unit was attached to his belt and a microphone clipped onto the lapel of his cream linen jacket, a souvenir from London. Della Torre sat in the truck while the Americans wandered a short distance into the night to give the radio system a last-minute run-through. All four were on the same speech-activated channel. Della Torre was astonished at how well it worked, even when more than one person was speaking.

Rebecca collected one of her cases from the back of the truck and took it with her into the old town. The rest of them settled into the truck to wait, the silence broken only by Snezhana's involuntary low grumble and grinding teeth. Della Torre thought he felt her tremble. But then he realized it had been him. He'd slept badly the night before, going over the permutations of Rebecca's plan, and he was cold with fatigue and nerves. He reached into his jacket pocket for a cigarette but then stopped himself. He wasn't going to smoke in the truck with the little girl there, and he didn't want to leave her.

"Number one in position," he heard Rebecca say through the earpiece.

"Number two heading out." Rob left the truck, taking a rucksack from the back with him.

The sky lightened at the top of the mountain overlooking Dubrovnik, and slowly they began to pick out more and more of the city's walls in the pre-dawn wash.

"Time to go, Mr. della Torre," said Bill.

They walked along the walled road, over the wooden drawbridge that connected the wider world with the ancient town, and through the massive gatehouse. They followed the twisting stone passage to the edge of the Stradun. He could see the full length of the wide white pedestrian road, which ended at the square by the walled harbour.

No one was awake in the city. The street lights were still on, though dawn filtered down onto the rooftops. Della Torre sat with Snezhana on the edge of the Onofrio fountain, the broad white stone cylinder that marked the Stradun's northern limit. The little girl sat on della Torre's lap, wrapped tightly in the blanket. Bill stood somewhere in the darkness.

"It will be fine," he said softly into her ear. "It's almost over and you'll be fine. You're a brave girl."

She murmured something in his ear, but he couldn't understand what she was saying.

"She will die," she repeated, her voice laboured.

He felt his scalp tighten and a ripple of cold trace his spine. Something in him believed the girl.

They sat still for a while. Della Torre checked his watch for the third time and then got up, the little girl straddling his left hip, and started walking down the Stradun.

"Gringo, where are you going?" Rebecca said in his earpiece.

He looked around and up. He knew she was somewhere above. At this time of morning, access to the walls was prohibited. The main entrances were barred until the ticket sellers arrived, though they weren't selling many these days. But he remembered how when they'd visited, playing tourist, she'd climbed up a tree and the ruins of a building on the seaward side of the wall, where the high walk had been nearest the ground.

"Just stretching my legs," he said.

"You'll have time to stretch them. Right now I want you to sit," Rebecca said into his earpiece.

He remembered how Rebecca had spent time crouching so that she could only just see through the arrow loops. She'd spent the most time over the Pile gatehouse, looking down along the Stradun with field glasses. And she'd had him stand, stock still, three-quarters of the way along. Two hundred and fifty metres from the top of the Pile gatehouse.

He looked up but couldn't see her. He returned to the fountain and sat down, willing control into his muscles, which had become as rigid and trembling as the girl's. He sat her on his lap again, pulling back his jacket sleeve so that he could keep an eye on the luminous dials of his watch. He watched the seconds turn. At exactly twenty minutes to the hour he stood up again.

"The girl needs a pee. I'm just taking her round the corner to a gutter," he said, speaking into the mike on his lapel.

"Wait for Bill."

"Sorry, got to run, poor girl."

"I said wait for Bill."

"Can't. It's an emergency. She can barely hold it in."

"Don't make me shoot you."

"You're going to shoot me because a little girl needs to pee?"

He was running now along the Stradun, counting the side streets as he passed. They all looked the same. He prayed he hadn't missed one. Two. Three. There it was, the fourth along. Snezhana was feather-light, but it was still awkward carrying her, and his left elbow hurt. He worried it would give way under the strain but dared not stop to swap her to the other arm.

"Gringo . . ." Rebecca said, her frustration audible.

He heard the footsteps behind him, the flat pancake sound of running shoes on stone. His were leather-soled and he was afraid he might slip on the glass-smooth paving slabs. But he'd reached the narrow alley he was looking for, one of the ones that spread perpendicular to the Stradun like the bones off a fish's spine. He ran along it, up a flight of steps, and then along another flat section and another flight of steps rising towards the city's massive east wall. The Stradun alone was unbroken by stairs in this hilly city carved out of stone.

Could he remember the place? It had been night when he'd been there. He thought it was close but he still hadn't reached it. Had he gone up the wrong street? He didn't know Dubrovnik that well and didn't have the luxury of getting it wrong. If he screwed this up, he wouldn't be given another chance. Rebecca would make sure of it. She'd probably replace him with Bill, make Bill sit with the girl on the bench.

"Lost the girl," he heard Bill say in his earpiece.

"Where are you, Gringo?" Rebecca hissed, her voice betraying impatience and strain.

Where was he?

Giving up on his objective, della Torre ducked into a smaller side passage.

He heard footsteps, though he couldn't tell where they were coming from. The city was still, silent in its early morning sleep.

He tried to control his breathing, but the run had winded him and his lungs wheezed. The girl ground her teeth as she made a heroic effort to stay quiet.

A man passed, moving in the direction della Torre had just come from. Shit.

Della Torre ran back to the mouth of the passage and saw the man moving cautiously, uncertainly, staying firmly in the buildings' shadows. Della Torre called out in a hoarse whisper, "Here."

The man was holding something. When he turned, della Torre could see it was a big pink stuffed bear wrapped in a hotel beach towel. Higgins. Della Torre held his finger to his lips.

Higgins came running up to him. Della Torre gave him the little girl and took the bear in return. The transaction passed in silence, though Snezhana made quiet guttural moans. Without saying a word, Higgins wrapped her in the beach towel. Della Torre made a motion for him to stay while he left, the pink bear covered by Strumbić's blanket. He kissed Snezhana on the forehead and then went back down the alley stairs to the Stradun.

"Done," he said. "I'm just coming back."

"We were getting worried about you," Rebecca said.

"Like I said, it was an emergency."

"Where'd you go?"

"In an alleyway."

"Okay, go back to the fountain. And don't do anything like that again."

He held the bear covered in the blanket tight to him and returned to the fountain's white stone lip. Bill flashed him a dirty look as he passed, breathing hard from his dash around Dubrovnik's dark alleyways.

Della Torre waited.

"Car," he heard Rob say in his earpiece. "Subject exiting alone. Has found rucksack. Doesn't look like he trusts it."

"Talk to him, Gringo. Bill, put what della Torre says through on the rucksack radio channel." Rebecca exuded calm authority.

"Mr. Djilas?" della Torre said. "Mr. Djilas?" There was a long pause. "Mr. Djilas?"

"Gringo?"

"That's me. Do you have the money?"

"In my bag," the Montenegrin said.

"Are you alone?"

"I'm alone. Do you have my daughter?"

"Yes."

"What do you want me to do?"

"Walk down the middle of the Stradun towards the Pile gate."

"Am I being set up, Gringo?"

"No, Mr. Djilas, you're not being set up."

"Because if I am, I know where your wife is. She is working at the hospital in Vukovar. I have a man at that hospital. If he hears nothing from me in two hours, your wife is dead. I know where your father lives in Istria, Gringo. He too will be dead. Anything you have ever touched or loved will be dead. Do you understand, Gringo?"

"I understand, Mr. Djilas. Now come the way you're meant. Quickly, please."

There was silence.

"Contact switched off between della Torre and subject," Rob narrated. "Subject entering the south gate, walking towards the main square. Will pursue once subject has gone sufficiently far along the high walk."

"Well done, Gringo," said Rebecca.

"Where are you?" he asked.

"Somewhere I can see you," she said.

There was a long wait. He listened. Dubrovnik was starting to wake. Somewhere in the distance, beyond the east walls, he heard a cock crow. A dog bayed in response. The faint strains of a transistor radio made their way from one of Dubrovnik's tall, tightly packed houses. The grey light of shadowed morning was starting to lift.

Away in the distance he heard footsteps. He shifted a little to see all the way down the Stradun. Pink dawn crept into the centuries-old man-made canyon of stone. He saw the form of a man enter the Stradun from the city's inner harbour. The man's movement was deliberate, slow, as if he was listening for something. He had in one hand the Americans' rucksack and in the other a holdall.

The man hadn't gone far, two of those narrow Stradun blocks, less than a quarter of the way along the broad main street, when he stopped, disappearing into a blind arch.

"What's he doing?" della Torre heard Rebecca ask.

Backing up against a wall to look up the side street, the Montenegrin had all but disappeared. Della Torre guessed he was roughly where the little alleys rose from the Stradun to the city's only eastern gate.

Without warning, he heard a metallic clank from somewhere overhead and behind him. That same instant, the Montenegrin sprinted across the width of the Stradun and into the opposite passage. Della Torre heard the clank again, and then the crack of splintering stone.

The Montenegrin was gone.

"Where is he? Where the fuck did he go?" Rebecca shouted so that he not only heard her in his earpiece but could hear her from the city wall far above him.

Bill was already racing along the Stradun.

"Subject disappeared toward the eastern gate," said Rob.

"Get on his tail. The walls go too far around for me to catch up with him. I'll stay here. Gringo, you move a muscle, you move an inch, and you're a dead man. I mean that. You are in my sight right now. You sneeze and your head comes off. Show me the girl."

"What?" della Torre said.

"I said take the girl out of that blanket. Let me see her."

"Subject is with accomplice. Accomplice holding bags. Subject seems to be carrying something big. Out of sight again." The American was breathing hard. "Subject and accomplice disappeared."

"Show me, Gringo."

Della Torre slowly unwrapped the bear from its blanket.

"What the hell? What is that?"

"A bear. From the Argentina."

"The bear from the Argentina? Gringo, you are in a world of shit. You hear me? You are in a world of shit."

"Subject disappeared. Seems to have left in car. No further sight of him."

Della Torre kept still, sitting on the edge of the Onofrio fountain, holding a large stuffed teddy bear on his lap, his heart pounding, any happiness mitigated by fear of what would happen to him next.

**37**

THE FEW PEOPLE making their way to work in the heart of Dubrovnik might have noticed the two men, one sitting on the lip of the Onofrio fountain with a large pink stuffed bear on his lap, the other pressed up against him, a blanket draped over his arms. But no one was curious enough to stop. It was a tourist town. Plenty of oddities happened there.

Della Torre felt the gun, wrapped in Strumbić's blanket, pressed against his kidney.

The other American was approaching along the Stradun.

Della Torre suppressed a sudden suicidal urge to make a weak joke, something along the lines of the Bill needing to be paid, or being caught by the Old Bill, though he didn't think it would translate to anyone who hadn't spent time in England. Or about being Robbed. Robbing Bill to pay ... whom?

Rebecca walked quickly towards them, carrying her hard case.

"Let's get to the truck. Quick. We'll deal with him later." And then, turning to della Torre, she said, "You do anything, anything at all to piss me off, and you're a dead man."

They hurried through the fortress's massive northern gate and across the wooden drawbridge back to the truck.

"You drive, Bill." She gave the man her keys. "Rob, you sit with our friend here in the back and make sure he doesn't do anything stupid. The slightest movement, shoot him."

She jumped into the bed of the truck, facing backwards, and quickly reassembled her rifle. "Gun it, Bill. I'll bet three to one that Djilas's people want to repay one of those bullets he didn't catch."

She was right. As they moved off, so did a light-coloured Ford Bronco that della Torre had seen circulating further up the road. It slid behind them as the Hilux hurtled through Dubrovnik's northern suburbs. Della Torre turned to look back, only to feel his nose nudged forward by a Beretta.

"I think the order was for you not to move," said Rob.

"I just wanted to see what was happening."

"You'll be looking through an eye in the middle of your fore-head if you don't sit still and face forward."

It was the most della Torre had heard the man say at a single sitting. He did as he was told, though by leaning slightly forward and to the side, as if in prayer, he could see what was happening behind them in the driver's mirrors. There were at least two men in the Bronco, but he couldn't tell whether anybody was in the rear seat. The passenger was holding what looked to be a submachine gun.

The Hilux bellowed disapproval as Bill ripped it through the gears. Hard on the clutch and brake, harder on the accelerator. The truck's high centre of gravity meant that they swayed with every twist of the wheel. The same must have been true for the Bronco, which was struggling to keep pace. Palm trees flashed past on his left, and then the harbour's blue-green waters. Della Torre figured the Montenegrin's man would fire once the Hilux went into a curve, hoping to catch them with a broadside.

Rebecca fired a round into the rear window, exploding the glass. She kicked out the remaining shards. The Bronco's gunman responded by firing off jackhammer rounds. They heard the thud of hail on sheet metal. Della Torre and Rob ducked in unison.

For a moment della Torre wondered whether Rebecca had been hit. But then he heard the metallic clank of her rifle, and in the mirror, he saw the Bronco weave unsteadily.

They turned sharply to follow the short, narrow inlet that marked the northern reaches of Dubrovnik's suburbs. The road was even tighter than the one through town. They passed slower traffic at vertiginous speed. But the Bronco stayed behind them.

They made their way around the other side of the inlet, pulling away after the switchback as a turning car delayed the Montenegrin's truck. To the left, della Torre saw the little island that guarded Dubrovnik's harbour.

Without warning, Rebecca fired off another series of shots as they went around a bend. Across the corner of a tiny bay, she'd managed to draw a bead on the Bronco. He turned to look back, ignoring the gun aimed at his side, and watched the Ford rock unsteadily and then, like a drunk, slide with a total lack of drama off the road and into the Adriatic.

A couple of cars pulled over but the Hilux kept going.

"Bill, they're off our case. I don't see anybody else, so slow down. Drop us off at the village and then carry on up the coast to that little cliff. Drive the truck off the edge. We'll pick you up at the bottom."

They stopped at the village and got out of the car. Rebecca made della Torre leave the pink bear behind.

They got into Strumbić's boat while Bill carried on up the coast in the Hilux. Rebecca steered the boat, hugging the shoreline. They'd lost sight of the truck on the main road, high up the hill. Half an hour later, the American called them on the radio. He'd spotted them and guided them into a little rocky cove.

Bill splashed through the shallow water and pulled himself into the boat. Rebecca, who'd kept the motor running, gunned it before he'd managed to gather himself together.

"I didn't see anyone stop when I pushed the truck over," Bill said.

"Good," Rebecca said. And that was all she said on the passage across the channel to Šipan. Everything seemed to be on autopilot.

Things changed when they got to the villa.

As soon as Della Torre stepped through the front door, he felt his knees give way under him. He hardly felt the first blow, but the next one, the kick between his legs, sent pain rocketing through his belly.

"Jesus." He breathed shallowly.

Rebecca ignored him. "Guys, see if you can get him in a chair a couple of feet from the wall."

They picked him up and bound his hands expertly behind him, tying his ankles to the chair legs. She tilted the chair so that his head rested against the wall.

"Okay, Mr. della Torre. Care to tell us what happened?"

"The girl needed a pee—" he began. The chair was knocked out from under him. His head hit the floor hard, causing sparks to fly in front of his eyes.

"Pick him up."

They leaned him up against the wall again.

"You can tell I'm not feeling very patient. What I need is correct information from you. I will get it. When I have the correct information, I will determine a course of action. But I can't do that until I have the information. You have the choice between a very big headache and then a bullet to make it go away, or to cooperate, and then we'll see what we can do with you. Say yes if you understand. Say anything else if you want your head to hit the floor again."

"Yes."

"Good. Maybe then you can tell us what happened."

"I took the girl to an alley. I met one of the Montenegrin's men. He swapped the girl for the bear and I came back. When Djilas was walking along the Stradun, his man called him over, and that's why he ran."

"All right. I'm not convinced, but you've made a start. Do you want to tell me again what happened, the right way?"

"That was—"

His head hit the floor again. This time he heard the booms that went with the fireworks.

"Okay, let's try him again."

Della Torre's head hurt. But so did his shoulders, arms, and neck from the fall, and the anticipation of the fall.

"Gringo, I've found that most people can take about five or six of these falls before they pass out. They're generally fine for more interrogation after a couple of hours, but we can't play the same trick anymore because their brains get scrambled. There's the risk of hemorrhaging and all sorts of nasty stuff. So we move on to other things. I need to know everything before you pass out, so we'll try this one more time and then we move on to the other things. Understand?"

"Yes," he said. He realized he'd bitten the side of his tongue with his back teeth during the last fall. He could taste blood.

"So tell me what happened. Exactly."

"I took the girl into an alley..."

"I believe you."

"There, a man patted me on the shoulder and said, 'I believe my card is marked for the next—'" He hit the floor hard again. "—dance."

Red lights exploded in his brain like a field of blooming poppies.

"Funny boy. How's your head?"

"Attached...to the floor." Della Torre wasn't sure if he was smiling or grimacing. He wasn't sure whether everything was blurry because of the tears in his eyes.

"I think we go straight to Plan B. The kitchen table will do, boys."

They had della Torre on the table, facing upward, his hands tied behind him. It was agony for his shoulders and back. His legs were tied to the table legs, and that end of the table was lifted by a couple of bricks. One of the Americans stuffed a rag in his mouth and a hand towel was placed over his face. Blinded, tilted back, his terror of what he suspected they were doing made it hard for him not to cry out, to scream. He'd been told about it in the commandos but hadn't been subjected to it. It was too effective. Maybe some of the commandos who'd trained in North Korea could take it, but he wasn't sure about that either. They'd tried to teach the soldiers how to resist, but when the soldiers saw how easily they could be broken, their morale crumbled. So the trainers stopped doing live trials sometime before he joined, and instead merely described the procedure and its effects.

Even though he knew what was coming, the water was a shock. It flowed into his nostrils. He held his breath as best he could. The damp towel stuck to his face. He blew air out of his nose and then tried to breathe. But he could no longer tell if he was breathing out or in. Nothing came. No air. The towel stuck to his face and panic sent his heart racing. He rocked his head wildly, tried to shake himself free, but couldn't. He couldn't breathe. He was lying on the table, drowning.

They took the rag out of his mouth and he gulped air.

"Okay, Mr. della Torre. Do you want to answer some questions or do you feel like trying that again?"

He thought maybe he could last one more go. But then he'd break. Just one more go. But it wasn't worth it.

"I'll talk," he said, tears in his voice.

"What happened?"

"He was. He was...Strumbić," della Torre lied, wondering why he didn't just tell them it was Higgins. Wondering why he was exposing himself to the risk of being tortured again. He could handle one more time, he told himself. One more time. So it'd be Strumbić until they found out otherwise, because Strumbić was expendable.

She looked at him skeptically. "Strumbić? What's he doing in Dubrovnik? I thought he was back in Zagreb."

"He came back straightaway. He took a flight back that afternoon. He had some deal he wanted to do down here, some business venture."

"I don't believe you," she hissed.

"He flew to Zagreb with your Mr. Dawes and some other guy. A friend of Horvat's, who Strumbić said had an American passport. They landed in Zagreb and then the other man flew right out again. Strumbić knew because your Mr. Dawes left him at the airport, didn't make sure he went back into town. So Strumbić stuck around in a café and then caught the next flight south."

All that was true. He'd heard it from Higgins. Strumbić really was in Dubrovnik. Back at the hotel. God rest his soul, and may he forgive mine too, della Torre prayed to himself.

"Where is Strumbić?" Rebecca demanded.

"At the Argentina."

"How did you set it up?"

"I called him. I called from the shop where I bought the girl clothes."

She looked at Rob, who shook his head, denying it, though he looked uncertain enough for Rebecca to turn back to della Torre.

"How did you know he'd be at the hotel?"

"He told me he was coming back."

"That doesn't tell me how you set it up. You didn't know what was happening until last night, after you called Djilas."

"Strumbić came here. He took the ferry over and I met him at the little *pension*. I saw him in the afternoon, and then we met up when I went for a walk after the call. I gave him the details. He went to the north side of the island and then paid for a fishing boat to take him back to Dubrovnik," he said. It was all true, except it hadn't been Strumbić who'd come to Šipan. It had been Higgins.

He'd waited for della Torre at a room in a little *pension* at the edge of the village, according to their hastily made plans. The old woman whose house it was hadn't wanted both men to be alone in the room until della Torre had paid her extra. Even then she'd muttered about Germans and their morals, confusing the languages.

Higgins had listened as della Torre explained himself. Cicadas buzzed outside the window, the sudden trill and staccato whistle of a nightingale, and frogs calling in their hundreds. Higgins didn't say much, and then only to confirm points or to check details.

At the end he'd extended his rangy frame and smiled. "I'm guessing you'll owe me one," he said.

Rebecca's voice brought della Torre back to the present. "What did Djilas know?"

"I don't know. Nothing, I think. I told Strumbić—" He'd almost said Higgins. "—it would be too dangerous to get in touch with him. That Djilas was being monitored by everyone. It would have to be done in the morning."

"Rob, the man you chased who was with Djilas—was he Strumbić?"

"Couldn't tell. I don't think so, but they were well up toward the top of the stairs. I'd have said he had blonder hair and looked thinner and taller."

"Maybe it was one of Djilas's men. There could have been somebody else," she said. "Okay, Mr. della Torre. Now we've got a little problem. I had Djilas in my sights but I missed. I shouldn't have missed from that distance. Boys, maybe we should put Mr. della Torre back in a chair. It's hard to talk to a man lying on a table."

They manhandled him upright. He offered no resistance, his body a burden. Pain flared through his shoulders, his neck, his wrists, his ribs. He stared at the floor, breathing deeply, savouring the air like a half-drowned man.

He was beginning to regret sacrificing Strumbić. But Strumbić could take care of himself. The Canadian journalist wasn't in the same league as these people. These Americans were no different from the UDBA.

He thought about the tortures the UDBA routinely used, most of them crude weapons of pain. Though there was psychological terror too, fear for one's parents, one's children. Was that why he'd been so reluctant to have children? He prayed that Irena was safe.

"Right, Mr. della Torre. What do we do now? How do we get to Djilas now that we have no leverage and he knows we're after him rather than his money?"

Della Torre wouldn't lift his eyes from the floor. "Gorki," he said.

"Gorki? The paramilitary gentleman who was so kind to us at the border?"

"Yes."

"How badly does he want Djilas?"

"I don't know. But Gorki hates the Montenegrin. You knew they were enemies. That's why we got through that border post. You know more about him than I do. Talk to your friends. But if you want the Montenegrin, Gorki's the person you want to be dealing with. Offer him money. Asylum, after all this is over. Guns. I don't know. You do these things better than I do. Either that or have a submarine sink the Montenegrin's boat."

She nodded. "Maybe that's what we should have done in the first place. Dealt with the other side," she said, mostly to herself. "Rob, you stay here. Sit with him. Keep a gun on him. If he moves, shouts, anything, kill him. If anyone comes to the house—I don't care if it's Strumbić or his cleaner—kill them.

Bill, get on the radio to our friends. Tell them to organize a pick-up tomorrow morning, first light. Can they get here that fast?"

Bill looked at his watch and did a quick mental calculation. "Shouldn't be a problem. They can't travel in these waters at night. The Yugoslav patrol boats are keeping traffic on a curfew, but they'll be able to get here once light breaks."

"The American navy's extracting you?" della Torre asked.

"Us. Picking us up. In the plushest yacht you've ever seen. Even the jail on board is comfortable. You'll have a little luxury before a tribunal decides what to do with you, Gringo. Though I happen to think you'll be put away for a long time, so don't get your hopes up." She turned away from della Torre. "Do that, then, Bill. And when you have, we're going for a little trip down to the Argentina. How long do you think it will take for Strumbić's boat to get us there?"

"About an hour, maybe a bit more," Bill said.

"Fine. Though I think Mr. Strumbić will have made himself scarce. But if we find him, we'll see if we can't persuade him to come back here, to confirm Mr. della Torre's story."

They left della Torre in the kitchen, tied to the chair. Rob took a seat in a corner of the room, his eyes locked on his prisoner. Della Torre listened to Rebecca and Bill leave the house, and then he heard the motorboat's engine start up. For a long time he could feel only pain, but then exhaustion got hold of him and he slipped into and back out of unconsciousness. His head hung forward, chin against his chest, shoulders straining because his arms remained tied behind the chair. When he woke, it was with a whimper, his eyes narrow slits taking in the emptiness of his lap and the floor's ancient, worn stone. He felt defeated. He was defeated.

At least the girl was safe. He wondered what would have happened to her otherwise. Would she have been allowed to live?

Would he? Or Strumbić?

He wondered whether he would have saved the Montenegrin had it not been for the child. The Montenegrin was no less a killer than Rebecca. No less an executioner. They'd both worked for their governments to the best of their abilities. Warriors in a time of peace. No different from the gunners pulling the lanyards on artillery pieces pointed at Vukovar.

Irena. He prayed for her. He prayed hard to a god the Communists had tried to crucify into oblivion.

·   ·   ·

Some time later, he couldn't tell how much, Rebecca walked into the kitchen. She turned on the lights and took some food out of the refrigerator. He asked for water, but she ignored him, left without saying a word.

He dozed, and when he woke it was dark. The light had been switched off. His shoulders and back hurt almost as much as his head. He felt damp across his crotch and realized he'd pissed himself. It could have been his thirst that brought him back to consciousness, or it could have been the sound of the engine, an outboard that ran at a lower pitch than the one on Strumbić's boat. It was hard to tell at that distance. Maybe it was one of the fishermen returning late to the village in the bay.

He heard movement in the house, people walking on the floorboards overhead, steps on the wooden staircase. He tried to call out to them, to one of the Americans, to tell them he needed water. But his mouth was sticky, dry, and uncooperative. Someone left the villa. He heard the door swing shut. He waited, hoping they'd be back soon, only to be startled by explosions, the timpani of war. And then silence again.

He heard the door open behind him, then footsteps. More than one pair. The Americans must have come back. The

kitchen door opened and he croaked, "Water," without bothering to look up. His head was too heavy to lift.

"Ah, Gringo," said the Montenegrin. "What a sad state of affairs when you're reduced to drinking water."

**38**

## BELGRADE, APRIL 1986

**THE OFFICES WERE** elegantly furnished, though in a dated style. Nineteen-fifties internationalist, he guessed, though, thinking about it, maybe it was modern. He'd never been much for fashions in furniture. Or in anything else.

The waiting room was grand, with tall windows looking out over the Danube. On one wall was a bookcase made of blond beech with clean, simple lines. The books—law reports and Communist dogma all bound in the same green leather and embossed with gold lettering—looked like they belonged to a dark, fussy library. Not this place.

He wore his major's uniform. He'd placed his peaked hat emblazoned with formal piping on the neighbouring chair, but he kept his briefcase on his lap. The uniform had that new look about it, but only because he wore it so rarely. It was grey with a hint of green, adorned with only a couple of ribbons and the insignia showing his rank. He'd polished his shoes to a high shine, though they were beginning to crease, showing signs of age. He'd had them re-soled recently.

The briefcase was also old. An antique. It was made from good, thick hide. As a young officer, he'd bought it as a present to himself, from an old man selling off his possessions in the

Sarajevo flea market. The old man had been a lawyer between the wars, but when the Communists came to power he'd been put to work in a factory. He'd kept the briefcase as a last link to his bourgeois life, but eventually he'd found the luxury of eating more appealing than old memories.

The case was just a prop. The Montenegrin always took it with him to these official meetings. It contained a fountain pen made in East Germany, a pad of paper, and a few pages of cryptic notes he'd typed up for the UDBA archives. A word-sketch of his mission with so few details or facts that the document would be useless to someone who didn't already know what it was about. It would be collated with other, similarly opaque reports and then stuffed deep into the UDBA's hidden files. One day all these papers would crumble into dust. But they wouldn't disappear entirely. Against all orders, he kept copies of whatever documents he could. His insurance.

In the days after he'd come back from Stockholm, it had been like stepping into a vacuum. He reported in, went to his desk at the Interior Ministry in Belgrade, and waited. There had been no debriefing, either official or unofficial, if only because so few people had known about the mission. None of his colleagues or immediate superiors had been aware of it. As far as they were concerned, he'd been on a temporary secondment to the Foreign Ministry. The reports from the Stockholm embassy were either classified or bland. All the useful information he got had come from the newspapers, especially the English press. There were plenty of accounts of Palme's killing, but apart from one vague description of the killer and an uncertain identification of the type of gun used, there was nothing of substance. Nor had there been any sign the boy's body had been found, or, if it had, that it was in any way connected to Palme.

He waited, wanting to go back to Montenegro but knowing he couldn't until they decided what to do with him.

He knew he was in a dangerous position. He knew that

whoever had ordered the killing was nervously watching to see whether the UDBA would be implicated. The Montenegrin wondered how he'd be handled if suspicion drifted his way. A cell in the Belgrade headquarters and a sudden bullet in the back of the head. It reminded him of Svjet, the old man from London with the hollow, haunted eyes of someone who'd known his fate the moment he'd stepped into that Trieste hotel room.

More than once the Montenegrin had thought of escape. In his job it was never truly far from his mind. Take his youngest daughter and go somewhere, to someone who might offer him sanctuary in exchange for information. The Americans.

But that was an idle fantasy. Nowhere was safe from the UDBA. Twice, after the failed Croatian independence movement of the early 1970s, he'd hunted renegade UDBA agents. One had disappeared to Australia, where under a different name he'd bought a vineyard with money accumulated over years of graft. The other he'd tracked down to an American suburb near Chicago. The man was staying with relatives.

The Australian had tried to run, had seen him and had fled through his vineyards. The American had long been resigned to his fate. He was sitting in a big, comfortable chair in the basement, watching television. He made a brief move to stand, but gave up and wept for himself. Both men had died.

Inevitability was a hard master.

If he hadn't known it already, he'd learned it standing in the corridor of that hospital, offering bargains to a god he'd long neglected, as the doctors fought for his wife's life. At some point, he'd learned, events set in motion can not be halted. His wife's fate had been sealed by her determination to have a last child. Physics, chemistry, biology all conspired against her once she'd started the mechanism of her fate spinning. No, once *they'd* set it spinning.

In the end, as the winds of fate had blown for her, they'd blow for him. His destiny also floated like the willow down.

And if it landed in the sea, there he would drown.

What then for his daughter?

The UDBA had no compunction about killing children. The memory of the boy in Sweden rose in his gorge, as green and bitter as bile. He had an atavistic urge to cross himself, as his grandmother had whenever a shadow swept past her cataract-fogged eyes.

All he could do now was wait and see what fate held in store for him. But he swore to himself that if he survived this, he would build a fortress around himself and his daughter. He realized that the protections he'd built for himself, the files of secret documents, were frail barriers against bullets. He'd had a thought that the UDBA would be afraid of having its assassination program exposed to the world at large. But then it dawned on him that the Germans, Americans, Australians, Italians—every government—had colluded with the Yugoslavs. It had suited them to turn a blind eye to these judicial killings, in exchange for Yugoslavia's promise to remain neutral between the West and the Soviet bloc. He'd have to do more, to learn from his forefathers. Neither the Venetians nor the Turks had ever completely conquered Montenegro. The Montenegrins had negotiated, bribed, blackmailed, built fortresses, and fought, and they'd always kept a measure of wild independence. He would build his own citadel in Montenegro, man it with his own people.

For now, he would have to survive by doing his job so well that his masters would find it a greater loss to sacrifice him.

It was during those days that he learned the details of another operation, also an unusual one, that had overlapped with his. Unusual because the target was not a Yugoslav dissident and had no connection, as far as the Montenegrin could tell, with Yugoslavia or its émigré community. It was strange enough that he wondered whether it had something to do with the Palme killing. Or whether the timing had been purely coincidental.

The morning after Palme died, a unit—two killers from the Kosovar mafia who did occasional work for the UDBA— had driven to the house of a German industrialist in Cologne. Because it was a Saturday, they had to wait for him to collect the morning newspapers from the letterbox fixed to the neat picket fence that bounded the tidy garden around his suburban house. They'd parked the car behind a hedge, where they could watch for him.

They stationed themselves before daybreak. No one passed on the pavement to wonder why the two men were sitting in a car on a suburban street. The man was an early riser, even on weekends. It was in that watery light of a winter's morning that they spotted him, dressed in casual trousers and a thin jersey— too thin for the weather—as he hurried down his walkway, braced against the cold, to collect his newspapers.

The car's passenger got out in the same instant, leaving the door open. The industrialist and the man from the car approached the letterbox simultaneously.

The industrialist noticed the other man only at the last second, too late to react to the gun. The man shot him twice in the chest. The industrialist had a surprised expression as he fell back, the impact of hitting the ground causing his slightly tinted bifocals to bounce onto his forehead. His light green sweater turned a deep brown where the blood soaked through. The noise of the gun had been suppressed, and not a curtain twitched that cold morning.

The assassin walked back to the car and the driver pulled away smoothly, unobtrusively, back to their temporary residence in Cologne, where everything was packed and ready for them to return to their Stuttgart homes. They only stopped long enough to call in a message to Belgrade from a phone box. Like the call he'd made to Germany from a Swedish phone box.

All that information was in the official file, pulled together by the UDBA resident in Bonn from a debriefing of the assassin and local newspaper reports. Another killing the Montenegrin couldn't understand.

So he waited in purgatory, staying at the UDBA officers' barracks, an east European version of a gentlemen's club, though with linoleum instead of polished marble and a bar that looked like a workingmen's café. The rooms were comfortable enough and the food was close to home-cooked. In the mornings, including Saturdays, he went to his office, and there he pushed bits of paper around his desk, read files, and stared out the window at melting snow on the Belgrade streets, waiting, forever waiting for a tap on the shoulder and a military escort to take him to the subterranean questioning rooms and prison. He'd waited like that for more than two weeks when the handwritten note was brought to his desk by an orderly, requesting his presence at the Foreign Ministry the following morning. The same offices he'd been taken to, just before the new year, by the Dispatcher, to discuss the assignment.

As he had the previous time, when he'd come for his orders, he arrived early and then regretted not bringing something to read. They kept him waiting through much of the morning; finally he was called into the chief translator's office by a male secretary.

"Major," Comrade Chief Translator to the Presidency Ivan Dragomanov said from behind a broad desk. "Thank you for being so patient. Things always come up at the last minute when one is at the beck and call of the presidency."

The order from the presidency to kill Palme had been implicit. But not signed, not issued on paper. The first irregular job the Montenegrin had ever done.

"I understand," said the Montenegrin.

Dragomanov smiled with the corners of his eyes. He was elegant, tall, his thick salt-and-pepper hair combed back over his head to give him a leonine air. The suit he wore was expensive, the French cuffs on his shirt held together with gold-and-onyx links. The tie, the Montenegrin guessed, was Italian silk. And the glasses the sort one saw on Americans in films.

"Please sit," Dragomanov said, waving the Montenegrin towards a chair. "Would you like a coffee? Yes, I think that should be two coffees. Unless you prefer a little glass of something stronger?"

"Thank you, a coffee is sufficient." The young man who'd shown him into the room left without being told to, closing the tall double doors behind him.

Dragomanov offered a cigarette, a pastel Davidoff, from a cedar box on his desk, but the Montenegrin declined. He would have liked a cigarette just then, but he abstained for fear that his hand might be seen to tremble.

"Don't smoke? Very good. You'll live longer. I can't remember a morning I haven't woken up coughing," Dragomanov said.

His eyes had that wetness of chronic smokers; the skin on his otherwise handsome face had thinned and was heavily lined.

There was a moment's silence while Dragomanov put the cigarette into a short ivory holder and lit it. The Montenegrin wondered whether the holder was an affectation; Dragomanov's fingers were as yellow as the ivory.

"I must thank you for how successfully and professionally you performed your service for us. I had wanted to call you in earlier, but first I wanted to make sure we kept our side of the bargain. You will have word of your impending promotion soon, I'm told. May I be the first to congratulate you, Lieutenant Colonel. I understand that when your service comes to an end, when you retire, you will be given the rank of full colonel with a full colonel's pension. Am I correct in saying it is three years before you are eligible for your pension?"

"A few months more. Thank you," said the Montenegrin, genuinely relieved. They needed him, it seemed.

"I'm afraid some conditions will apply to the remainder of your service and retirement," Dragomanov said, contemplating the delicately carved holder. "I'm sure the terms won't surprise you. The only one that really interests the Foreign Ministry is that you won't be able to leave the country for a period of ten years after you leave service."

The Montenegrin shrugged. He knew he would be kept under surveillance during that time as well. There were ways around those things.

"Both the Interior and Foreign Ministries will do our utmost to ensure not just that you have a contented retirement, but that however you choose to occupy yourself is made easy."

"Thank you," the Montenegrin said, encouraged but still cautious.

Former UDBA men often opened bars and restaurants to keep themselves busy and to earn some extra money. Belgrade could smooth many difficulties: red tape having to do with planning restrictions, hours of operation, access to low-interest loans, finding adequate staff and ensuring their loyalty. All that was necessary to make business lucrative.

"It is the very least we can do. The very least."

There was a brief knock on the door, and the young man came in with the coffees and then left just as quietly.

"You have written a report?"

The Montenegrin nodded. "The barest details."

"Good." Dragomanov looked relieved. "Nothing else is to be committed to paper. No mention of this anywhere. Including the agency."

"As far as anyone is concerned, Pilgrim is a blind file. It ends here."

"Good. Of course, this isn't just for our benefit—I mean, for the presidency and the ministry. You must rest assured that we will not be producing much documentation either. And it will be stored carefully. I'm sure the UDBA archives are safer than any other for the material, so it will be compiled there."

"Thank you."

"This is why you were chosen. No one is more...capable or discreet in the Interior Ministry. In fact, I don't think I know of any diplomats with your reticence. It's a shame we didn't scoop you up when you were young."

The Montenegrin smiled in a perfunctory way. The Foreign Ministry would never have considered him for anything. A boy from the wilds of Montenegro who hadn't even gone to gymnasium, much less university, who'd gone straight from school to an apprenticeship? It would have been a capital joke.

They drank their coffees in silence.

"Colonel, should you ever need a favour in return..." Dragomanov said, though he left the offer hanging there. Implied but not explicit.

"Thank you. Is there anything else, sir?"

"Only to wish you as much luck in the future as you have had in the past," Dragomanov said.

The Montenegrin stood up to go. He shook the tall man's hand. Dragomanov looked even more handsome in the flesh than he did in photographs of days past, when he'd stood beside Tito as the dictator's official translator and general advisor on foreign affairs. It seemed such a modest title, official translator to the presidency, for a man who had for so many years been the helmsman, navigating Yugoslavia through international affairs.

The Montenegrin had walked as far as the tall double doors when something made him turn back to Dragomanov, who had already shifted his attention to the papers on his desk.

"Sir?"

"Yes, Colonel?"

The Montenegrin knew he shouldn't ask. Knew it was senseless, unprofessional. That any answer he got would be worse than silence, would leave him in even more clouded ignorance. But the urge was there. One day, he sensed, he would be made to pay for his Swedish luck. He wanted to know why.

"Why?" Why did the innocuous leader of an innocuous country have to die, an act that, from all he'd read, could glean no advantage for anyone anywhere? An act whose consequence was also a boy's death.

"Why?"

"Yes. Why Palme?"

"You surprise me, Colonel, asking such a question. You must know I couldn't possibly answer."

"I'm sorry, sir. It was an impulsive question."

"I understand. You're right, it is very different from anything we've ever done before. Let's just say it was a favour to a very important friend of the presidency's, a friend of Yugoslavia. Leave it at that, shall we?"

## DUBROVNIK, AUGUST 1991

H E WAS IN a big wooden fishing boat. It had a cabin at the front, but he was sitting on a bench near the stern, facing inward. His arms were tied behind his back and looped around a cleat so that he couldn't move, but he was no longer parched. They'd given him something to drink.

Rebecca sat across from him. She was also trussed up, with a gag in her mouth. She was even paler than usual in the moonlight. The dark stain on her side might have had something to do with it. She'd already been in that position when he'd got into the boat, so he hadn't been able to talk to her. But her eyes told him she didn't have much to say. They shone with contempt. If she was injured, the wound hadn't been deep enough to weaken her will.

Della Torre wondered whether the Montenegrin was taking them back to the Bay of Kotor. But that didn't seem right. His internal compass told him they were going north. Then again, what could his internal compass know on such a night, in a strange sea?

"Comfortable, Gringo?"

"Better now that I've had something to drink. Thanks."

"That's the problem with choosing an inconsiderate hostess."

"How is she?" della Torre said, pointing his chin towards Rebecca.

"She won't bleed to death."

"Do you think maybe you ought to take the gag out of her mouth?"

"No, because, quite frankly, there's nothing I want to hear from her."

"How did you find us?"

"My daughter told me. She's a very observant girl. So good that she even knew the depth of the dock. Said the water came up to your shoulders at the end of it."

"How is she?"

"Astonishingly untroubled by her misadventure."

"She's quite a girl."

"It's easy to underestimate her. I'm glad you discovered how special she is."

"What happened to the others?"

"The two men? Fish food. I'm afraid I only asked for you and her to be kept alive. My men were very unhappy about what had happened to Snezhana. They took their revenge."

"So what now?"

"Now?" The Montenegrin pressed a button on his watch to illuminate it. "We wait for another ten minutes or so. With this current and in these channels, I need to get things right."

Della Torre didn't understand, nor did he feel like pressing the man.

"I will leave you to contemplate the moonlight," the Montenegrin said, standing up. "But I won't be gone long."

Moonlight. It made him think of Harry in England. Listening to Britten, watching her look out over the broad Suffolk marshes and the North Sea. The melancholy bars of the third *Sea Interlude*, "Moonlight."

His memory matched the rocking boat, the cantering motion of waves in a choppy sea. The wind had picked up, lifting the swell against them. The great silver and green moon.

Rebecca's eyes were focused on him. She wasn't communicating anything, just watching him, as a caged panther might gaze at a visitor through its bars. They were at the Montenegrin's mercy. But the Montenegrin was a professional. In his career he'd never shown himself to be a merciful man. Nor was he cruel. There would be no long wait, no torture, no gloating bloodlust such as might be expected from Gorki. A professional, like Rebecca. Maybe that was the defiance in her eyes. Whereas della Torre retreated into sentimental nostalgia.

The Montenegrin came back to the fishing deck. Della Torre could see the moonlight glint off something in his hands. A knife. The Montenegrin was steady on his feet, unaffected by the boat's motion. He walked over to Rebecca, reached behind her. For a moment della Torre wondered whether he'd stab her, gut and fillet her like a fish. But the Montenegrin had only cut the ropes holding her to the cleat. Her hands remained fixed behind her back and her legs tied. The Montenegrin put away the knife in a holster on his belt and pulled Rebecca up.

Then, in one smooth motion, he lifted Rebecca above the fishing boat's gunwales and threw her over the side.

Della Torre watched her surface behind the boat. He watched her through the green and silver light, the seawater rope knotted about her neck, her copper hair gone black in the night water, her face, sick of sin, gasping up towards heaven, nostrils flared above the bound mouth. He watched her flounder, strive.

And then, with all the horror and terror suffered by a battle-shy youth, he watched her drown.

The boat pulled away.

She'd felt no sickness or remorse in murder. For her, death was absurd, and life even more so. For the Montenegrin too. But it shook della Torre. He gasped, breathing for the drowning woman and himself.

There was a long silence. The Montenegrin stood watching over the boat's transom.

"Even at my age, you live and learn," the Montenegrin said without turning.

"Die and forget," della Torre said to himself, but audibly enough for the Montenegrin to hear.

"And then, yes, you die. But if you're lucky, someone carries the memory of what you learned." The Montenegrin looked at della Torre. "You mustn't be surprised. It would have been less cruel to have shot her first, but this was the punishment prescribed by Snezhana. She said Milady sends her greetings. Whatever that means. I'm afraid I'm not as bookish as she is. Anyway, she said an honourable death was too good for the red-headed woman, so it was death by drowning. She told me to tell you."

Della Torre nodded. Snezhana. *Snow*. Winter's snow. Milady de Winter. The child who'd been fearless. The ten-year-old girl, light as a feather but with an iron will, had known. Had seen. She was right. Only Milady had that sort of strength, courage, ferocity. Understanding just how cruel life can be, compared to the sentimentality of the Musketeers. Who had she thought Rebecca was? Buckingham? Constance? The wretch Fenton? And who was he? D'Artagnan? Athos? No. Planchet.

"Rebecca nearly had you," della Torre finally said, swallowing his words. "On the Stradun."

"Did she? I thought I heard a bullet fly past, but I assumed it was my imagination. It must have come very close for me to have heard it so clearly. She was a good soldier."

"Is Irena..."

"Your wife? She's unharmed. But she's in danger still. No longer from me. But now she's in the thick of war."

"Thank you for not taking your revenge on her."

"Thank you for my life. And for tending to Snezhana. There was a price on your head. Had she been hurt, you would have learned how the Turks exacted vengeance when they owned much of this country. Though never Montenegro." He laughed. "People learn the hard way that Montenegrins are difficult to subjugate, no?"

Della Torre stayed silent.

"When you called and I warned you that I would accept no trickery, that any deceit would be met harshly, you said, 'Trust me.' I laughed. But later, I thought about it. I had always trusted you. And you had always been trustworthy. And when you freed my daughter and had your friend save me, you were again trustworthy. So when you brought that American woman to me, did you know what she intended to do?"

Della Torre thought in silence and then knew it would be worthless to lie. "Yes."

"You knew she meant to kill me?"

"Yes."

The Montenegrin turned to face him and nodded.

"I didn't know that she would use Snezhana," della Torre said.

"Yes, this seems apparent. Did they know that Gorki would help you?"

"Maybe. That's not something they told me. There was much they didn't tell me. I don't know why they wanted you dead. I know what they said. That it was because you'd run the liquidation program and had arranged the assassination of people on American soil."

"But you don't believe it?"

"No."

"Gorki wasn't the only one who helped the Americans." The Montenegrin sat next to della Torre now, the boat rocking in the light swell.

"No, he wasn't," della Torre agreed. "Horvat had something to do with it too."

"Horvat is easy. He was doing the Americans a favour, an

easy favour. He was sacrificing a former UDBA agent to kill another former UDBA agent. I'm pretty sure he wouldn't weep too much at your funeral. And he'd dance on my grave. Because without me he could develop a monopoly on smuggling down here. He's got one up in eastern Slavonia. He has a little power base in Vukovar, which means he's sewn up the smuggling routes to Hungary. I hear he's doing something similar in Istria, though there are plenty of established interests that are proving hard to budge. He's got links with Bosnia through Zadar, and he's building up his interests on the Austrian border. He's a busy man."

"Yes, I hear he's a clever businessman."

"He's very good, very forceful, canny. People underestimate him because he's crass. They shouldn't," the Montenegrin said. "Horvat, I understand. But I find it interesting that the Americans know about my difficulties with Gorki. Did you tell them?"

"I didn't know anything about it. I thought he was in Vukovar until I found out he was here."

Somewhere over the water, della Torre saw a beam flash towards them.

"Ah, we have a shepherd. We'll have to continue our conversation in a little while, Gringo."

It was a signal demanding identification. One of the naval patrol boats. They'd become increasingly active in these waters. The Montenegrin used a heavy waterproof torch to flash out a code towards the ship. Della Torre read the Morse without having to think about it, his army training so deeply embedded in him that he'd never forget it. A...T...H...O...S, it read. There was a delay and then the navy ship flashed back: P...O...R...H...O...S.

"Stupid signaller," the Montenegrin said. "Drunk conscripts."

He flashed a repeat signal and the ship repeated it correctly: P...O...R...T...H...O...S.

The Montenegrin replied again: A...R...A...M...I...S.

And there was nothing more from the navy.

"They're being very...how shall I say it? Fastidious. They're being very fastidious with the night shipping. Too many smugglers." The Montenegrin laughed. And then, more seriously, he said, "And I think they're getting ready for something."

"So are the militias."

"Yes, the militias too." He fell silent and then slapped the locker he sat on. "Would you like anything, Gringo? I should have asked, but the conversation was so engrossing. Some water?"

"No. My thirst is gone."

"You certainly drank enough to burst."

"Maybe a cigarette."

"Of course. But I'm afraid I can't untie you. You understand."

"That's okay. If you hang it off my lip, I can do the rest."

The Montenegrin went forward and came back with a lit cigarette from one of his crew. Gently he put it up against della Torre's lips. For a moment della Torre thought he might kick out at the other man; his legs were untied. But to what end? He'd never manage to free himself.

"So, we were talking about Gorki. You don't know why he would want to help the Americans?" the Montenegrin asked.

"I can only assume it has something to do with UDBA." Talking with a cigarette in his mouth made della Torre sound like some gangster from an old black and white Hollywood movie, like the ones they'd shown on Saturday afternoon television when he was living in Ohio. In any other circumstance, he might have found it funny, made a joke about it.

"The old UDBA never had that much use for him, though he had defenders in the hierarchy," the Montenegrin said. "He was an operative. Before my time in command they'd used him on a couple of liquidation teams. But he was unreliable. He had a bad habit of robbing banks and getting caught. He was always in one prison or another. Unfortunately he is a very good linguist; he has very good English, French, German, speaks some Dutch, some Italian, and enough Swedish to get by. I imagine he's probably got Russian as well, but I never asked. His friends are now even more senior in the Serbian UDBA. So he grows in strength. Maybe he does what he likes, sees that there are advantages to being friendly with the Americans. Maybe he was doing a favour for his masters."

Della Torre sucked on the cigarette, the smoke coursing into his lungs and the nicotine washing through his body so that he felt he could withstand anything.

The Montenegrin had grown quiet again. The boat's engine was chugging regularly. It felt like they were making steady progress through the night sea. Where they were was littered with islands and dangerous channels. Della Torre could understand why they would be cautious. In the distance he could see the occasional cluster of lights. Villages, some on the water, others in the hills. But not many lights. No one wasted electricity here.

"You asked about Pilgrim."

"And you never answered."

"No," the Montenegrin said. "Pilgrim was a secret file. All reference to it was supposed to have been destroyed. But these things never are, are they? Files are cross-referenced and little side notes are made. The important things, though, they were never written down. Not with Pilgrim."

"I know."

"What do you know about Pilgrim?" the Montenegrin asked.

"It had something to do with nuclear centrifuges. Swedish centrifuges sold to Belgrade that Belgrade then sold on."

"Ah, that was part of it, a little part. Though I don't know what part. But Pilgrim was a person."

Della Torre looked up at the man, ash dropping on his lap from the half-spent cigarette.

"I did that assignment. Alone. No backup. No one else party to it, except a boy who didn't know anything and didn't live." The Montenegrin sighed. "That target was Olof Palme, the Swedish prime minister."

The cigarette fell out of Della Torre's mouth onto his leg, burning him before dropping onto the deck, where the orange-red ember hissed and then fell silent in damp darkness.

"Who asked you to kill the Swedish prime minister? The Dispatcher?"

"The Dispatcher had almost nothing to do with it. He merely passed me on to the man who made the order."

"The presidency?" Della Torre asked.

"Yes. Though not in the normal way," the Montenegrin said. "The orders were passed on by a mandarin, rather than through the usual channels. They made promises and arrangements that I couldn't refuse. I was made a colonel, given the department, and allowed to build my little militia in Montenegro. My insurance."

"Who was the mandarin? Why would they want Palme dead?"

"Who? Dragomanov. Why? I don't know. You shouldn't be surprised. Good soldiers do as they're told."

"Dragomanov? Tito's translator?" Della Torre was puzzled by the convolutions he'd involved himself in — what had once been merely meaningless bits of paper to sell on, in exchange for enough small change to buy himself cigarettes.

The Montenegrin laughed. "You say it as if he was Tito's baker. Or tailor. Dragomanov was Tito's voice to the world. Foreign ministers came and went, but Dragomanov was permanent. Even after Tito died. Do you not know that he ran Yugoslav affairs with the rest of the world? Titles were meaningless under Tito. All that mattered was how close you stood next to him. And no one stood closer to him than Dragomanov. No one. Not even Tito's wife. You want to know why Palme had to die, you have to talk to Dragomanov."

Della Torre licked his lip, imagining he tasted cigarette ash on it. "It's too late to be asking anyone anything."

"Gringo, you sound defeated. Never be defeated," the Montenegrin said. He'd sat down on the bench next to della Torre, leaning forward slightly, his hands together on his lap, like a father confessor. "Can you swim?" he asked.

It took della Torre a moment to understand the question, to filter it through the conversation of the past few moments, through his enormous fear of dying.

"Yes."

"Good. If you couldn't, you'd either have to learn fast or pray hard."

The Montenegrin reached behind della Torre with his knife, cutting the cords. Della Torre's arms felt almost frozen from having been bound so long. He started to work the blood into his hands but wasn't given a chance to revive them before the Montenegrin threw him overboard. For a moment della Torre thought he might drown, unable to orient himself, his limbs barely functioning.

The membrane of cool water stretched and broke over his face as he surfaced. He gulped air and opened his eyes to see a sky pinned with stars by clumsy hands. He turned, and there was the Montenegrin standing over him in the stern of the boat, its engine idling gutturally.

"Behind you, you'll see lights. That's Orebić," the Montenegrin shouted. "We're about a kilometre offshore. The current's favourable for you here. If you can swim, you should get there without too many problems. You can thank Snezhana for your life. D'Artagnan, she calls you. Pray that you never see us again."

The engine throttled up, chugging loudly, and the boat quickly disappeared into darkness. For a moment della Torre thought the Montenegrin had lied to him. But then he saw them, the lights. They seemed to be arranged in a crucifix, a beacon to guide him. His arms were sore, but it was no struggle to swim. The water was cool but pleasant. The distance manageable. So he swam towards the lights, the silver lights, through the green phosphorescence of the Adriatic.

# COMING SOON
## FROM HOUSE OF ANANSI PRESS
### IN JANUARY 2015

Read on for a preview of the next thrilling Marko della Torre novel, *The Heart of Hell*.

# PROLOGUE

## BARI, ITALY, SEPTEMBER 1991

I am Lazarus, come from the dead,
Come back to tell you all, I shall tell you all
— *The Love Song of J. Alfred Prufrock,* T. S. Eliot

THE WATERS OF Croatia's Adriatic are crystalline blue and turquoise to a depth of ten metres and more, so that the coral fans and black round balls of spiny sea urchins on distant bare rocks appear to be no more than an arm's length below the surface. The clarity engenders a sense of vertigo. Schools of fish are seemingly suspended in unaccountable space between the skin of surface and the seabed, where they flow and flutter like leaves on the wind, while the swimmers' shadows undulate far below.

That the waters are kept so pristine is thanks to friendly currents that carry rubbish to Italian shores.

Which was why the Italian state police in Bari, on the western Adriatic where Italy's heel meets the rest of the boot, eventually turned their attention directly east, two hundred kilometres to Dubrovnik, in Croatia's extreme south—a corpse had washed up on one of their beaches.

It was September 1991 and Yugoslavia was hurtling towards civil war after Croatia had declared independence only a couple of months earlier. In the past, formal requests for police cooperation would have been made by Rome to Belgrade; they would then have been passed on to the local authorities in Croatia's major coastal towns. But with the Croatian leadership no longer speaking to Belgrade and the Italian government not formally recognizing the Croatian state, the head of the state police in Bari took it upon himself to make an informal call to the senior detective on the Dubrovnik force, with whom he'd worked before and who he knew spoke good, if German-inflected, Italian.

This was how Detective Brg found himself taking the ferry from Dubrovnik to Bari. The crossing was slow, but there were no longer any direct flights, and to have gone by way of Zagreb and Rome would have taken as long and cost eight times as much.

Detective Brg's first instinct had been to send someone else or to regretfully refer the Bari police to Zagreb. He just didn't have the time to take a day off from his other duties to inspect a corpse in a foreign jurisdiction on the off chance it might have floated over from his shores. He was handling an ever-growing number of responsibilities in the Dubrovnik police's increasingly depleted squad.

And that too was down to politics.

Dubrovnik is a distant appendix in Croatia's far south, at the end of a narrow strip of land along the Adriatic coast, separated by a chain of mountains from Bosnia and Montenegro, two republics that were still within control of the Yugoslav federation. Though an ancient and massive fortress city, Dubrovnik would be all but impossible to defend against a modern military onslaught. Theoretically, that didn't matter — it had no military value. It was a site of purely historical and touristic interest, and the Croatian government assumed it would be left alone so long as nobody there provoked the Yugoslav army.

But the Dubrovnik authorities weren't so sure. Within their modest means, they set about quietly creating a defence force. Unfortunately, it was built around the police, leaving regular policing duties to a small, very overworked team, led by Brg.

What swayed him to make the trip was the description of the body. A red-headed woman, a little above average height and probably in her late twenties or mid-thirties. He'd been working on a case involving the violent deaths of two American men in a villa on an island less than twenty kilometres to the north of Dubrovnik, and a missing American woman. A redhead, age thirty-two, 170 centimetres tall and weighing around fifty-eight kilograms. Zagreb had official control of the investigation, but inept bureaucracy and a diplomatic impasse with the local American consulate had left Brg's team working on the case more or less unaided.

A detective from the Bari force was waiting for him at passport control. Because Brg was pressed for time—he was adamant that he had to be on the overnight ferry back to Dubrovnik—they skipped a courtesy visit to the station and had the driver take them straight to the morgue.

The medical examiner was a locum, a retired professor called Dr. Angelo Albini. In Brg's experience, pathologists tended to be supercilious stuffed shirts, irritated at being questioned, intolerant of the smallest sign that a cop might not understand the jargon. Then again, he thought, with that sort of bedside manner it was just as well they were inflicted only on the dead.

But Dr. Albini was unlike any Yugoslav pathologist Brg had ever met.

The professor looked like a pink-cheeked elf, with white hair, bright eyes, and an ebullience that belied his age. He moved with obvious discomfort, with a heavy limp, but his incessant chatter was that of a ten-year-old boy expounding, with end-less digressions, on his latest enthusiasm.

"Detective Brg, Detective Brg, very interesting case, this one. Very interesting. Brg? Sounds German somehow. German, is it? You speak Italian with a German accent," Dr. Albini said, leading Brg to a bloated and bleached body on a stainless steel table in a sterile, windowless room.

"My father's family was from the north, near the Austrian border. They're all German-speaking. Brg is the Slavicized version of Berg," Brg said, trying to sound detached as his stomach turned over at the smell and sight of the once-living flesh before him. He understood now why his local police liaison had another, suddenly urgent piece of business to attend to.

"Ah, of course, of course. Austro-Hungarians, the lot of you up there. Our own Tyroleans speak with a German accent. Very interesting, very interesting." Brg couldn't tell whether the professor was referring to his name or to the dissected corpse he now leaned over. "I must apologize for the aroma. I'm told the compressor on the air conditioner failed." He lifted an arm to expose the corpse more fully. "New parts. Take forever, eh."

New parts for the corpse or the compressor? The old man was beginning to overwhelm Brg as much as the gruesome yet somehow sanitized effigy in flesh.

"German, eh?" Albini said. "You should have been here three days ago. You could have talked to the German couple who found her. Camping. Not her — the German couple. She was bobbing around on the beach. Must have been a heck of a shock. Well, probably for her too. But the German couple, you should have heard them. You'd have thought they'd found a body on the beach." He tittered at his little joke. "Have to feel sorry for them. Well, for her too. But the German couple ran all the way back to town to raise the alarm, and what do our police do? Say thank you very much? Not likely. Fined them for camping illegally. Not just fined them but didn't issue them a receipt. We all know what that means. You Yugoslav — my apologies — *Croatian* police probably don't know much about corruption." Here he stopped to give Brg a theatrical wink. "But we Italians can write whole encyclopedias about it. Shame nobody ever thinks to bribe medical examiners, eh? Never think of it. Poisoners might, I suppose, but never get around to it. Anyway, here she is, our inanimate guest."

Brg nodded. He pulled from his briefcase a thin, shiny sheet of fax paper showing a photograph of the missing American woman. It was hard to reconcile the image with what was in front of him.

Albini hobbled over to Brg's side of the table to have a look at the fax.

"Gout. Me, not her. Terrible. Look at my poor leg."

Albini pulled up his trouser leg to expose his limb, swollen to twice the normal size and as red and purple as a bottle of claret. It looked like it might have belonged on a corpse. Brg nodded with what he hoped looked like sympathy, but the old professor had already switched his attention back to the subject at hand.

"You wouldn't think a girl who looked like this could look like that, but that's what a couple of weeks in the water will do to you," Albini said.

"A couple of weeks?"

"Probably. I'd put it between ten and twenty days."

Brg nodded. The Americans had been killed a little more than two weeks before, and the woman had gone missing around the same time.

"The weather's been cold but the sea's still warm, and that usually speeds up decomposition. She's been nibbled at by some of the sea life, but she's in much better shape than you'd expect. Probably because the Adriatic has been all fished out. Nothing left to feed off corpses, eh? Just as well, wouldn't do to be served corpse-fed fillet of mullet."

Albini hobbled back around the table, nodding knowingly at the body, its bleached skin made all the more stark by the cold fluorescence of the overhead lights.

"What can we say, what can we say? Haven't written my report yet, of course. That'll take another few days, and with the time it takes to get processed you might not see anything official for another month. This is just me and you talking informally, right?"

Brg nodded and began to say "Of course," when the old professor cut him off.

"Well, if you look at her musculature and fat content, she was very healthy. Very healthy indeed. Athletic, even. All the organs clear of disease. Officially, I'd put her age between twenty and forty, but unofficially I'd say mid- to early thirties. Don't ask why. I've been doing this sort of work for fifty years. Eventually you figure things out in ways that aren't worth explaining. Hair, red. Real red, no dyes. No indication of poison or heavy metals or drug use in the hair samples. Teeth, very good. A bit of dental work. The quality suggests northern European or North American. When I say North American, that could mean Australian or New Zealand too. We found some coral embedded in the skull. That and the pattern of abrasions suggests she drowned at a rocky part of the coast. We're sand on this side, so it means more likely the western Adriatic. Head's heavier and tends to sink lower, gets dragged along that way until the gases associated with decomposition float the body again."

Brg had taken out his notebook. He was finding it hard to transcribe the professor's remarks while translating into Serbo-Croat at the same time, and instead ended up writing in a pidgin Italian. He prayed he'd be able to decipher what he was writing later on.

"Drowned, you say?" Brg asked.

"Oh, yes. Quite a lot of water in the lungs, and residuals of foaming that you only get with drowning. Though the foam doesn't tend to last this long. Saltwater drowning too. There's that movie, can't remember what it's called, where somebody was found drowned in a pool, except the water in the lungs was salt." Albini paused for a moment. "Or the other way around. Something we always check. Too easy to drown somebody in a bath and then pop them in the sea. Except it's not very easy to drown somebody in a bath. People tend to struggle and then you get all sorts of other indications that the drowning wasn't accidental. Abrasions, odd bruises. And then they have to get the body into the sea. People tend to notice bodies being lugged around. What was I saying?"

"She drowned."

"Oh, yes, quite clearly. And not an accident or suicide either, in my professional opinion," he said.

"Why is that?" Brg asked, intrigued by the professor's methods.

"Tied up. She was tied up in such a way that she couldn't have tied herself up. Needed somebody else to do it. Suppose you could be a suicide and get somebody to tie you up and pop you overboard. But then it's not suicide, is it?"

"Somebody tied her up and threw her in the water?"

"Oh, yes. Proper fishermen's knots. Houdini couldn't get out of those. Maybe they drowned her because they failed to kill her some other way."

Brg looked puzzled. Albini pointed to an injury high on the fleshy part of the corpse's hip.

"Puncture wound. Probably from a projectile. Bullet would be my guess. Pattern of bruising suggests not too long before she died. But it didn't cause her death. Would have been painful, but not fatal. Well, might have got infected, and then would have killed her a few days later. But it wasn't the cause of death."

Once again the old professor paused, shaking as if a small tremor had run through him. "Aye. Never get gout. Hurts like the devil but doesn't kill you. Maybe I'll get somebody to truss me up and toss me off a bridge. Sorry, that's a joke, by the way. Pathology, very funny business."

Brg nodded, overwhelmed. By the corpse. And Albini.

"Right, what more can I tell you? Ropes were probably Yugoslav-made, judging by the fibres, but we're running tests on that still. She wasn't. Yugoslav-made, that is. Or if she was Yugoslav, she didn't live there. Wasn't just the teeth telling us. Her clothes were all American-labelled. Everything down to the underwear. She'd also been fitted with an American inter-uterine device — that's birth control, to you. No evidence she'd ever borne a child, but these things can be deceptive. What more can I tell you? Oh. She probably floated over from around the Dubrovnik coast."

"Let me guess," Brg said. "She had a postcard in her pocket."

"Oh, no. Nothing like that. Wouldn't have been very useful anyway. People carry around postcards from all sorts of places. No, it's the hydrological office that tells us. Normally the stuff that washes up on the beach here comes from further north, north of Split, towards Fiume. What do you call it? Oh, yes, Rijeka."

Albini smiled slyly, watching to see whether Brg would take the bait. Fiume had been an Italian city with a majority Italian population, but was nonetheless given over to the Yugoslavs after the First World War, as part of the postwar redrawing of boundaries. The Yugoslavs renamed it Rijeka. Both words meant "river." The port town was briefly "liberated" by the Italian nationalist poet and adventurer Gabriele D'Annunzio and a handful of his followers. D'Annunzio then went on to declare war on anybody not supporting Fiume's return to Italy. Including Italy. D'Annunzio was eventually defeated and the postwar settlement was reimposed, though he emerged a hero. For many, that rebellion marked the beginning of European fascism. For some, Croatia's nationalist rebellion against Yugoslavia was merely a continuation of something D'Annunzio had started.

Brg ignored the comment. Living under Communism had taught him that debating history or politics only ever led to an argument at best, and jail at worst.

"Most times the body would have originated further north," Albini continued, "but a big bora was blowing last week. Surface currents would have taken her on a much more direct course across the sea."

The bora was a cold wind that blew from the north and the east. In the winter it could freeze sea spray onto lampposts and ship's masts and rage with near-hurricane strength. The one Albini referred to had been strong enough to keep yachts in harbour for days on end and had caused a number of the Dubrovnik-to-Bari ferries to be cancelled. Which was another reason Brg did not want to miss his boat back. The bora could rise again very quickly. He looked at his watch.

Albini smiled at Brg. "I think our officers would like very much that it's your corpse. Makes less work for them. But anyway, they're pretty sure she's not ours. Doesn't fit anybody in our missing-persons files. There was almost a match, but our lady here still has her appendix."

And then, with an exaggerated shrug and raised hands, Albini made it clear the interview was over.

"Thank you very much, Doctor Professor," Brg said. The identification wasn't conclusive, but it was good enough for him. He'd pass her on to Zagreb, and maybe with some luck they'd give him a pat on the back and send somebody down to investigate the dead Americans. So far, all they'd done was to take the corpses back north. Now they had a full set.

He looked at his watch again. Just as well he wasn't hungry. There wasn't enough time to stop for an early dinner before getting the ferry. He wasn't looking forward to the journey back.

1

## DUBROVNIK, SEPTEMBER 1991

STRUMBIĆ'S TONGUE FELT its way uncertainly around his mouth, as though it was travelling an alien landscape. He was once again surprised by the jagged corner of the bicuspid two back from his left upper incisor. The gouge inside his left cheek was no longer hot and swollen, but it itched and demanded to be prodded at until the pain came back. The bitten flesh on the tongue itself had become a knot, lumpy and huge as it slowly healed.

A sharp, pungent odour hit him. It took him a few seconds to realize it was his own clothes he smelled, his own stench. They hadn't let him change his suit for... how long was it? Two weeks? At least he'd been allowed to shower in that time, a special privilege, as his jailers let him know. But Strumbić had a talent for getting things out of people.

He'd been waiting in the interview room on his own for a good ten minutes before the detective showed up, carrying a case file.

"So, Mr. Smirnoff, shall we try this again? Maybe a few days in the cells cleared your head. Let some of those memories fall back into place."

Strumbić hadn't met this cop before, the third one to interrogate him since his arrest. He was a few years younger than Strumbić, dark hair, medium height, and solid build. He wore a cheap suit, the tie hanging loose around his collar. A moustache followed the full length of his top lip. His stubbled cheeks, puffy eyes, and sagging expression spoke of very long nights. The detective didn't seem dissolute, so it must have been work keeping him up.

It was unconscionably early. Strumbić hadn't even been fed breakfast yet. He'd had to be roused from his bed, though he wasn't quite sure of the exact time. The clock on the wall was stuck on half past two. The first thing they'd done when they booked him was take his Rolex. He'd signed a receipt, but he was certain he'd never see it again. If he was lucky, they'd replace it with a cheap East German Timex knock-off. He knew how these things worked.

"Okay, so, for the record, could we have your name again?"

Strumbić hesitated, almost said his own name, and then remembered his alias.

"Julius Smirnoff," he said.

"How is it that the only identification on you is a . . . what is this, a loyalty card for a British department store?" the detective asked, stifling a yawn. "What the hell's a loyalty card?"

"Well, Detective . . . I'm sorry, I seem to have forgotten your name."

"It's Brg. Mister or Detective to you."

"Not from around here, then, Detective Brg?"

"Perceptive," Brg said. It wasn't a conversation he was interested in having right then. "So where's 'Smirnoff' from? Other than a bottle of vodka?"

"Russian. I still have spiritual ties," Strumbić said.

Brg nodded. Too tired to appreciate the wit. "You were explaining the . . . loyalty card."

"I'm loyal, it's a good shop. Marks & Spencer. They do nice suits," Strumbić said. "You should try them anytime you're in England."

The wallet Strumbić took on his jobs only ever had cash in it. Not all criminals appreciated doing business with a cop. Explaining a lack of ID, when it came to it, was easier. The card must have been an oversight from when he'd been in London earlier that summer. Stupid.

Brg rested his eyes on Strumbić. Yet another middle-tier crook. All Brg wanted to do was get home and go to bed, but he had to deal with this asshole first. He wished he hadn't gone back to the office to drop off the documents from his Italian trip. He wished he hadn't seen the prosecutor's note sitting face-up on his desk: "You've run out of time on this guy. Charge him or let him go. This morning."

They'd have done it two weeks earlier if he hadn't somehow fallen through the cracks. If the arresting officers had taken proper interview notes. If somebody had been paying attention. Well, it was down to Brg. Quick interview and then a quick charge. Leave the rest to the prosecutors.

"So maybe you can explain how it is you came to be in possession of two thousand compact discs and to be consorting with people who shoot at police officers?" Brg asked.

Two thousand? Strumbić's eyebrows climbed. It had been three thousand dockside. It seemed a couple of Dubrovnik cops were richer not to the tune of just an expensive Swiss watch but also a thousand pirated compact discs.

A wave of regret washed over Strumbić. The scam had had so much potential. A Turk copied American rock and heavy metal CDs in Istanbul, packaged them with photocopies of their proper labels, and packed them into boxes. His associate took them up the Adriatic, along with other goods for other clients. Some Montenegrin fishermen picked up the cargo in international waters and delivered it to Strumbić at night in the mainland village. All Strumbić had to do was load them in his car and drive them up to Zagreb. He'd lined up buyers, quoted keen prices to whet demand. Restricted his initial investment in case they were duff, but he'd had a good feeling about this line of business. He had interest in five times as many CDs as he'd ordered from the Turk.

And then it went sour.

How was he to know the Dubrovnik cops were staking out the village dockside? Bad timing. The stakeout had nothing to do with him or the Montenegrins. The village was opposite a pretty island called Šipan, where unbeknownst to him or anyone other than the local cops, there'd been a double murder a couple of days before. Pure coincidence.

Though maybe not so coincidental. Strumbić had chosen this particular loading point because he knew the area well, and he knew the area well because he owned a villa on Šipan.

The Montenegrin smugglers had shot at the cops and got away in their very fast boat. And Strumbić had been left flat on his belly, licking the salt off the stone breakwater as he tried not to get in the way of any passing bullets.

Once things had calmed down, Strumbić's first reaction had been to do what any Communist apparatchik did as a matter of course. Because that's what he was. A senior detective on the Zagreb police force recently seconded to Croatian military intelligence as captain. High-intensity beams still on him, he jumped up and, looking as pissed off as a bear who'd lost his dinner, made ready to tear strips off the cops for ruining what he was going to tell them was an undercover sting operation.

Only he didn't get the chance.

The cops were still shaking with anger, fear, and adrenaline over being shot at. And the bigger one of the two hit Strumbić hard enough to chip a tooth and knock him down onto the stone breakwater before he'd managed to say more than two words.

By the time Strumbić's jaw worked well enough to string a comprehensible sentence together, he'd worked out that he was better off keeping his mouth shut. Better off praying the cops didn't figure out who he was.

"Two thousand?" Strumbić asked. He was surprised only a third of the CDs had gone walkabout. Had the tables been turned, he'd have taken half. More, even. Leaving only enough to give the investigating prosecutor sufficient evidence for a smuggling conviction.

"That's how many my officers tell me were in the boxes," Brg said, his look challenging Strumbić to contradict him.

"Seems an awful lot," Strumbić said mildly. "Didn't think there was a big enough market for the things. On account of how nobody has any money these days."

"Couldn't say. I'm not much of one for economics."

"Nor accounting, it seems," Strumbić said.

Brg started to say something, but thought better of it. He took on a chillier formality. "So what were you doing with those CDs, Mr. Smirnoff?"

"Me? Like I've been telling your colleagues, I had nothing to do with any CDs, Detective. I'd just been out for a bit of night fishing and these gentlemen landed the boat and started unloading the boxes."

"An innocent who just happened to be at the wrong place at the wrong time."

"Exactly."

"So what happened to your rod and reel?"

"Must have fallen off the dock in all the excitement."

The detective paused to rifle through the thin file in the blue folder.

"So you're from Herzegovina, are you, Mr. Smirnoff? The Yugoslav army's between here and there. How'd you get over?"

"Hitchhiked. A tank stopped for me, said they were heading in this direction anyway," Strumbić said.

Brg nodded, cursing himself for expecting anything other than obstruction. There was a long silence. Brg's eyes became slits. Sometimes cops did that because they thought it might catch the suspect off guard. Sometimes they did it because they were finding it hard to stay awake. Strumbić figured Brg was on his last legs.

"And you didn't tell us where you were staying in Dubrovnik, did you, Mr. Smirnoff?"

"Hadn't gotten around to finding a place. Nice of you folks to help out, though I don't like abusing your hospitality. Shouldn't you have charged me with something by now? Or let me go?"

The police jail cells weren't bad. It had taken Strumbić a couple of days to sort himself out, but he knew how cops operated, he knew the rulebooks, and, more than anything, he had a roguish charm that made people warm to him, do things for him that they might not otherwise. Besides, anyone who owned a Rolex and wore British suits was given the benefit of the doubt.

He'd organized a private cell and decent food and even clean underwear, though he hadn't managed to get his suit laundered yet.

Life wasn't bad. And it had been as good a place as any to stay safe, as long as he remained anonymous.

"Bags?"

"I travel light."

Brg stood up, walked around the desk, and perched on the corner. He must have seen that in a movie, Strumbić thought. Be friendly with the suspect. Coax a confession out of him. Or maybe it was the best way for him to keep from falling asleep.

It was the opening Strumbić had been looking for.

In a breach of interview protocol, Strumbić stood up too, catching Brg by surprise. Strumbić moved in a way that deliberately wasn't threatening, shifting his limbs as if they creaked from the hard bed of the past couple of nights. A supplicant approaching the great lord.

Strumbić knew that if he tried anything, the cop stationed just outside the interview room would finish the amateur dentistry his colleague had started the night he'd been arrested.

Brg wasn't alarmed, just taken aback slightly.

Strumbić knew he had to work quickly, that he had maybe a minute before the detective put him back in his place. He took the detective's hand, grasping it gently but refusing to let go. He used the pressure of two fingers on the inside of Brg's wrist so that Brg swivelled slightly, opening up his body. As he did, Strumbić stepped deeper into Brg's personal space, forcing the detective to rise up off the desk. All the while, Strumbić kept up an inane patter.

"Detective, I know you're a kind man, you're so gracious in seeing me. I mean, someone of your seniority taking time over such an irrelevant little person like me, I know it will be no time at all before a man of your capabilities will be able to resolve the matter…"

The fingers of Strumbić's free left hand brushed the detective lightly, like a tailor taking pride in a suit he'd just fitted. Even above his own jailhouse stench, Strumbić could smell that Brg was a smoker. A heavy one. He hadn't lit up yet but it wouldn't be long.

What Strumbić was doing wasn't so unusual in ordinary life, though maybe it wasn't quite normal for the subject of a police interview. People in the Balkans often had a strange sense of propriety, needing to touch the person they were talking to, to get as close as lovers, especially when dealing in confidences.

Strumbić continued to work quickly. Brg might have been tired, but he was still a professional and didn't seem stupid. Adrenaline sharpened Strumbić's wits. He had thirty seconds left maybe. He lifted his forearm so that it hovered at Brg's chest, not touching but close. Now he finally let go of the man's right hand.

Working, the whole while working, Strumbić's fingers remembering everything they'd learned two decades before as a rookie cop. The things he'd learned watching the street criminals and gypsies, interviewing them, standing them drinks in bars to draw out their secrets. And if they were recalcitrant, he'd make them talk by arresting them and threatening to break their fingers.

Distract the mark's attention. Shake his hand and keep hold of it while drawing closer, into his space. Use a forearm as cover to keep him from seeing what was happening. Keep the friendly, subservient chat going. Apologize for not being more helpful, tell him it was a misunderstanding. All the while, the hands move fast, lightly touching the mark, feeling pockets, patting his back.

Not once during Strumbić's brief performance did Brg show any sign that he realized what was really happening. Strumbić sat back down after less than the full minute. Brg, ever so slightly nonplussed but not entirely sure why, returned to his side of the desk.

"Detective, can I ask you a favour?" Strumbić said.

"What?" A wariness had crept into Brg's expression.

"Could you spare a cigarette?"

Brg gave Strumbić a look that said, *You're pushing your luck.* But he clearly needed one too. The detective patted his jacket pockets. One side, then the other. He patted the front pockets of his trousers and then his jacket again. A cloud of consternation passed over his brow and then he stood up, patting himself over again.

"I seem to have left them in my office. I'll be back in a couple of minutes. Try anything stupid and the officer outside will have something to say about it," Brg said and left the room.

Strumbić counted twenty seconds after the door shut and then reached forward for the phone on the interview table. He picked up the handset. It was for cops to make internal calls only. But internal calls could be switched through to other police stations—it was one of the country's few communication systems that actually worked properly.

Strumbić called the Zagreb police department's automated switchboard. Once he had a connection, he dialled the code to get an external line. And then, from memory, the private number he needed. Easy.

The phone rang. And rang. Della Torre didn't answer.

Strumbić figured he had five minutes. Maybe ten at most. He held the phone to his good cheek with his shoulder, reached into his pocket, and pulled out a packet of Lords and a transparent orange imitation Bic lighter.

Brg's Lords and Brg's cheap plastic lighter.

As the phone continued to ring, he checked the contents of Brg's wallet and took out a couple of thousand dinars, just in case he needed money to bribe the guards. He didn't know how long he'd be a guest of the Dubrovnik police. But he left enough that Brg wouldn't immediately suspect he'd been robbed, and then he flipped the wallet under the table so that it sat just under the detective's chair.

Strumbić had spent years perfecting his pickpocketing and lock-picking skills, which he had learned from the masters. Thieves as good as the Serb Borra, who'd become famous travelling around Europe in circuses, entertaining people with his magic: his ability to take watches off men's wrists; ties from around their necks; hell, even glasses from their faces, without their noticing. Strumbić's gypsies were just as good. Only for some reason they'd never managed to become as rich as Borra.

Where are you, Gringo?

He pressed down the receiver. He had to find somebody to get a message to della Torre. Anzulović? No, too risky.

He dialled another number. A squeaky voice answered.

"Hey, doll, it's Julius."

"Yes?"

"Listen, it's urgent. I need a favour from you."

"Julius? No one here by that name. I'm afraid you have the wrong number," she said, hanging up.

"Bitch," Strumbić said aloud, grinding the cigarette butt onto the linoleum floor. This time, he'd really sort her out. Like he'd done for her cop boyfriend. Even now it galled Strumbić to think that one of his own men, one of his own police officers, had been sleeping with his mistress in the secret little apartment Strumbić had set up for her. He gave her money and she'd done the dirty on him. Stupid cow. And now she refused to help him.

For some stupid, sentimental reason he'd let her stay in the place after finding out her deceit. He was too soft. No, it was her tits that were too soft to give up. But Strumbić'd made sure the squaddie got busted down to traffic—and then, when cops were being transferred into the civil defence force, Croatia's proto-army, that he was sent to the front line in Vukovar.

He wouldn't forgive her again, though. He'd sort her out properly this time. He'd put her back on the street, where he'd found her.

His mental clock was ticking down. Three minutes? Four, tops? There was one last chance. One last call. He had to make it count. He knew he had no other choice. He'd do it only as an act of desperation. Not just because he'd rather have his teeth knocked out with a chisel than talk to his wife, but because he knew they'd be monitoring his home phone.

"It's me."

"Where are you?" Her voice grated on him like steel on slate. "Light in the toilet has gone again, and all sorts of people have been trying to get in touch with you. Phoning non-stop. Constantly at the door."

"Listen. Take a message, will you." He tried not to raise his voice, tried not to yell.

"Minute you leave the apartment, that light stops working. What did you do to it? You rig it up to make me miserable, don't you? Have to use candles. A month you've been gone without word."

"Will you shut your trap and just listen for a minute, woman," he hissed. He could see her pinched face, top lip pursed under her sharp nose as if she'd detected a bad smell. Her thin frame, desiccated by a lifetime of bitter complaint. How many times had he told himself that if it wasn't for her strudel he'd have left her long before?

"Don't you be swearing at me. If my father was still alive, you'd be watching your tongue."

"Well, the old thug isn't, is he?" he said, exasperated. "Will you just for once in your life stop yammering at me and listen?"

"So that's how it is, eh? What's next? You going to beat me? You going to break my arm like Franz down the way did to his old woman? Knocked her right into hospital and left her blacker than blue. Only last week..."

Strumbić felt every second evaporating with a pulse of cold dread. He'd have happily beaten her. He'd have beaten her for twenty years now. But not while the old man, Zagreb's thuggish ex-chief of police, had been alive. No, not now either. If he'd ever laid a hand on her, he knew she'd cut his throat in the night. And no one would blame her.

He caught himself. Forced himself to be calm. Forced his voice to become even, neutral, pleasant.

"I'm sorry, darling. Really, I didn't mean to get off on the wrong foot. I will get a good electrician in to look at the light. A proper one, not like the monkey last time."

"And a new washing machine..."

"And a new washing machine. Could you please do me a favour? Please?"

"And all sorts have been looking for you."

"Who?" he asked.

"How do I know? Police," she said. "Detectives. People. Past couple of days."

Anyone trying to discover who he was phoning would only be able to trace this call to the Zagreb police department. But he'd still have to be careful about what he said.

"Can we get back to that favour?"

"What?" She didn't sound mollified, but it was an opening.

"Could you please write this down?"

"I'll remember it."

"Please could you write it down."

"I'll remember," she said. "My memory's as sharp as it was when I was seventeen, and when I was seventeen I could recite, verbatim—"

"Okay, okay," he said, trying to hide the exasperation in his voice. "Use that seventeen-year-old memory. Can you get in touch with Marko della Torre? He's in military intelligence. My new office. Get in touch with him, get a message to him. Tell him I'm with our colleagues—" He paused, trying to think of something della Torre would understand that no one else would. "—near that Italian staircase he liked so much."

Della Torre had marvelled at the staircase in Strumbić's villa on Šipan Island. He'd know that the Italian staircase meant down south and that the colleagues were the Dubrovnik cops.

"Why can't they get in touch with him if they're colleagues?"

He felt a hot, wet tear on his cheek. It was as much as he could do to control himself. "It's an undercover job. Top secret. Inside stuff."

He could almost hear her snap to attention. Why hadn't he thought of that before? A top cop's daughter knew her duty.

"Della Torre," she said.

"Tell him that I'm a guest of our colleagues but I'm using my pub name."

"Your name's a pub?"

"My pub name."

"Your pub name?"

"Yes. He'll know what I mean. That's as much as I can say." Smirnoff was the name he'd used in London. Della Torre knew all about that. And pubs were found in London.

"I'll make sure he gets the message," she said, all efficiency.

He heard the door open behind him and put his hand on the phone's kill switch without saying goodbye to his wife. For once, he knew she'd do as she was told.

"Calling someone, Mr. Smirnoff?" Brg asked.

"I was just about to ask them to page you. I was starting to feel lonely."

Brg nodded and went round to sit on his side of the table. As he pulled out his chair, he stopped for a second and stared down at his feet. He bent over, picking up his wallet. He slid it back into his pocket without looking at the contents and sat down, staring at Strumbić with a strained expression.

"Did you manage to find some cigarettes?" Strumbić asked, as sweet as candy floss.

"Why don't we get back to those questions, Mr. Smirnoff? I don't have a lot of time to waste on you. I've got three dead Americans to worry about."

For the first time that morning, Strumbić felt a chill. He didn't like the way the detective said "Smirnoff." Nor did he like that the number of dead Americans had risen to three.

In the back of the patrol car the night he was arrested, he'd listened to the cops talking about the two dead Americans on Šipan. They were keeping an eye out for anyone making the crossing from the island. The mention of dead Americans had quieted Strumbić, made him think twice about revealing who he was.

He'd been dealing with some Americans on an official job only days earlier, while setting up his distinctly unofficial CD-smuggling scheme. In fact, one of them had stayed at his villa on Šipan. She still had the keys to the place. Two dead Americans on Šipan. A third now.

He had nothing to do with their deaths. But it wasn't something he wanted to argue from a jail cell. He knew it would be hung on him, on Captain Julius Strumbić of military intelligence, unless they found out what had really happened. And as far as he could tell, they had no clue.

Strumbić hadn't a scintilla of doubt that della Torre was somehow tied in with the deaths. Della Torre would have to get him out of the mess. Just as well then that, however much trouble della Torre kept landing in Strumbić's lap, he was also the only man Strumbić trusted with his life.

"I don't really know how I can help, Detective," Strumbić said, helping himself to one of the cigarettes Brg held out, not allowing himself to show any of the unease he felt. "Like I said, I was fishing and suddenly found myself in the middle of the O.K. Corral."

The Dubrovnik detective rifled through a second file he'd brought into the room, pulled out a sheet, and contemplated it for a long, quiet moment. He raised his tired eyes, took a final long drag on his cigarette, and trapped the other man in his gaze. Strumbić's amusement at having so thoroughly picked the other man's pockets faded a little. His certainty of having found a safe haven, a comfortable little hideaway, was evaporating. He found himself feeling increasingly unsettled. It wasn't an emotion he was used to. Brg ground out the cigarette in a cheap tin ashtray.

The Dubrovnik detective contemplated the man in front of him, more seriously than he had less than half an hour earlier.

Brg had gone back up to his office, pissed off at the petty smuggler he was having to deal with when all he wanted was sleep and then to report back to Zagreb that the American redhead had been found.

Brg was sure that in his tiredness, he'd left both his cigarettes and lighter on the ferry. He got another pack out from the carton he kept in the bottom drawer of his desk. But the spare matches he had to hunt for on his desk.

It was while he was shifting the papers that the roll of fax paper with the dead woman's photograph fell on the floor. He picked it up and it unspooled. As he looked down the pages, folding them so that they'd fit more neatly into the file, his eye lighted on a photograph of a man: middle-aged, greying, receding hairline, flabby face, and tired eyes. Captain Julius Strumbić of military intelligence, formerly detective lieutenant with the Zagreb police. Missing, wanted in connection with the deaths of two men in a villa on the island of Šipan and a suspect in the disappearance of the American woman Rebecca Vees, now in an Italian morgue. He must have seen Strumbić's photograph a dozen times before without noticing it. It was fuzzy, barely bigger than passport-sized. Unlike the woman's picture, it hadn't been posted anywhere in the station. No one else in the force had seen the picture. Why? Because the note next to the photograph said the suspect had probably fled the country, most likely destination Italy or the United Kingdom.

England. Marks & Spencer.

Seeing the picture now was like a shot of slivovitz injected into a vein.

Detective Brg brought the incriminating fax with him to the interview room. He sat comparing the photograph with the man in front of him for long minutes. The other man didn't break the silence. Brg's eyes prickled from the cigarette smoke and fatigue. At last he spoke, quietly, without aggression.

"Why don't we stop playing games, Detective Lieutenant. Or is it Captain Julius Strumbić?"

Brg gave Strumbić credit for not betraying any emotion. Strumbić merely smiled.

"I'm sure you're mistaken, Detective. My name is Smirnoff."

He turned the fax towards Strumbić.

"This piece of paper says it isn't."

Strumbić leaned forward and pulled the thin thermal paper across the stained blond wood table, turned it with three fingers, and considered.

"It's a reasonable likeness, though it's a pretty small picture and not particularly clear. Could be me. Could be any one of a hundred men within a kilometre of here. What did you say you want the man for?"

"As a witness, probable accessory, or possible perpetrator of three murders."

"Three? The Americans? Sounds like a dangerous fellow. But like I said, it's not me."

"What do you say, Mr. Strumbić, would you like to have a friendly chat with me or do you want to wait for the Zagreb investigators? I hear they're a lot less friendly. Plenty of former UDBA types."

Silence. The UDBA was Yugoslavia's hated former secret police. Strumbić knew more than a few of them. Like della Torre.

"What I don't get is if you killed those men, why, just a couple of days later, you'd want to be smuggling stuff onto a dock in a village on the opposite side of the channel," Brg continued. "I mean, you don't strike me as being stupid. They don't make stupid people detectives in the Zagreb force, do they?"

"Detective, those are all very good questions. But you're asking the wrong guy."

Brg was fading. Questions kept crowding his mind. Irritating, tiny details overwhelmed his brain. It was as if Strumbić wasn't there and he was asking himself.

"Says here you own that villa in Šipan. Where two of the Americans were killed. We had a look and it's not in any official records. All we could find was that it was registered to an Italian company. Your company, Mr. Strumbić?"

Strumbić was surprised at the turn of questioning, but played along.

"Thought Italians could only own up to forty-nine percent of a property in this country," Strumbić said.

"Oh, well, that's the clever thing. One Italian company owns forty-nine percent of the property and a Yugoslav firm owns the rest. Except forty-nine percent of that Yugoslav company is owned by an Italian company. Coincidentally, the same Italian company. The rest is owned by another Yugoslav company. You guessed it, forty-nine percent of that is owned by the very same Italian company. In the end, the only domestic owner-ship we could find was some lawyer in Varaždin who owns less than one percent. You won't be surprised to hear that he is only holding on behalf of a company based near Venice. Illegal, but what can you do? Lawyers. Anything to do with you, Mr. Strumbić?"

Strumbić shrugged sympathetically. "What our country's coming to." He shook his head sadly. "All the ills of capital-ism have already filled in the cracks left by the noble but failed Communist experiment."

Brg felt his head nod forward. He needed sleep. He knew that dwelling on stupid details was just a sign of how tired he was. The villa's ownership? Who cared about the complicated scheme designed to hide the owner. Strumbić owned it. And Strumbić was there, sitting in front of him.

Brg needed to be sharp to deal with Zagreb. And he needed to be even more on the ball to handle as wily a character as Strumbić.

Four hours of solid shut-eye. If he left for home now, he'd get that much rest and be awake again by lunch, have a bite to eat, and then come back to the station, refreshed. Call Zagreb, tell them he'd wrapped up the whole of the mystery, found the missing woman, had the lead suspect in a jail cell. Formally charge Strumbić with everything from smuggling to murder to fraudulent property ownership.

Hell, how could it hurt to delay calling them by a couple of hours? The woman wasn't going to get any more dead, and Strumbić, well, he'd already been sitting around in prison for more than two weeks. Another quiet morning wouldn't do any harm. Just in case, Brg would have a cop stand sentry outside

Strumbić's cell. Keep an eye on him the whole time.

*Four hours.* Brg thought. *What could possibly go wrong in four hours?*

# ACKNOWLEDGEMENTS

Olof Palme's assassination on that cold February night in 1986 remains one of Europe's great unsolved crimes of the postwar era. For anyone who wants to know more, *Blood on the Snow: The Killing of Olof Palme* by Jan Bondeson is a well-written and detailed account of the murder and the Swedish authorities' botched investigation.

There are numerous theories about who might have been behind the killing and why. One is that the Yugoslav government was somehow involved. This isn't particularly far-fetched. The UDBA may not be in the popular imagination like the KGB or the Stasi, but of all the organs of state security operating from Europe's Communist bloc, the Yugoslav secret police was perhaps the most murderous beyond its borders—even if its known targets were Yugoslav dissidents or somehow related or associated with them.

Della Torre's Department VI, however, is a work of fiction, as are all the characters in the book, apart from Palme. Some of the events I write about leading up to the Yugoslav wars of independence in the early 1990s, such as the police assault on Borovo Selo, actually happened. But any similarities between the people in my book and anyone who ever lived and breathed is coincidental.

That's not quite true. Steve Higgins, an American journalist and a friend, was real flesh and blood. He had nothing to do with former Yugoslavia, and he was a far more charming, clever, and gently ironic man than the one who appears in my book. And he'd have been a fine novelist had he only been given the time.

I owe thanks to numerous people for help and support in writing this book. I've dedicated *Killing Pilgrim* to my children, but my wife, Lucy, deserves top billing for her understanding and patience with a husband who spends far too much time at the computer and far too little doing the stuff he ought to be doing.

Janie Yoon is what every novelist dreams of but few are blessed with: an editor who has both the skill and determination to make the very best book possible.

I owe a debt of gratitude to my agent, Hilary McMahon, a realist in a world of fantasy. And to friends, readers, and family who made deep if not always obvious contributions, especially Andrew Steinmetz, Fred Biggar, Luke Vinten, Robert Kirkby, Nives Mattich, Bill and Elaine Vinten, and my parents.

**ALEN MATTICH** is the author of *Zagreb Cowboy*, the first novel in the Marko della Torre series. He was born in Zagreb, Croatia, and grew up in Libya, Italy, Canada, and the United States. He went to McGill University for his undergraduate degree and then did postgraduate work at the London School of Economics. A financial journalist and columnist, he's now based in London and writes for Dow Jones and the *Wall Street Journal*. The third Marko della Torre novel, *The Heart of Hell*, will be published in February 2015.

# KILLING PILGRIM

Also in the Marko della Torre Series

*Zagreb Cowboy*